Targeting DART

SATAN'S DEVILS #4

MANDA MELLETT

AUTHOR'S NOTE

Targeting Dart is the fourth in the Satan's Devils MC Series. While this book can be read as a standalone it picks up on a story that began in *Slick Running*, and which will be continued in the fifth book, *Heart Broken*. To get the full benefit I advise you to read books 3, 4 and 5 in the right order.

If you're new to MC books you may find there are terms that you haven't heard before, so I've included a glossary to help along the way. I hope you get drawn into this mysterious and dark world in the same way I have done—there will be further books in the Satan's Devils series which I hope you'll want to follow.

If you've picked this book up because, like me, you read anything MC, I hope you'll enjoy it for what it is, a fictional insight into the underground culture of alpha men and their bikes.

GLOSSARY

Motorcycle Club – An official motorcycle club in the U.S. is one which is sanctioned by the American Motorcyclist Association (AMA). The AMA has a set of rules its members must abide by. It is said that ninety-nine percent of motorcyclists in America belong to the AMA

Outlaw Motorcycle Club (MC) – The remaining one percent of motorcycling clubs are historically considered outlaws as they do not wish to be constrained by the rules of the AMA and have their own bylaws. There is no one formula followed by such clubs, but some not only reject the rulings of the AMA, but also that of society, forming tightly knit groups who fiercely protect their chosen ways of life. Outlaw MCs have a reputation for having a criminal element and supporting themselves by less than legal activities, dealing in drugs, gun running or prostitution. The one-percenter clubs are usually run under a strict hierarchy.

Brother – Typically members of the MC refer to themselves as brothers and regard the closely knit MC as their family.

Cage – The name bikers give to cars as they prefer riding their bikes.

Chapter – Some MCs have only one club based in one location. Other MCs have a number of clubs who follow the same bylaws and wear the same patch. Each club is known as a chapter and will normally carry the name of the area where they are based on their patch.

Church – Traditionally the name of the meeting where club business is discussed, either with all members present or with just those holding officer status.

Colours – When a member is wearing (or flying) his colours he will be wearing his cut proudly displaying his patch showing which club he is affiliated with.

Cut – The name given to the jacket or vest which has patches denoting the club that member belongs to.

Enforcer – The member who enforces the rules of the club.

Hang-around – This can apply to men wishing to join the club and who hang-around hoping to be become prospects. It is also used to women who are attracted by bikers and who are happy to make themselves available for sex at biker parties.

Mother Chapter – The founding chapter when a club has more than one chapter.

Patch – The patch or patches on a cut will show the club that member belongs to and other information such as the particular chapter and any role that may be held in the club. There can be a number of other patches with various meanings, including a one-percenter patch. Prospects will not be allowed to wear the club patch until they have been patched-in, instead they will have patches which denote their probationary status.

Patched-in/Patching-in – The term used when a prospect completes his probationary status and becomes a full club member.

President (Prez) – The officer in charge of that particular club or chapter.

Prospect – Anyone wishing to join a club must serve time as a probationer. During this period they have to prove their loyalty to the club. A probationary period can last a year or more. At the end of this period, if they've proved themselves a prospect will be patched-in.

Old Lady – The term given to a woman who enters into a permanent relationship with a biker.

RICO – The Racketeer Influenced and Corrupt Organisations Act primarily deals with organised crime. Under this Act the officers of a club could be held responsible for activities they order members to do and a conviction carries a potential jail service of twenty years as well as a large fine and the seizure of assets.

Road Captain – The road captain is responsible for the safety of the club on a run. He will organise routes and normally ride at the end of the column.

Secretary – MCs are run like businesses and this officer will perform the secretarial duties such as recording decisions at meetings.

Sergeant-at-Arms – The sergeant-at-arms is responsible for the safety of the club as a whole and for keeping order.

Sweet Butt – A woman who makes her sexual services available to any member at any time. She may well live on the club premises and be fully supported by the club.

Treasurer – The officer responsible for keeping an eye on the club's money.

Vice President (VP) – The vice president will support the president, stepping into his role in his absence. He may be responsible for making sure the club runs smoothly, overseeing prospects etc.

Brothers protecting their own

CONTENTS

CHAPTER 1

Dart

I suspect I'm not alone in disliking hospitals with a vengeance. First off, it's the smell, that odour of disinfectant that permeates the air and from which there seems no escape. It invades everything you're wearing, so no matter what you do it's impossible to shake the aroma that lingers even when you leave. Pain, sickness, and death are all around, and whether or not any effort's been made to brighten up the décor, it does little to help raise your mood.

Of course, it's better to be here as a visitor rather than an inmate, but that brings its own challenges, particularly when the patient I've come to see is very inaptly named. Heart could more properly be called an 'impatient', fed up of being confined to his bed, and visibly suffering under the burden of the news that was delivered to him shortly after he regained consciousness. He'd been in a coma for almost a month.

It's not particularly easy visiting with a man of action who's used to being out riding his bike but is now immobilised with one leg badly smashed up and broken ribs. Couple that with someone who has been told he's lost his wife, and you've got one angry, devastated man whose emotions swing constantly like a pendulum. My club, the Satan's Devils MC is determined never to leave him on his own, even if spending time with him is becoming an increasingly uncomfortable and soul-destroying task.

Tonight I've drawn what's become known as the short straw, and it's my turn to keep him company for a while. As I exit the elevator on his floor, I'm mentally trying to prepare myself for the ordeal ahead. Don't get me wrong, I love Heart like a true brother, and not just in the club sense. We'd joined at the same time, prospected together, and formed a strong bond while we were having all manner of shit thrown at us. But now he's changed. Oh, he doesn't look or sound any different, it's just he's not the same man that he was before the accident. Last time I was here I barely recognised him.

I rap gently on the door and, as Beef steps out, ask in a low voice, "How is he today?" while hoping against hope I'll be told there's some improvement. I'm not asking for a medical update, his body's healing alright, it's his mind that's still got a long way to go.

Beef shakes his head, and I pull back my shoulders, prepared to be disappointed. "Bad, man. The doc's talkin' about lettin' him out at the weekend, but there's no fuckin' way he can deal with comin' back to the clubhouse and Crystal not being there."

Beef's words are not unexpected. Nevertheless, I'd hoped to hear different. Closing my eyes, I press my hand against the wall, lowering my forehead to rest on my arm. Fuck, not only has Heart got to cope with his debilitating physical injuries, but his mental anguish on top of everything else.

Just four weeks ago, everything was normal. Heart was riding back from a visit to Tombstone, an enjoyable afternoon out with his old lady, when they were deliberately knocked off their motorcycle. The incident leaving my brother fighting for his life, a battle which proved too much for his wife, losing it on the operating table shortly after being admitted.

They'd had to sedate him when he was first told the news and, as much as I love my brother, I'm grateful I wasn't the one who had to break it to him and watch him go to pieces. Now, a week later, he's still not pulled back together. The man behind the door is a different person to the one that set off on that ride with his old lady.

"How we gonna do this, Beef?" On top of his loss, Crystal's bitch of a mother buried her daughter without waiting for Heart to regain consciousness, taking away his chance to say his final goodbyes. While I've never experienced a love like Heart and his old lady had, having seen their relationship from outside in, I know how distressing this must be for my brother.

Beef, named for the fact he looks like a fucking bull, shrugs. "No fuckin' idea, Brother. Fuck, it's hard for everyone. We all miss Crystal bein' around. But Heart? This has darn near destroyed him, man. He loved her so fuckin' much."

He did. If ever there was a match made in heaven, it was theirs.

There's nothing I can say. Sure, we've lost brothers before— only this past year we've lost Hank, a prospect, and Adam, a fully patched member—but losing a woman we all adored has affected every member of the club in a different way. And it's so much worse for him. Heart's not just lost a friend; he's lost his soul mate. Already I'm wondering if it's even possible he'll be able to ever recover. Up to now he's certainly showing no sign. Beef pats my shoulder, a gesture given in solidarity as though to support me through the hours when I'll be here. Then he strides off down the corridor in the direction that I've just come from, his head hanging low. Visiting with Heart is always depressing.

Taking a breath, and then bracing myself, I enter the room, seeking any change from the last time I was here. There's not much. Heart's leg's still in plaster from his hip to his ankle, but the bandage has been removed from his head. Having been shaven to treat the wound, his blond hair on one side is at last growing back, but short and stubbly, the other side left long.

3

Inanely I wonder whether he'll get it all shorn off to match, but how his hair is styled is probably the least worry on his mind. Eased off the pain medication, his eyes for once look sharp and bright as they track my approach, a change from the slightly dazed look he had before. I pick up the chair by the side of the bed and turn it around then sit astride it, my arms leaning on the back, and my chin resting on my hands. Neither of us speak.

When the silence gets too grating, I'm the first to break it. Nodding at the crutches he's obviously been given to use, I start, "Beef tells me you've got your ticket out of here. In a few days you'll be home, Brother."

His eyes widen and his nostrils flare. "Home? I ain't got no fuckin' home."

It's not the first time he's snarled at me, but I ignore it and remind him, "You've got us, your brothers. You've got the club…"

"What's the point of the fuckin' club when I ain't got no ol' lady."

"You've got yer kid." Yeah, he's got a three-year-old daughter, Amy, who he's consistently refused to see.

"She's better off without me. Fuck, let her gramma have 'er. She wants her."

We haven't told Heart the whole story, it's too much for him to handle in the state he's in now. But yeah, he's right. Crystal's mother wanted the kid, but only to sell her to pay off her debts. She'd started the ball rolling that ended with their accident. It's only the fact we don't take out women easily that she's still breathing air. And I won't be alone in hoping she gets hold of some bad shit, or overdoses and removes the problem herself. All we've said to him is that she's entirely unsuitable to look after a young child. He's got too much to deal with without adding that information just yet.

But I emphasise what's already been explained. "Heart, she's so into the shit she can't even look after herself." Yeah, she owed people for the crap she injects into her veins. "Well, let the kid stay with the prez and his ol' lady. They seem to have taken to her." We've all noticed he doesn't even use the child's name. And yup, Drummer and Sam have been looking after her, and well. But, "She needs her dad." Heart sneers and looks down at himself. "Ain't no fuckin' good to anyone like this."

I don't remind him she won't care, that she just needs to know one of her parents is still there for her, whatever shape he's in. All of us have tried, but Amy, the spitting image of her mother, is the one person he won't allow into his room. I keep my mouth buttoned up and my thoughts to myself. Better people than me have tried to persuade him. *When he's home it will be different.*

Pulling a brochure out of my cut, I try to interest him in something else. "Club's replacin' your bike. We've voted to get you a new model. Want to have a look at what you could get? Don't know about you, but the new Low Rider looks fuckin' ace to me." His own was totalled as a result of the crash.

But he's closed his eyes and turned his head, pretending to sleep. I end up flipping through the pages by myself. It's par for the course. Heart's hurting so badly he just lives in his head, unable to move past what he's lost and get on with his life. If neither the thought of his daughter or getting a new bike can start bringing him out of his fugue, then I've no fucking idea how to get through to him.

A gentle tapping at the door gets my attention, and I look up to see an unwelcome but familiar face entering. It's the fucking heat, one of the detectives who have been buzzing around Heart's accident. Detective Hannah. Her erstwhile dirty partner,

Archer, is long dead. Not that she has that intel yet, all she knows is that he's disappeared off the face of the earth.

I nod at her, and pretend to look past her into the empty corridor. "Detective. On your own today?" I hide my smirk. Oh, we've solved the mystery of who ran Heart and Crystal off the road. Archer admitted it himself. But that secret we're keeping close for obvious reasons, including that Slick shot off his dick before our Vegas brother cut his throat. The cops won't be finding a body either, Slick made sure of that. Just a few charred pieces of bone, which will take them time to put back together.

"Detective Archer is unavailable," Hannah says tightly.

Oh, he definitely is.

The new voice has disturbed Heart. He stirs, opens his eyes, and impassively regards the detective. From his expression, I take it they've met before and that he's not particularly pleased to see her.

Hannah's viewing him just as intently. She clears her throat. "How are you today, Mr Norman?"

"The name's Heart," he growls. "And how d'ya fuckin' think I'm doin'?" He sneers as his left hand indicates his plastered leg. Painfully he goes to pull himself up. I go to help, knowing his wincing comes from his broken ribs that are still healing, but he waves off my assistance, grimacing through the pain. I push the button for his pain meds closer to his hand, but he ignores it.

Hannah takes a step closer. "I need to know if you've remembered anything more about the accident?"

Accident? Murder more like.

Heart touches his hand to his head. "Can't remember fuck all as I've told ya already. Last fuckin' thing I remember was ridin' back from Tucson with my ol' lady ridin' bitch behind me." It's impossible to miss the moisture gathering at the corner of his eye.

"What have you discovered so far, Detective?" I probe. It would be useful for the club to know how far they've got.

She looks from my brother to me. Heart doesn't seem at all interested. Even when we explained what had happened and that the man who caused Crystal's death has been dispatched to meet Satan, he seemed to focus on the loss of his wife rather than the punishment meted out to the perpetrator.

Just when I don't think she's going to speak, she sighs. "We've tracked the vehicle down to a rental agency, seems the person who rented it used a fake name and papers."

Doesn't surprise me. The Herreras, the crime family in Tucson to which Archer had a distant connection, wouldn't find it difficult to create a false identity.

"Oh, and we found the vehicle. Burned out."

"No evidence?" I ask, hoping that Archer had left fingerprints. We all know, and that includes the detective in front of me, that he was a dirty cop, but proving his involvement in what happened to Heart is going to be impossible. He'd only admitted it to us. And then we made sure he wouldn't be saying anything at all.

The detective shakes her head. "No. No fingerprints." When I think she's finished, she continues, "But we got a description from the rental agency."

And then she clams up. It would be to our benefit if they find evidence it was Archer. Perhaps knowing his culpability, they wouldn't be too concerned when they eventually identify what's left of his body. Literally burying a cop on the make would be easier than going through the rigmarole of taking him through the courts.

Hannah tilts her head to one side, and once again tries to engage Heart. "I'm pleased to see you conscious. I hear you're going to make a full recovery. I expect you're looking forward to being with your daughter again."

Oh fuck. She did not just go there, did she?

Gasping, Heart leans forward and points a shaky hand toward her. "Pig, I suggest you stay out of my fuckin' business. Your job's findin' out who killed my fuckin' wife, and you can keep your filthy nose away from anythin' else."

For a moment she looks taken aback, and then a fleeting look of sympathy comes over her face. "I'll keep you informed as to what progress we're making." As Heart gently lies himself back, unable to escape the groan of pain, she gives a stiff nod, then turns and walks out of the door.

"Fuckin' cops," Heart grumbles, and closes his eyes once again.

After a while, gentle snores begin showing that this time he's dozed off for real. I try to make myself as comfortable as I can on the hard chair, and think about Hannah's visit, smiling to myself as I realise this is one of the few times that a brother's actually told the police all he knows. We've asked him ourselves, but he really has no recollection of the Ford F-250 hitting his bike. Can't recall seeing it at all. His last memory is of Crystal's arms wrapped around him, speeding along an open road. That he has no recollection of seeing her broken body on the ground has got to be better than remembering everything and reliving it over and over again in his nightmares. He must have fought hard but been unable to prevent the bike leaving the freeway, and I can only imagine the panic and fear he would have felt. Thank God for small fucking mercies that he's got no memories at all. I hope the detail never comes back.

Eight hours later, and Blade's entrance marks the end of my shift. Heart being asleep meant the time had passed with no further conversation. My muscles feeling seized, I stand and stretch, then give our enforcer a similar update to the one Beef had supplied to me, and we exchange sorry shakes of our heads. I update him on Hannah's visit, and once that's completed, at last I'm free to leave. While we're all elated to see Heart physically improving, I walk out just like Beef had done after spending time with him, head down and dejected.

Outside the autumn sun is shining, a pleasant temperature, not as harsh as it is in mid-summer. Monsoon season has passed, making it one of my favourite seasons to ride. Starting the engine, I point my bike towards the clubhouse, more than ready to go home, using the miles and the time to give the breeze a chance to clear sombre thoughts from my head and the condition of my injured brother from my mind. But when I arrive at the clubhouse, where I've been is obviously written on my face. It's an expression we all seem to wear when we come back from visiting Heart.

Drummer, our president, standing at the bar, notices and waves me over. Jekyll, one of our prospects, puts a beer into my hand. After a quick look at me, Drum nods to the top shelf where his best whisky is kept. Declining ice with a shudder, but grateful to have something stronger, I pick up the shot glass, knocking the spirit back in a couple of swallows.

"How is he today? Any mention of Amy?"

Sadly, I explain, "I tried, Prez, but he's adamant he won't see her. Fuckin' shame for the kid. She doin' okay?"

Drum turns and points to where his pregnant old lady, Sam, is playing with the little girl. "Kids are resilient, she's settlin' in with us fine. But she needs her father. And Heart needs to see her."

That he does.

"Hannah came sniffin' around."

"Oh? She got anythin'?"

"Nothin' at all. 'Cept they may have a description of the fucker who rented the Ford."

Drum taps his fingers against the bar. "Could be interestin' if that matches Archer. 'Bout time they put the clues together."

I nod. My thoughts exactly. "We gonna make a move on Clyde? Heart still doesn't know she's a problem." Susie Clyde was Crystal's mother, and as far as I'm concerned should be in the ground for her sins.

"Want Heart to be part of that decision. We'll set him straight on what she did when he's in a better state of mind."

I suppose that's the right thing to do. Turning around, I survey the room, freshly painted and with all new furniture. There's no doubt it's freshened the place up, but the reason for the redecoration is something else that fucker Archer was responsible for, he and his cop friends had destroyed the place using a trumped-up search warrant. As I'm glancing around, I see the sweet butts are just coming in, and a good fuck might be just what I need to clear the last few hours from my mind. I nudge the prez and indicate Paige. "Think I'm gonna give her a try." She's been here a couple of months now, but to date I've not been with her.

His sympathetic eyes meet mine, and he gives a quick nod. "Yeah, go get laid, Dart."

He turns back to take a sip of his drink and I wonder how he deals with his pent-up emotions now he's restricted himself to an old lady. Sure, the fucking's probably good, but having no variety? My eyes fall on the other new girl, Diva. I've already seen they're both up for threesomes. Having two girls service me tonight will surely bring me out of this funk that I'm in. Drummer used to be up for multiple partners before he tied himself down.

Before I move off, having gestured toward the girls I've chosen and received their eager nods in response, I ask him, "How can you cope with having just one pussy, Prez?"

He swings around and a smile comes to his lips. "Ain't the hardship you're thinkin', Dart. One day you'll find the one, and she'll be so good that you'll never want your cock to go anywhere else."

I laugh, and shake my head so violently my long hair comes loose from my bun. "Ain't no one girl alive could satisfy me, Drum."

His lips remain curved as he replies, "Perhaps you just haven't found the right one yet." He pauses and points around the room, indicating the whores ready and waiting. "There are girls you fuck, and girls you make an ol' lady."

I chuckle, not persuaded in the least. I'm still moving my head left to right in negative dismissal as I walk away, going over to the Paige and Diva, who stand and enthusiastically link their arms with mine. Within moments we're in one of the crash rooms, clothes scattered over the floor, and I'm lying flat on the bed while Diva sucks my cock into her talented mouth and Paige sits on my face. God, this is the life!

Tomorrow I could go with another of the club girls, or perhaps one of the hangarounds who come to our parties. A different experience every night. No siree, I'm never going to find a woman who's got everything I want in one package. *Uh uh.*

After I've come in Diva's mouth and in Paige's cunt, I'm totally drained. Having ensured both girls have been satisfied, I send them away and, too tired to go up to my suite, settle down to sleep where I am.

My last thoughts before my eyes close return to Heart. When we thought we were going to lose him, it wasn't only me who felt the loss, he is my best friend after all. It affected us all, and some of the soul went out of the club. Heart was our conscience. Heart was a lover, a peacemaker, though he'd fight alongside any brother when needed.

Heart, Crystal, and Amy were our resident family, their love for each other making all of us smile, cheering us up on the darkest of days. When he came round, I thought at least we now had him back. Damaged for certain, that was a given, it's hard for anyone to deal with the devastation that comes with losing a mate. But what none of us expected was he'd be totally broken. That man in the hospital bed? I don't know him at all.

CHAPTER 2
Alex

Celine covers her mouth and leans toward me, whispering conspiratorially from behind her hand. "See those two men at the bar? I'd give them both at least an eight, and probably darn near a nine."

Only vaguely interested, I turn to see what my sister has pointed out, and it only takes a second before I'm agreeing with her assessment. "For whites, they're okay." And my, that's an understatement. The two tall men are stunning, particularly the one on the right. He's got his dark hair tied up in a man bun, and when he turns my way his features are aquiline with well-defined cheek bones. His stance and bearing show he's all man, almost too much for one woman to handle. As I watch, he laughs at something his companion has said, then slaps him on the back, drawing my attention to the strange leather vest that he's wearing. "That one's not bad. But what's he wearing?"

Celine narrows her eyes. "The threads show they're members of the Satan's Devils," she tells me. "It's an outlaw motorcycle club based here in Tucson. Have you not seen them around?"

I haven't, no, but then I haven't been here that long. Then I latch onto something she's said. "Outlaw?" Now intrigued, peering up through my eyelashes, I risk another glance at them.

"Yeah, they live outside the law. Or that's the word."

"Criminals?"

"Christ, girl. Don'cha have bikers where you come from?" As she picks up her glass and drains it, I think about it. No, I don't think I've come across them before, not unless I've been driving and had to put up with a group of motorcyclists splitting lanes, making me ultra-careful to keep to my side of the road. Tilting her drink toward the bikers, she continues, "There are rumours they kill people and bury the bodies."

"Kill? Who? Anyone?" I can't help shifting nervously and shrinking back into my seat.

She throws me a disparaging look. "Jesus, Alex. What stone did you crawl out from under? No, not random peeps. Just people who cross them."

Making a mental note not to do anything to upset them, I risk another look, trying to assess just how dangerous they are.

Celine must see that's she's made me nervous, and gives a little laugh. "They're just rumours, Alex. If they were criminals, don'cha think the cops would quickly be along to arrest them?"

They certainly don't look like wanted men, standing at the bar and enjoying a joke.

"And they own this place. The Wheel Inn. Or so most people believe. That's why they're here, I expect. To check it's running smoothly. And to keep trouble away."

Which they'd have no problems doing just by their presence. You'd have to be mad to take on big, tough men like them. And something about them being tattooed and dangerous, I'm ashamed to admit, sparks my interest. What would it be like to have one of them in your corner? Or in your bed. Especially the one with his hair in a bun. God, I bet he'd know what to do to keep a girl satisfied. Mnnn mmm.

Celine resumes the conversation. "I think they've gone, or are trying to go legit. They own a number of businesses in Tucson…" She breaks off and looks at me with a gleam in her eyes. "Hey, girl, that's a thought. They own a strip club."

I shrug, having absolutely no idea where she's going with that comment.

"Yeah," she carries on enthusiastically, "that could be an idea for you. You're desperate for a job, ain't cha? And I doubt they'd be worried if you didn't want to give them your social security number."

It was the wrong time to take a sip of my drink, as I now spit it out all over the table, and my resultant choking fit has the bikers, and everyone else in the vicinity, spinning around to look at me. Feeling the blood rushing to my cheeks, I grab hold of her arm. "What the fuck you talking about? Me? Work in a strip club?"

"Babe," she looks at me as though addressing a child, "you've got no real work experience to offer. What's the one skill you have got?"

Suddenly I regret telling my sister as much as I had. There were definitely some things I should have kept quiet. But she's right. Having run away to Tucson with little more than the clothes on my back, the money I had managed to bring with me was fast running out. I'd be unable to rely on her generosity for very much longer, and needed to earn enough to pay my way somehow or other. It's not that I haven't been looking for work, I have. But either I'm not wanted as I've no resume to offer, or if someone was willing to give me a chance, I baulked at having my name officially entered on employment records. I may be overly cautious. Ron might not even be trying to find me, but if he is searching for me, I don't want to make it easy for him.

Hopefully he wouldn't even think of looking here, even if I did come and impose on my sister. Ostracised by my overly strict family when she'd got pregnant and had an abortion at the age of eighteen, I'd kept in contact with her in secret, and as far as I know, am the only one who knows where she ended up.

Even if Ron did find out her address, there's no reason for him to think that this is where I would run to.

Thinking about my plight reminds me how overwhelmed I was by her easy acceptance of my situation, and the help both her and her husband have extended to me. Not only putting a roof over my head, but also refusing much more than a pittance toward the food they willingly share. It is well past time I begin to repay them and, hopefully, manage to bring in enough money so I can put some aside. *But a strip club?* I bark an incredulous laugh.

She's looking at me strangely. "I think it's worth a try."

I just give a disbelieving look. "Me, a stripper? Working for bikers? You have got to be kidding me. Just look at me, Celine. I'm not the type." I know what I am. Christ, I find it hard enough to get clothes to fit. *Which wouldn't be a problem if I'm taking them off.* I give myself and mental slap around the head. *I'm not seriously considering it, am I?*

"I'm black," I add. And coming to Tucson I'm finding it strange how few of us there are.

She tilts her head to one side. "You're different is all. And from what you've said…"

"I said too much, obviously." My eyes narrow at her.

Her sudden change of subject catches me off guard. "Want another?" She points to my empty glass.

Thank goodness! She appears to be done with her preposterous suggestion.

When I nod, she takes the empties and goes over to the bar. I watch as she meanders around the tables instead of taking the direct route, and ends up, *oh shit*, beside the bikers. Showing such rough types can also be gentlemen, they move aside to let her through, but I can see from here they're undressing her with their eyes as they do so. Oh, Celine got the figure, looks, and the height. She's the total opposite of me. As usual, I can't hide my envy at the way the dice fell.

What they see must be enough to tempt them, but she dismisses the comment they make with a confident laugh, then turns and places her order. As she's waiting for the bartender to bring the drinks, she swings back around and starts having what becomes an animated discussion with the men clad in leather. Anxiously biting my lip, I half look away, but continue watching them out of the side of my eye. *What is she up to?* But luckily there's not one glance coming my way to suggest the topic of the discussion seems to concern me. The biker taps something into his phone, and I'm hoping it's not her number. She's happily married, or that's what I thought.

After a few moments she returns, and a fresh drink is placed in front of me. There's a gleam in her eye that I'm not sure I like.

"Thanks, Celine." I regard it for a moment, feeling guilty. "You know you didn't have to bring me out tonight. I'm so sorry I can't pay my way."

"Oh shush, girl. It's good to get away from the house and have a girls' night out. Craig's all well and good, but I can go out with him anytime. And I can't eye fuck the men while he's around."

I smile, thinking she doesn't have to. She landed herself a good'un with him. *So, what was she up to?* I make a small gesture that no one else would notice. "What was that all about?"

"What?" she replies innocently, but something in her eyes flares.

"You, talking to the bikers."

She laughs, shrugging it off, and points to the drinks on the table. "You'll soon be able to return the favour once you're earning again."

She's changing the subject by reminding me of my sorry predicament. I lift my chin and lower it, while thinking it will take a long time before I find anyone willing to take me on. Though, surprisingly, in Tucson it's not the colour of my skin that's much of a drawback. There are relatively few blacks in the city, and therefore we're not viewed as any kind of threat. No, it's the fact I've never worked a day in my life that's against me. A half completed law degree hasn't proved to be of any use.

Celine's looking at her glass, and then peers at me over the top. "Hey, get that look off your face. Things are looking up, girl. I've got you an interview. Well, maybe audition's the better word for it."

Hang on. She said nothing about this earlier, and that flick of her eyes toward the men at the bar gives her away. Oh shit, don't tell this mama it's something to do with the bikers. I put my hand to my mouth, suddenly feeling very afraid. "Celine, what have you done?" I hiss. My eyes return to the bar just in time to see the two men disappearing out the back. "What do you mean, an audition?"

"At Satan's Topless Angels."

I growl low in my throat, "Which is?" But deep down I already know the answer. The name gives it away.

"The strip club owned by the Satan's Devils Motorcycle Club." Her reply is nonchalant, as if she was speaking about nothing more edifying than the weather forecast.

Now my head drops into my hands. What the hell has she gone and done?

"It's tomorrow morning," she continues, as if she's not given me anything out of the ordinary to consider. "At eleven o'clock."

For a moment I peer through my fingers, staring at her. *What the hell is she thinking?* There is no way on earth that I'll be making that audition. For one thing—the only thing that matters—I don't have what it takes. All at once, anger takes over as I look at my sister who, though has the same skin colour, unlike me, has been blessed with a tall, slender physique, taking after our father. "Celine, just be sensible. Look at me," I hiss. "I'm short, overweight, and my boobs are totally out of proportion. Hardly stripper material."

As quickly as mine had, her ire rises to match. "You're beautiful, Alex, and don't you ever forget it. And strippers come in all shapes and sizes, they have to. Men are attracted to many different types."

"Not mine." My husband had criticised my body for years, not that there was much I could do about it. All the dieting and exercising in the world hadn't altered the basic shape God had gifted me with. My legs are too short, my breasts top heavy, and as for my ass... I, as Ron had so often said, am a joke.

She waves her hand in dismissal. "It's what you do with it that matters the most. And boy, have you got some moves."

Maybe I have. Who am I to judge? But I'd spent months trying. Not that Ron had appreciated it at all. He'd seen the same video I'd sent to Celine and he'd laughed his head off before telling me I made him feel sick and walked out, presumably to find a whore to stick his dick into.

I'd never told him anything about my strange hobby again. But I'd continued my lessons, performing for nothing other than my own enjoyment. But the legacy of the reaction of the man I'd left was what made me so nervous showing myself off to strangers. If he was repulsed, wouldn't they be too?

"Look, Alex, I think you ought to give this a try..."

"Celine. You know I love you, and how much I appreciate you taking me in. And I know you need me to start paying my way, but there must be something else I can do..."

"You haven't found anything so far. And," she holds up her hands to stop me trying to talk over her again, "you need to get some confidence back. I think this is a great way. Go to the audition, show them what you've got, shake that little booty of yours, and if you get the job, great, you don't have to take it. If they offer it to you, at least you'll start believing that bastard Ron was just trying to wear you down."

But what he'd said was the truth. I could use a mirror as well as the next woman. It will just be one more situation where I'd make a man laugh. "But it's a strip club," I snarl. *Shit, how did I end up with this as my only option?* "I can't do that."

"Why not? Plenty of women do. And it's not as though you're going to be a hooker. Damn girl, just give it a try. For me?"

"I am not getting naked in front of strangers." My hand wanders down and smoothes across the curves of my stomach.

"You don't have to do anything you don't want. Wear a body-suit or something. I'm sure you can work something out." The airily way she dismisses all my protests makes me realise with a sinking feeling of dread, she's actually serious about this.

My eyes narrow. "They didn't even look at me. They weren't at all interested." Yeah, they'd looked around at my coughing fit, but away just as quickly.

She shrugs, pushing her artificially relaxed and straightened hair over her shoulders. "I may have led them to believe it was going to be me."

"Well you can fucking go instead." There. If she's so keen for one of us to take her clothes off in public, let it be her.

"Alex," she starts, sounding like she's addressing a slow learner. "I might have been blessed with a typical figure and reasonable looks, but I can't do with it what you can. You've got the rhythm and movement. I'm just a stick on two legs."

That brings a small smile to my lips. Unfortunately, she's right. But is my ability to move enough for people to overlook my other major shortcomings?

She leans forward and covers my hands with her own. "Babe, sleep on it, okay? If you don't turn up, they won't be too bothered. They only know to expect an Alex in the morning. If you really don't want to do this, then don't. But if you want to give it a try, then I'm behind you all the way."

Again, my teeth worry my bottom lip. If I wasn't so desperate for money I wouldn't even consider it. I start to wonder what the wages are like, the thought of being able to put dollars in my wallet suddenly sounding attractive. But her confidence I can pull it off is surely misplaced. I glance at my sister, not for the first time in my life, wishing I'd won the looks lottery instead. "You really think I can do this?"

"Why not?"

I can think of a hundred reasons why. Including, "I'm not a whore."

"Of course not!" She looks shocked. "Look, I used to know one of the girls who stripped there—lovely girl, actually. She told me nothing like that was expected. The bikers are protective of the girls, and make sure there's no touching. Sure, some give lap dances, but none are pushed into it if they don't want to. And woe betide a man who puts his hands on a girl unasked. She was like you, desperate for a well-paying job, but because of the positive environment she actually enjoyed it. She ended up marrying one of the patrons."

Our glasses are once again empty. Celine gathers her jacket and picks up her purse. As I copy her actions her words go around in my head. *Don't be stupid. It's ridiculous.* In my mind I can hear Ron laughing his head off.

And I pull myself up straight. What the fuck do I care what my soon-to-be ex-husband would think? Part of the reason I left was to change myself into someone different from the housewife he'd modelled me into, the Stepford wife clone he wanted to keep his house.

I got away. I'm free. I can do anything.

CHAPTER 3

Dart

Striding into Satan's Topless Angels, I notice, not for the first
time, how sleazy the joint looks by day, when all the overhead lights are on, casting their glaring white light on the
shabby velvet sofas and red satin chairs covered with stains, the
origin of which I don't want to think of. Table surfaces are pitted
and worn with numerous rings left from glasses. The red carpet
looks threadbare in parts, and the gold decorations of the
curtains framing the stage look gaudy and tarnished. But by
night, with the lights down low, the place looks very different.
And let's face it, the men who come here haven't eyes for their
surroundings. No, they just want to see what's happening on the
stage. And as long as we provide the talent, they keep coming
back.

Angels happens to be my domain, the one I manage on
behalf of my club. Recently we've lost a couple of strippers,
leaving us short. Candy, I know, didn't want to go, but her other
half got a job up Phoenix way and she moved to be with him.
Don't blame the girl at all, but she was a great loss. A favourite
with the customers. We left on good terms, her saying how
much she enjoyed working here, and that's down to Satan's
Devils taking care of our women, whether they be old ladies,
club whores, or our employees. Strip clubs which turn a blind
eye to some of their more handsy customers lose their best
dancers fast. While the girls here know we're always watching

out for them, they're happy, and reward us by giving their all on the stage. Yeah, it pays that they know we've got their backs.

Throwing a nod toward Road, one of our prospects who's come in early to restock the bar, I glance around at the cleaners doing the best that they can to clear up the mess left from last night. Vacuums are humming, cloths scrubbing at the wood-work, trying to turn this place into something it's not. But it will be good enough, and will bring in the cash. Money that will make Dollar, our treasurer, happy. And the draw of this place isn't what it looks like. Fuck, even if it was bright and shiny no one would notice. Our success depends on the girls who strip off. The right ones will bring in the dollars, good tips for them, and more customers through the doors for us.

I'm here bright and early as a result of a short conversation in the Wheel Inn last night when I'd been approached by a woman. At first taken aback, Beef and I had discussed her proposal back at the club. Tucson is made up of mainly whites, with Hispanics coming in a close second. African Americans make up only around two percent of the half-a-million total population. Satan's Devils is, of course, like most one-percen-ters, historically a whites only club, and to date, the Angels have had only white dancers. A black girl could add a bit of spice, if she can use that body of hers, of course. And from what I can recall, she was slender and shapely. Alex was her name, and that's who I've come to give a try-out today.

We might have a strict club rule of being hands off—no employee of ours will be bothered by a brother—but we're only men after all, and when there's an opportunity to watch a new girl dance and strip, I'm not short of volunteers offering to help with the interview and audition. Today it's Blade who's won the honour, and it's him, our enforcer, who's currently walking toward me. Well, with all the shit jobs he has to do for the club, he deserves a reward.

"Dart! Beef tells me it's dark meat on the menu today. Bit of a change from the ordinary?" Blade slaps me on the back as he approaches.

"Thought it was worth seeing what she's got."

"She stacked?" He holds the palm of his hands over his chest as though his words alone weren't enough.

I take out my phone and check the time. "You can see for yourself in five minutes."

"Unless she chickens out."

Yeah. We get that a lot. It's one thing to think you can be a stripper, quite another to actually take off your clothes in front of strangers if you haven't done it before. I realise I'd been so caught off guard being approached as I had, that I'd omitted to query about experience. Shit, I hope this isn't going to be a waste of my time, and Blade's.

A bell rings. Road leaves the bar and goes to answer it. Together, Blade and I turn around in expectation. We don't have to wait long before a woman comes into sight.

Well, fuck me! How I manage not to burst out laughing I'm really not sure. Blade coughs and covers his mouth with his hand. I try and peer around the prospect to see the other girl who's surely coming in behind, but the only one entering is the one that's causing me to almost lose my shit.

Oh fuck!

"Is that her?" Blade asks incredulously, his eyes opening wide. At my shrug, he suggests quietly in my ear, "Let her down lightly. She looks like a lamb goin' to the fuckin' slaughter."

And that she does. Her mocha-coloured skin doesn't completely hide the darkening purplish flush on her cheeks, and I can see her shaking from here. Christ! I don't like hurting women, but there's no way, just no fucking way. Leaning over to the enforcer, I let him know I agree. "I'll just have a word with her first, then tell her gently. Don't think I could bear to see her try and strip."

"I've just had breakfast, man." As he pretends to make a vomiting sound, I bat Blade's arm, knowing I'll be unable to hold it together if he doesn't stop.

Road brings her over. I look her down, and then a little bit up. There isn't far to go. Then being polite, I hold out my hand. "I'm Dart, this here's my brother, Blade. And you are...?"

The little thing answers in a surprisingly husky and sexy voice. "I'm Alex."

My eyebrow rises. "I was expecting someone different."

"You spoke to my sister, Celine, last night." She looks down at her feet.

And she'd misled me. I feel a twinge of anger. If she'd been upfront and honest we wouldn't be going through this charade now. Blade nudges my arm, and when I look at him, gives me a pointed look. He knows me too well, so I tamp my rage back down. Fuck it though, this is a waste of my time. Did she encourage her sister? Make her ask on her behalf? Thinking back, there were two of them there last night. Though one quick glance had been sufficient for me to dismiss this one. Did they plot it together? And for what reason? Is this some kind of a joke?

I look down at her face, the woman's biting her lip. She looks nervous. I glance again at Blade, and he just shrugs. Oh fuck it, might as well get on with the pretence. She wouldn't be here if she didn't want to strip. All I have to do is talk to her a while and find a kind way to explain why it wouldn't work. Yeah, like that's going to be easy.

"So, Alex." I'm still trying to adjust fitting the name to the girl in front of me, having been expecting her sister instead.

"Yes. Er, that's me. Er, hi." She gives a little wave, then drops her hand as though realising it's not quite the way to greet bikers.

"Well, let's sit awhile and you can tell us about yourself and your experience."

As her face drops I realise it's worse than I thought, and she's probably never done anything like this before. I indicate the stools sitting by the bar. I take one for myself, Blade pulls up another for him, and we sit, waiting for her to hop up. Which she tries to do. But she's too short, and the stool's too high. After a couple of failed attempts, Blade growls beside me, then stands, lifts her up, and plonks her down on the seat. This time I can't help myself chuckling at her outraged expression.

Blade doesn't notice. "You a midget or something?"

"The correct term is dwarf," she replies haughtily. "And no, I'm not, I'm just short. I'm four-foot eleven."

That's tiny to me, I'm over a foot taller. But at least she's spoken up for herself and shown she's got spirit. And her words have made me look at her mouth, which is luscious and full, just right for putting those lips around a man's cock. Her eyes are large, and so dark with gold flecks. Her cheeks are a little on the chubby side, but attractive for all that, and her nose flares slightly. Her hair is tamed with some sort of gel, tight curls framing her face. All in all, she's pretty enough. At my blatant inspection one eyebrow rises in challenge. Hmm, no shrinking violet here.

Her breasts are enormous, or perhaps they just look out of proportion on her small frame, and her ass seems to hang off the seat. Her stomach is rounded, she looks like a fucking ripe mama. Wiping my hand over my face, I wonder how quickly I can tell her the bad news.

But I'll go through at least some of the motions so I don't disappoint her. "So, you want to be a stripper, doll." The endearment comes naturally, she's such a tiny thing.

"No," she replies quite seriously, shocking me. *She's come to an audition in a strip club, for fucks sake.* But I come back to myself as she continues. "I really don't. But I don't mind being a dancer, and I'm left with few options. I'll tell you upfront, if you need information to put me on the books, I'll not waste your time further."

Blade's quick on the uptake. "Someone looking for ya, darlin?" He's gone tense, and if there's the slightest chance we'd take her on, well, there isn't, but if we did, we'd need to find out who's looking for her. Can't afford to bring trouble to the club.

She gives a little shake of her head, "No. Yes." Then as she realises her answer's probably confusing, adds, "I really don't know. But if he is, I don't want to be found."

"Who we talkin' about, darlin?" Again, Blade gets in first.

There's a slight hesitation, as though she doesn't want to tell us. "My husband, ex-husband."

"Well, which is it? Husband or ex?" I ask for clarification, a little impatiently.

"Husband, unfortunately. I have good grounds for divorce, that won't be a problem, but I don't want him to find out where I am, so I've not yet started proceedings."

There's normally few reasons why a woman doesn't want to be found. I go for the most common. "He hit ya?" She's so tiny, well, in stature, the rest of her is quite large. But even so, for a man to raise his fists to someone as little as her? The thought makes me angry.

There's a flare in her eyes as she replies, her hand going to her cheek. "Only the once."

But, good girl. So many women hangaround, lapping up the excuses until they're too broken to run, or end up dead. That she only let him hurt her just one time shows she's got backbone. Looking closely, I notice while it's somewhat disguised by the dark skin and makeup, she's got some scarring. I'm incensed on her behalf.

"To be honest," I realise she hasn't finished, "we'd been married six years and that was enough for us both. I believe he'll be glad I've gone, but..."

"You're not takin' any chances."

Gratefully, she nods at Blade.

"You got a place to stay?" I'm not sure why I'm asking. It must be the fact she's so petite that brings out my protective instinct.

She smiles—the expression transforming her face, revealing she's really quite pretty—and nods. "Yes, with my sister and her husband."

"The girl you were with last night." I'm glad she's got family looking out for her.

Another nod, but this time the sides of her mouth turn down. "I'm sorry, I suspect that's who you were expecting. She set this up. Set *me* up."

"But you need work, and a job off the books." Blade looks at me, and lifts his chin. It seems he's taken a liking to this little pixie, and fuck me if I haven't too. Perhaps we can find her some waitressing work. We do own the Wheel Inn restaurant, there might be something for her there, where her out-of-proportion figure wouldn't be such a drawback.

I decide to be blunt. "Look," I wave my hand at her. "You're not really the type we employ here."

Before I can finish my sentence, she interrupts, saying forcefully, "You haven't given me a chance yet to show what I can do."

Surprised, not normally used to someone cutting me off, it pulls me up. Part of me wants to teach her a lesson. "So you want to take your clothes off, show us what you got?" I suspect my harsh question will have her running. Berating myself, I wish I hadn't spoken so sharply. Something about her makes me hope she'll accept the challenge. While we've been talking, I've started to see her in a different light, and now I'm intrigued to see what's under her clothes. She's not giving away very much at the moment, though she's wearing skin-tight yoga pants, her chest concealed by an ill-fitting sweatshirt. Though her top's baggy, it doesn't hide that she is indeed, as Blade had hoped, stacked.

She licks her lips. *Fuck girl, just stop.* I'm amazed as my cock twitches when my attention is drawn to her mouth once more.

"I don't want to strip totally naked, I couldn't do that. But I do want to dance. I'll show you what I can do, and then you can decide."

"You want to dance for us?"

"Yes, Blade, wasn't it? Yes, Blade. I do."

Her back straightens and a look of determination comes to her face. Blade looks at me and raises his eyebrow. I return his stare. A silent conversation between us of, *What could it hurt?* A few minutes of our time, that's all it will take. I only hope I can hold off from busting my gut laughing.

Reaching inside the purse on her lap, she brings out a disc. "Can you put this on for me, please?"

At least she's come organised. Calling Road over, I pass it to him. He looks at the title.

"Got this on the system already, Dart."

"Go cue it up then." Road knows his way around. Before becoming a prospect he worked here full-time as a bouncer.

She slides off the stool, a major achievement, but lands surprisingly lightly on her feet. Taking her purse along with her, she ascends the steps to the stage and approaches the pole in the middle.

"Oh fuck. I don't know if I can fuckin' bear to watch." Blade covers his eyes with his hands, fingers splayed so he can still peer through.

But my attention has been caught as she rips off her sweatshirt. She's wearing a tight tank underneath that reveals curves my fingers actually itch to touch. Next, she opens the purse and brings out a couple of items. A spray bottle is one, and she squirts it at the pole, another is a tube of something she squeezes onto her hands. I nudge my brother. "Looks like she at least knows what she's doin'."

"If she falls off, that ass is gonna dent the floor."

"Can it!" I growl, for some reason wanting to give her a chance.

Suddenly the sound of claps and the first beats sound of Enrique Iglesias' Bailando start to play. Her face splits into a grin as she approaches the pole, her body already swaying to the beat in perfect rhythm. As she takes hold and pulls herself up and performs some sort of cart wheel around the base, the way she's pointing her toes seems to make her legs look longer. Then she's hooking her leg around the pole, balancing with just one knee and leaning back and, oh fuck me, her back arched to the floor shows her breasts just begging to be caressed. In an amazing display of flexibility, the moves just keep coming, and all the time she's keeping to the beat. When I get a glimpse of her face she's smiling, her eyes flashing. She's loving this shit.

I exchange a look with Blade. He's fucking entranced. She's doing some serious progressions, she fucking owns that pole. I've seen dancers aplenty, more than I care to count, but I can't remember anyone quite so elegant, and at the same time so fucking sexy. What seemed to weigh her down when she was on the ground appears flattering when she wraps herself around the metal. She might not be naked, but she's alluring enough as it is.

SATAN'S DEVILS #4: Targeting Dart

Oh, hell. What's she doing now? She's off the pole and taking a deep breath, her body still moving to the rhythm though. *Is that it? Has she no stamina?* She glances across to me, now her smile's smaller and appears nervous, then her shoulders come back as she seems to come to a decision. Without hesitation, she takes her yoga pants off, and there's the tank gone. It wasn't the best striptease I've ever seen, but I'll be fucked if it wasn't worth it. Now all she's wearing is a red satin bra and panty set, the colour contrasting well with her dark skin, and revealing the gentle curve of her stomach. *She'd feel soft under my hands.* And now she's shimmering up the pole again. Christ, did I say she was sexy? What's a word that means she's even more than that?

She's back on the pole and I can see more of her now, her muscles rippling, her skin glistening from the effort she's putting on. How she can keep hold with just one hand, or just her ankles, I've no idea. She's must have a lot of strength, particularly in her arms and thighs. But it's not her athletic ability that gets to me most. No, it's that ass and tits, and everything else she's got. It's the whole fucking package, and the whole way she's shimmying and not once missing a beat.

My jeans get uncomfortable, and I reach down to adjust myself. One glance at Blade and he's doing the same. He catches me noticing, and sends me a wry look.

"I'll be the first to admit I'm wrong, Brother."

"Me too, Blade, me fuckin' too. If we can compromise she'll wear a thong and pasties and does a striptease as she's comin' down that pole, the customers will go wild for her."

"She fuckin' owns it, Brother."

I watch her again. She seems lost in her own world. Her lips are curved up in a satisfied smile as she twists and turns, pulls herself up, and lets herself slide again. *She's loving it.* She's not dancing for me, she's dancing for herself.

Blade's right. The patrons would fucking love it.

CHAPTER 4

Alex

Spraying vodka on the pole to clean it, and then chalk onto my hands, I prepare to dance as though my life depends on it. Which, in essence, it does. I *need* this job, need money going into the bank so I'm no longer a burden on my sister, and hopefully can start to save up. *I can do this.* I must.

The music starts, the beat's counting me in. I begin to forget everything else and lose myself in my routine, stretching out my legs with my toes pointed, the move my instructor would tell me seemed to lengthen my legs. All the time keeping to the rhythm, I plant the toes of one leg square with the base and hook my knees around the pole, when I arch my back with my head and hands hanging down, knowing I'm making the most of my ample bust in this pose. Now I'm back on the pole, gripping it halfway up and opening my legs gracefully into a V, then keeping my legs out straight, raise them over my head so I'm upside down in the inverted position. I then transition smoothly into the plank, and follow that with one hand above my head and the other in line with my waist, then raising myself up to perform the boomerang spin.

I feel constricted in my clothes. Normally when I'm on the pole I'm wearing just a leotard. My first thought is that original audience of one, and my memory of Ron watching the video, his face first mocking then twisting in disgust. Now, this time I'm dancing it's in front of two, no, three bikers if you include

SATAN'S DEVILS #4: Targeting Dart

the one behind the bar who's stopped his work to look. Their eyes rapt as they watch. Before my nerves catch up with me, I gracefully dismount and rip off my yoga pants and top, glad I'd had the foresight to wear my best underwear today. Red satin against my black skin.

Then I'm back on the pole, enjoying the freedom, letting my mind escape as I twist and twirl, my muscles stretching and contracting. I'm completely oblivious to anything else as I lose myself in the dance, unable even to name the positions I move through, lost in the beat of the song. My arms and legs moving, stomach and thighs working to support me in contorted positions, spinning and moving in time with the music. To the floor and back up, posing, then twisting again.

The music comes to an end. I time it perfectly, sliding down, and end up doing the splits, my head bowed low to the floor. I wait. It's completely silent. Then the room is filled with the sound of clapping and whistles.

Embarrassed now to be wearing so little, I pick up my tank and pull it over my head and quickly slip into my pants.

Ron had complained about my figure, told me to do some exercise. Telling him I'd joined a gym, I let him assume what he wanted, but had taken up pole dancing lessons instead. At first even I thought myself mad, but I soon found my talent. I'd practiced and practiced, and then got my teacher to film me. I'd dressed as sexy as I could, cooked Ron his favourite meal, then hooked up my phone to the TV, hoping my display would have spiced up our non-existent sex life. All he'd said was what an idiot I looked like. How ungainly, and such a joke. He'd bring up his dinner if he watched any more, and other unflattering comments. We never spoke of it again, but without him knowing, I continued to dance. From that point on, just for myself.

Now I stand rigid, not daring to look. *Are they laughing at me too?* Their response didn't suggest it, but they might just be being kind for the short chubby girl who'd given it her all.

My back is turned toward my small audience, and I've tears in my eyes. I couldn't have done more. Now I should pick up my purse and go home. I start bending to the floor to take hold of it as the sound of heavy motorcycle boots clomps toward me. Not wanting to be hurt by seeing his expression, I don't turn around.

"Pasties and a thong. We'll settle for that. When can you start?"

My back straightens as I have trouble processing the words. While I never dreamed of ending up working in a strip club, I'm desperate and destitute. This compromise he's offering of not getting completely naked is one I'm sure I could make. Without turning, disbelieving I've passed the audition, trying to stop my voice shaking with excitement, I ask for confirmation. "You're offering me a job?"

"Fuck, doll. Never seen anythin' like that before. Of course I'm offerin' you a fuckin' job. Would be out of my fuckin' head if I didn't."

Now I twist around, my head first, followed by my body. The man called Dart is standing in front of me, admiration shining out from his eyes. And, if I'm not mistaken, the outline of a very stiff dick pushing at the denim of his jeans.

My lips curve into a small, self-satisfied smile. My moves certainly hadn't had that effect on my ex. I feel like fist pumping the air, and my mouth widens into a grin. "I'll agree to the terms. And I can start whenever you like."

Dart reaches out his hand and helps me off the stage. "Fuck, woman, where the hell did you learn to dance like that?"

"Classes," I explain, my feet on the floor, but I'm strangely reluctant to let go of the biker's hand. A feeling reciprocated, as he doesn't drop mine, but leads me back to the bar where Blade is beaming at me.

"You fuckin' owned that, darlin'."

Nodding at his compliment, I can't stop myself from smiling. I'm in a strip club run by bikers, and I feel appreciated for the first time in my life. *There Ron. Suck that up.*

"It's what I love doing." I feel brave enough to try to explain. "I feel weightless and free, as though I'm flying."

As though he's been doing it all his life, Blade puts his strong arms around me and lifts me back onto the stool, this time with no comment about my lack of height. His actions force Dart to let go of my hand, and as I catch a glimpse of his face, I see his mouth tighten.

"Stop manhandlin' her, Blade."

"Whatcha gonna do, get lower stools?"

Their interaction makes me laugh. "One with cross bars would help, so I could climb up."

"You ain't gonna be sittin' at the bar, doll. You'll come on, do your set, then get the hell back stage."

Blade's eyebrows rise as he glances at Dart, but he doesn't say anything. I don't think anything of it, just feel relieved. I've been given the confirmation that all Dart wants me to do is to dance.

We spend a few moments talking about wages, and they explain I'll be able to double that or more with tips. I'm pleased, as it sounds more than sufficient for me to pay back my sister, and, if they're right about the money that will be thrown on the stage, enough to start a savings account. I'm on cloud nine and can't wipe the grin off my face.

Then Dart takes out his wallet and peels off a few bills. "Get somethin' sexy, doll." As I glance at him, perplexed, he adds, "You obviously need money, so I'm guessin' you could do with an advance to get some suitable costumes. You'll need to incorporate a striptease durin' your dance. You know how to do that?"

I offer a guilty nod. Yeah, my teacher had taught me, and I'd done that on the video I'd shown to Ron. My only reward had been a sneer accompanied by gagging sounds. I try to push my ex out of my head. "Will I have access here, during the day? I'll need to work up some routines, vary it up a bit."

Dart's eyes roam over me, and he widens his stance. "Anytime you want, doll." He waves around to the cleaners I hadn't realised were there, so quietly and efficiently doing their job. "As you can see, we have people workin', so just come in when you want and do your stuff."

And will he be here, watching me? The thought makes me shiver.

We've gone through all the necessary arrangements, me, of course, making sure they agreed to that so important cash in hand. Just when I'm about to slide off the stool and make my way out, Dart stops me with a hand to my arm.

"Your ex. We need to know if he's gonna cause a problem."

I bite my lip, unable to totally reassure them, but doubting it myself. "He doesn't know where I am. I could be anywhere in the country for all he knows."

"Where's he live, darlin'? Anywhere close?"

Answering Blade, I shake my head. "Not really, he's in San Diego."

"But you're stayin' with your sister. Surely that's the first place he'll look?"

I raise my chin toward Dart and sigh. I don't really want to tell them my life story, but I can appreciate why they wouldn't want a furious ex-husband bursting into the club and causing trouble. "I'm the only one in my family who's kept in contact with Celine." I pause to take a deep breath and then let it all out. "When she was eighteen she was raped. Got pregnant. She had an abortion, and my parents threw her out. I was forbidden to stay in touch with her, but I disobeyed their rules. She was held over me as an example of what I shouldn't do." And that's when they pressured me into marrying a man of their choice. A respectable alliance that wouldn't bring shame on the family. "They don't know, or care, where she ended up."

Blade and Dart seem to have a silent conversation. An eyebrow raised here, a grunt there. But they don't press further, hopefully having heard enough to satisfy them I'd gotten away cleanly.

Dart's hand has remained on my arm, causing a strange tingling sensation. He squeezes his fingers, and what he says next surprises the hell out of me. "You're workin' here now, which means you're under our protection. One sniff of trouble and you come to me, okay?"

Now that was totally unexpected. I'm not particularly worried about Ron, suspecting he'll just be pleased that I'm gone, though there's always the outside chance he'll want what I brought with me. Tears prick at the corners of my eyes as men I don't know give me the security I didn't know I even wanted until it was offered. Ron's got a bad temper. I only allowed him the one chance to get physical with me, but now that he's started, he might not be able to stop. He was barely able to last time.

Dart clears his throat. "Club's open Tuesday through Saturday. You'll dance every night."

Sounds fine to me, gives me a chance to earn more.

"You can start tomorrow if you want."

That gives me the time to sort out some clothes easy to take off, and, of course, a few nice underwear sets. I give an eager nod.

"You think you can do it?" Blade seems concerned. "A roomful of men is different than just the two of us."

Having assured him that won't be a problem—as I think I've demonstrated, I get lost in my head when I'm dancing, and who

I'm in front of doesn't bother me at all, I don't even see them—at last this strange interview comes to an end.

I leave the club, and once outside, stand for a moment with my head resting on the wall. A giggle bursts out of me. How the fuck did I end up like this? My plan for life had been to be a lawyer, to stay in school and study hard. But then Ron had turned up, introduced by my parents, paraded in front of me as a suitable mate. And stupidly, I'd not put up much resistance, unwilling to disappoint them. And Ron was easy enough on the eyes. I'd been flattered, if slightly aghast at the speed, by his swift offer of marriage. In fact, my parents had been in the room, and had accepted on my behalf.

From then I was caught up in an avalanche, unable to escape what was bowling down that hill. I was wed before I knew it, and barely finished the first year of college when Ron decided he wanted a full-time wife.

And look at me now. Christ, my parents would disown me. A stripper dancing in a men's club? But then, they've probably already decided they didn't have a daughter anymore. Leaving my husband would have shamed them enough.

I might not have become a top-notch lawyer, but I've got this job on my own, and I'm allowed to feel some pride.

After driving back on cloud nine, I enter my sister's home to find her waiting for me, her face impassive, ready to react to whatever news I've got, either to transform her features into a sympathetic frown or a smile of delight.

For a moment I keep her in suspense, my expression equally set. Then I can't hold it in any longer. "I got the job!" I cry out.

She beams, then squeals. "I knew you could do it! Alex, that video you sent me of the way that you work that pole, showed you had talent." Then her face falls. "You gonna be okay working in that club? I know this can't be what you wanted."

"Are you kidding me? Dancing every night? They don't expect me to do more, Celine. They made that clear. I'll be doing something I love, and getting paid for it." Taking hold of her hands, I look up into her face. "You might have got the height, *big* sister, but I got the moves. And I'll be able to pay my way and have more besides." I twirl her around me and shake my butt. She tries to copy me and stumbles, making us both laugh.

Then she pulls away and grows serious. "You know I'll always help you out. Anything you need me to do."

She'll have to, as I'll be working nights.

CHAPTER 5

Dart

"Snake's offered to help."

I nod to acknowledge our prez's announcement. It's our Friday night church, the weekly meeting all brothers are required to attend, and which is traditionally followed by a party, an alcoholic fuck fest. Normally nothing would keep me from participating, happy to leave Satan's Topless Angels in the safe hands of Road and the rest of our staff. But tonight, I'm eager to see how the new girl will cope having to perform in front of a live and very lewd audience, and decide while I'll stay after church, it will just be for a couple of drinks. For once, forsaking the chance to get my dick wet doesn't worry me none. If yesterday was anything to go by, and if Alex hasn't had nerves and decides not to show, I suspect after seeing her on that pole I'll be straight back here to drag a sweet butt into the nearest room to give my poor throbbing cock some relief. Even the memory of how she moved to the music has me already swelling. *Fuck it. I'm in church!*

"We know where he is?" I try to concentrate on the meeting I'm supposed to be contributing to.

"SoCal is all we know, but Mouse has been trackin' him. He's not tryin' to stay under the radar. Which suggests he doesn't know we're lookin' for him."

"Yeah, I got a hit on his credit card in Escondido of all places." Our computer nerd indicates his laptop, always open in front of him. Sometimes I think his fingers are glued to the keys.

"Can Snake tempt him out into the open?" I ask.

"Yeah. The plan is for him to reach out. He's puttin' out rumours that the San Diego chapter wants to break off from us." We're the mother chapter of the Satan's Devils MC. Snake is the president of our chapter down in San Diego. If they really were pulling away, it wouldn't seem strange they'd be gearing up for a fight and would want to bolster their ranks. And floating the suggestion might tempt a rogue Demon to join their numbers.

It was five months ago that we took out the Rock Demons, and we didn't do it quietly, we blew up their club. Only two escaped, and the fact they got away didn't bother us much at the time. Not being officers, we thought them unlikely to cause problems. That is, until we found out what they'd done to Slick's wife, Ella, and that one escapee was the nephew of their now very dead president. Always wary of trouble, we took the vote on cleaning up the remnants. Then we can stop looking over our shoulders.

I listen as Peg throws out some thoughts, and pull out my smokes as Blade adds his bit. He breaks off midway to point at my pack. When it's returned to me, having gone around the table, it's half empty as usual. Pulling the ashtray toward me, I shake my head.

The vote comes around, and I record the decision in the book, while wishing Heart was here to take over the task. In his absence I'm acting secretary, and although that gives me the hallowed, albeit temporary officer status, I'd rather my brother returned and took back his rightful role.

"What's the latest with Heart?" As the prez speaks, I wonder if Drummer can read my thoughts.

"He's not in a good place," Wraith replies.

"Can understand that." Viper frowns.

Lady puts up his hand, the prez gives him a chin jerk. "He's not plannin' on comin' back to the club." *What?* Various expressions of disapproval go around the table as Lady continues, "I was with him last night. Seems he's makin' plans to visit an ex-Army buddy up in Utah."

"If it's the one I'm thinkin' of, I thought there was bad blood there." I frown. "He never agreed with Heart bein' in the club." I hope he won't be persuaded to turn in his patch.

Lady shrugs. "Don't know about that, but the fucker's pickin' him up Sunday."

"He needs his real friends, his *brothers* around him," Beef snarls.

"And his fuckin' daughter needs *him*. He takin' her with him?" Joker seems incredulous Heart's not coming back.

"He comin' back when he's healed?" I couldn't think of Heart permanently being gone from the club. Fuck it, he couldn't be pulling away, could he? His choice of place to convalesce gives me no good feelings.

As Lady shrugs again, obviously not knowing the answer, the prez snarls out, "He doesn't quit the club without talkin' to me. And we don't take brothers leave lightly." Drummer's face has gone dark.

"Don't shoot the messenger, Prez. Just repeatin' what he told me."

"Okay, well I'll go visit him tomorrow and see what the fuck he's thinkin'." The prez glares around the table as if it's our fault. He probably doesn't even know he's doing it, but when Drum gives *that* stare, everyone shrinks back into their seats. Then he pushes his chair back and puts his foot up against the table while tunnelling his hands through his hair. When he speaks next, he changes the subject. "Heard you've taken a new girl on, Dart?"

"Yeah, Prez. Tonight's her first night. I'm be gonna go along in a bit to make sure she's doin' okay."

Blade's grinning. "Strange lookin' bitch. Dark meat, Prez."

"A black?" Drum looks surprised. "Well, I suppose it's different. She fit?"

Now Blade and I exchange glances. How to describe someone who you wouldn't look at twice if she wasn't swinging around that pole? In the end, I plump for something fairly non-descript so Drum won't think I'm out of my mind to hire her. "She's got what it takes to interest the customers." Yeah, those fuckers will be all over that. But I'm visualising her in my head, pretty face, gorgeous tits, luscious ass, but all in a very small package. Nothing there to attract me, except for the way she can move.

"She uses what God's given her," Blade adds, chuckling.

The prez nods. "Well, see how it goes. We've got a reputation to maintain. Good girls bring in the money."

"I'll keep an eye on her, Prez."

"Any other business we need to fuckin' discuss?"

Nothing's offered. Drum bangs the gavel and sends us on our way.

Tonight, it's the prospect Hyde who's minding the bar and passing out beers. I take one and have the bottle halfway to my lips when Blade appears.

"You're gonna go watch her first performance, then?"

"Yeah, thought I would."

"You're takin' a risk on her, you know that? Sure, she can dance, but when those fuckers start getting their hands on her..."

"Ain't no fuckers gettin' near her," I snarl.

Blade, the bastard, laughs. "Like that is it? You fancy tappin' somethin' different?"

Christ, I've got to shut him down fast. There's a myriad of reasons why he's way off the mark. "I'd break her in fuckin' two, man. Not my taste at all. You see how tiny she fuckin' is?" I scowl at him for even thinking I'd go there.

"Not in the tit or ass department." He's right there. But it's the parts in between which are a bit lacking. And what's more, I'd lose my patch if I gave her a trial run. It's a written rule we don't touch our employees.

Two hours later, I'm walking into the Angels. It's a full house tonight, every table filled, which will put a smile on Dollar's face. Topless waitresses walk around, evading groping hands and carrying drinks to the customers. My sharp eyes fall on a table of men, their raucous behaviour suggesting they're out on a stag night.

I nod to Fergus, one of our bouncers. "Keep an eye on them."

"Already on it, boss."

He's a good man. Knowing I can safely leave the potentially rowdy group to him, I make my way out back to the dressing rooms. The girls are all strippers and used to me giving only a brief knock to warn them before walking in while they're in various states of undress. All except one, that is, who yelps and goes to cover herself in a robe. I smirk, thinking she hadn't really thought through what working in a strip club entailed.

My lips quirk as I step forward to greet her. "You doin' okay, doll?"

"I'm here, aren't I?" she answers in a spirited voice.

"Nervous?" Her expression tells me I'm stupid even to ask. "You'll be fine," I tell her, sincerely, and remembering how she'd blown me away when she danced, it's no false platitude.

She rubs her hands together and looks up with a cheeky grin. "As long as I don't slide off the pole."

I've scheduled her early, as we tend to lead up to the best. She's yet to prove herself, so we'll try her with one number to see how she goes down. That goes okay, we'll have her on again later. She's biting her lip, a habit I've noticed. "Spit it out."

"Will you be watching?" she asks in her husky voice.

"Yeah, doll. I watch all the dancers." When I'm here I usually do. There are perks to this job.

But her face lights up, and her eyes sparkle as if that was the right answer. Then she sets those dark eyes on me and drops her robe, making me inhale a sharp breath. Fuck me, I can see she's obeyed my instruction. Under several sheer red veils, I can clearly see matching red pasties and a thong. Around me other women are half naked, but none of them make my cock stir. But her? Unable to understand my reaction, I turn away to leave and get on with my business, but I don't miss the little smile of satisfaction which comes to her face.

Fuck me. If I didn't know better I'd think she was flirting with me. Well she can think again on that. She's so far from the type of woman I go for it's laughable, and even if I wanted to, anyone who works for us is off limits to me and all of my brothers. As I walk back to the stage area I realise I might have to make sure she understands that.

Lyndsy comes on and starts off the night. She's in good form, and sufficient dollars land on the stage to show we've got high rollers in tonight. Then a now-familiar tune starts to play, the house lights go down, a spotlight comes up, illuminating a small figure coming onto the stage.

There's a ripple of laughter, which makes my heart break, and a voice beside me says, over-loudly, "Didn't realise it was comedy night." I cringe, hoping she hasn't heard it.

But, completely oblivious, Alex walks onto the platform and approaches the pole as though she's been doing it all her life. Her eyes half closed, she swings herself up and begins her routine. Dry ice wafts around her, and within moments she has everyone enthralled. As she works that pole, she transports every man watching away.

No one speaks. The laughter has stopped. All eyes are upon this dark-skinned beauty going through her moves, transfixed, as one by one those veils float to the floor. When she slides down as the music comes to an end, a thunderous roar goes up. *She's done it.* Watching for the second time with the right lighting is even better than when I first saw her routine. The magic she wreaks by the way she uses her body, somehow transforming her awkward shape into something amazing, so fluid, so sexy. My jeans feel too tight, as I suspect do every man's here. Just the effect the dancers are supposed to cause. Something to fuel the patrons when they go home to their wives. Or in my case, when I hammer into a club whore tonight.

She's waiting, head bowed. Money floats down onto the stage. With a beautiful, almost angelic expression, she starts to gather it up. I jump on the stage, my hand to the small of her back, and push her toward the dressing room.

"I'll get it for you." My voice sounds gruff. Though she's got some covering, I don't want the men ogling her as she bends and twists, showing that ripe ass split by just the string of the thong as she picks up the money in her hands.

It makes sense to give her another spot. When she comes back for her second set the room is silent with anticipation. Now knowing what to expect, they wait breathless for her to start. Men getting lap dances push girls off them in order to watch. Employing her was no mistake.

Her dance finished, I again collect the tips on her behalf, pocketing the money in my cut to give to her later. Then, not interested in seeing the girls I've watched a hundred times before, I go to the bar.

"She's fuckin' amazin'," Della, our bartender tells me with a wide grin, as she hands me a beer.

"She's somethin' else, isn't she?" I'm just pleased that I gave her the chance to show what she could do. Yeah, I'm giving myself a pat on the back for that.

"She'll bring in the customers." Della's correct, and her observation pleases me. Even another woman can see Alex's worth.

I nod, thinking I'll need to get photos taken, hoping a still on a poster would show how magnificent she looks. Perhaps in that pose she does with her head flung back and tits pushed up. Maybe it's her dark skin, but there's an air of mystique, an unknown and forbidden aura that surrounds her.

Leaning back against the bar as Della fills a table order, I look around at the men in the club, still rapt. A waitress approaches me. "Dart that table there…" she points to the stag party I noticed earlier. "They want to know whether the new girl is available for lap dances."

No fucking way. "No, she's not," I say shortly.

She nods and goes away to deliver the disappointing news. I see her telling the group, then indicating myself. A man gets up and comes over. He's fishing out his wallet and taking out high denomination bills.

"Here," he says as he approaches, "we'll pay good money for the black bitch."

My fingers curl into my hands. Men think they can have anything they're after at the right price. But they're not going to get Alex. *Perhaps she could use the money.* I'm not giving her a choice in the matter.

"No," I say curtly, hoping that word is enough. If he doesn't take the hint then I'll follow if up with my fists.

He sneers. "Your loss." He pointedly puts his notes back into his wallet and then goes back to his friends. I watch him, and don't like the way he and a couple of the other men are whispering, *plotting.* Hmm. We've had trouble with the likes of them before. Just because a woman takes her clothes off on stage doesn't mean she's up for anything more. Like Alex, most of them are only here because they have no alternative.

Making a quick decision, I go backstage to the dressing room, but the person I'm seeking isn't there.

"Alex? The new girl?"

"Oh, you're talking about the coloured girl? She left after her set." Bambi shrugs as she answers.

Again my fists clench. "Don't call her that." *Is her skin the only thing she sees?* I stare until she can no longer meet my eyes and turns away with a huff. I spin on my heels and go to the back entrance. Philby, another bouncer, is stationed out here to make sure the girls get to their cars unmolested, and to make sure no one tries to sneak in this way.

"Have you seen the new girl? Alex?"

"The black? Yeah, she left some time ago. Drove off in her car." *What is it with these people?* I feel incensed on her behalf. Snarling, I tell him, "She's Alex, okay? She's a person, not a colour."

He shrugs as if it's of no matter.

"And she's a fuckin' good draw for the customers. I don't want anyone upsettin' her." That seems to sink in. "Keep your eye out, got a stag party in. They might try to get to the girls as they leave."

"Thanks for the warnin', boss." He taps his two-way radio. "I'll call for backup if I need to."

Job done, I glance back into the club and decide I've had enough for the night. My mission accomplished, which was to make sure the new girl didn't fall flat on her ass, I cross to my bike and return to the compound.

The clubhouse is still packed when I return, more like an orgy than a party. All my brothers are occupied with sweet butts or the hangarounds who've come up from Tucson. Dicks getting sucked, girls getting fucked over any available surface. I seek out someone currently unoccupied. Ah, over there, that's definitely the type I go for. Long, straight blonde hair and legs that go on for fucking miles. They'll be great wrapped around my ass, she can keep those high heels on too. Breasts a bit on the small side, but fuck, what do I care?

Pausing only to snag a beer from Jekyll, I go over. Now I'm not a modest man, I know I've been blessed with good looks and a body girls like. I've no fear of rejection as I take her hand and pull her out back to one of the crash rooms, not wasting a second once we get inside.

"Get naked and on the bed."

Her face flushes at my terse instruction. But shit, she's come here for one reason, and that's for biker cock. And yeah, baby, that's what you're getting tonight.

"Keep your shoes on."

She grins. She probably paid a fortune for those. Quickly she dispenses with her clothes—it doesn't take long, she's not wearing much. And now she's naked and she's lying on the bed on her back, her ribs clearly showing, her breasts looking even smaller now. But it's her pussy I'm focusing on.

"You ready for me?"

"You going to lick me out?"

It's late, I'm probably not the first she's had tonight, so the answer is a definite no. "You're gonna take my big cock," I tell her, a demand, not a question. Without invitation, I put my hand on her cunt, checking and finding it sopping wet. Yeah, she likes the man to be in control.

"Now slide those legs up baby, show me what you've got to give."

She does as I say. I take off my cut, placing it carefully down, then slide off my tee. Her head's turned to the side and I see her eyes widen and she writhes as my tattoos and abs come into view. My mouth twists. "Gonna give it to you hard and fast."

Her face flushes again. *Yeah, she likes the sound of that.*

Undoing my zip, I free my cock, slip on a condom, and then kneel on the bed. Her eyes are studying everything I do.

"Yer a dirty bitch, ain't cha?"

Her eyes open wide as she nods. Her pupils are dilated and her breathing comes fast.

Without waiting a moment longer, I hold her thighs apart and thrust inside, and then start hammering to get myself off. Her legs come around me, trying to hold me close. I use no finesse, but my assault is exciting her. When I hear little gasps and a slight tightening of her pussy, I press hard on her clit, then pinch it. Her cries get louder. Thank fuck she's not going to take long.

When she goes over I let myself follow, the release that I needed pumping out into the condom.

Finished, I slide off her, go into the bathroom and deal with my shit. She's still lying naked on the bed and staring up at me with adoring eyes when I return. Like I said, I'm good looking, and quite a catch. Though no one's come close to hooking me yet, all the girls seem to think they're in with the chance of being on the back of my bike. But with all the willing pussy on offer, except for the sweet butts who know the score, it's rare, if ever, that I go back for a repeat performance.

In a breathy voice she tells me, "That was amazing." Yeah, it probably was. With all the practice, I should know how to fuck.

Ignoring her comment, I pick up her clothes and toss them on the bed. "Thanks for that, sweetheart."

Her face falls, then she gets the message and starts slipping into her tight short skirt, leaning forward as if to make the most of her breasts. It does nothing for me. I've got my rocks off, and now I just want a drink. But I wait, like a gentleman, until she's ready, then opening the door, gently push her out.

"Can we do that again?" She turns, puts her arms around my neck, her intention clearly to kiss me.

I rear back, having none of that, and tell her quite frankly, "Enjoyed it myself, it was a good fuck. But I don't do repeats, babe." And I'm not one to kiss. The girls I fuck may well have sucked one of my brothers off already tonight. And the thought of tasting another man's cum holds no appeal at all.

But she just stands in the doorway, placing one hand onto her hip, the other she brings to her mouth, sucking her finger in between her lips. It does nothing to tempt me.

"I could make you feel good."

I'm tired and thirsty. And now she's just pissing me off. "Look, babe, you've got great legs, but not much going in this area." I point to her tits. "To be honest, you're really not my type."

Her mouth drops open as if she's unused to being rejected in such a direct way, then, muttering something angrily under her breath, storms off.

Jesus. Women! Always wanting to make more of it than what it is. I turn around and pick up my tee and cut. Then it hits me. Why did I tell her she wasn't my type? She's exactly the kind of girl who attracts me, and the reason why I made a beeline for her in the first place. What the fuck's wrong with me? It's true that I wouldn't have been up for another round, but even though she'd started to annoy me, it's not like me to be quite so cruel and blunt.

As I slide my arms into my leather, my hands land on the bulge in my pocket. *Shit.* I forgot to give Alex her tips. And suddenly my mind conjures up a woman with a completely different figure. I huff a laugh. She doesn't fall into the category which would capture my interest either. No fucking way.

CHAPTER 6
Dart

After chasing the girl off last night, I'd gone to the bar and drank more than I normally do, with the predictable result that this morning that I've woken with a headache which feels like someone's banging a drum in my head. Twisting my torso around, I grab my phone to see it's already noon. Fuck. I hadn't meant to sleep in so late, not with that money burning a hole in my pocket. What if Alex thinks she isn't going to be given the money she's earned? And she'd taken a fair amount in tips, a couple of hundred dollars by the feel of that wad. I need to give it back to her as soon as possible. If she thinks I've taken it, she may have second thoughts about turning up to dance tonight.

I'll call her. *I don't have her number.* Fuck. Still holding my phone, I tap it against my mouth and then do place a call. Within seconds I've got her address. Now I've just got to drag my lazy ass out of bed.

A quick run through the shower, a couple of Advil and a coffee, and I'm ready to go. Not being the only one to have over-partied last night, there's hardly anyone around as I make my way to the gate. Hyde slides it open, and I drive on through, onto the freeway, and make my way through the city and to the suburbs where her sister lives.

Drawing up outside, I notice it's a pleasant enough brick home, probably only a two-bed looking from the outside, the front yard well maintained and welcoming. I park in the driveway and make my way to the front door. As I raise my hand to knock, the door swings open.

"Like your bike, mister." A high-pitched voice greets me.

I knew I'd have to look down, but I have to lower my gaze even further and eventually meet an eager face looking up. It's a young boy, five, possibly six at most. And my first thought is, fuck, he's got something to learn about opening doors to strangers.

He must be the sister's kid.

"Hi," I start, softening my voice. "I've come to see Alex, is she home?"

"Yeah, Mom's in the shower. Is that a Harley?"

Fuck! She's got a kid?

"Is your…" I quickly work it out in my head, having to swiftly change the roles I'd assumed, "aunt home?"

"Nah, Auntie Celine and Uncle Craig have gone out to the mall."

And this young boy is opening the door while his mom's naked with water running over those breasts… *Fuck man! Don't go there.*

Then it gets worse. "Do you want to come in and wait. She won't be long."

"Um, yer mom ever spoken to you about opening the door to someone you don't know?"

The boy's eyes widen, and it must have been the tone of my voice as he asks, "Have I done something wrong?" His lower lip trembles.

Luckily I'm saved when, *fuck me*, Alex appears, dressed only with a towel around her. "You okay, Tyler?" she asks as she continues drying her hair, and only when she's checked he's alright, notices at last that the front door is open.

Her eyes and mine meet at the same time. Hers widen as mine narrow. Fuck, I saw her almost naked yesterday, but there's something about knowing she's completely unclothed beneath that barely ample covering, with water drops glistening on her dark skin, that makes me feel very uncomfortable. She opens her mouth, I get in first and say the first thing that comes into my head just to get my mind off her body.

"Tyler and I were just getting acquainted."

"Tyler!" she snaps. "What have I told you about opening the door?"

Her son turns and shuffles his feet. "I know, Mom. You told me not to open the door without asking you first." Then he adds in an excited voice by way of explanation, "But he's got a motorcycle."

I swallow a laugh as Alex tries to keep her face stern. She fails, and steps forward, affectionately ruffling the boy's hair. "That makes it alright then, does it?"

He leans in close. "Sorry, Mom."

"Just don't do it again. No matter what. Not without asking me or your uncle or aunt."

When the boy nods to agree, she seems to remember I'm here, and now it's hesitation on her face. "Why are you here, Dart? Don't tell me you're firing me."

"*Firin'* you? Hell no. You did great last night."

She offers a hesitant smile and laughs awkwardly. "Oh, well, I'm glad."

I continue, "In fact, you made decent tips. You left last night before I came lookin' for ya and I wasn't able to give you your money, so I brought it today. Didn't want you to think I'd pocketed it myself." Reaching into my cut, I pull out the wad of notes and hold it out to her. She takes it awkwardly, struggling to keep hold of her towel, and for a second, looking at a loss where to put it.

In the end, she offers it to the kid. "Can you go put this in my purse, Tyler?"

The boy's looking from her, and then to me. He seems reluctant to leave.

I suss out the reason. "Go do what your mom says, Ty, and then I'll show you my bike, if your mom agrees."

As he turns and runs off, I don't think I've ever seen a kid looking so happy before. I raise my eyebrow at Alex, waiting to know if there's any objection. She peers around me out the door, seeing my bike parked close by.

"Look, why don't you go and dress while I show Tyler my sled. I won't be takin' him anywhere. And then we ought to talk." Her ex might not be trying to find *her*. But what man lets his kid go? There's pricking at the back of my neck, which suggests there could be trouble on the horizon.

Looking puzzled, she considers and then gives a little nod. "I'll only be a moment. Watch him carefully, won't you?"

For some inexplicable reason, the thought she's trusting me with her son gives me a warm feeling inside. As she disappears, Tyler comes back, almost jumping up and down in excitement.

"Is it a Harley? I'm right, aren't I? How fast does it go?"

By the time Alex reappears, Tyler knows almost as much as I do about my bike, including that it's been modified to have a chain drive instead of a belt to make it go faster. I'm almost out of things to say, and explaining that I can't take him for a ride, when Alex comes out of the door wearing form-fitting jeans and another of her tank tops, which clings to her tits. Man, *that ass!* And her breasts must be three times those of the girl I was with last night. *And I bet I wouldn't be able to feel her ribs.* I could slide my cock between those tits…

"Come on, Tyler. Let's see what we can put on for you to watch. You mustn't wear yourself out now."

He's being a normal kid. Full of energy. Wondering whether she's an overprotective mother, uninvited, I follow her inside. She fiddles about with the TV, puts on a cartoon, and then points towards the kitchen. Leaving Tyler to amuse himself, I follow her, then lean back against the cabinets. She fidgets as though she doesn't know what to do with her hands, and looks down at her feet.

"Er, Dart. Thank you for bringing the money, but you didn't have to. You could have given it to me tonight."

"No problem. The ride cleared my head." I nod toward the pot on the worktop. "Could do with a coffee, doll."

She seems flustered as she goes about refilling the pot and then pouring a cup for both me and herself.

I wait until I've taken a sip before starting in. "So, Tyler." As she lifts her eyebrows, I explain my concern. "He seems a good kid," I say, partly to settle her, and partly because it's the truth. I've not been around many children, three-year-old Amy's about the closest I've come, but from what I've seen, Tyler's polite and well brought up, and any man would be proud to call him his son. Which is the point that brings me to ask, "I can understand if you don't think your ex is comin' for you. But what about him?"

As she brings her hands to cup either side of her face, I read in her expression that concerns her as well. "That's why I don't want him to find us." When she looks up, her eyes brim with tears. "Before he raised his hand to me, he was getting impatient with Tyler. I couldn't risk him taking it further."

I grit my teeth, having a particular hatred for anyone picking on someone weaker than themselves.

"He didn't like all the questions he keeps asking. He's an inquisitive kid."

I didn't mind at all. Liked someone showing an interest in fact.

"Give me your phone." I make a decision.

"What? Why?"

"So I can give you my number. You get a sniff that he's around, and you call me."

"I haven't got a phone. One of the things I left behind and couldn't afford to replace."

I begin to think there's more she isn't telling me. She left quickly, that's for sure. What woman leaves her phone behind? There's a story I'm yet to hear, and one way or another I'm going to get it out of her. Wouldn't look good for the club if her ex turned up making trouble. Of course, that's all I'm worried about.

Suddenly there's a scream from the family room. Coffee sloshes from her cup as Alex put it down fast and rushes to her son. I follow. Tyler's rolling on the sofa, gripping his leg.

"Where's the pain, baby?" Alex looks frantic. When Tyler points to his calf, she starts massaging the muscle. The boy's crying now, tears rolling down his face. I may have only just met him, but his distress is so real it gets me in the gut. Looking around the room, I don't understand what's happening. There doesn't seem anyway that he could have hurt himself. *Is it just cramp?*

His pain appears genuine and severe, I'm driven to help. "What can I do?"

It's as though she's forgotten I'm there, but at my question she turns and nods down the hallway. "Could you run a hot bath?"

"Sure."

Not really certain why she's asking, I do as she asks, easily finding the small room I'm looking for. When I return, she's giving him a tablet and making sure he drinks a whole glass of juice. Then I follow as she takes him into the bathroom and helps him undress. Still hovering, feeling useless in the doorway, she strips off his clothes and, after testing the temperature, puts him in the warm water.

I continue to watch as she gently strokes his head, her action mesmerising. "Breathe, baby. Deep breaths, in and out. That's it. I know it's hard, but try to relax."

As she slows her breathing, the boy begins to copy her, and I find myself doing the same. Gradually he begins to stretch out in the warm water. It's a while later when he looks up at Alex. "It's getting better, Mom."

Alex closes her eyes, and I see, more than hear, her sigh of relief. It's as if she doesn't want to show her own stress to her son.

"Feeling tired, baby? Want to take a nap."

Obviously somewhat better now, the boy nods his head. Whatever has happened, it's taken it out of him. I have no place here, but am strangely reluctant to leave. I wait while she dries and dresses him, and then while she lays him down. She's back surprisingly quickly, but I notice she's left the door to the boy's bedroom open.

She startles, as if surprised I'm still here, and I notice she looks exhausted herself as she explains, "These episodes take it out of him."

I remember the instruction I'd thought was superfluous, that now gives me a twinge of guilt. "He was running around when I was showing him my bike. Was it…?"

"It was nothing you did." She inhales, and then lets the air out again, and her shoulders slump. She points to the sofa, and as I sit, starts to speak. "I suppose you're curious."

I can't deny it. Throwing a nod towards the open door I can see, I ask, "What's wrong with him?"

She takes a deep breath before telling me, "He should never have been born."

It was the last thing I expected her to say. I pull myself up, but her hand on my arm stays my movement. *And I thought she was a good momma.* Does she resent the kid?

Before I can say anything, she gives me the explanation. "I'm a carrier for sickle cell disease. Ron, that's my ex, told me he wasn't, and I just believed him. Had I known... And anyway, that was in the future. I was going to finish my degree and qualify as a lawyer, and hopefully get established before thinking about having kids. Huh, those were my plans for my future." She breaks off and stares at nothing, as if considering how her life might have turned out. And then continues, "But Ron had other ideas after we were married. One night we were having sex and he took off the condom without me knowing and without my consent."

I suck in air. To my mind that's as bad as rape, even if they were married. But looking at her face, the worst was yet to come.

"I got pregnant. But my baby was going to be healthy. If just one of us is a carrier, there wouldn't be a problem. Ron said the tests were too expensive and unnecessary. But I, I had them done anyway. Even before Tyler was born..." Her voice breaks off as she chokes on the words. "I knew he was positive for sickle cell. I might have not wanted a baby at that time, and certainly wouldn't have taken the risk if I'd known, but by then I couldn't think of getting an abortion, even though my poor baby had already been condemned to a lifetime of hell."

My teeth clench. "Ron was mistaken? He hadn't been tested?"

"Oh, he knew alright. He knew there was a twenty-five percent chance of our child getting the condition. He was just blasé that we'd win those odds. He thought the risk was insignificant as neither him nor his sister had developed the disease. He played with my son's life."

"Jesus!" I stand, brushing my hands over my head. "Fuck, woman. Is the man fuckin' insane? And you stayed with him?"

I can hardly keep up as the words tumble out. "I didn't have much choice. I had a baby to look after. My parents told me they wouldn't help if I walked out of the marriage, and at that point I'd lost touch with my sister. But that's when I started to hate him. Oh, to anyone else he played the part of a devoted husband and father, but he had a child who was broken, and he couldn't handle it. He came home later and later—sometimes not at all—and would start arguments. Celine made contact, and I told her everything. She offered me a place to get away if I ever needed it. But I stuck it out as long as I could, too nervous about striking out on my own. Then came the final straw. He took his hand to me, and I knew I had to leave. Staying was no longer an option, so, well, as you can see, I came here."

I hope he does come to find her. *I'll kill him.*

"You regret having Tyler?"

Her sharp look tells me all I need to know. "I could never regret that. But I would never have had children with another carrier if I had known. What Tyler's going through? You saw his pain just now. No child should have to suffer like that."

She's silently weeping now, tears falling down her face, but she's making no noise. I've never seen a woman cry this way before, it seems she just can't help it. I take a seat beside her again, and it feels natural to pull her into my body. "What's his prognosis?"

She starts talking as if quoting from a book. "People with sickle cell disease have a shortened life expectancy, but they're coming up with new things all the time. And not everyone has painful episodes like the one you just witnessed."

"He get these a lot?" Poor fucking kid.

"Too many." A sob escapes. "The doctors want to try out a drug to limit the frequency, but I've found out all about it, and it might be dangerous at his age and have serious side effects. If he takes it, he'll need biweekly blood tests for the first year to check he's not having adverse reactions. They're even talking about regular blood transfusions if it keeps getting worse. And it costs money, Dart. Money I haven't got." She half-turns to look at me, but it's through her eyelashes, and she swallows a couple of times as if she's guilty of something. "Ron gets insurance through his job…" She breaks off, stares at the floor, and mumbles, "But now he's getting worse…"

"That's why you haven't started divorce proceedings. To stay on his insurance."

"No. In fact, if I get a divorce I might be able to get Tyler's additional needs taken into account as part of the child support."

Something is niggling at me. I test out the waters. "If you've nothing to lose, file for divorce, doll." I hate the thought of her being tied to that motherfucker.

My arm still around her, I can feel her go tense. "I told you he hit me. That sounds like nothing, doesn't it?" Her hand goes to her cheek and traces the scar I'd noticed. "He knocked me out, then left me bleeding on the floor. He didn't care if I was alive or dead. When I came around I managed to call for an ambulance. They kept me in as I was in quite a bad way. I needed stitches and had a concussion."

She breaks off, as if there's something else that she should be saying, but I don't push. After swearing under my breath, I keep my voice fairly calm as I ask instead, "What caused the argument?"

"The same thing that caused all the others before it, only those were just verbal. That both Tyler and I were a waste of space. And that he'd be better off without us." She grabs hold of my hand, and I can feel her shaking. "I thought he was going to kill me, Dart. I think he thought he had. And he'd have passed it off as an accident, I slipped and fell. There was a bottle of oil lying spilt on the floor when I regained consciousness. It hadn't been there before."

There it is, the real reason she ran. She was afraid for her life. And from what she's told me, she had good reason. Just who is this man who'd leave his wife quite possibly dying, and set it up so it looked like her own misfortune? What am I dealing with here? "Doll, what does Ron do for work?"

"He's a detective."

Shit. She's tried to keep under the radar, but from his job I'd bet good money he knows exactly where she is. *Why hasn't he come for her?* One answer is that if she's too scared to go through with a divorce, he won't have to pay support. The other thought I can't now get out of my mind is that if she's right and he really does want her out of his way, he could be biding his time. If I, we, the club, give her our protection, what possible blowback could come down on us?

Parking that thought, I get back to the subject of her son. I don't know anything about this disease he's got. "Is there no cure for what Tyler's got?"

"For Tyler, maybe." Her words take me by surprise, I didn't expect that. She's still trembling, my arm holding her tightens. "Sickle cell carriers seem to have a higher incidence of carrying twins. And that certainly happened to me." She takes a gulp of air., As there doesn't seem to be another child around, I have a gut feel how this story is going to end. "They're usually identical, but in my case, they weren't. And oh yes, I won the lottery with my babies. As well as discovering Tyler had sickle cell, they discovered his twin, a girl, had anencephaly, a rare condition that stops brain and skull development. She was likely to be born dead, or only live a short while. I couldn't abort her, as I could risk losing Tyler, so I carried them both to term. They were born early, at thirty-four weeks. Tyler seemed healthy, we knew she was going to die."

I'm a tough biker, but there's moisture in my eyes at her story. *Fuck! She's one hell of a strong woman to be able to cope with all this.*

She resumes without prompting, "I'd already had so many discussions with the doctors by the time she was born, and they tested her immediately. She didn't have sickle cell, and being a twin, there was a twenty-five percent chance she'd be a match as a tissue donor for Tyler, should he need a transplant in the future. She only lived an hour, but they harvested stem cells from the umbilical cord and were able to confirm she was a match."

This is all alien territory for me. A cure? So why hasn't she already gone for it? "What happened to the stem cells…?"

"They were frozen. The idea was if Tyler's condition worsened we could try a bone marrow transplant using the cells. If it works, that will cure him."

It sounds simple. Easy. But if it was, I wouldn't have seen that boy suffering. "Why didn't he have the procedure?"

"Money." She breathes. "Sickle cell manifests in different forms. By the time we knew how much his disease was affecting him, we found that we weren't covered for a stem cell transplant. The insurance company won't pay, as it's too expensive. They want us to go with the alternative and cheaper treatments. But they're not a cure, just something to keep it under control."

"If you need to pay out for this procedure, we're possibly talking tens of thousands here, aren't we?" I say the cold statement, not having a clue how I could help. Her nod, followed by a few more tears, tells me I'm right.

"At least half a million, possibly double that."

Shit. That's more than I thought. "And without the transplant, there's no other cure?"

She shakes her head. "It's the only chance he's got, and even that might not work. His red blood cells are shaped like a sickle, that's what gives the disease its name. They can get stuck as they pass through his veins. The idea of the transplant is to encourage his body to produce properly shaped cells."

I'm processing that when she adds, "Time's against us. And it could already be too late. I've looked into it. Though I've read some research that suggests frozen stem cells are good for up to fifteen years, doctors don't normally use them after five. Tyler's six." She waves her hand toward the bedroom her son is currently asleep in. "Blood transfusions could help him, reduce his episodes, but if we resort to that, the chances of the transplant being successful drastically diminish. And if he experiences organ failure, then it will be too late." She nods her head toward the short hallway. "That episode today, the cell must have got trapped in his leg. Many sufferers get heart attacks…"

I can fill in the gaps for myself. Fuck, that child I was so impressed by is a fucking time bomb. And it sounds like she's got a long list of impossible decisions to make. Amazed at how strong she is, how she's holding herself together, all I can think is, poor kid, poor mother. I want to help, but I have no fucking idea how.

CHAPTER 7

Alex

I knew that it had shocked Dart seeing Tyler have one of his episodes, but the difference between his reaction and that of my ex couldn't be more different. Ron just used to walk out and leave me to deal with it. Dart had stayed to help, even though he's just my boss and owes us nothing at all. But he's sitting beside me, his arm around me, and selfishly I'm taking all the comfort I can. It feels a relief to get it off my chest.

What mother ever wants to learn they've given birth to a child who has a lifelong disease with complications which could arise at any time, shortening or ending his life? It's the first thing you do, find out everything to watch out for, wanting to make every moment precious.

I'm trying to give Tyler as normal a life as possible, and to be honest, since we've come to Tucson the frequency of his episodes have reduced. Until this afternoon, I'd been hoping the change to this dry heat and no longer being exposed to the stress of my strained relationship with Ron had been beneficial to his health.

Dart's gone silent, as if he knows there's nothing he can say or do to help. Slowly he pulls his supportive arm away and stands up. He stares at me for a long moment. "Doll, take the night off. Stay here with Tyler."

"No, Dart. I can't do that. Celine will be home and she's happy to watch out for him. I need the money. If I save enough, I might be able to pay for the procedure."

He gives me a sad nod. He understands my plight, and that I'm fooling myself that I could ever get enough dancing for tips, but I won't give up trying, I owe that to my son. I watch him fidget for a second as though he doesn't know what to say or do, and it doesn't surprise me when he tells me he needs to go.

Of course he does. I've taken up too much of his time. I get to my feet, wiping the last of my tears away. It's unusual for me to cry, normally I'm stronger than this. I cried my heart out in the first year of Tyler's life, before realising getting upset about what can't be fixed doesn't change anything. Just as I'm stepping up to get the door for him, it opens.

"Hey, we got a visitor? Who has the bike?" My brother-in-law Craig swaggers in, his muscles bulging as he carries in heavy bags.

"That would be me." Dart steps forward and holds out his hand. "Dart." He introduces himself.

Craig drops one of the bags and complies with the hand-shake. They seem to hold it a little too long, as though testing each other out.

"He's my boss," I explain. "He just dropped by to give me my tips from last night."

"Nice sled, man." Craig jerks his head backward.

"You ride?"

"Sure do. Got an Indian out back." And then they're off talking bikes. Craig drops the other bag and they both go outside to inspect Dart's bike.

Celine's standing wide-eyed in the doorway. As the men disappear she pretends to fan herself. "My, but he's hot, girl."

"I work for him," I hiss, pretending like I haven't noticed. But I'm not blind. It's just right now I'm more concerned for my son and sorting out my predicament than getting laid, and the last thing I would do is risk my job by making things awkward with Dart. Sure, I'm not blind, and he's been so kind and caring this afternoon, but I need to squash any thoughts in that direction down. Knowing how easily my sister can read me, I change the subject fast. "Tyler had an episode."

She closes her eyes and takes in a breath. "Is he alright?"

"He's come through it. He's having a nap." My sister loves her nephew as though he were her own. I know she'd like a child herself, and she's the lucky one, Craig doesn't carry the sickle cell gene. "Dart offered me the night off, but I need to go to work."

"Of course you do, Tyler will be fine with me. I'll keep him quiet."

"Yes, but don't fuss." It's important to me that Tyler is treated like the six-year-old he is, the cotton wool I'm wrapping him in kept invisible. He goes to school and plays like any child. We just have to watch him so he doesn't get over-fatigued, dehydrated, too hot, too cold, too anxious... The endless list of possible triggers continually goes around my head.

I nod at the bags. "Want help putting those away?"

She accepts my offer, and we're still putting packets and jars in the cupboard when I hear the roar of an engine start up, and then the sound slowly fades. *He's gone.* Why do I feel this sudden emptiness?

When I enter Satan's Angels later on that night, I'm still trying to suppress any improper feelings toward my boss. I mean, he's hot as fuck, but I've so much on my plate. I can't do anything to risk losing the one job I was able to get. Everything between us must be kept strictly professional, and I must forget that I spent the good part of the afternoon in his arms. Yeah, I'll just be casual when I see him, I've too many complications already to add anything else into the mix. Already I regret telling him so much, but having such a sympathetic ear that's not been offered before, somehow everything just came spilling out. When I see him tonight, I'll just be polite, and maybe offer an apology for taking up so much of his time.

Yesterday I was a bag of nerves when I arrived, tonight I walk in with confidence. The tips that I'd made showed me while Ron had never appreciated my pole dancing, other men have no such aversion. Ironically, I'm being well rewarded for doing what I love. That they've made allowances and I don't need to get completely naked is the icing on the cake.

Despite my resolve to treat him no differently, I'm more disappointed than I should be when I don't see Dart, and it's another biker who comes into the dressing room to check on us girls.

"Hey, you must be Alex." Well, as I'm the only black girl here, that's a fair assumption to make. "I'm Joker." In the middle of putting on makeup, I just give him a nod. Perching his backside against the counter he stands with his arms folded. "Dart told me to watch out for ya. You get any trouble, you come to me, okay?"

"Hey, Joker! Why's she so special?" One of the other girls calls out. I haven't really bothered to get to know them as yet. Last night my nerves kept me to myself, and today I've been preoccupied with thoughts about Tyler. But my back goes up at what could be a catty comment.

Joker turns around, and glancing up I can see him glaring. "Because she can dance." He waves his hand around, indicating all the girls who have now stopped what they're doing to see what's going on. "All of you are important to us. If we don't keep you happy, you won't make us money. And Alex is new, she doesn't know the score yet."

The girl who'd spoken comes over and lays her hand on my shoulder, looking at my face reflected in the mirror. As our eyes meet, I can see she's smiling. "I'm Vida, anything you want to know babe, just ask me."

As I nod, Joker pats my shoulder and goes. Now the others introduce themselves, and I'm surprised to find no obvious bitchiness at all. In fact, they all seem to agree it's a good place to work, knowing that the bikers are there to protect them.

Vida sits down next to me. "Hey, there was this one guy, he was a bouncer. Started laying his hands on us girls, thinking his job gave him privileges, you follow?"

Yes, I do. "What happened?"

"One day he went too far. The girl said no, he ignored her. Slapped her. Huh. He got a beat down to remember and was tossed out on his ass."

"I didn't want to work here," I start to tell her. "But I couldn't get any other kind of job."

"Why do you think any of us are here? Not many of us would be here by choice, hun." She stares at me for a moment. "And you're certainly not the normal type."

I freeze and wait for her criticism, my obvious differences to their slim, slender forms.

"Watched you on the pole last night. And boy, Joker's right, babe. You can dance."

"Those tits real?" Another girl who'd introduced herself as Bambi joins in the conversation. She's holding her own up as if for inspection. Hers are obviously fake.

"Unfortunately, yes," I reply, wincing as they make me top heavy.

"Alex, time to go on," a voice calls from the hallway.

I smile at the girls, who I didn't expect to be quite so friendly, and walk out on the stage with a spring in my step.

When I'm dancing I can forget everything and live only for the moment. It's my respite from all the worry in my life. Even the audience fades into the background as I twist, turn, climb, and slide for myself, not for anyone else. It's only when the music ends and I finish my set that I'm suddenly aware that all eyes are upon me, but the smile on my face is for me, the satisfaction of another flawless performance.

Money flutters around me, and with no Dart today, it's me who gathers it up. I use the assets God gave me, a wiggle making my tits bounce, a little shake of my ass. More bills are thrown, accompanied by cat calls and whistles. Then a man gets too close when I'm at the edge of the stage, his hand wrapping around my arm...

And then he's gone, holding a hand to his bleeding nose.

"What the fuck?"

"You don't touch the fuckin' dancers," Joker growls, then says over his shoulder, "you okay, darlin'?"

I'm rubbing my skin where his fingers have pinched. "I'm fine." Then I hurry back to the dressing room. Yeah, this job will obviously have its seedier moments, but the girls were right, the bikers seem to look out for us well.

My next two sets pass without incident, and the tips I've collected are more than I could earn in any other job. But even the tips won't pay for a procedure that's perhaps already too late.

As I take off my makeup I gaze at my reflection. After tonight, I've got two nights off. Though I'll enjoy the extra time with Tyler, I smile to myself. It's strange, but I'm actually going to miss my time on the pole, hearing the shouts of encouragement, the sort of things Ron had convinced me I'd never hear. *Roll on Tuesday when I can dance again.*

I might have been driven to working in a strip club, but for the first time in my life, I'm starting to have confidence in myself.

CHAPTER 8

Dart

Riding back to the compound, I couldn't get Alex or Tyler out of my head. And, of course, that bastard Ron Thompson, her ex. Or not quite an ex yet, she's still fucking married to the man. And that's a fact I don't like.

I got on okay with her brother-in-law though, he's alright, and he rides a decent bike too. As he showed it to me, we'd had ourselves a little chat, and I found out more about the man Alex was still shackled too, and none of it I liked.

I've every intention of going to Satan's Topless Angels tonight, but when I get back my plans go awry. After being impressed by Tyler and then having to witness his pain, learning that kid was going to suffer episodes like that for the rest of his life, understanding even that could be cut short at any time, well, that had hit me hard. As soon as I walk into the clubhouse I head for the bar, and instead of beer, grab a bottle of Jack and a shot glass. Going over to an unoccupied table, I sit, pour myself a drink and throw it back, quickly chasing it with another. Then my head sinks into my hands. Life's so unfair, it doesn't seem right that a child has to suffer such pain. Though I know he's not the first, and certainly won't be the last, he's one I've personally met, not just heard about on a TV documentary.

Fuck! I feel so useless. And so full of admiration by the woman who's been handed such an impossible task. The way she coped when her son was in such distress astounded me. The weight she carries everyday would overwhelm even the strongest. Yet she carries on, never giving away how she's feeling inside. *Tyler shouldn't have been born.* Terrible words, having met the boy. But if that fucker of a husband had told her the truth, he might not be here and wouldn't be suffering. The vision of Tyler so excitedly looking over my bike comes into my head. I'd felt an immediate connection to the kid, even before I knew he was ill. And suddenly I interpret what Alex had said. Perhaps no, a child shouldn't be conceived if there's a chance he'd suffer for all of his life. Or at least she should have gone into the pregnancy with her eyes open. Thompson had lied to her, and worse than that, stealthly removing the condom without consent, and getting her pregnant.

But despite everything, it's clear to see she doesn't regret having him for one moment, and will do anything she can, even take her clothes off for strangers, to give him the chance of a better life. Fuck, what an amazing woman she is.

The sound of a glass banging down on the wood makes me look up to see Blade not taking the hint I purposefully chose a corner table as I wanted some space.

"What's got your underwear knotted?" he asks.

"Leave me a-fuckin'-lone," I snarl, wanting to process this afternoon's conversation by myself.

Overhearing me, Lady comes over and takes a seat, placing his beer on the table. "If you want time to yourself don't come to the fuckin' clubhouse. You're fair game here, Brother."

And now Dollar's appeared. "What's up, Dart?"

Fuck it. They're not going to let me wallow. I pour another shot. Blade gets out his smokes—what the fuck? I must look bad—and passes me one. He even hands me his zippo so I can light up.

The drink warming my throat and the smoke soothing my lungs loosens my tongue. "I've been to see Alex." Everyone except Blade looks confused. "The new dancer," I clarify, then take another sip and another nicotine hit before continuing. "Fuck, has that bitch got problems." And then I let all of it out.

When I finish, there's stunned silence around the table. Then Blade catches on to the problem of her ex. "She didn't tell us the half of it when we took her on."

"No. And he's a fuckin' cop."

He sucks in breath. "What's the bettin' he knows exactly where she is and is bidin' his fuckin' time until he makes a move?"

I jerk my chin. "My thoughts exactly. There's somethin' between him and her parents too, somethin' that made them pressure her into marryin' him. Some benefit for them, perhaps."

Dollar wrinkles his nose. "Smells like a dirty cop to me."

"She bring her car with her?"

Glancing at Lady, I dip my head. "I assume so. How did she get here otherwise?"

"Tracing the licence plate would be easy for a cop."

Suddenly I feel a hand clamp down on my shoulder. "What's goin' on? You lot look fuckin' serious."

Blade answers, pointing his cigarette toward me. "Dart's woman might need our help."

I splutter. "She's not my woman."

Drum sucks in air. "Whenever brothers get involved with a woman that means trouble for the club. What the fuck is it now?" He can talk. Sam, his old lady, definitely got us up to our necks in things we'd rather have stayed out of. There are twenty decaying bodies buried up the top of the compound that can testify to that. But before I can remind him, Prez continues,

"Better get talkin'. Sooner I know what's goin' on the fuckin' better. Dart, Blade. My office, now."

"Prez, I've got to get to the club…"

"Joker?" Drum shouts out. "Fancy babysittin' the strippers for a night?"

It seems that will cause Joker no problem at all. After telling him to watch Alex closely, while having the weird feeling I'm letting her down by not being there, I follow Drummer into his office. In all honestly, I don't know what the fuck I can do to help, and not even knowing whether it's my place to do anything at all. I just know her situation doesn't rest easy with me. Having more brains look at it might be better than stewing on it alone.

Half-an-hour later, Prez starts to sum up. "We've got a stripper who's left her ex, who's a cop with a violent streak. We all know what a close-knit club that is. He'll have cop friends all over and quite likely here. They could be keepin' tabs on her."

"In which case, I doubt he'll like her new occupation."

Drum glares at me for interrupting. "Or he may feel he's well shot of her. And the kid. Which brings me to the second issue. We don't offer insurance plans for our employees." He breaks off as we chuckle. Nah, we tend to stay away from citizen stuff like that. "To help Tyler, she needs a fuckload of cash. She got any immediate needs, Dart?"

I shake my head. "From what she's told me, no. But if she gives up the idea of the transplant and goes along with the new treatment, the kid will be having hospital visits every couple of weeks, and that's bound to mount up."

"Which her ex's insurance might cover. Or could be part of a divorce settlement."

"And might be the reason why he'd prefer her permanently out of the way. We don't know what his deductibles look like." Tapping his fingers against the desk, the prez looks deep in thought. "She's an employee, but not part of the club. Don't see how we can use club funds to help, and even if we could, they're not a bottomless pit." His brow creases as I open my mouth and his eyes narrow. I shut it again. "And if the transplant route has anythin' goin' for it, seems like she needs to explore it as soon as she can." He raps his hand on the table. "So she needs money, and she's not gonna make enough however good she twirls around that pole. What about a charity run? Might bring in a bit to help."

Well, fuck me. I raise my head and stare at him, never expecting he'd come up with anything like that. It's a great fucking idea. Fun for us, and if we get enough people involved, money that can at least be a start toward the procedure Tyler needs. It's a good time of year for it too. Summer heat is just a memory, and so are the fucking monsoons. While I'm thinking on the prez's suggestion, Blade's still stuck on her other problems.

"She safe with her sister?" Blade looks concerned.

"Yeah." I laugh. "The brother-in-law seems pretty protective. He's a big fella, and not many people would take him on. The sister is very supportive too, doesn't have a problem watching the kid while Alex is at work."

"I'll get Mouse investigatin' this Thompson, see what he can find. You say he's based in San Diego? I'll get in touch with Snake. It's in his area, he might be able to put out some feelers. At the very least we should be able to put pressure on him to pay child support."

"Thanks, Prez."

A frown appears on his face. "Hate to think of kids hurtin'. Bad enough with Amy going through losin' her parents, but that kid Tyler's in a world of pain, as well as havin' been through fuck knows what before she ran." He pauses and scratches his chin. It crosses my mind he might be thinking about Sam being pregnant, and hoping to hell their child's born healthy. It would explain why he's so eager to help. Suddenly Drum looks up. "Got a family cookout here tomorrow afternoon. Why not bring her along? Kid like bikes?"

"Loves them." I grin, remembering his face when I'd let him sit on my Harley.

"Yeah, bring your woman."

"She's not my woman." I've got to shut that shit up fast, for fucks sake and say the first thing that comes into my head which, for some reason is, "Prez, she's black."

Drum's face darkens. "Bylaws say we only have white brothers in the club. Don't say nothing about ol' ladies."

Christ! He's going too fast for me. Blade laughs at the look on my face.

"She ain't gonna be ridin' on the back of my bike. Fuck, Drum. When you meet her, you'll see she ain't nothing any of us would go for." I summon up the mental image of the tiny woman with her top-heavy breasts and wide ass, and quickly shake my head to clear it from my mind as my cock twitches. *I need to get laid.*

Tossing me a strange look, Drum actually laughs. "She's got to you though. You wouldn't be wantin' to fix all her problems if she was just some bitch whose pussy you wanted in. You'd just do that and be gone."

Again, I only get so far as opening my mouth before he subjects me to his steely stare. "You'll bring her to the club, tomorrow. Let the brothers meet her and the kid. You want our help? Let's see what we're dealin' with. Be one fuck of a lot easier if they all take to her and the boy."

There is that, I suppose.

I go to stand up. "Dart. Just remember, you want to go that step further she can't be working at the club." And he thinks I don't know that?

I scoff, trying to replace the picture of her with an image in my head of the women I like to fuck, and she certainly doesn't fit into that description. "No worries there, Prez, I know the rules. And that's the last thing I'm thinkin'. There's no chance I'll be goin' there." I walk out shaking my head. I do want to help her, but only as a friend. No way I'll be tapping that. As I've tried to tell him, she's not my type, and even if she was, anyone can see she's not a one and done girl, and I'm not up for anything other than that.

Lunchtime the next day I find myself in the club's truck despite that I fucking hate riding in the cage. Especially in autumn when the weather's at its best for riding. Vowing the next thing I'll do is get her a phone—I mean, who hasn't got a phone nowadays? Fucking madness. I'm sitting at red lights with the air conditioning turned up full to get me some airflow, while on my way to see if I can persuade her to come to the clubhouse. I know Tyler will be game, the promise of twenty Harleys to check out is sure to attract him. His mother? I'm not too sure what she'll think of an invitation to a biker compound.

Driving along her street, I'm relieved to see her car sitting in the driveway, and, as I pull up, the sound of childish laughter coming from inside. Today it's Celine who opens the door. She beams as she recognises me, even without the cut that I'd get a fine for wearing in a cage, and steps aside to let me in.

"Someone for you, Alex," she calls as I enter.

Tyler's the first to see me, and struts over like a real little man, his shoulders pulled back. "Dart." He throws me a very adult chin lift, making me stifle a laugh.

Returning the gesture, I work on keeping my face straight. Alex appears soon after, she's wearing a simple tee and shorts, her short legs exposed. For once I don't compare her with the other women I know, but see her for herself, and it dawns on me she actually comes in quite an attractive package. Her proportions are just different than what I'm used to. *That ass...* Mmm mm.

"Dart?" My name falls off her lips as a question, and then she gives a cheeky grin. "I've already got my tips from last night."

I smile at her. "You got anythin' planned' this afternoon?"

Her eyes narrow. "No? Why?"

"Good. Got you an invite to a cookout at the club. I brought a cage so there's no need for you to drive."

"Cage?" She looks at Tyler and then back at me as if I'm going to crate him or something.

"Cage is a car to us bikers."

Tyler's listening carefully, and is quick on the uptake. "Can we go in Dart's cage?"

Fuck, this kid's going to have me cracking up in a moment.

Again, she looks at the boy, then at me, and her head tilts to one side. "Is it family friendly?"

"Yeah. There'll be the old ladies there."

"Old ladies?"

Now I do laugh, realising this is new to her. "That's what we call the women who belong to my brothers. Oh, and there's young Amy as well. She's younger than Tyler, but at least there'll be another kid around. And probably Jayden, she's a teenager but enjoys playing with the youngsters."

Celine nudges her sister. "Go on, why don't you? You could do getting out of the house and having some fun. It will do Tyler good too. You don't get much chance to socialise, so why not take it?"

She's wavering, not sure whether to come or not. I decide to sweeten it. "Look, if you come and feel uncomfortable, I'll bring you back home. Or, drive yourself if you prefer."

"How far is it?" It doesn't take a genius to realise she's probably calculating the cost of gas.

"Not far, about six miles from the city."

Again, it's Celine who encourages her. "Why not let Dart drive you? It would do you good to let your hair down for once. If you get stuck Craig can always come pick you up. And we know where you are."

Suddenly her face lights up, and I swear it's like the sun coming out from behind a cloud as she makes her decision. "Okay, we're in."

After some reassurance she's dressed fine as she is, she gets Tyler ready with a mandatory visit to the bathroom, and then brings him outside. She switches a child booster seat from her car to the truck, and then buckles the kid in. I wait by the passenger door until she's finished, then close it after she's got inside.

Sliding into the driver's seat, I switch on the engine, turning the air conditioning up to max as the interior's already warmed up from the heat of the sun. Immediately she places her hand on my arm.

"Not too cold, Dart. Sudden changes of temperature can trigger an episode."

Fuck. There's a lot I'm going to have to learn if I'm going to be around them. I point to the controls. "You're in charge. Have it the temperature you want. *And I'll just have to suffer.* But if it's to save Tyler going through pain, I won't complain.

She twists to check Tyler, who seems excited by the outing. In fact, he can't stop talking, and I've no chance to discuss anything with her, as he fires questions at me the whole way about what models of bikes he's likely to see, and who's got the fastest, and other shit like that. Fuck me, there's a biker right there in the making. *But not in our club.* It's the first time I've been pulled up thinking about our rules.

CHAPTER 9

Alex

I wanted to ask Dart to explain more about what I'm apparently about to walk into, but don't have a chance as Tyler doesn't give up for a moment. But hearing him so excited as he prattles on about his beloved motorcycles puts a smile on my face. As does the way Dart so patiently answers him, so different to Ron, who'd have told him to shut up. Hmm. I grin as I catch the last part of the conversation. Dart has the fastest bike? I think I might need to take a spoonful of sugar with that.

It doesn't take long before we've navigated the city and turn off the highway and head up an asphalt track that's a bit rutted in parts. I don't know what I expected from a biker compound, but as we approach, anything I imagined could have been nothing like what appears in front of me.

As we wait for the gates to be opened, I hush Tyler and ask a question of my own. "What is this place, Dart?"

"It's an old vacation resort. Club bought it for a song after it was burned out. We rebuilt it, and now it's a pretty good home for us."

He's now pulling up in front of a long, low building. "See? That used to be the reception area of the old hotel, with bar and restaurant. It's now a damn fine clubhouse. We all live in the units you see up the roadway."

Tyler's impatient to get out, bouncing in his seat as he spies the lined-up Harleys.

"Hey, patience, little man. You'll be able to see them all." Dart's laughing as he gets out, then comes around to my side while I release my son and lift him out. Dart places his hand on Tyler's shoulder, holding him back. "Right, Tyler, some things for you to understand. You never touch another brother's bike without permission. No climbing up or sitting on them, okay?"

Tyler's eyes widen, and he nods at Dart, taking in everything he says so seriously. I suppress a grin, wishing I could get through to him like that. I'd probably have got a sullen look accompanied by an 'Oh, but Mom'.

There's a couple of heavily tattooed men standing, beers in their hands, bikers I haven't met before. They look tough, muscular, and rugged, and if Dart wasn't with me, would make me feel uneasy. They're staring at us. Dart takes a deep breath, then starts walking over to them, swinging around and gesturing we should follow him.

"Peg, Tongue. This is Alex and Tyler." Both men look down at me and give me a lift of their chins. Then, lowering their eyes even further, take in my son.

"Hear you like bikes, kid."

Tyler gives a shy nod, then shrinks back into the protection of my body. Both men look one step away from violence, and I don't blame him for seeking my comfort.

The one introduced as Peg ignores his reaction. "Wanna see my ride?"

Another little nod. Tyler's thumb has gone into his mouth, a soothing action left over from babyhood when he's not sure of a situation.

But the biker called Peg has got it in hand. "I've got a Wide Glide Sports. Which do you think it is?"

Tyler pushes away from me, and with an intent expression starts looking along the line of motorcycles. I have no idea if he knows what he's looking for, but his thumb comes back out of his mouth. Eventually he makes a decision. "That one?"

Peg laughs. "No, but close. It's that one there. Wanna see it?" As Tyler nods, Peg holds out his hand, and my son takes it. "You gonna look at the bikes with me and Tongue while Dart takes your mom out back?"

While I might be a little apprehensive, Tyler has lost any qualms he might have had as he almost drags Peg along. Peg grins, and calls back over his shoulder, "Go on, Momma. Little man and me, we'll be just fine."

Dart links his arm through mine, and with his free hand, waves towards the two bikers who dwarf my small son. "I'd trust them with my life, doll. They won't let no harm come to the boy. Come, let's go around the back and you can get to know everyone."

With a few lingering reservations, and one last look at Tyler, who seems to be having the time of his life, I let Dart lead me through their clubroom and out the back where fire pits are burning and a couple of bikers are manning grills. There are several women around who are going back and forth, bringing out dishes of salad and stuff. Apart from the preponderance of males and that all the men are wearing those leather cuts, it could be any large family barbeque.

There's a small child, laughing and giggling, being chased by a girl in her mid-teens. Fondly looking on is a biker who barely seems out of his teens himself. A small smile plays on his lips as his eyes follow the girl. Turning my attention away from him, I watch the other men, amused and put at ease by the way the burly bikers just sidestep when the girls almost run into them, and the doting smiles they cast their way, help to remove the last of my apprehension.

Having been engrossed in watching them, I hadn't noticed we'd been approached until a man's standing right in front of me. The flash on his cut is directly at the level of my eyes, so it's easy to read the word 'President', making me swallow knowing this is the man in charge of all these men, and, the boss of my boss. A pretty woman comes up alongside him.

"Alex. I'm Drummer. President of this unruly lot. Pleased to meet you, and glad you could make it. Have you brought your son?"

I smile to acknowledge his warm welcome, and then say with a chuckle, "Lost him already, Drummer. Couple of your men are showing him their bikes. He's in seventh heaven."

As Drummer raises his eyebrow toward Dart, the man still with his arm entwined with mine informs him, "Peg and Tongue."

"Your son likes bikes?" The woman now asks, and then remembers her manners. "I'm Sam, by the way, Drum's ol' lady."

She seems to be about my age, not old at all, making me remember this is how they refer to their women. "He's bike mad," I reply with a chuckle. "His uncle's got a bike and I suppose he's learned it from him."

"What does he ride?"

Again Dart answers for me, thankfully, as I wouldn't know. "Dude's got an Indian."

Drummer seems interested, but Sam steps in. "If—Tyler, isn't it?" At my nod of confirmation, she continues, "If Tyler likes bikes, why don't we show him yours, Drum?"

Drummer draws her into his side and plants such a deep kiss on her lips it almost makes me blush to watch them. At last pulling away, he says, "Ain't got no problem with that, darlin'. Later, perhaps. Now, Sam, d'ya wanna go introduce Alex to the rest of the ol' ladies?"

"Okay. Alex?"

As Dart pulls his arm away, I again nod my head. "Come on then. They're sorting out the food over there." She leads me in the direction she's pointing.

I hadn't missed the fond way the president looked at her stomach before walking off, or the way her hand unconsciously rubs the small bump there. A woman's intuition makes me ask, "How long you got?"

"I'm only three months along, but I'm already showing. Think it's going to be a big baby." She grimaces and points back at her man. "But just look at its father. He doesn't do anything by halves." I laugh, but her face is serious as she continues, "Can't imagine what you went through when you had Tyler. Drummer's told me your story." For a second I'm taken aback that Dart's shared what I told him, but hell, it's no secret, so it doesn't bother me none.

Eyeing her up, I wonder if knowing what I'd been through concerns her. After all, I understand more than most how pregnant women worry about their unborn child. I try to set her mind at ease. "In my case, having a child with a severe problem was a probability. If my husband had been honest, I wouldn't have taken the chance. But," I continue more fiercely, "Tyler's here and he's a wonderful child. While I hate he has to suffer in the way that he does, I could never wish he hadn't been born."

"I can't wait to meet him."

But there's something more I want to say. "We all hope for a perfect child, Sam. But in the end, we cope with whatever's thrown at us. I've no regrets. Wishes that things could be different of course, but no regrets."

She stares at me for a second, her hand again poignantly rubbing her stomach, and then nods. "Hey, there's Sophie. She's a bit further along than me." Drawing me over to the table, she points to a lovely blond woman, and then to the auburn-haired girl sitting alongside her. "This is Ella, she's with Slick. And if she's not pregnant yet it's not for want of trying."

Ella gasps and reaches out to mock slap Sam's arm. Sam jumps out of reach, laughing. Then she introduces an older woman. "Sandy's with Viper, who's my dad."

"And *we're* definitely not pregnant," Sandy says with a laugh.

"I'm Carmen, I'm married to Bullet. And I just love your hair!"

Self-consciously, my hand goes up to my head as the last woman introduces herself. "It needs a trim, but I haven't found anyone to do it yet in Tucson."

Sandy laughs. "There's your chance, Carmen." Then explains to me, "She's a hairdresser."

But Carmen's shaking her head. "I've never learned to do Afro hair, and I suspect that's your problem. I can ask around, see if I can find anyone to recommend."

"Is it so different?" Sophie asks, looking perplexed.

"Yeah, it's a different texture and needs someone who knows the right cutting techniques."

Sam chuckles. "First time I've seen you stumped, Carmen. We'll have to call Alex, the one who got away."

Carmen purses her lips. And now everyone's laughing at her.

"Move your asses and let Alex sit down."

When they do as Drummer's woman requests, I squeeze myself onto the bench. The autumn sun's blazing down, but it's a comfortable temperature and, for some reason, these women seem to accept me as one of their own. Ron had dissuaded me from making friendships, and his sneering attitude discouraged me from bringing anyone back to the house. Apart from my sister, I can't remember the last time I had female company like this. I settle back to enjoy it, and happily listen as they tell me a little about themselves and their men.

"A wedding in Vegas? And you rode up the aisle?"

Ella's grinning widely. "Yeah, it was only three weeks ago. It was a complete surprise. I'm still getting used to it." As she's talking, the teenager I'd noticed earlier comes up with the young child.

The little girl climbs on Sam's lap, and the older girl rests her hand on Ella's shoulder. "When's the food ready? I'm starving."

"The hungry one's my sister, Jayden. Jayden, meet Alex." We exchange smiles.

"And this here is Amy." As Sam introduces her, I notice the child is staring at me. She cocks her head on one side. It suddenly hits me she might not have seen a black person in the flesh before, or perhaps not up so close. We're not exactly common in Tucson. Suddenly Amy leans forward and curls her fingers into my hair.

"Pretty."

I'll take a compliment from anyone. And when she reaches her arms to me, it's natural to let her slide off Sam's lap onto my own.

Sam's grinning widely, as if something good has happened. The other women seem pleased about it too.

"She's coming along," Carmen says, quietly.

Sam nods, then seeing my quizzical expression nods at the child and tells me softly, "I'll tell you later."

I'd assumed she was her daughter, but I might be wrong.

There's a jug of margarita on the table, and I'm offered a glass. Can't remember the last time I had one of those. Ron didn't like me to drink. What the heck, he's not here and I'm not driving. I take a glass, and even accept a refill. Then the meat is ready, and we're filling our plates. As if summoned by some magical intuition, Peg appears with Tyler. Once we've eaten, Tyler gets involved in a game of chase with Amy and Jayden. I'm pleased to see he's gentle with the small child, pretending to be unable to catch her.

Noticing, Sam nods at him. "He's a good kid, isn't he?"

I have to agree, while keeping a close eye to watch he's not getting out of breath.

And now she tells me something that breaks my heart. That Amy's mum has recently died, and her father's recuperating away from the club. The thought that these men and women have looked after a child who wasn't theres, and succeeded in making her happy, makes me realise what a good bunch of people they are. Even if they're a one percenter club and thought of as criminals by most of the outside world.

The kids come back to the table just as Drummer and Dart step up. Dart leans over and speaks into my ear. "Drum wants to discuss somethin' with you. Wanna come up to his house and Sam can show Tyler the bikes he's got there? He's got some vintage ones he might be interested in."

"Can we, Mom?" There's obviously nothing wrong with Tyler's hearing as he tugs at my sleeve.

I slide off the bench, and take hold of his hand. "Haven't you seen enough bikes for one day, Ty?"

As he pouts, Drum puts his hand on his shoulder. "Ain't possible to see too many sleds, is it young man?"

Tyler straightens and gives his serious nod, a sharp dip up and down, which he seems to have copied from the men. "No, sir," he replies, earnestly.

Dart snorts as though disguising a laugh.

Wondering what the president has to talk to me about, I walk alongside Dart as we go up to the top of the compound. I'm taking it all in as we go. There are a number of interlinked blocs which were presumably originally built to house guests. This really is an unusual biker compound. Not that I have much to base my observation on.

At the top, there are some more traditional-looking houses, one of which belongs to Drum and Sam. Using the side entrance, we go around to the garage. As Drum hits the remote and the interior is revealed, Tyler squawks and starts jumping on the spot. All I can see are a few bikes, some looking rideable, others decidedly not. Sam takes hold of his hand and walks him over to one that's little more than a frame. In a patient voice she begins explaining, pointing things out. Tyler's lapping it up.

Tilting my head in surprise, I listen to Sam spout all kinds of jargon. Drummer notices my expression and clarifies, "Sam knows her way around bikes almost better than I do. And," he points to my son, "reckon we've got a little mechanic there in the makin'."

The interest Tyler's showing suggests that he might be right. With ease of long practice, I successfully choke back the sob which threatens whenever my son's future is discussed.

Drummer points to a work bench and, without asking permission, Dart picks me up and puts me down on the top. He leans by my side, and only then looks at me and shrugs. His action so natural, as if he'd been doing it all his life. A startled laugh bursts from me.

The president stands in front of us, his arms folded. Before he speaks he twists around and gets thumbs up from Sam, and I realise she's keeping Tyler occupied.

"Your son needs treatment," he starts without preamble. "And you need money for that."

I raise my shoulders, Dart's obviously told him.

"We're thinkin' of doin' a charity ride to raise some funds. Ain't gonna be a lot, but a start perhaps."

My head jerks forward and my eyes open. Out of everything I could have thought he might say, I never expected something like this. It's the first time anyone's offered me anything, well, apart from my sister, but she can't afford to do much more than give me a roof over my head.

"Drummer, I don't know what to say." Tears come to my eyes. These people don't even know me.

"You're one of ours now."

"As you work at the club," Dart explains quickly, and as my eyes flit to his I see them narrowing at his president.

Giving a quick grin, Drummer continues, "A poker run, we're plannin'. Dart can explain what that is. And we'll get as many clubs interested as we can takin' part."

"It will take some organisin', so won't happen tomorrow," Dart adds, presumably so I don't get my hopes up too fast.

"I don't know what to say." I really don't. I've no idea how much they'll be able to raise, but anything could help. I've never thought about soliciting money, it goes against the grain to ask strangers to give up their hard-earned cash, but this is my son's life we're talking about. Up to now I've been fighting just to help him live day by day. Why shouldn't I up it a notch to give him a real chance at life? As long as I can find a doctor willing to give the op a try at this late stage.

The corners of my mouth start turning up. "I don't know how to thank you," I tell Drummer.

The president turns to where Tyler is studying an engine with Sam. I can see from here he's got grease on his clothes and a smudge on his face. It's simply adorable how much fun he's having today. Drum chuckles. "Dart told us he was a good kid. He deserves everythin' we can do for him."

I turn to Dart, and, unable to resist, put my arms around him and give him an impulsive kiss right on the lips. Embarrassed, I immediately go to pull away, but his hand whips up and presses against the back of my head, holding me to him. His lips are softer than I expected, warmth transferring from him to myself. A tingle that I haven't felt for years starts building between my legs. *Oh my God. I can't deny it any longer, I really am attracted to this man.*

He doesn't push for more, our contact is only for a second. When we part I see a slightly dazed expression in his eyes, which I suspect is reflected in mine. He steps away from the workbench, offering me a hand to get down, then both of us turn our heads, looking in different directions.

CHAPTER 10
Dart

She kissed me. And I kissed her back. An innocent meeting of our lips, no tongues involved, no promise or expectation of anything more. But I had to step away from the workbench, as I started to feel the tell-tale swelling against my thigh. I looked away from her, and my eyes met Drum's. The fucker looks like he's grinning at me, but with him you never can tell. He might very well be thinking of taking my patch and burning my fucking Satan's Devils tattoo off my back. I can't start anything with Alex, she works for us. I try to recover fast.

"Well, best get you and Tyler home. Looks like he's had enough excitement for one day." And then I'll come back and lose myself in a sweet butt. This woman's so wrong for me. I don't know why my cock's responding to her. Nothing she's got would have had me hardening before. *Except those tits look amazing, and I could see myself holding onto that ass as I...* I put my hand to my forehead as though I can stop all the thoughts swirling around. Her tits and ass might be okay, but she's so short and stocky. *But she's so supple, and the way she moves...*

Perhaps I could go there just once and get her out of my system? She's just offering something different and I'll come back to my senses once I've had a taste. Nah, she'd never go for that. She's got a kid, wants a man to look after her, not a one-night stand. And, on top of everything else, she's black. I shouldn't even be considering it. But the strange thing is, when

I look at her, I see her clear complexion, notice the dark depths of her eyes. Her colour doesn't seem as important as I first thought it was. And Tyler? Well, he's just the same as any young kid. A boy any man would be proud of to call a son. Just not this man. No way. Never in a million fucking years.

While Alex agrees it's time to go home, it takes longer than I expected to make it off the compound. First, we have to drag Tyler away from the bikes, which is only achieved with a promise he can come back again soon, then all the women want to say their goodbyes. Fuck, men just simply jerk their chins at each other and get gone. I've never had responsibility for a woman before, just fucking the whores and kicking them out of my bed, or having a hook-up with a like-minded woman in town. The social niceties and rituals the old ladies need to complete takes me by surprise. Eventually I'm able to pull them both away and get them in the cage to take them home. Tyler's worn out and falls asleep on the short journey. When Alex frees him from his seat and looks like she's going to try to carry him in herself, it seems natural for me to take him in my arms.

The smile she gives me as she gets out his booster seat and I take care of her son is worth it.

I'm inside her house with no reason to stay. She's fidgeting as if she doesn't know what to do. We're boss and employee, though, I believe, on the way to becoming good friends. I like her and respect her for the way she takes care of her kid. It will not, and cannot ever go further than that.

I walk to the front door, open it, then turn, resting my hands on the top of the frame. "I'll see you Tuesday evenin' at the club."

She closes the distance between us, and has to look up. "Thanks, Dart. I'm so very grateful. I enjoyed today, and so did Tyler. And wow, I don't know what to say about your president offering to help."

"All my brothers wanted in on it," I tell her gently. "It's a fuckload of work, but all of us enjoy a poker run, there's no disputin' that."

She glances down at her feet. "Well, thank you anyway. And whatever I can do to help…"

"I'll let you know."

"Okay."

I have an overwhelming desire to kiss her, just to prove her taste wasn't as addictive as I first thought. I can't. I mustn't. There's nothing to start here.

She's still looking down. Placing my fingers under her chin, I raise her head to face me.

I can't. I have to resist. But her lips, so full, and now I know so soft, are tempting me. I swallow, then tell her, "Goodbye, Alex."

"Goodbye, Dart."

It's still a moment before I turn and walk away, get into the hated cage and drive back to the club, trying to focus my mind on finding a sweet butt to take care of my needs, but at the thought of any of the club whores my cock seems to deflate. When I dare think of that dark flesh that I've seen almost all of when she flaunts herself on stage, it starts to come to life again. *What the fuck is wrong with me?* For a start, she's an employee, completely off limits. Why is it so fucking difficult to remember that?

As I drive the truck through the gates I make a resolution not to see her again outside of Satan's Topless Angels. That's far for the best, and once I keep her at a distance my cock might forget it's strange desire to sink into her soft, warm depths.

Having totally lost any desire to fuck, I make my way to the bar. The long, straight dark hair hanging down the back of a man standing and talking animatedly to the prez shows Mouse, for once, has ventured out of his cave. Realising they're deep in conversation, I walk to the other end of the bar. Jekyll's eyes have plotted my progress across the room, and there's a cold beer ready and waiting for me. Nodding to the shelf behind him, I also request a chaser of Jack. If I'm not going to get my dick wet, I might as well indulge in a different type of pleasure.

I only have time to enjoy the spirit warming my throat when Drum is at my shoulder, Mouse close behind him.

"My office, now," he instructs.

Unable to refuse such an invitation from the prez, I follow them both in. Mouse and I take seats in front of the desk, my companion placing his laptop on the wooden surface.

Going around to his normal chair, Drum nods at Mouse. "You wanna lead?"

Mouse nods, his long hair swinging around him. "Thompson," he begins without preamble. "He's a decorated cop. Commendations on his record."

I smooth my hands over my hair, idly teasing the bun at the back of my head. "So?"

"So..." Mouse taps at the keyboard and a picture of a cop in dress uniform appears. "He's gonna have a lot of support. Fucker like that garners respect."

"Unless he walked all over someone to get it," Drummer throws in.

I look at the screen. Mouse flicks onto another picture, this one where Thompson's surrounded by other officers, most standing a head taller than him. "Anythin' to suggest he's comin' after his wife and child?" I ask our computer expert. If there's anything to find, he'll dig it out.

"No. But I did find something interestin'. Alex had a restrainin' order prepared, but it was cancelled before it got filed. Judge must have refused to sign it."

"Can't have somethin' like that tarnishin' his career." He's obviously got some clout and uses it.

Drummer leans back in his chair and puts his hands behind his head. "A cop with a restrainin' order out on him can't carry a weapon. His department probably closed ranks."

She'd done the right thing, even if she hadn't succeeded. If he'd hit her hard enough to leave her for dead, she was right to try to take the official route to keep him away. I wished she'd been more upfront the first time we met, I feel like we're playing catch up now. Darn woman tries to deal with shit on her own. But now she's got me in her corner. I'm her concerned boss wanting to keep her safe so she can earn the club money.

Drum closes his eyes and thinks for a moment. When he snaps them open, he leans forward. "I think it's time we talked to Snake." A man of action, he's already taking out his phone as he speaks and places it on the table in front of us, putting it on loud speaker.

"Yo, Drummer."

"Snake. How's it hangin', my man?"

"Hangin' fine here, Drum. What's up with you? Got trouble again?"

"Maybe we have," Drum admits, and throws a nod toward me. "But first, any news on our Demon?"

"You know he's been spotted in Escondido? We've got a couple of brother's doing the rounds, lettin' themselves be overheard about dissent between us and yourselves. Hopefully it will be enough to draw him in. Reckon he'll be missin' bein' part of a club."

Yeah, once a brother, you'd miss the life if you didn't have it anymore. The chance to be part of something again might just be enough to get him to stick his head above ground.

"Appreciate it, Brother."

"You got anythin' else? Or just callin' to chew the fat."

"Yeah, I got somethin'. Cop by the name of Ron Thompson, a detective based in your parts. Put his hands on his woman and she's come to us, workin' at one of our joints. Wondered if you've ever crossed paths?"

"Hey, San D's a big city, not surprisin' I ain't. But I can have a dig around."

Drum doesn't answer for a second, then makes a suggestion I didn't expect. "Thinkin' of sendin' a couple of brothers down. Slick, as he's itchin' to get his hands on the fuckin' Rock Demon who hurt his ol' lady, and Dart, who's lookin' out for Thompson's bitch."

"That would be fine by me, Drummer. Get them down here and we can show them what we got."

Me? Go to San Diego? I frown. That would mean me leaving Alex alone. But if it means I can get to the bottom of what's going on with her ex, it would take one worry off her mind. After a moment, I give Drum a nod.

The prez ends the call by agreeing to keep Snake informed of arrangements, then looks at me. "That okay with you, Dart?"

Mouse waves his hand. "I don't mind taggin' along, Prez."

I huff a laugh. "Getting out of your cave? Be a first for you, Mouse."

The half Native American looks at me and grins. "Yeah, but I took a likin' to Alex and the kid. Don't mind lendin' a hand."

I suppress my frown at the thought Mouse is showing an interest in Alex, and consider it might be safer if he comes out of town with us, she doesn't need brothers sniffing around.

"I'll tell Slick," Prez announces. "But I don't doubt he'll be up for it. He's got a debt to repay for Ella."

"When you thinkin' of, Prez?" I'm working out the logistics of getting cover for the Angels, and particularly someone I trust to look out for Alex.

"No time like the present," he replies sharply. "Let me talk to Slick and you can leave tomorrow if that sits well with him."

I think about it, with luck we'll only be down there a couple of days but I'll need someone to stand in for me. Hopefully Joker will be free, he seemed to look out for Alex okay last time, and when she was here earlier he showed no sign of acting inappropriately toward her. *No, that's just me.* Belatedly I realise Drum's probably looking for an indication of my agreement. I lift my chin.

"Mouse, you give Dart anythin' he fuckin' needs, okay? And Dart anythin' you're plannin', I'd appreciate you runnin' it past me."

Mouse and I both speak at once, slightly different variations, but we're both in on the same page.

Slick's eager as fuck to get after his Demon, so first thing the next morning we leave. The freedom of the road. The wind in my hair. It's what every biker lives for. The four-hundred-mile journey to San Diego is exactly what I need, having been a while since I've been out on long run.

As a temporary officer I take the lead, Slick and Mouse falling in behind me. I take in the scenery as we pass, admiring the sand dunes of Yuma, then tolerate our progress being briefly slowed at the Winterhaven check point as we cross over into California, but not delayed long as there are fewer nooks and crannies to search on a bike. We're riding clean, and are not wearing our cuts as we're out of our area, so are quickly waved on. Next we come to the unusual signs as we approach Jacumba —being only half a mile from the Mexico border, there are warnings of possible immigrants taking their chances with the traffic as they cross the road desperate to enter the States.

We hit the approaches to San Diego mid-afternoon, and turn off to head to the SoCal chapter's compound. I've visited before, so it comes as no surprise to find it's housed in a converted hanger on a disused airfield, the surroundings making me grateful for the relative luxury where I'm based in Tucson. I'm totally spoilt back home, my own suite away from the club-house, and a swimming pool to take advantage of in the hottest days of summer. Here, at least we escape from the dry heat that's found further inland, and the view, looking down over the sprawling city does makes up some for the lack of facilities. In the distance, the Coronado Bridge is clearly visible, with the Navy base close by.

The three of us back up with our pipes towards the building and a familiar face appears, almost as if he'd been watching out for our arrival. As temporary leader of our little group, I step forward to greet him, stretching out my hand then pulling Lost, Snake's VP, in for a hug. When I let him go, Slick does likewise, holding him for longer. Lost had a hands-on role helping us get rid of the Herrera threat a month or so back, fighting alongside his Tucson brothers.

"Good to see yer, Brother." Mouse gets in on the greetings as well.

"Welcome to San Diego. Fuck, we're always happy to help brothers out. Got a couple of rooms for ya. Two of you gonna bunk up together, okay? We ain't got as much space as you have." Slick and I shrug. A room's only for sleeping, I don't much care, as long as he doesn't snore. Mouse we'll leave to himself, it's not unknown for him to be tapping away at his keyboard half the night.

Satan's Devils, wherever we hail from, know how to greet brothers from another chapter, and the San D lot aren't any different. Lost leads us inside, shows us where to dump our stuff, then brings us back down and starts introducing us around. A few of the brothers I've met before, but being a bigger chapter, one name soon starts to merge into the next. We meet Smoker and Tinder, Snips and Grumbler, and their sergeant-at-arms, Poke. Snake puts in an appearance. Unlike back in Tucson, there seems few old ladies, or none that are putting in an appearance tonight. We're invited to share fried chicken, strangely cooked by Snake's mother, who seems to be in charge in the kitchen, with sweet butts following her direction. It's a completely different vibe to the one back at home, much more male orientated and less of a family feel.

We drink, I let a sweet butt put her mouth on my dick without even bothering to learn her name, admiring Slick for resisting the temptation to try out new flesh. Wouldn't have been so long ago he'd been all over that, but now that he's got an old lady he refrains from sampling the pleasures on offer. Can't understand it myself, a hole's a hole, and any one will do when a brother's got the urge—only having the one woman must get boring after a while. After thanking the girl and pushing her away, now thoroughly sated in every way, I go to the luckily king-size bed that I'll be sharing with my brother tonight, already finding him asleep and gently snoring.

I don't want to be mistaken for his old lady and wary of wandering hands in his sleep, so I keep my pants on, and to my side of the bed. Then, the long drive, good food, more than enough beer and shots all add together and soon I'm fast asleep.

As expected, Mouse must have spent most of the night doing research, but that doesn't stop him banging on our door first thing in the morning. Slick's still sleeping like the dead as I open it, wiping at my own bleary eyes.

"Give us a sec, bro. Need to visit the head." After a long, much needed and satisfying piss, I return to find Mouse's door open.

"What you got then, Brother?" Before he can answer, a vibration alerts me to a text.

As I take out my phone, Mouse nods towards it. "Just sent you Thompson's address."

I shake my head. "Already had it, Brother. It's Alex's old house."

I'm surprised when he smirks. "Oh, no, it's not."

"No?" Still half asleep, I'm not sure what he means. "He's moved?"

"Nah, got two residences. One he owns, one he rents. Both in his name."

I rub my hands over my face then smooth them down over my sweaty chest, wishing I'd taken the time to run through the shower to wake myself up, knowing I'm being a bit slow on the uptake. "Anyone else live there?"

"Not that I can find on the records. The houses are only in his name. But I thought it was worth taking a look?"

Hmm. I agree, it's a puzzle I'm going to have to sort out. Alex never mentioned him having a different place.

A hand rests on my shoulder. "Whassup, Brother?"

I point to Mouse and then update Slick. "Fucker's got another house we didn't know about."

"You still planning on talkin' to him?" Yeah. That had been my plan if Mouse hadn't turned anything else up. Just have a polite chat to make sure he was going to leave Alex alone and wasn't going to be an ass about supporting his kid. If he didn't take to the words, I'd have followed up the conversation with my hands if he needed extra persuasion to get my point.

I'm quiet for a minute, thinking things through in my head. There are clearly things about Thompson we hadn't known, and where there's a whiff of a smell there's often something rotting underneath. It's my first inkling this might not be as straightforward as I'd hoped. "Which one is rented?" I ask at last.

"The address Alex gave us." And that's probably another reason for not rushing through with the divorce. If she knew they didn't own their home she'd know there was no collateral in it, and nothing to help her get the money she so desperately needs. *The bastard's been hiding something from her.*

And it would be useful to find out just how much he hid. "I'm gonna go take a look," I decide at last. "See what I can find out."

"You plannin' on knockin' on the door, Brother?"

I'm planning exactly that. "Don't see why not. Easiest way of having a word with him, and sends a good message, don't ya think? *We know where you live.* And that a biker club's looking out for her."

"I'll come too," Slick's quick to offer.

"And I've got ya six, Dart."

I direct a chin jerk toward each of them.

There's food in the kitchen, breakfast here seems a buffet-style help yourself affair, the cooking once again done by the club girls under the watchful eye of the prez's mother, a dour, non-communicative woman. After filling our stomachs, we waste no time going to our bikes, storing our cuts again in the saddle bags, not wanting to step on anyone's toes or wear some-thing that so clearly proclaims where we're from. Though we suspect he knows exactly where Alex has holed up, just in case we're wrong, there's no sense in giving Thompson a fucking signpost.

With directions from Lost and the GPS on Mouse's phone, it's not long before we're driving up to a decent enough one-story to the south of San Diego. There's a car on the drive, a Chrysler hatchback, and not a particularly new model. Not a vehicle I would have expected a cop to drive. As my engine ticks, I swing my leg over the seat and get off. Slick comes to my side. Mouse nods, but stays with the bikes.

Slick and I exchange looks, then I march up the neatly kept front yard and approach the front door.

There's sounds from inside, so I know someone's home. Another glance shared between us, then I roll my shoulders, loosening myself up and getting prepared to meet the man who last spoke to Alex using his fists, the reminder making me clench my hands. Slick notices and gives me a warning growl.

"Thought we agreed we'd just talk, Brother?"

We did. But...

Before I can finish the thought, the door is opened by a blond who's covering her mouth in an effort to hide a yawn. Her eyes widen. "Oh my."

The sight of two bikers on her doorstep, and a third waiting in the road, take her aback. Too slowly, she tries to close the door, but is prevented by my well-placed boot. My hand applying gentle pressure on her shoulder, I push her inside.

"I've got no money," she squeals, looking around in dismay.

"Ma'am. We're not here to fuckin' rob ya," Slick barks to reassure her.

"We just want to ask a few questions is all." I back him up.

Her eyes flicking wildly between us, she seems completely confused. "What? Who?" She swallows and tries again. "Why are you here?"

"Thompson. Ronald Thompson. You know him?" When I'd seen her, the immediate explanation that would fit was that she's just the tenant, and him her landlord.

"He's my boyfriend." And like that my previous assumption is blown right out of the water. "He lives here with me."

We've clearly woken her up. She yawns again, widely, as I process what she's just said. Fuck me, he's not missing Alex at all. Didn't take him more than a minute to find someone else.

"You been with him long, sweetheart?" Slick's followed me into the house.

She shrugs, and frowns as though considering whether it's any of our business, but clearly can't see the harm in telling us as she replies, "Six years, give or take."

What the fuck? My eyes widen as I realise Thompson's had a bit on the side all the time he's been married to Alex. Tyler's only just six for fuck's sake. He must have started it while she was pregnant, if not very soon after the birth. And it doesn't make sense. Why did he stay with Alex and keep up pretences? Why not just leave her and live with the blond? Something doesn't add up. I owe him nothing at all, and have no qualms dropping him in it. "You do know he's married?"

She doesn't even flinch. "Yeah. The bitch gives him hell. Refuses to give him a divorce. He left her, but she's being a right cow about it. Won't let him see his son unless he pays her money."

But Alex isn't getting a penny from him. And he doesn't even see the kid. Right about now, the conversation I wanted to have with him is getting rewritten in my head, and it's going to be fucking harder than ever not to push his teeth down his throat. But I'll have to hold that in check until I get some fucking answers. I was right about that smell, and the need to track down the source.

"Where is he?" Slick growls.

"Not here."

"He at work?" Not that I really care. I'll be waiting here when he arrives home.

"No, he's not." Now that she's woken up a bit she's come to her senses and her body language starts screaming that she doesn't like us being in the house. "He had some rest days, has gone out of town for a week."

Fuck it! I thought this would be over and done within a couple of days, now it seems my stay in Cali will be longer. But where's he gone? And why alone? "You didn't get to go with him?"

"I work. I'm a nurse and work nights," she explains, confirming we had indeed disturbed her rest. "He's gone to visit a friend."

You don't survive my kind of life by ignoring any prickling feeling suggesting something's wrong. "Know where this friend might live, darlin'?"

My body is already tensing as she replies, "Tucson, he said."

Fuck!

"When did he leave?" I ask through gritted teeth.

"Yesterday morning."

Double fuck!

I start pulling Slick out of the door and back toward our bikes. He remembers his manners, throwing a quick thank you over his shoulder. I've got my phone in my hand as I swing my leg astride.

"Prez. We've got a fuckin' problem. Seems Thompson's come up to Tucson. Left yesterday. We must have fuckin' passed him on the road." Yeah. While I was getting my dick sucked last night, Thompson was on fucking his way to the city where Alex and Tyler are hiding out. "Can you send someone to check on them?"

"What? No. She doesn't have a fuckin' phone." I meant to get her one and it had slipped my mind. "I don't know her sister's number either."

"Thanks, Prez. I'm on my way back. "Sure, send Tongue and Beef to see if everything's right. Can they let me know they're okay?"

I hear voices and then hurried instructions. Drum's not wasting a moment making sure Thompson hasn't gone after Alex. I bang my hand on the handlebars, utterly frustrated I'm not there to help. Fucking coincidence I've come to San D when her bastard of an ex is in Arizona. Prez is still talking.

"What? What do you mean don't come back?" I listen to the words he's saying and I don't like it one bit, but he does have a point. There's probably nothing I can do back home that my brothers can't do equally well, but it doesn't sit right with me, I want to be the one to ensure Alex's protection. But as Drummer goes on to explain, I can't fault his reasoning, and albeit reluctantly, I agree.

A few more words then we hang up. Mouse comes alongside and puts his hand on my arm. "Steady, Brother. You can't travel alone. Slick and I will come with."

"Not going back, Mouse." I rub my hand over the short beard on my chin, realising I'm worried sick about Alex and *I can't even fuckin' ring her!* "Drum told us to head back to the San D clubhouse and wait until we find out what's going on. Tongue and Beef are on their way to see her now, and depending what they find, might get them to go to the club for safety. He said they'll contact us as soon as they know the score and we'll decide what to do from there."

I put my key in the ignition and press the button, my Harley starts with a roar. Fuck, and I thought this would be easy. Come here, meet Thompson, get the lay of the land and sort things out for Alex and Tyler, either with words or whatever other persuasion he needs, then get the hell out of Dodge. But now I'm playing a waiting game, and that isn't something I do easily.

A quick look behind me shows Slick and Mouse already on their sleds. Waving my hand over my head, I'm off, only just able to stay within a respectable range of the speed limits to avoid getting pulled over. Wouldn't be no use to anyone sitting in a cell. As I ride, all I can think is why this great fucking coincidence? Why has Thompson waited until now before staking his claim?

It's a question we address as soon as we get back to the clubhouse, well, after Slick's rounded up a sweet butt to make coffee for us. With a possible six-hour ride coming up, all of us make our own decision to stay off the beer.

"Why now?" Slick puts my question into words.

"Been givin' that some thought." Mouse refreshes his ponytail, making my hand go up to check my bun. "We know cops are a pretty close-knit family, and I reckon he had the Tucson guys keepin' an eye on Alex. This visit coincides with her taking a job at the Angels. Fucker like him might be the possessive type and not like the thought of other men eyein' his woman."

"Can't be that fuckin' possessive to have another woman on the side."

"Don't work that way, Dart. She's married to him, he could still see her as somethin' that's his. A possession. But hey, I'm just guessin' at reasons. It's the only thing that makes any sense to me."

We can't know why, but just need to deal that Thompson's in a place where I'm not.

"I feel sorry for her." I'm not only sorry, I'm angry. "She's tried so hard to stay under the radar. Did everythin' right. What she wasn't aware of is his contacts in different police forces. Bet he's known where she's been almost since the day she arrived."

"I said that before," Mouse agrees. "She thinks he doesn't know about her sister, but he's a cop for fucks sake. He would leave no stone unturned. Be shit easy for him to send some of the Tucson colleagues to the locale and check it out."

If she'd come to us earlier, we'd have found her someplace better to hide. But then, why should she have? She's a law-abiding citizen who doesn't know fuck about how the underworld works. And that includes the police.

Our coffee arrives. Fuck, I wish it was something stronger, but I need to keep my head straight. When my phone rings in my pocket I take it out without delay, almost dropping it on the floor in my haste.

"Tongue?"

"What's happened?"

"*What the fuck?*" Mouse and Slick look at me intently, straining to hear the voice at the other end of the phone.

"You've spoken to Celine and Craig? Did they see anything?"

"FUCK!"

"Keep me posted, okay?"

"What's going on, Brother?" Slick's half out of his seat, prepared to go, stay, whatever I need him to do.

Brushing my hand over my hair, I shake my head, then look from one to the other, not quite sure what to say. "Alex and Tyler have gone missing. Celine got home yesterday and they were gone. Her car's still there, her clothes... But they've disappeared." The fear smashes into me, making my heart lose its rhythm and sweat to break out on my hands. "They've fuckin' gone," I yell, unable to keep my pain and anguish inside. It hits me that she's not just a dancer. In the short time I've known her, she's become a friend. And having a woman as a friend is alien territory for me. I care about her, and the fact she's disappeared hits me as hard as it would had I lost any one of my brothers. And add that smart kid into the mix... I slide my hands around until they're cupping my cheeks, feeling helpless for the first time in my life. I want, have, to help her. I want to be there to protect her. And I don't have a clue where to start. *Fuck.*

"Calm, Brother. She might have got wind of Thompson being around and took off on her own."

With my voice rising I tell him the rest. "There's no fuckin' doubt about it. Tyler was picked up from school. By his fuckin' father."

My outburst has attracted attention. Snake and Lost have appeared.

"What the fuck's going on?"

My watering eyes show my torment, and while it's not correct, I don't argue with Slick's phrasing when he responds to the San Diego prez. "Dart's woman. She's disappeared. Bastard ex of a husband has taken her and her young son."

Snake stares at me, but only a second later he's circling his hand over his head and shouting as only an MC prez can. "Church, boys!" Then he rests his hand on my shoulder. "Whatever you need, Brother."

Turning my head toward him, I can't find the words, but raise my chin to him in thanks. I might not be in my own club-house, may not even know the names of some of the men, but we're all Satan's Devils. Pushing myself up out of the chair, unsteady on my feet, I walk beside Slick and Mouse and enter into the hallowed room. I hover for a moment, until I'm pointed to a chair. I'm on automatic pilot. *Alex, where the fuck are you? And how's Tyler coping seeing his dad? And is Thompson keeping his hands off them both?*

CHAPTER 11

Alex

The barbeque I'd gone to at the clubhouse had been nothing like I'd expected. Sure, it was very man heavy, and all of them looking like the rough bikers they are, but I didn't feel threatened or out of place for one moment. The old ladies—it seems strange to refer to women my age as that—had been welcoming, and everyone, both male and female, so kind to both me and my son.

The chance to get out and make new female friends had been wonderful, and I'd already been thoroughly enjoying myself when their president dropped that bombshell on me. Not only had they extended the hand of friendship, but they'd come up with an idea to help raise money toward getting Tyler the treatment he needs. It might end up only being a small drop in a very large ocean, but what had blown me away was they cared enough to make the suggestion.

I'd still been bemused when I'd got back to Celine's, still unable to believe this group of strangers are going to help me raise money for Tyler. Why would they bother? They owe me nothing, the tenuous link is only that they own the club where I work, and I've only been there for less than a week. Other people I've told my son's story to might have offered sympathy at the most, but not a suggestion of practical assistance.

Realistically, I know time's running out. Tyler's now six, and that means it could already be too late to convince any doctor to try a transplant. We're at the point now that we have to try something. If I do nothing, he lives with that threat hanging over him every day of his life. A stem cell transplant could be a complete cure and might give Tyler the chance of a normal life. For the first time in months, maybe even years, Drummer's offer to help raise money has made me feel optimistic. Maybe there's more I can do to get what I need myself. Instead of wallowing, it's given me the push to begin coming up with ideas myself. The kick up the backside to do *something*, anything. I owe it to my son to try.

When I awake Monday morning it's with a sense of purpose to do more than just cope and exist. Ron never cared, but suddenly, with this club of bikers behind me, I wonder whether there might be light at the end of the tunnel after all. People raise money for causes all the time, perhaps I should bury my pride and see what's available to help my boy.

I don't have long to think about it, Tyler's up already, running into my room wearing his cartoon pyjamas, and I take a moment to notice he looks like any other kid as he jumps on my bed and gives me a hug and a kiss. It's our way in which we start the day, and I can't think of anything better as I tickle my son, making him giggle and squirm.

The rest of the morning proceeds as normal. Cutting an end to his antics, I get myself out of bed and dressed, and him ready for school. Having seen him off to the bus, I'm suddenly at a loss. Yesterday's amazing outcome has got me buzzing with energy, a nervous excitement, and my mind's working ten to the dozen.

I've got the whole day to myself, no working tonight, and the house is empty, both Celine and Craig are at work. While my brain's racing, thinking of possibilities, I decide to keep myself active by being useful. Even though I'm now bringing in some money, Celine will only accept the minimum for food. Doing housework will keep my hands occupied, and help her in some small way.

By mid morning, I've cleaned the kitchen, started a load of laundry, and tidied all the toys in the living room away. I take out the vacuum and go to plug it in when there's a loud knock.

My heart leaps when it shouldn't. *Maybe it's Dart?* But I realise I hadn't heard a loud motorcycle pull up, so tamp down my anticipation as I go to open the door. Despite my warnings to Tyler, I'm not even cautious, just fling it open wide. And then I have cause to remember my own instructions. *Always check before opening the door.*

"My dear wife." The words might be sweet, the tone of delivery anything but.

Quickly I try to slam the door closed, but I'm not fast enough. He's ahead of me there, putting his foot in gap to stop me.

A chilling shiver runs down my spine, but I try to stop my voice from shaking, imbibing it with a strength I don't feel. "Why are you here, Ron?" I've been here two months, apart from thinking he'd no idea where I'd gone, I hadn't expected he'd even want to look. Now that he's standing in front of me, it's like my nightmare turned into reality. Although my voice might be steady, my trembling hand still holding onto the door betrays me. And when he reaches out his arm, his fingers painfully biting into mine, I feel a flicker of fear.

"I've come to take you home. Back where you belong."

The coldness in his voice does nothing to reassure me. My heart starts to pound in my chest. Going anywhere with him would be a bad mistake. I try to shrug of his touch, he just tightens his hand.

While knowing it's probably useless, I try to reason with him. "You can't want me back, Ron. Let's be sensible about this. I'm out of your hair and not asking for anything. Surely you're better off living on your own?"

His face darkens, and his features rearrange themselves into the expression I'd last seen that day in the kitchen just before he'd hit me. "I'd have left you alone if you hadn't brought shame on the family. Fuck, Alex. You've been whoring yourself out."

Oh shit. He knows I work at a strip club. *But how does he know?* His description of what he thinks I'm doing gets my blood boiling. "I'm not *whoring myself out* as you put it so nicely. I'm dancing."

"You're taking your clothes off." He's getting angry now, and I regret speaking back to him. That flicker of fear rapidly morphs into full blown panic.

The words to try and justify myself tumble out quickly. "I don't take all of them off. No one's ever seen me naked, except for you Ron."

The slap around my face isn't totally unexpected, but there was such force behind it, for a moment I see stars. He takes the opportunity to uncurl my fingers from the door and drag me out onto the porch. There's a car waiting, engine still running. *I can't let him take me away.*

Regaining my senses, I pull hard against him, but he's too strong and is winning, inch by inch. My mind's working. At least he's only come for me and not Tyler. Celine will look after him as if he was her own. *If I go with him, he'll kill me.*

A sense of self-preservation makes me scream, but it's a workday and the houses around appear empty. Either that or no one wants to get involved.

"Shut up!" he snarls. "If you don't want to worry the boy, you come quietly."

What?

"Yeah, that got your attention, didn't it, bitch? I went to the school and collected Tyler. He's waiting in the car and watching us right now. I suggest you do what I say and don't fight me."

One side of his mouth turns up in a twisted grin. "There's no way you'd win, Alex. And Tyler will witness what happens when you disobey."

He's got Tyler? How? The school wouldn't let anyone but me or Celine take him, would they? Then I realise there's little doubt he's telling the truth, probably all he needed to do was flash his police identification. All resistance leaves me, I can't abandon my son to this monster. Reluctantly I let him take me to the SUV and get me settled in the front. As he's doing so, I turn and try to summon up a smile for my son sitting in the rear seat. His bottom lip is quivering, but he says nothing at all. Par for the course around Ron. I notice he's at least remembered to bring a booster seat. Jesus, how long has he been planning this?

The car's too cold, but there's no point saying anything. Ron's all for his comfort and not anyone else's. I compare that with how Dart was so kind, letting me keep a comfortable temperature for Tyler. Ron doesn't give a damn. There's no point in mentioning it, I'd only get another back hander, and I don't want my son to see what a violent man his father has become.

As he puts the SUV in drive, I try to sound calm as I ask, "What about our things? I can run back and pack…"

"I've wasted enough time. You've got stuff at the house at San Diego." Yeah, when I'd run I'd left everything behind. *So he's really taking me home. Why? To pick up playing house where we left off?*

Again, I look over my shoulder. Tyler might be young, but as his eyes flick to me he knows this is wrong, but thank God he's not uttering any protest or objections. Ron's wound up tight, it would take little to set him off. I want to hold my son, to cuddle him, to reassure him, but Ron's never approved of what he calls mollycoddling. I have to content myself with offering another forced smile. It's meant to be comforting, but from Tyler's expression I've not been successful.

And then the SUV's moving, taking me away from the only place I've ever felt safe or happy, and the new life I was building for myself and my son. I feel a tear escape from my eye and turn to look out of the window so as not to give Ron the pleasure of seeing it.

I'd knew there was something lurking beneath his civilised façade, even when I'd first been introduced to him. I'd never have married him if I hadn't been so young and pressured into it. I'd been a virgin, he'd taken me roughly, and that side of our marriage didn't improve after our wedding night. All too quickly, I learned my own pleasure meant nothing to him. When he'd done what I now know is called stealthing, removing the condom and getting me pregnant without my permission, the beast inside him began to come to the fore.

He dropped all pretence as soon as we knew the fate of the babies, but at that time he hadn't hurt me physically, it was just mental abuse and starting to avoid me. Staying out nights and hardly coming home. The one good thing, was he'd never had sex with me again. He put the blame on me, for being so unattractive.

I was only eighteen, and accepted it was my fault. Beaten down until I was ashamed that our marriage wasn't working, I did what I could to try and improve it. When that hadn't worked, I just settled into a loveless relationship. I shouldn't have stayed, but I was young, stupid, and naïve. My parents had no sympathy, siding with him and insisting the failure of my marriage was down to me. I should work at it harder, they said.

What choice had I got? I had no skills and no money, my only option to keep up the pretence with my man. If I left him with no job, and nowhere to go, he might have got custody of my son.

And while his hate had only been expressed verbally, I could cope with just words. I wasn't stupid, despite my inexperience I

SATAN'S DEVILS #4: Targeting DART

read the signs, and had known for a while that his anger was building, but still, he hadn't raised his hand to me. Until that day he exploded and given vent to six years of pent-up rage. *I don't trust him.* Not with myself, and definitely not with Tyler. He got away with hurting me once, and now I know he's going to put me through hell again. He tried to kill me last time. Now that he's got his hands on me again, he'll probably succeed.

Casting him a sideways glance, I realise the man driving the SUV bears little resemblance to the man my parents first introduced me too. He's let the animal inside him out in the open, and now it's never going to be put back in its cage.

"How did you find me, Ron?" I'd asked why before, but didn't get an adequate response.

"For fucks sake, Alex. You're so fucking stupid. I'm a cop. I've got contacts in all police departments. You thought you hid that you were in tight with your sister? I knew about that all the time. Your phone records told me." He thumps his hand on the steering wheel. "Didn't really care you were gone, at least you took the brat with you. But I've had people watching you. When you started stripping I couldn't allow that! Fuck, I'll become the laughing stock of the department when that gets out. And liaising with a fucking outlaw biker club? Probably whoring yourself out to them? That was the last fucking straw."

If I was a good mother I'd stop him swearing in front of my son. But if I was a proper mama, I'd have left him years before. I bite my lip, not knowing where this is going. And I'd been so foolish, thinking he would have been glad that I'd left and not bothered to find me. And I never considered he'd be able to use the tools of his job. He's right. *I've been stupid.*

Another few miles pass, and I look at my son. The smooth vibration of the car has lulled him to sleep.

I take the opportunity to find out what I already know I'd rather not hear. "What are you going to do with us, Ron? Surely you don't want to pick up from where we left it? The marriage hasn't been working for years." *If it ever had.*

He doesn't answer, just leaves me guessing. And while he doesn't let me into his plans, I doubt there's a rosy future in it for me. Or for Tyler.

Miles pass, and then we're approaching Winterhaven, the border between Arizona and California. *Maybe this is my chance.* I could shout out we're being abducted, but when we slow ready to stop at the checkpoint, Ron gets out his police ID and we're waved on past.

If only I'd been able to get that restraining order. With that in place there'd have been a reason to report him. But I'd found how hard it is to prove something against a cop. His colleagues had rallied around him, and it had never been filed. Clearly his team were more worried about not having him on their side than they were about what was happening to me. Briefly my mind flicks to the bikers who people call criminals, and how different they were to the man beside me, and the colleagues who rallied around him.

No one had believed me, except the doctor who'd treated my injuries.

"Mom. I wanna go potty."

Ron swears loudly as I glance at my son. Having woken, his face is scrunched up, his legs crossed, and he's fidgeting. Sure signs an accident is close unless we do something about it.

"We've got to stop, Ron."

He heaves an impatient sigh and swears under his breath, but pulls off at the next rest area. "Stay in the car," he tells me. "I'll take Tyler to the bathroom."

"I need to go too, Ron." And perhaps there'll be someone I can talk to in there, tell them I've been kidnapped or something.

"Once Tyler's sorted I'll come back and get you. I'll escort you inside."

SATAN'S DEVILS #4: Targeting Dart

"You can't go into the girls' bathroom."

"I'm a cop, babe. I go where I like. Anyone asks I'll say you're a fugitive." He leans over and painfully entangles his fingers in my hair, pulling me toward him so he can whisper straight into my ear. "Stay here like a good girl. Be quiet and don't attract attention or speak to anyone. I'll have Tyler with me, remember." Then he gets out, grabs Tyler from his seat, and locks up the car with the windows closed. Tyler throws a look of panic over his shoulder, but there's nothing I can do to help him. I try to give him a reassuring smile. Surely Ron wouldn't do anything to hurt his son? But he's scared me enough that I bide by his threat and do nothing to make my predicament known.

I heave a sigh of relief when they're both back safely. By that time I'm overheating and finding it hard to breath the stuffy air. Not wanting Tyler to be trapped in a hot car, I refuse the opportunity to relieve myself. Only minutes later we're back on the road, and I'm being driven to a fate that I can't try to imagine. I only suspect it won't involve me playing house like I did before.

CHAPTER 12
Dart

Once seated in church, Snake wastes no time getting down to business. He takes out a smoke but doesn't pass them around. After he's lit it he waves the glowing tip toward me. "Dart, here, our brother from Tucson, has a problem he may need our help on. Wanna fill us in, Dart?"

Despite my despair, I'm heartened that every man here turns and gives me a nod, chin lift, or other such indication they'll try to help sort whatever is wrong.

"We run a strip club," I begin, knowing that's not news for anyone around the table. "One of the girls came from San D, as she'd had problems with her man. Got a young son, he's got sickle cell disease."

Poke, the sergeant-at-arms, scrunches his face. "She black?" he asks, his mouth gaping.

Immediately I'm on the defensive. "Yeah, she's black. So what?"

"White club, man." Tinder's shaking his head.

Slick bangs his hands on the table and goes as if to stand up. "If you fuckers gonna take exception to my brother's ol' lady, then we'll do this alone. Come on, Mouse…"

Snake knocks the gavel loudly against the table. "Sit down, Slick. Everyone just calm down. We might not have a black brother in the club, but our rules don't say nothin' 'bout the ladies. Fancied myself a bit of dark meat a time or too."

I bite back my anger, and note the way Slick's said Alex is mine and that I don't rush to refute it. Applying the ownership label might get us more help. Getting our relationship straight in their minds can come later. Right now, I just know that I want to have her and Tyler back safe and sound.

"When you're ready, Dart."

I nod at Snake. "Her old man's a cop. Ronald Thompson is his name. Based here in San Diego."

"And that's who's taken her?"

I look at his flash to remind me of his name. "Yeah, Snips. That's what we believe. Me and my brothers came here to have a chat with him. The kid needs treatment and he's not payin' up." I go on to explain how we'd visited Thompson's second home and what we'd discovered.

"You reckon he's bringin' them back to San D?"

I shrug my shoulders. "He could be takin' them anywhere. But here's a good place to start. My feel is he'll want them somewhere on his home turf."

Grumbler leans back in his chair and folds his arms over his chest. "What d'ya reckon he wants to do with them?"

"I've got no fuckin' idea. But my gut tells me whatever it is won't be good. She was afraid for her life when she ran. He tried to kill her once already."

Smoker gets out his cigarettes, which makes me reach into my pocket for mine. He pauses before lighting up. "I think I know Thompson. Detective, you say? Well, if he's who I'm thinking of, he's one sadistic motherfucker."

Snake sits forward. "That wasn't who…"

"Sure was, Prez. Yeah, that's who arrested Stickler a couple of years or so back."

The murmurs and protests around the table suggest I'm going to hear something I'm not going to like.

"You were there, Grumbler. Want to tell the Tucson boys what went down?"

Grumbler shuts his eyes as though he's remembering the details. "We'd been out on a run. Stickler had some dope with him. For personal use." He rubs his hand over his beard. "Stickler had served and come back with PTSD, got severe depression. He was legally prescribed marijuana. Had the letter with him an' all."

Snips grins. "Yeah, but while we know that, instead of carryin' eight ounces, knowing him he probably had double that."

Giving Snips a frown for interrupting him, Grumbler continues the tale. "The rest of us were clean. They pulled Stickler off his ride. He tried to show them the letter he had — he'd carried it around with him for ages, so it was crumpled and dirty. Cop arrestin' him wouldn't even look at it."

Tinder takes up the tale. "Those fuckers had it in for him. Maybe they were down on their arrest record, I don't know. Anyway, they were treatin' him roughly. Stickler's PTSD cut in. He'd been taken prisoner out in the sand pit, so he didn't like bein' manhandled or restrained, and started to fight back."

"He'd have gone willingly had they just spoken to him calmly and cuffed him, but they were too rough. The way they were handling him hit one of his triggers," Snips snarls.

"Yeah. Anyway, cop car pulls up with your friend Thompson inside. Came out swingin' a baton…"

I haven't seen anyone called Stickler around. "And…?" I prompt, already having a bad taste in my mouth.

"Last we saw of him he was unconscious."

"Word was he died resistin' arrest."

"Man, that blow was fuckin' hard. Heard his skull crack."

"And you just stood there and watched?" Slick sounds appalled.

"Wasn't much we could do, man. They took him away, said they'd get medical help. There were only three of us, and by the time Thompson arrived with his partner, four of them. Without killin' all the cops we had to trust they'd do what they said." Lost, their VP, silent up until now, is obviously still upset at what happened.

Again, Smoker leans forward. "Bird kicked up a fuckin' fuss. But couldn't shake them from the official story. Made sure he got a hero's fuckin' funeral, press there, Patriot Guard Riders, the lot. There was a story in the paper sayin' he'd been legally carryin' and that the cops had fucked up." My brow creases, and then I remember Bird was in the prez's chair before Snake.

Grumbler lifts his hand, letting me know there's more to this story. "Strange thing was, Thompson's name was kept out of it. Accordin' to the police, it was one of the traffic cops who'd hit him too hard."

"So how d'ya know?"

"Apart from that we saw it with our own fuckin' eyes?" he scoffs, then shrugs. "Cop who got blamed wasn't too happy about it. Had a loose mouth. We sent one of the prospects into the drinkin' place they prefer and he heard him mouthin' off."

"If you want help takin' that motherfucker down, we're right there behind you. And I don't think we need to take a vote on that." Snake eyes up his men, every one of them nodding. While I feel chilled inside. To kill a man for legal possession of dope? What would Thompson do to his wife who'd run off? Or Tyler, come to that.

Something's niggling at me. "Why didn't you tell us this before, Snake, when Drum asked if you knew the fucker?"

Snake shrugs. "I wasn't in the chair when it happened, and didn't immediately remember. Fuck, Dart, I don't carry the names of all the fuckin' cops in the city in my head."

No, but wouldn't you remember the one who'd killed a brother? I shake my head. Still, whether or not he'd have told us earlier wouldn't have made much difference. Couldn't make me hate Thompson any more than I already do.

Mouse has been tapping away at his laptop. He's also been exchanging muttered asides to Token, who's apparently Snake's go-to computer guy. Apparently, his full handle's Hard Token, but fuck knows what that is.

Suddenly Mouse looks up. "Can't link Thompson to any more properties than the two we already know about. Can't find a lock-up or anythin' like."

"Doesn't mean he hasn't got somewhere else."

Token points to the laptop screen. "Mouse has looked everywhere I would. Even into his financials." He breaks off and nudges Mouse. "Show me how to do that sometime, will ya?"

Mouse looks smug. "Got expert help from an Arab hacker, man."

I'm getting frustrated. "When you've finished your fuckin' bondin' session, can you put that in English?"

"Yeah, Dart. We couldn't find any regular payments goin' out for anywhere he might have rented."

"He's a cop," Snake says drily. "He'll know all sorts of places and all kinds of types."

My leg's bouncing and I'm finding it hard sitting here doing nothing. "Why don't we start with visiting the houses we know about first? Good thing is, he won't know anyone will be lookin' for him."

Slick's running his hands over his bald head. "The girlfriend might have more info about places he'd go."

"Good point, Brother. Think it's time we put a bit of pressure on there." We hadn't thought we'd needed to question her further. The only thought on my mind when we'd left her was how quickly we could get to Alex and her kid.

I glance toward Snake. I want to get moving, but protocol says he's got to wrap this up. He must see my impatience, as he raps on the table. "Okay, we split into two groups, visit both houses. Dart, where d'ya wanna be, man?"

And that's my conundrum. Do I want to go to their marital home, the obvious place where he might take her? Or, on the assumption he's stashed them somewhere else, be the one interrogating his girlfriend? Fuck, I don't know. I just want to find her safe. He's already had her for a day and a half, fuck knows what he might have done. An image comes into my head of the way she owned that pole, and it hits me I can't handle the thought of not seeing her again. What do I do? Go after more information, or on what could turn out to be a wild goose chase?

Slick sees my confusion. "Brother. My gut feel is he wouldn't take her to the house, not unless he wants to resume playin' happy families. And from what you said, I'd say there was fuck all chance of that. But it needs to be checked out, just in case. Let's go question the girlfriend. I didn't like hearin' that story about him and Stickler. The sooner we get hold of Alex and Tyler the happier I'll be."

You and me both, Brother. But what he says makes sense. I just don't like the thought that she might be in the most obvious place and I'm not there to rescue her.

Snake is staring at me, his hands playing with his long hair. As he twists it around his finger, he clears his throat. "Dart, understand your concerns. I'll take point goin' to this fucker's house. If the girl's there, I bring her and the kid back here and keep them safe." He gives a wicked chuckle. "Hell, I'll throw in that fucker Thompson as well. Reckon we'd all like to have a chat with him."

'Fuck yeahs' and 'bet your fucking ass we do' fly around the table as brothers vocalise their agreement, and Grumbler cracks his knuckles.

"Right," I step up. "Slick and I'll go question the girlfriend. If Thompson is there we'll bring him back. That means we both need trucks of some sort?" Snake nods to show he's got that sorted. "If we find anythin' else we'll keep in touch."

"We've got your ass, Brother. Soon as any of us know anythin' we'll share the news." He assigns various brothers to accompany me and Slick, Mouse offers to go with Snake as Alex and the boy know him, then the prez picks up the gavel. "Anyone else got anythin' they wanna say? Okay, brothers, get out of here and go do what ya got to do."

As I walk out, Slick pulls me aside. "Wasn't sure of the support we were gonna get here. Not after they sent Buster our way."

That thought had occurred to me. Buster had transferred to the Tucson chapter and all but raped Wraith's old lady. Of course, he's no longer alive to tell the tale. Some of the San D boys have no reason to love us, but I hadn't picked up on that vibe around the table. Thank fuck.

Without wasting any more time, we go to our bikes. Apart from Slick, Lost and Tinder are coming with us, as well Snips and Smoker. Poke is going along with Snake and Mouse, along with a couple more of their boys. Two trucks are already waiting for us, each being driven by a prospect. Prepared as we can be, we peel out of the lot and once more retrace our steps back through the city.

We don't try to be quiet as we thunder up to the house. Knowing the loud pipes will have announced our arrival, I send Tinder and Snips around the back so no one gets out that way, and then approach the front door, which flies open before I raise my hand to knock. *Thank fuck Tyler didn't take his mama's message to heart.*

For a second I just stand there open-mouthed as the boy leaps into my arms. It takes me a second to realise tears are falling down his cheeks and he's hanging onto me as though his life depended on it.

After disentangling myself from his tight hold, I lean back so I can see into his face. "Where's yer mom?" While I'm waiting for an answer, I look behind him. Slick pushes past and goes inside.

"Daddy took her away. I don't think she wanted to go, Dart." He sobs out the words. "She was crying. I saw him hit her." My arms automatically squeeze him, trying to give him comfort, while inside I'm burning with rage. Thompson dared hurt her? And in front of the boy?

Slick emerges from a back room, his hand curled around the girlfriend's arm. He's being none to gentle, but I don't give a damn.

"Where the fuck is Thompson?" I hiss through my teeth, not wanting to yell and upset Tyler any more than he already is. "And where's he taken Alex, his wife?"

Her eyes are flicking around in horror. "Please get out of my house. Tyler. Come here, son."

Tyler only holds on to me tighter.

"Please." She sounds panicked. "He left the boy with me. Said we were going to be looking after him now. Please, just go. I won't call the cops if you leave now. But you've got to leave Tyler here."

She won't be calling the cops anyway. A polite conversation won't cut it now I know Thompson's started hurting Alex. And we can't leave her here, we can't afford for her or one of his pals to get him word we're looking for him.

I exchange a few glances with Slick, a chin jerk over my shoulder, he lifts his head in return. "Prospect," I yell, letting Tyler down, but keeping hold of his hand. As the prospect approaches, I hold out my other hand for his keys and chuck him mine in return. I don't trust anyone else to drive the truck, not with both Tyler and the woman on board.

Slick's already got her hands bound behind her, and for good measure puts a gag in her mouth. She may well be innocent in all this, but I'm taking no chances, and I don't want her mouthing off in front of the boy. As we're putting her in the truck, Lost emerges from the house shaking his head. I know he's been searching. There wasn't any doubt in my mind, but we had to make sure. Tyler is right, his mom isn't here.

"Hey, Brother. Grumbler and I will stay on for a bit. Search for any paperwork that might give away another location."

Nodding my thanks, I turn to Tyler. "Hey, little man. You're going to sit up front with me, okay?" I wink at him. "But don't tell your mom." It's a little bit of normality, a small reassurance he'll be seeing her again. That's all he needs to climb confidently in and allow me to fasten the seat belt. Illegal, I know, but I've not got much choice. I'm not leaving him in the back with a woman I don't trust. She's already damned in my mind by her association with that bastard.

Tyler's sitting wide-eyed. "Are you taking me to Mom?"

Now how the fuck do I answer that? "You'll see her soon, buddy. You'll see her soon." I'm crossing my fingers, hoping that's the truth.

I risk another glance at him, seeing his bottom lip trembling, but fuck me, he's trying to be brave. The brothers returning to the clubhouse with me start their bikes, and we pull away, and Tyler goes quiet as we navigate the San Diego traffic then drive out of the city and up to the clubhouse. As I'm pulling up the handbrake my phone rings.

"Yeah."

"Snake, what did you find?"

"Fuck." I bang my fist on the steering wheel. Alex wasn't there, and Thompson's clearly not taking her there to resume their married life. All her clothes are trashed, and things that obviously belonged to her, hairdryer and such, have been

SATAN'S DEVILS #4: Targeting Dart

smashed. That's not the action of a loving husband who wants his wife back. Like we left Lost and Grumbler, a couple of Snake's boys are staying behind to search through his stuff. Mouse is apparently dismantling the computer he found in the study to bring it back to the clubhouse.

As I help Tyler out of his seat and put him gently on the ground, the one thought going around my head is, *Alex, where the fuck has that bastard taken you?*

Chapter 13
Alex

He won't tell me what he's done with Tyler. I'm going out of my mind worrying about where he might be, and who's looking after him.

When we arrived in San Diego Ron took me back to our house and left Tyler in the car while he dragged me inside then handcuffed me to the bed. I was crying, begging him to bring my son to me, but without a word he'd left, leaving me to survey the wreckage of my bedroom. All my clothes have been shredded, everything I'd owned broken. What sane man would do something like that?

Although the house is warm, I grow cold at the realisation my son has been taken away by a madman. *He wouldn't hurt his son, would he?* But now that Ron's shown me his true colours, I can't be certain of anything anymore.

I can't stop the tears rolling down my cheeks, all full of fear for Tyler. I don't give a damn what happens to me, just as long as my child isn't harmed.

I don't know how long he's been gone, but when Ron returns sometime later, frees me from my restraints and drags me out to the SUV, I'm devastated to find there is no little boy sitting in the back seat. My worries about where he'd left my son, with whom, and in what state override any concerns about myself. "What have you done with him?" I growl.

"That doesn't concern you."

I see red, and spit out angrily, "Ron, I'm his mother. I need to know he's safe." *I need to know you haven't hurt him.* "Tyler needs his medication. You know he takes antibiotics daily to stave off live-threatening infections, and needs his painkillers for when he has his episodes."

"You smother him." His voice is flat and cold. "He doesn't need all that shit."

And we're back to the old argument. If Ron doesn't listen to me, he'll be signing his son's death warrant. Even a mild infection could have severe ramifications. I have to make him understand. "Ron, for fuck's sake. Tyler's a sick child. You know that."

But he never wanted to admit he'd fathered a weak son. "He's only sick because you wrap him in cotton wool. He's got to man up." He gives me a calculating look.

Christ! There's no getting through to this man. My fears for Tyler increase ten-fold. *I need to get away from him.* Knowing I'd prefer to take my chances throwing myself onto the road, I reach for the door handle only to find he's used the central locking. I press all the unfamiliar buttons, to unlock the door, or open the window at least so I can yell for help. Frantically I bang on the window trying to attract attention. Someone must see and help.

Sharply he pulls the car over into an alley and parks up. In one quick move, he pulls something out of his pocket and roughly takes my arm. I try to pull it away, but he's got hold of me too tightly. The syringe plunges into my arm.

"What are you doing?"

"It's your fault, you wouldn't keep fucking quiet." And that's all I hear. Almost immediately a wooziness comes over me. I struggle against it as he turns the car around and gets going again, but it's no use. I can't keep my eyes open.

When I come around, I'm lying on a couch in a place that's familiar, but with absolutely no idea why Ron's brought me here. It's my parents' old cabin up in Big Bear, a couple of hours outside San Diego. *How has he got the key? Have they given it to him?* The thought that they might be complicit in my kidnapping is chilling. *Would they force me to go back to him? Do they know I'm here? Have they any idea he means to harm me?*

Groggily sitting up, trying to stop looking for explanations and instead seeking out a route of escape, I look around the room, noticing it hasn't changed much since I came here in my childhood. There's a musty smell as if it hasn't been used for years. But the fact he's brought me somewhere familiar gives me a moment of comfort. My sister will have raised the alarm by now, reported me missing to the police, and she might remember the cabin. Would she think of pointing them here? Then I remember what he'd told me, the police are his colleagues, his friends. They'll believe what he tells them. It wouldn't matter whether Celine has gone to them or not. They might pretend to go through the motions, but won't follow through. Cops stick together.

No one will come looking for me here. *Unless my parents know. They wouldn't let him hurt me, would they?* But deep down I know they'd be more concerned about me bringing disgrace on the family.

I stand and walk to the window, looking out on the beautiful but desolate view which only serves to remind me how isolated the cabin is. There are no neighbours, meaning he can do anything he likes, and however loud I scream there'll be no one coming to help. Still weak from the after effects of whatever he'd drugged me with, I sink to my knees, wondering whether I'll ever see Tyler again, praying with everything I've got that while Ron might hate me, he would take care of his son.

And where has Ron gone? Is this my chance to escape? Trying to clear my head, I pull myself up and go to the door. It's locked. I try a window, it's been nailed shut.

"You can't get out." Thinking he'd left me, I jump. I hate that voice and its sneering tone. "Not if I don't want you to go."

I try to swallow my fear down. "And will you? Let me go?"

"What do you think?"

I'm silent, already knowing the answer. Instinctively I know I've not got long on this earth. Why else would he have brought me to such an isolated place?

"Tell me, Alex. How do you think it felt to know you've sunk so low? That my wife was stripping for money? Letting men leer at the body that belongs to me?"

"I danced," I try to tell him again, biting my lip, knowing even if I could convince him that's probably bad enough.

"Show me how you strip, Alex," he lazily commands. "If the bikers employed you, perhaps you do have some moves. Let me see what I was missing all those miserable years."

That's the last thing I want to do for him, and I shudder at just the thought. I'm scared but try not to let it show, keeping my voice calm, not wanting to provoke him into losing his temper. "I pole dance." I wave my hand around. "There's no pole here, so I can't show you."

"As if I want to see your fat ass contorted around a fucking pole," he scoffs. "Just take your clothes off."

"No."

"No? Don't make me force you." His threat makes me shiver. He takes a step toward me, I take one back.

"If you do as I tell you, I'll let you see Tyler."

Can I believe him? But why does he want me to take off my clothes? *Is he going to rape me?* I'd let him do anything to me if it means I get to see my child again. And it wouldn't be much different to how he'd taken me in the past. If that's what it takes to see Tyler, I can do that.

"Strip, Alex," he repeats.

"Why?" I'm having difficulty believing he wants to see me naked. In the past, he'd tell me my body disgusted him. I can't see anything would have changed now.

"*Take off your fucking clothes!*" And there's that tone he used that last day, the one that carries a touch of madness.

I see a vein pulsing in his forehead, and realise he's getting to the end of his tether. If he kills me I'll never see Tyler again. *My son needs me.* Making a quick decision, feeling like insects are crawling across my skin, I reach for my top and pull it over my head, and then unbutton my shorts, close my eyes, and slide my shorts down and shrug them off over my shoes. It's cooler up here in the mountains, and goosebumps rise on my body.

"Huh!" He sneers, leaning himself back against the wall. "If that's how you stripped in the club I'm surprised they gave you the time of day. Fuck, Alex. You're an ugly piece of work to begin with. Now take the rest off. And do it how you did it for them."

Feeling humiliated, telling myself it's not showing him anything he's not seen before, I undo my bra and let it drop. Then I slip out of my panties. I shiver, from cold and despair. Is he going to leave me here without any clothes as a way of ensuring I don't escape? It's the only explanation I can come up with. I can see I'm not turning him on. One glance at his crotch is all I need to confirm that.

He smiles at me, the expression showing me I can expect trouble. He's not a big man, but he's enough to overpower me. He approaches menacingly, and although I struggle and try to fight him off, I'm still feeling dizzy, and it doesn't take much effort on his part to drag me into one of the two bedrooms. As I look at the bare mattress, it's clear what's he's been doing. He's set all this up.

He uses his greater strength to immobilise me on the bed and uses two pairs of handcuffs to fasten my arms over my head, and another two sets to secure my feet to the bottom posts. I'm spread-eagled before him.

As I pull at the metal cuffs holding me prisoner, he stares at me and then says, his voice now calm and reasonable, "The thing is, Alex, if I let you go, you'll just go back to the club and embarrass me like you did before. Do you know what it feels like to be a cop and know all your colleagues are snickering behind your back because your wife's become a stripper? And can you imagine how I felt, *as your husband,* to know you were taking your clothes off and letting other men see what belongs to me?"

Any other man would just have divorced me. There's something I'm missing, something I don't understand. "Why does it bother you? You never wanted me!"

"And ain't that the truth!"

"Why did you marry me if you found me so unattractive?" I scream out, realising I've never come out with it and asked him before, even though I'd often wondered.

Suddenly he laughs. "You stupid bitch. You really don't know, do you? Did you really think it was ever you that I wanted? You're fucking crazy if you do. Truth is, your parents gave me money to take you off their hands. I'm surprised you never guessed."

What? Why would they do that?

"You really don't think anyone would want a sad bitch like you without having a sweetener, do you? Fuck, it's been hell living with you and that fuck-up of a son you had. But it was hard to turn down the money they paid me."

My parents paid him? While it's hard to get over that blow, I realise I have to know. "How much, Ron? How much did they sell their daughter for? And why did they do it?" *And what has he done with the money?*

He shrugs, and chooses to answer the second question first. "They wanted you tied to a man who could control you. You'd started going to college, became independent. They didn't want you to turn out like your sister. One daughter running off they could explain, but another getting pregnant or bringing home the wrong sort? They didn't want to risk the embarrassment. A police officer could help them, and provide a good influence on their errant daughter. And as for the money? Not a lot in the grand scheme of things, but it came in handy enough. Allowed me to live the life that I wanted, which wasn't with you. They gave me a down payment of a hundred thousand dollars, then twenty-five thousand a year after that, which increased to fifty once you had the kid. Unfortunately, if they know you've left me the money will stop."

"So, you need me to come back." And there it is. Money is at the bottom of it. Tears prick at my eyes, he never wanted me at all.

"No. I don't need their money any longer, I've made other plans."

I shudder, grasping it probably would be preferable for him to want me back. If he asked me now I'd put up with anything just to have Tyler back in my arms. Whatever scheme he's alluding to will almost certainly bring nothing good my way. If he no longer needs the money… "You never wanted me, did you?" I don't phrase it as a question.

But he answers anyway. "No man in his right mind would want a fat tight-assed bitch like you. And now I'm going to make sure they never will."

What's he talking about?

I might not know what exactly he intends to do next, but he's got me at his mercy, and I'll be unable to prevent it. I try to keep him talking. While I doubt anyone's searching, the longer I can delay him, there's a chance I could be rescued. "You were worried about losing the money then, when I left? I thought you'd be happy that I was gone, and took Tyler with me."

He smirks. "You can't believe how great it was not having to come home to you. Yeah, you did me a big favour by walking out." Then he leans forward, his face so close to mine I can smell his foul breath and his sweat. "But eventually you'd have started divorce proceedings, and then money would have stopped. And, my dear Alex, no one leaves me. Not unless I want them to. No one causes me shame like that. You leave on my terms, or not at all." He stands back and stares at me. "Six years being tied to a bitch like you. Six fucking years when I had to put my life on hold. You owe me for that, owe me for every minute of having to sleep next to your disgusting body, owe me for all the suffering you put me through."

I don't have much time to ponder his warped reasoning as he pulls something out of the bag that's been lying, unnoticed, at his feet. My eyes widen as he pulls out a packet of cigarettes. *He doesn't smoke.* But he certainly looks like he's taken up the habit as he lights one and sucks in, making the tip glow orange. He coughs, and huffs a short laugh. "Can't think why people do this." Then he comes closer to me, his mouth twists. "Six years Alex, and you're going to make up for every fucking day." Before I realise what he's doing, he presses the burning cigarette end into the tender skin of my breast, slowly pushing it in until it's stubbed out.

I scream. God, the pain! An intense burning and stinging sensation. I try to curl up to protect myself, but secured as I am, I can't move. There's nothing I can do to ease the agonising throbbing on my tender flesh. My eyes have closed, a sound makes me open them. Smoke reaches my nostrils as he lights another cigarette. He brings it closer to my breast, the same one as before, this time torturing me by holding it only just above the skin so I can feel the heat from the tip.

"Please, no," I cry out. Now that I know the level of pain to expect, the anticipation is made worse. And the look on his face

135

shows he's got no mercy at all. The end comes down and I scream again.

Tears run down my cheeks. I squirm, but there's no relief. He lights another cigarette, and then another. I start thrashing, but he easily holds me down with one hand while pressing that burning tip to my skin time after time again. Now I'm breathing in the scent of my own scorched flesh, and turning my head as far as I can to the side, I retch.

"You know, I could get used to this," he says conversationally as he flicks the lighter again.

When will it stop? My throat feels hoarse from screaming. Any noise I make is futile, there's no one to hear me, only the man who's relishing my cries. I've lost count of the number of times he burns me, but after a while he pays the same attentions to my other breast.

"It's looking good. Maybe I'll start a new trend." He pauses for a moment to admire his handiwork.

I've almost given up, my body automatically jerking as I try to evade the torment he's dishing out. My screams have become wails which run into each other, pleading and begging for him to stop.

At last he appears to have run out. He grabs the back of my head and pulls it up, holding me roughly by the hair, a further pain which doesn't even register over the burning agony of my breasts.

"Open your eyes. Look." He shakes me by his grip on my curls, and reluctantly I obey him. From this point of view, I can only see the top of my breasts, each now marked by a semicircle of angry looking burns. I can only assume the rest of the ring is underneath. He breathes a sigh of satisfaction. "Now no one will ever want to look at your tits."

He's scarred me and marked me, quite possibly for life.

I want to hold myself, want to rush and jump into a cold shower. Anything to take the agony away. But I can't move. My eyes squeeze shut as my mind battles with how evil this man is, as waves of pain wash over me.

"That was fun," he pronounces. "But not quite enough."

Oh Jesus. What's he planning on doing now?

"I mean, you've tortured me for years. Making me sick just with the sight of you, and bearing that diseased brat you saddled me with, I deserve some payback, don't you think?"

I have to swallow to get moisture into my mouth, made dry by my screams and the pain. "I tried to be a good wife," I whisper. And I had. Devoting my time and energy to looking after him, but nothing I ever did satisfied him.

"You don't even know what a good wife looks like. A wife, my dear Alex, is someone her husband wants to fuck. And no one would ever willingly fuck you."

"Open your eyes, Alex. Watch what I do."

As an answer, I squeeze them shut.

His hand grabs my hair, pulling it so painfully for a second it overcomes the discomfort of the burns. "Open your fucking eyes, bitch!"

I do as he says. Oh no. He's got a knife. My breasts are throbbing, and that gleam in his eyes tells me it isn't enough for him. Has my torture just started, or is he going to kill me now? *Tyler. What will he do if I'm gone? Who will look after him?* The only thought in my head is for him.

Looking almost bored, he presses the tip of the blade just underneath a couple of inches below my breastbone. *He'd have to move it over a bit if he wants it to go through my heart.* Why I'm mentally giving him directions, I've got no idea.

Then the blade pushes in and I start at the stabbing pain. It's different to the burns. And then gets worse as he drags the sharp knife downwards in a straight line. He's cutting deep, I can tell.

At first there's no pain, then blistering agony. His face is creased with concentration as he digs the blade into my side and drags it through my flesh, down and then up. I'm barely aware as he starts cutting again, my brain unable to isolate different areas of pain, and I feel blood welling up and dripping down my skin.

I think I pass out, a slap to my cheek brings me around to a world of pain I could never have imagined.

"Look, bitch. Now I've marked you with exactly what you are. Fucking look, will you?"

It's hard to open my eyes. When I do, it's to look into a mirror he's holding up. He's carved five letters right into my chest, and even backwards I can read the word WHORE. In my semi-faint state I know what he's done as I watch his handiwork rapidly being disguised by the blood flowing freely. He's made it so I can never take my clothes off again, in front of anyone.

This must be it. This must be the end to my torture. Even a tormentor as evil as he must be satisfied now. I'm hurting so badly it's hard to summon up any desire to live.

But I was wrong, it's not over. He reaches into that bag of implements once again. I'm so weak my head rolls back onto the mattress, almost uncaring of what else he might do. *Just kill me now.* If by the blood flowing out of my wounds he hasn't already.

"Tyler." The word escapes my lips as though on my last breath.

He laughs almost manically. "Just shut up about that fucking brat. He's no concern of yours anymore." His hand slaps my pussy. "Fuckin' dry cunt you always had. You couldn't even bring anything fuckable to the marriage. Six years of hell, that's what I went through. When I was lying beside your frigid ass I'd dream up ways to get even with you. And now I've got my chance."

As I'm wondering how on earth he can put it all on me, I feel a stinging and pulling sensation. *Fuck!* What is that. Jesus! With one last effort, I lift my head to see him with a needle and thread, and he's using his body to keep my legs wide apart. No! He can't…

"Nooooo," I wail out. No, not that. No! Such an invasion worse than anything else he's done.

He looks up and laughs. "You can lie here and think on the fact I was the last man here. And how I'm ensuring no man can ever go there again."

Then, with a look of total absorption, he goes back to what he was doing. He's stitching my labia together. Each time the needle and thread pushes through it causes a sharp tearing. His lips are pursed as he focuses on his task.

And then I'm only able to manage a whimper, my only protest at this final indignity.

At last he's finished and steps back. "I've marked you, made you even uglier than you already are." He puts his hand on my sore pussy. "You should never have whored yourself out. And now you'll never be able to anymore."

Just finish it.

"Right," he starts conversationally. "Well, it's been nice catching up. But now I've got a boy to deal with. So I'll be off. This is our final parting, dear wife. We won't be seeing each other again." He pauses and his hand touches my face in a parody of a caress. "I would say it's been nice knowing you, but I don't want the last thing you hear to be a lie. Goodbye, Alex. And enjoy the rest of your fucking miserable life."

With that parting shot, he turns.

He's leaving me? Like this? Lying in agony?

But he lingers for a moment. "You'll probably bleed out, or die of infection. Or hunger or thirst or the cold. I don't much care. Just think on your sins, woman. If you'd not left me I wouldn't have had to go this far. You did this to yourself, it's all your own fault. If you'd stayed we could have kept up pretences."

I'm too weak to argue, but I know that he's wrong. If I'd stayed he'd just have found another method of killing me.

Passing in and out of consciousness, I don't hear him leave, but in periods of lucidity I hear no sound. Weakly I call out, but he's gone. I test my restraints, only to find I'm still tied up.

Even if I had the strength, there's no way to get myself loose. These must be police issue handcuffs, designed so a criminal can't escape. I'm destined to die a slow painful death, alone with no hope of rescue. And with no way of protecting my son from a monster.

I try to stay conscious and fight off the darkness, but I'm losing too much blood and becoming weaker all the time. My eyes flutter open, and then closed again, and this time, they stay shut. My last waking thought is for my son.

Tyler.

CHAPTER 14

Dart

As the old lady epidemic hasn't hit the San D chapter, I ask Snips if any of the club girls would be dependable enough to look after a young boy. Before I finish getting the question past my lips, a pretty woman who looks to be in her mid-twenties approaches, her eyes fixed on Tyler.

"And who have we got here?" She's got a pleasant, musical voice, and I immediately take to her. She's different from the typical club girls, not so flighty, and with a caring expression on her face.

"Yep, her." Snips claps his hand on her shoulder. "Dart. This is Eva. She's got a kid herself, 'bought the same age, I reckon."

"That I have." She gives an easy grin. "He's with his dad this week. And I happen to know all little boys like cookies."

Tyler, who's hiding behind my legs at the moment, gives a small nod as he cautiously eyes the strange men around him. Then his face looks up at the woman. "And bikes," he tells Eva in a solemn voice.

"Hey, kid likes bikes," Snips announces to one and all. "Anyone 'ere got one?" He's greeted by a round of laughter and sarcastic comments.

Putting his arm around Eva, Snips plants a kiss on her cheek then turns to me. "Dart, Tinder will show you where to take the woman you brought back to get some answers, and Eva and I will entertain young Tyler here." He crouches down to Tyler's level. "Cookies, then we'll take a look at some bikes? How does that sound?" As Tyler lifts his chin, and even in the tortured state of mind I am currently in, the gesture brings a half smile to my face, Snips continues, "Bet we've got better ones here than at the Tucson Chapter."

I give Tyler a little push, and bend down to speak into his ear, but loud enough for Snips to hear. "And I bet they haven't. You'll have to tell me later."

A little more at ease, Tyler gives a small grin then skips off, holding Eva's hand. I hold my middle finger up to Snips. Better bikes, my ass.

Thompson's girlfriend is brought in and pushed alongside us as Tinder shows Slick and myself down to a basement. It looks like it's used for much the same things as our storage room back home. Pulleys are attached to a ceiling with chains hanging down, and various tools are scattered around. There's a faint lingering odour of blood and urine, not totally disguised by the slightly stronger smell of disinfectant. The woman is looking around with scared eyes and looks almost ready to piss herself.

Ignoring the equipment, I pull a chair into the middle of the room. "Sit."

Her eyes flick around her surroundings, and she's gone very pale. She opens her mouth, then clears her throat before speaking. "I don't understand why you brought me here. And why you've taken Tyler. My boyfriend's a cop. You won't get away with this. He'll be angry if you hurt his son."

Thinking causing Tyler any harm is the last thing on my mind, I pull up another chair and turn it around, straddling it with my forearms resting on the back. I regard her intently until her eyes shift away. "Way I see it, it's your boyfriend who's in trouble. He was the one doing the kidnappin'. He took his ex-wife and her kid away from their home."

"His kid." Her voice has more spirit in it. "His wife was keeping him from seeing Tyler."

I nod as if she's said something completely reasonable. And then bark out, "He brought his wife to San Diego too. Now why the fuck d'ya think he'd do that?"

Again her mouth opens, but all she does is gape like a fish. She's not got an answer. In the end she resorts to denial. "I don't know anything about his wife coming back."

I wonder whether she'd spoken to Tyler, but she must have. Tyler's first words to me had been concern for his mom. She's lying. "Where's he taken Alex?"

Something in my face communicates I'll have nothing but the truth. Her eyes narrow as she snaps, "I don't know what he's done with that bitch. All I know is I haven't seen her. He wouldn't bring her to me, not after the things she's done to him. She's a cruel, cold-hearted woman. That kid's better off with us."

"What do you know about Tyler?" I wonder how deeply she's involved, and how much Thompson's told her. "You know that he's sick? That he needs tablets and stuff?"

She sneers. "That was just his wife being over protective. There's nothing wrong with the boy. Ron says he just needs toughening up."

Even if I was going to make damn sure there wasn't any possibility of it happening, there's no way I'd consider leaving Tyler to be 'toughened up' by his dad. The memory of that child's pain when he had his episode that day makes me go cold. What would they do to help him through that if it happened again? Which reminds me, I've got to keep a close eye on Tyler here and make sure everyone's aware how to help him.

Her head's gone down, and now comes back up, and her shoulders slump. "Alright, I admit I know she's in San Diego.

Ron told me she insisted on coming to keep the boy company for the journey. Ron left her at their old house so she could get some of her stuff, and then was going to get rid of her."

Slick comes up alongside and stands with his arms folded across his chest. "Get rid of her? Your words or his?"

"His," she replies sulkily.

Slick bends his head to mine. "Move along with it, Dart. We might be runnin' out of time."

That was exactly my thought too. "Look, lady. Hell, I don't know what your name is."

"I'm Belle. Belinda."

"What's your last name?"

"Winscott."

"Look, Belle, Belinda. I don't think you understand what this boyfriend of yours is capable of." In the back of my mind I recall the story of the Satan's Devil he'd killed. "When Thompson says he'll get rid of her, he doesn't mean put her on a train or buy her a bus ticket to get home. He's going to stash her somewhere, kill her, or at least hurt her."

Again, she glances down at her feet. "He wouldn't do that. He's a good man."

Slick's eyeing her carefully. Suddenly he moves and pulls up her sleeves. There are fingermark shaped bruises on one of her forearms. He raises his hand and touches her cheek and she flinches. "Wearing a lot of makeup there, sweetheart. Your man did this?"

She refuses to answer, neither to deny or admit it.

"I think you do know what he's capable of. And that includes gettin' off on makin' people hurt." Perhaps that's why she's not talking. She's more afraid of Thompson than of us.

"He wouldn't kill her. He's a cop." Or very naïve.

Cops can do anything, and get away with it too. Who better to know how to disappear a body? Well, except perhaps for us.

I decide to go straight for info. "Has Thompson any property which he owns, apart from the two houses? A garage? Lock-up?"

"If he has, I wouldn't know."

Slick crouches down on his haunches. "Look, Belinda. There may well be a woman whose life is at risk at this very moment. Even if we're wrong, we want to find her. Can you think of anythin' at all that might help?"

She scrunches up her face, and then shakes her head.

At that moment, Snake walks into the room. He nods at me, then his eyes narrow as he sees the woman sitting on the chair. "You got yer phone on ya?"

He's a striking man, a snake tattoo winding around his neck. His hair is almost as long as Mouse's, and currently tied back. At about six-foot-two and massively built, he can be quite intimidating. One look at his face and she doesn't delay putting her hand in her pocket to pull out an iPhone.

"Unlock it." He holds out his hand. She passes it over to him. Quickly he scrolls through the contacts, looks at something, and then shakes his head. "Doesn't look like he shares his location." This is addressed to me. Well, it wasn't going to be easy.

"Dart, Mouse is back. He's got Thompson's computer. Go and sit with him, see if the two of you can put your heads together and come up with somethin'. I'll stay here with Slick and we'll see what else she knows." And then he removes his attention from me and focuses on the woman in the chair. The last thing I see is her cringing in fear.

Going up to the clubroom, I find Mouse in a corner looking at a screen. "Anythin', Brother?"

"No. Token's gone to look somethin' up. I'm just seein' what I can find on here."

As if hearing his name, Token appears. "Got somethin', I think. I know she doesn't keep in contact much with her parents, but they own a cabin up in Big Bear."

"Why would he take her there? That's a long shot, man. There's not even anythin' linkin' him to them."

"That's where you're wrong. You missed somethin', Mouse." Token looks extremely pleased with himself. "He's got a separate bank account, they pay him an annual sum."

"Why the fuck would they do that?"

"Don't know, man, but there's obviously some contact there."

Mouse is rubbing his face. Suddenly he takes out his phone. "Got their number, Toke?"

"Sure have. Was wonderin' if you'd need it."

I'm not quite certain what he's going to do. I put my hand on his arm. "Mouse, if they're in tight with Thompson, don't blow it. They'll go straight to him…"

He shrugs of my touch and gives a grin. "Trust me, my man." Then he dials the number.

Well my mouth drops open at the poshest accent I've ever heard coming out of the half Native American's mouth. "Good morning, Mrs Argent. I'm very sorry for troubling you, but I'm ringing from the SD Vacation Resort Group. We understand you and your husband own a cabin at Big Bear and were wondering whether you were considering making it available to rent? It's in a desirable area, and I'm sure the rental income would be very attractive…"

"Uh huh."

"Mmm."

"Oh, well it's an ideal location for that."

"So sorry to trouble you, ma'am. But if you reconsider, please get in touch."

He ends the call and turns to us with a grin, while opening the phone and taking the battery and sim card out. He chucks the pieces of the burner phone into a nearby bin.

"Well?" I prompt, rising up on my toes in impatience.

"She might have been interested, but her daughter and son-in-law have started using it. It's an ideal place to take a young boy apparently. And," he pauses for effect, "sounds like she's fuckin' there now. Thompson picked up the keys last week."

She's hiding in plain sight? Some of the tightness in my chest eases. It would be a crazy place to kill her, far be too obvious, and able to be traced back to him. But it doesn't mean he won't hurt her.

"Someone give me the fuckin' address. I'm checkin' it out, now."

"Not on yer own, Brother," Snake growls from behind me. "Bitch downstairs had nothing else to give. But we'll leave her enjoyin' our hospitality until we find yer girl." I nod. If nothing else, if we find Thompson but not Alex, using his girlfriend as a bargaining point might make him loosen his tongue to tell us where Alex is.

I glance around. Both Slick and Mouse are standing up, ready to go. Snake nods at Lost, who raises his chin in return. Grumbler's close by and lifts his hand.

"Reckon we're only dealing with Thompson, so the six of us should do."

Then I hear a child's voice and know we can't all go. "Slick, man. You stay here and look after Tyler. You know his problems."

Slick looks puzzled. "I know what he suffers from and what you said, Dart. But what the fuck do I know about lookin' after a kid?"

"You've got Jayden." I try to explain to him my reasoning, by referring to the teenage girl he's all but adopted, and add, admittedly a bit lamely, "And you're tryin' to get Ella pregnant."

His eyes open incredulously and his hands open in a what the fuck gesture.

Snake's quick to decide. "Eva will stay with him. Her nursing skills might come in handy. But if he's got issues like Dart said, someone who knows somethin' about what his problems are could be useful."

Taking in a deep breath and letting out a sigh, Slick accepts he's staying behind.

"Thanks, Brother. I'd feel happier." I raise my chin at him.

A sudden slap on my back takes me by surprise, and I stagger slightly as Snake announces, "Let's go get the kid's mother back."

I need no further encouragement to leave the clubhouse and go to my bike, hoping and fucking praying we're right, and we'll find Alex at the cabin. I'd hate to waste more time following another false lead.

Snake's out in front with Lost and Grumbler riding behind him, Mouse and me at the back. The two-hour ride seems to take forever, and for once I just want it to come to an end, not even feeling the normal enjoyment of being out on the open road, and seeing none of the scenery we're riding through. My only desire is to get there, find Alex, and return with her up behind. Yeah, me, who's never had a bitch on the back of his bike before, and suddenly I can't think of anything better, having her breasts squashed against me. Ain't letting any of my brothers have that pleasure instead. Thompson's a dead man for even thinking of putting his hands on my woman. *My woman?* What the heck am I thinking? I admit I want her, desire her, but I also don't want or need a woman in my life. She's my friend. But the thought of those tits against my back… Perhaps I should just fuck her and get her out of my system once and for all.

But first, we've got to get her out of the hands of the man who's got a legal claim on her. But he won't that have for much longer. The shit he's put her through? Separating a loving mom from her kid if nothing else? I'm aiming to make their separation more permanent than any piece of fucking divorce paper.

At last Snake gives us the signal to slow down, and then waves us to a stop. Cutting our engines, we gather around him. "Cabin's aways up that track." He points it out. "I say we ride up, bust in and don't give Thompson a chance to escape."

"We gonna kill the cop?" Grumbler flexes his fingers as though getting ready. *Yes!* I mutter under my breath.

But I'm in Snake's territory, and have to be guided by him.

Snake only takes a second. "Play it by ear. See what's goin' down. But we already know it won't be a loss."

"If he's hurtin' Alex…"

"Dart! This is a cop we're talkin' about. If there's no other way we'll do what we have to, but got to do it clean so it doesn't fall back on the club."

I don't care what he is. I'd rather see him dead and unable to be a threat to her anymore. But I give Snake a nod, letting him know I'll follow his lead. He's a Satan's Devils prez after all.

Back on our bikes in the same formation, we ride up the track, kicking up dust as we come to a halt. Mouse and Lost slip away to cover the back as Grumbler goes to the front door. It's locked, and no sound is coming from inside. He lifts his leg and kicks at the flimsy wood. It gives on the second try and we walk into a living room which is musty and dim, crusted dirt on the windows as if no one's been here for some time. Snake tries the light switch, but I'm not surprised when there's no bulb glowing as a result. Out here we'd be able to hear a generator running if there was any electricity.

Snake heaves a sigh. "Doesn't look like anyone's been here in a while."

My heart sinks, realising we've come to the wrong place. Mouse and Lost come back, shaking their heads, they've found no rear entrance and nothing suspicious to the rear of the cabin.

Lost touches my arm. "Sorry, Brother. Wrong call. Seems we've wasted our time."

I can't give up. "Let's look around before we go."

"There's nothin' to see, Brother. You can tell that from here. The dust's undisturbed on the worktops. No one's been here." Snake's speaking patiently as though to a child. "Faster we get back to the clubhouse, faster we can start searchin' again."

"Dart's right," Grumbler says, going to the back of the room, giving me support. "Can't leave no fuckin' stone unturned. Let's have a quick look around. Won't take but a minute, and will make our brother feel better."

But I'm getting the feeling Snake's right. It doesn't look like anyone's been here in years. I'm impatient to get back now that there's no sign anyone's been here. I'm tapping my feet as Grumbler disappears down a short hallway, not even thinking it's worth going with him.

"*Dart!* Oh fuck! Get in here!" Grumbler's voice has me running in the direction he's gone. I meet him in the hallway outside a bedroom door. His hand swings out and bars my way. "It's bad, Brother. You need to prepare yourself."

But nothing will stop me. Reading into his words that she's probably dead, bile rises into my throat as I enter the room.

She's lying on the bed. Her chest has been cut up, and when I move closer I can see what appears to be cigarette burns all over her gorgeous breasts. And, *oh fuck.* With her legs splayed open, I can see the bastard has fucking sewn up her pussy! He's fucking violated her so badly. I can't help it, the sight makes me turn and vomit, the little I've eaten today coming back up. She's so still, she has to be dead. There's too much blood…

"She's breathin'!" Lost announces.

Turning sharply, I see his hand resting on the pulse in her neck.

"Get a fuckin' ambulance," I scream.

Snake takes out his phone. "Doc, need you to come to the clubhouse. Bring your emergency kit." Then he places a second call, requesting someone to bring up a truck, and Doc when he arrives.

"She needs medical care," I scream at him. "No fuckin' quack can fix this."

"Steady, Brother." The San D prez grabs hold of my shoulders and gives me a shake. "The medic on our payroll is a fuckin' qualified emergency room doc. If she goes to hospital Thompson will know she's alive. It's obvious he left her for dead. Until we know what the fucks going on, she needs to be kept under the radar." Turning away from me, he looks at Lost, who's fiddling with the handcuffs. "Can you get her out of those?"

"Give me a moment, Prez. Standard police issue, shouldn't take too long."

"He's fuckin' gonna die slowly for this!" I say, watching Lost work.

"That he is, Brother. That he is." Grumbler's hand is on my shoulder, his voice gravelly with disgust.

A snick, and one arm's released. There's no way Alex would have had a chance if we hadn't found her. Even if she was conscious, there's no way she could get herself free. *Just how long has she been left like this?* And now we've got at least two hours to wait until the truck and the doc gets here.

"We're wastin' time." I cross to the woman on the bed, now seeing her chest just about rise and fall as she's breathing so shallowly, and that's only if I look hard. *And there I was thinking she'd be riding back on my bike.* Fuck, now I don't know if she'll be getting to the clubhouse alive. I'm frightened to touch her, can hardly see her through the moisture blurring my vision. Gingerly I place my hand on her head, and then gently start massaging one of her arms, trying to get the blood back into them again. Mouse goes to the opposite side of the bed and mimics my actions on the other. We've all strung up men and know the pain and cramp that comes from being trapped in one position too long.

"Alex," I begin, my voice soft and low. And then stop. I don't know what to say, how to comfort her. To tell her I wished I'd got here in time before Thompson started hurting her? To tell her how sorry I am that we got here too late? I can't tell her it's all going to come out right.

He's maimed her. And violated her, almost worse than if he'd raped her and there's nothing to say he hadn't done that as well. Those fuckin' stitches are messing with my head. I leave her and go to the end of the bed, taking out my knife, wanting to cut them away.

Grumbler is quickly at my side. "You can't take them out, Dart. Think of infection. Leave it to the doctor to do it properly."

He's right, but it's killing me. "I can't stand it. That fucker..." *He'd touched what was mine. Violated her in such a horrific way.* And I hate that she's lying their naked. "Can't we at least cover her up?" I hate to see her so exposed.

"Look at those wounds, man? There's nothing here clean enough to put over her. I assure you, no one's getting a fuckin' hard on from this."

"She's fucking freezing to death."

Lost's looking around. "Try and find something that at least looks clean."

Which gives me an idea. Running out to my bike, I take a sweatshirt out of my panniers, and running back in, place it gently over her from the waist down. I'm not lifting her up to put it on properly, her injuries look too bad for me to want to move her. At least I've given her some semblance of dignity now.

"He's not gonna die easy," Lost growls.

No. He's fucking not.

Mouse is staring at her. I want to scream for him to give her some privacy, but then he looks at me, his eyes narrowed and angry. "Dart, it's hard to see through the blood, but have you seen what he's carved into her?"

I can hardly bring myself to look at the deep, angry wounds. But I force myself. And then scream out, "Motherfucker! For fuck's sake. Look what's written on her chest."

Lost's arms come around me. "Keep it together, Brother," he snarls. "Look to your woman. She's needs you more than fuckin' ever now, man. Breathe. The bastard's a dead man walkin', ain't no chance of him livin' now. Keep that in your mind, but your woman needs you."

I close my eyes and shake my head. My breath's coming in pants, and it's hard to calm myself down. Lost is right, even if we can save her she'll need my strength to help her through this even if I can only be there as a friend. Gradually bringing myself under control, I move back to her head, feeling about as helpless as I've ever done in my life. She won't be able to hear, but that doesn't stop me trying. "Alex, oh Alex, darlin'. Just hang on, doll. Help's on its way."

I watch as moisture weeps down her face, but that's the only sign that she's still with us.

Lost has got her legs free now, but she doesn't wake.

I go back to massaging her arm, and then wipe that tear from her eye.

CHAPTER 15
Alex

I've been drifting since Ron left me, losing all sense of how many hours have passed. Each time I come round, it's to a world of pain—my breasts burning, my chest smarting, my pussy stinging, and added to that I've cramps in my arms I can do nothing about. *He's not coming back.*

Tears flood from my eyes as I think about Tyler, the son I have to accept I'll never see again. Ron said he'd gone to get him, and I'm afraid for his life. Ron's imperfect son who he never loved. I dread to think how he could try to toughen him up. Ignoring what's wrong with him isn't going to help, and not getting him medical attention when he needs it could be fatal.

No one's ever going to find me. Hell, they won't even be searching. And if they were, why would they think of looking here? I was fooling myself, Celine would never think of the cabin, it was years ago that we last came here. And it's not a place many people would stumble across. Again I pull at the handcuffs, only confirming there's no way I can get free. And even if I could, I know I'd be too weak to leave and find help.

And then I'm too drained to even try to get loose, and I pass out again, to return to a brief period of consciousness, then the cycle repeats once again. I know the life is leaching out of me, it's getting harder and harder to open my eyes. Even with only the sun's movement to guide me, I can tell hours must have passed since I last was awake. I struggle to stay alert, not knowing if this is the last time I'll see anything at all. But this time, as I lose that battle and sink into darkness, I accept this is the end, my body's been too abused.

Now I must be hallucinating as I hear voices, my arms feel free, and God do they hurt. But there's a sensation as though someone's rubbing them gently, the returning blood causing a different type of pain. It must be a hallucination, miracles don't happen. *Has Ron returned?* No, I'd be waking to a nightmare in that case, not to the touch of caring hands.

If someone's here, I want to move, to show I'm awake, but the pain threatens to pull me under again.

But no one could have come. My mind must be trying to calm me, conjure up sounds to reassure me I'm not dying alone.

"Alex, oh Alex, darlin'. Just hang on, doll. Help's on its way."

That's Dart's voice. Now I'm certain I'm dreaming. He's in Tucson, not here. He'll be working at the club, wondering why I haven't turned up to dance. One more tear squeezes from my eye as I think of lost chances. He'll never know how inappropriate my feelings were towards him. I wanted him as more than just my boss, and more than a friend.

The voices keep talking, and the gentle touch on my arm continues. The thought I'm not alone is soothing. *Maybe it's not my imagination.* Maybe there are people here for real. I'm torn between forcing open my eyes to see nothing has changed and remaining under and accepting my fate. It might be better not to know, to simply fade away, enjoying the fantasy that people have come to help. *Perhaps this is how death will take me away.*

Someone's touching my face, wiping the tear from my eye. *Surely that must be real?* Facing disappointment head on, I make one last effort. The light is dim, but there's a face close to mine.

A face which I recognise. *He must be a vision.* But if that's what my mind's letting me see, I don't mind. If I'm dying there could be a worse last sight than of his beautiful features.

I see his eyes widen, watch as he starts, and then his mouth works. "Alex?" he offers cautiously.

I swallow, but can't manage to speak.

"Save your energy, darlin'. Help's gettin' close. We'll get you fixed up, sweetheart. Stay with us now."

Ignoring his instruction, I try again. "Hhhh… how?"

"How am I here?" He interprets my blink as confirmation. "Long story, darlin'. We came to San Diego to get Thompson to give ya what yer entitled to. Bad fuckin' mistake, should have stayed close to ya." I swear his eyes are glistening. "I'm so sorry, darlin', that we didn't get here in time. So fuckin' sorry."

I try to convey that it's not his fault. Nothing's his fault. But my mouth is so dry it's too hard to talk.

"Rest, darlin'. Doc's nearly here. He'll get you sorted."

I swallow again, trying to force out one word. Eventually I manage it. "Tyler."

Dart's hand covers mine. "Don't worry about him, Alex. He's safe. He's with Slick, my brother. He won't be letting Thompson anywhere near him. We'll look after him. I promise you that."

Such immense relief. I trust Dart with my son—more than I ever trusted Ron. "Look… Look after him for me." I don't know why, but I know that he won't abandon him.

"You'll be with him soon, doll."

But I feel so weak, I'm not sure I will. I want to keep listening to the voice that confirms I'm alive. But despite my desire and my effort, I drift off again.

The next time I wake there's even more voices and activity. I feel a pressure on the open wounds of my chest. Now a moan comes out as I open my mouth.

"Doc's tryin' to help you, darlin'. I know it hurts."

"Alex. I'm a doctor. I'm just covering your wounds with a sterile dressing, and then we'll move you down to the club where I can work on them better."

I groan again. While everything in me wants to get out of this place, I'm scared of being picked up and moved. But the doctor's got that covered.

"I'm giving you a painkiller and a sedative. Now just relax."

I feel a sharp stab in my arm and it all goes dark again.

I know nothing more until I wake to find I'm lying in a properly made bed, not on a bare mattress, and while I'm still in pain, it's at least bearable.

Tyler.

I try to sit up, but there's tubes running into my arm, and the pull on the wounds on my chest send pain shooting through me.

"Hey, just lie back. You're gonna be fine, Alex." Dart, who I hadn't noticed sitting on a chair by the bed, leans over me.

"I heard voices. Is she awake?" Dart mumbles a confirmation, and the new voice continues, "Doubt you remember, but I'm the doctor who's been treating you. Doc, they call me, okay? Unimaginative for sure."

"Tyler?" It might be rude, but it's all I can say.

"You'll be able to see him soon, but we thought it best to get you tidied up first. Didn't want to worry him."

"Dart's right, sweetheart. Now let me check your stitches. Dart, you want to give us a moment here?"

"I'd like to stay," Dart replies tersely.

My fingers tighten around Dart's hand. I'm frightened to see my own wounds, but I'm even more worried about him seeing them. Who wants the man you've previously had erotic thoughts about seeing that you've been disfigured for life? "Could you wait outside, please, Dart?"

There's a flicker of something I interpret as pity in his eyes, before he gives a slow nod of understanding and leaves. It's then I remember he'll have seen them before, back at the cabin. Ron had left me naked.

"Okay. You ready?"

I don't think I'll ever be. After a moment's hesitation, I lie. "Yes." *At least I'm alive.*

Having obtained my permission, Doc gingerly draws down the sheet and removes the bandages. I risk glancing down, and tears come to my eyes. God, I'm such a mess. Although the doctor's obviously an expert with a needle and neat stitches have now closed the wounds and cleaned away the blood, the flesh around them is puckered, red, and angry, and clearly spelling out that hated word. Ron had certainly succeeded in what he set out to do. With letters carved into my chest and burns around my breasts, I'm about as undesirable as any woman could possibly be.

"There will be scarring, I can't avoid that." Doc's only telling me what I already know. "The burns, less so. We got them treated quickly. There's creams we can use which will certainly help. It's infection that I'm checking for. The wounds on your chest were quite deep. You lost a fair amount of blood."

As detached as any professional, he pulls the sheet down lower. I cringe, my muscles involuntarily tightening at the memory of exactly what Ron had done. "Alex, you know what else he did?"

"Yes," I admit, as tears leak from my eyes.

"He was sadistic, messing with your mind. He didn't rape you, that's one thing to be thankful for, but I'm not belittling what he did. The mental anguish of being so violated is possibly worse than any physical damage. I know it's hard for you, but focus that there's no real harm done, though you'll be sore for a while. I'm assuming he didn't use a sterilised needle, so I'm giving you a topical cream to apply. You'll heal in time with no scarring down there."

Except in my head. Still reeling from the awful memories, I shudder as he pulls the sheet up, but thankful at least my pussy won't show signs of the abuse, though I doubt I'll ever be able to forget Ron's evil touch there.

"You're dehydrated and, as I said, you've lost blood. I'm giving you a transfusion, fluids, and antibiotics. You've got a catheter, so you don't need to get out of bed for a while. I'll be back regularly to check you out, and one of the club girls, Eva, is also a nurse. If you get hot and feverish, if you think something's wrong, then give someone a shout. Oh, and I've left painkillers for you."

"Thank you, Doc." Though I've tried to hold them back, tears start streaming down my face in earnest.

I hear the door opening and closing, and then Dart's voice. "Hey, we've got this. You're going to be fine." His hand brushes away my tears.

"You can't say that, Dart. I'm going to be scarred for life. I won't be dancing again."

"Don't talk about that!" he snaps. "It's too soon, and all you need to do for now is concentrate on healin'."

I shake my head. "You know why he did it? He wanted to make sure everyone thinks I'm a whore. And he, he wanted to punish me for him having to be married to me. He... He wanted to make it so no man could ever want or..."

"I know what he did to you, Alex. I saw. He's a twisted motherfucker. When I find him..."

"Dart, don't do anything. He's a cop."

"Don't worry about me, darlin'." Whatever he was going to say, he doesn't complete it as a knock comes at the door. He opens it, then turns to me with a grin. "You've got a visitor, you up for that?"

He doesn't wait for an answer, just goes to let the person in, and the best sight I could see comes through. My son approaches me carefully, a look up to Dart to check, before cautiously extending his small hand and taking hold of mine. I curl my fingers around him, holding him tight, wanting to cuddle him but knowing it's too soon.

"Dart's told me you're hurt, Momma." Tyler sounds like he's going to cry.

"What did I tell you?" Dart hunkers down beside him.

Tyler draws he's shoulders back. "That Momma's hurting and I've got to look after her."

Dart's hand squeezes his shoulder. "You gonna stay here and keep her company for a while?"

Tyler gives a nod and looks at me, his face scrunched in thought. "You want anything, Momma? I can get you some juice."

I smile. When he doesn't feel well that's what I offer him. "Water would be nice."

"Here." Dart passes him a bottle that's been left on the side. "Give this to your mom. She needs anything else, you come down and get me or Eva."

Another serious nod from my son. Watching Dart leave, it hits me how quickly a bond has formed between the two of them, which blows out of the water any connection he'd had with his father.

I use the straw that's been thoughtfully left for me, and then start to count my blessings. Ron didn't succeed in killing me. I might be scarred, but I'm alive, and reunited with my son who I'd given up hope of ever seeing again.

And I trust Dart to keep us both safe.

CHAPTER 16
Dart

Reluctantly I'd left the room to allow her to preserve some dignity while Doc examined her. I already know exactly what scars she carries on her body, and now I'm worrying about those she'll hold in her head. I think I deserve a medal for holding my temper when she told me why Thompson had mutilated her. And one thing's for certain, he hasn't succeeded in putting me off, and I make a vow to her here and now, if that's what she wants, when she's healed she'll be up on that stage one way or another. I'm certainly not accepting her resignation today.

I've no worries leaving her with her son, she's in good hands. Tyler's a great kid, perhaps his own health problems making him better able to understand hers. I'd had a long conversation with him when I explained why he had to wait before seeing her. His level of understanding and compassion surprising me for one so young. Not for the first time, I'm impressed with the lad, and proud of him too.

Alex had been out of it for twenty-four hours since we brought her back to the clubhouse. Once he'd fixed her up as best he could, I'd got the rundown on her condition from Doc, my brothers who'd been at the cabin lurking close by so they could hear too. I don't think any of us who'd seen what that bastard had done to her will ever forget the sight. As Doc said, what he'd done to her pussy wouldn't leave visible scars, but for her to have gone through a violation like that? It will have fucked badly with her mind. I shift uncomfortably and my hand goes to my groin. No one, of whatever sex, can easily cope with any type of mutilation in that area.

Even if Tyler hadn't appeared, I'd have to have left her. Snake's called a meeting, and one I wish to attend, its sole purpose to discuss how to fulfil our desire to find and take the man who'd caused her such terrible suffering, and wreak out our own vengeance on the sadistic motherfucker. *He left her to die.* And he would have succeeded if I hadn't had the help of my brothers to find her.

I'm the last to arrive, and Snake doesn't waste time on formalities.

"Right, let's get this meetin' started. I know we've got a few updates since you've been up with Alex. She doin' okay, Dart?"

"Physically? As well as can be expected, Prez. Mentally she's got a fuck of a long way to go."

"When we get our hands on Thompson, Dart, he can say goodbye to his dick." Mouse and I can't help but give a sideways grin toward Slick. Yup, when he was saving his old lady Ella and her sister, he'd got himself a reputation for removing a man's cock. But remembering just what Alex's husband had done to her, I couldn't argue the punishment wouldn't be apt.

Snake gives us an impatient look, not understanding what we found amusing. But it's not the time to enlighten him now.

"We've had prospects watchin' both houses. We need Thompson alone to take him."

"Any movement?"

"Give me a fuckin' chance, Dart." Grumbler's tone lives up to his name. "Yeah. The cops went to the marital home yesterday. Spent a bit of time inside. Thompson wasn't with them."

I cock my head to the side. "Why would they go there?"

"She got anyone else who'd report her gone?" Snake raises his eyebrow as he answers my question with one of his own.

Of course! "Yeah, her sister. She'd be quick off the bat to make a report to say she's disappeared. She'd have directed the cops straight toward Thompson."

"Wouldn't he have tried to come up with somethin' to delay them?" Kink asks. "Kind of defeats his objective if she's found too soon."

"He took leave for a week, remember? Maybe they don't know where he is and can't contact him."

"So we can assume her sister's reported her and Tyler missing. Cops start at the logical place and search the home where she'd lived before she left for Tucson." Token's thinking aloud.

I frown as I think. "Celine would kick up quite a fuss, the two sisters are tight. They'd have to try somethin' to appease her. She'd try to tell them about Thompson, and whether they want to believe her over another cop or not, he's the obvious person. They'd have to investigate, particularly when there's a child involved. And they'll be suspicious now that house is in a mess. All her clothes and possessions destroyed. That would raise a red flag if nothin' else."

Smoker takes a deep drag on the cigarette he's just lit. "We can presume they'll be pullin' out all the stops to find her. You think Thompson's stayin' out of sight so he can't be questioned?"

I'm less worried about what all the cops are doing, I'm just focused on finding one. "Any sign of him at all? Has he gone back to the house he shares with his girlfriend?"

"Nah, no sign, the prospect said. And that woman, Belinda, said he'd taken the week off work, so as far as he knows, she wouldn't be expectin' him back. For some reason he's being clever, keepin' his head down."

"What's happened to Belinda?" I'd been too tied up with Alex to ask.

"Sent her back home after puttin' the fear of God into her. She opens her mouth about comin' here, she's dead." Snake gives his evil grin. "I reckon I've convinced her."

"But she'll talk to Thompson. Might have already spoken to him on the phone. He'll know of our involvement."

"Yeah, it's a risk. But I took her phone, so she can't speak to him unless she knows his number by heart, and not many people nowadays remember things like that. And he'd not planned to go home for a few days."

Lost is tugging on his beard. "What I can't work out is why he used the cabin. He must have known it could be traced back to him."

"It's a fuckin' mystery, Brother." Slick comes in now. "On one hand, we're sayin' he's clever keepin' out of sight, while on the other we're sayin' he's stupid to be usin' such an obvious place."

"There's a plan in his head we don't know," Snake pronounces. "The girl say anythin' to ya, Dart? Any reason for takin' her there?"

I shake my head. It seems all he wanted to do was to hurt her.

"Got a man on the cabin in case he goes back. But there's been no sign up to now."

"Don't think he ever had any intention of returnin'. Wouldn't have left her so long, Prez, if he had. If he hasn't gone back by now, all he'd be going for is to dispose of the body."

My teeth gnash together, but my gut feel is that Lost is right. *If we hadn't found her…*

Token raises his hand. "He left her to die. And he had a reason." All eyes are now on the San D computer guy. "I've been doing some diggin', found somethin' of interest. A month or so ago he took out life insurance, for both him and his wife. A nice five-hundred-thou policy."

"But why kill her at the cabin? That makes no fuckin' sense." Snips is shaking his head. "The parents would link him to it fuckin' fast, and…"

"Hold up a minute." I say stopping him midtrack. "What exactly did her parents say when you spoke to them, Mouse?"

Mouse frowns and tries to remember. "That Thompson had collected the keys so that Alex could go there." Tapping his finger to his chin, he looks deep in thought, then adds, "Thinkin' back, while I assumed they meant them both, maybe I'd picked it up wrong." He pauses as though running back over the conversation in his head. "Actually, they only mentioned her. That she was goin' there on her own. No mention of a family vacation, just her and the boy." He frowns. "I must have filled in the gaps wrong about them saying the boy would be with her."

"So she's alone at the isolated cabin, and then becomes the victim of a vicious murder."

"You may have a point, Dart, but he carved WHORE into her chest. That smacks of something personal and someone who knows her."

"She's not a whore!" I shut that down fast. "She's a dancer in a strip club." My glare ensures no one contradicts me.

"Cops have enemies," Snake rasps. "Thompson could be intendin' to pin this on someone he's crossed."

"You mean someone with good reason to hate him?" Grumbler growls. "Doubt he'd need to look far for that."

"So why aren't they searchin' the cabin?" Slick shakes his head.

I snarl, "Because she might not be fuckin' dead yet. He'd want to give it some time." And again, the horrific thought hits me of what would have happened if we'd arrived too late.

"They might be waitin' on questionin' him. Or fuck knows what merry dance he could be leadin' them on, sendin' them off in the wrong direction to gain a bit of time," Tinder suggests while scratching his ear. He's right. Time in which he's thinking his wife is dying a long drawn out and painful death.

"Any chance you can get into the police reports, Mouse? See what they're doin'?"

Mouse opens his laptop, which unusually has been closed up until now. Token leans over, interested in what he's doing. Suddenly Mouse's tanned face pales. He sits back on his chair, and only one word escapes. "Fuck."

This isn't going to be good news, and it's Token who enlightens us, telling us through gritted teeth, "There's an APB out on Mouse."

"What the fuck?"

"Why?"

"How?"

As we all throw around questions without thinking of answers, Snake bangs the gavel, getting our attention back on him. "You in the system, Mouse?"

Mouse shrugs. "Yeah, did some time in juvie."

"You're fuckin' fingerprints were in Thompson's house. All over the crap when you unplugged his computer."

"So were ours, Prez."

"Scribe, Brakes. You got records?"

"I'm clean."

"They've got nothing on me."

Poke puts up his hand. "I have. Anything out for me?"

"Nah, Brother. Just Mouse."

"But why?" I wonder out loud.

"Could be just that he touched more stuff than the rest of us." Poke's nodding as though that make sense. "Next, she has no connection to us San Diego boys. And we've just put out word we're goin' up against the mother chapter—that was to catch your guy, Slick, the Rock Demon." Slick nods. "Most importantly, Stickler's death is too fresh in all our minds. Doubt Thompson would dare cross us again, especially to set us up for somethin' like this." There's obviously a reason why Snake was made president. He's putting things together a lot quicker than the rest of us. "Thompson doesn't want shit on his own doorstep. He knows she works at your strip club in Tucson. Could concoct a story that he brought her back as she was getting grief from one of the brothers."

"Planned? Or was he thinkin' on his feet?" Lost asks.

"Couldn't have been planned, or highly unlikely. We only decided on Sunday that Mouse was comin' down with us." Slick's shaking his head.

"Must have thought fast when they ran the prints."

Mouse is still frowning, though some colour has come back to his face. "When's Alex going to be fit enough to get out and about?"

"I don't know. What ya thinkin', Mouse?"

Mouse looks more animated. "Can we get the cabin cleared, Snake? Mattress taken out, blood-spatter cleaned up?"

"Consider it done, Brother. You think they'll go there next?"

"Yeah, and they'll probably find my fingerprints there as well."

"We'll clean it up."

"No, don't do that. Let them find my prints, just try and get rid of the blood stains and anything that looks suspicious. I'll just keep out of sight here for a couple of days. When Alex is fit we'll go to the cops. Thompson's havin' it all his own way for now, reckon we can fabricate a story every bit as credible as his. Especially if he thinks she's dyin' or dead."

I stare at my brother. Is he saying he'll willingly put his head in the lion's den? Not the normal way we do things.

As he correctly interprets my raised eyebrow, he gives me more. "The story will be somethin' like this. We met up in Tucson, she became my girlfriend. We came back to San Diego to collect some of her stuff…"

"It was shredded, Mouse. The cops will already have found that."

"Okay." One thing my brother's good at is pulling information together and sifting through it, fast. Sometimes I think he's a damn computer himself. "She got back, found the house trashed, someone must have broken in or somethin' like that. We'll have to firm up on that. Anyway, she took me to the cabin to have a few days break."

"And disposed of the mattress?"

"Hell yeah! We had fun on that, made a few stains." Mouse pauses to wait for the laughter and crude comments to die down before continuing. "Knew we needed to replace it, so threw the old one out. Since then we've been stayin' in a motel in the city." He looks around to make sure we're all paying attention. We are. "Anyway, the point is, they'll see her alive—her face is unmarked, we'll just have to make sure she's pumped up with sufficient painkillers that she can hide her other injuries. What the cops will see is an innocent woman in love with her man." The fucker pauses to wink at me. "We'll take Tyler with us, show he's a happy kid. Any alternative story Thompson can come up with will be blown out of the water. There'll be no suggestion of foul play." He lifts his chin toward me. "Think she can pull it off, Brother?"

I don't need to consider it long. She's a strong woman. "She'll need a couple of days, but yeah, she'll do it. But I don't like the thought of you turnin' yourself in." And it irks me he'll be the one pretending to have a relationship with her. But fuck knows why. Otherwise it's a good plan.

The corners of Mouse's mouth drop down. "Don't care for it much myself. But they won't have anythin' to hold me on. Anyone got any better ideas? It's me they're after, my head on the fuckin' block."

Snake puts his head into his hands, and when he looks up he appears to have come to a decision. "If she can pretend she's not injured or being coerced it could work, Brother. Get that fuckin' APB out of the way. Ain't no problem hidin' you in the meantime. Reckon it might be for a few days though. He may want to leave it a while before leadin' the cops to the cabin. VP, can you get those Arizona plates swapped on their bikes? Just in case the po-po come sniffin' around."

"Sure thing, Prez," Lost replies.

"Okay. I suggest, Dart," he defers to me due to my temporary officer status, "you get in contact with Drummer and update him as to what's goin' on. He needs the heads up if there's a chance they'll go lookin' for Mouse back in Tucson."

I wave my hand to show he can consider it done.

"And the rest of you douche bags—if the cops come callin', we ain't seen or spoken to anyone in the Tucson Chapter. Leave them in no doubt, we're preparing for war. Any one of our desert dwellin' brothers would get our fists in their faces if they decided to come to our compound." At that there's a few laughs and mock punches thrown in our direction.

"What if they've run my prints?" Now it's Poke's turn to frown.

"Go with the flow, Brother. Make somethin' up about you bein' best friends with Mouse, were visitin' with him or somethin' as long as you say nothin' to contradict Mouse's story it should work. Play it like you're stupid or somethin'."

"Wouldn't be hard for ya."

"We'll back ya up on that."

Poke glares and throws an empty cigarette pack toward Snips and Tinder.

With that, Snake wraps things up. Leaving church, I pop straight up to see Alex, but she seems to be sleeping peacefully and I don't want to disturb her. Quietly leaving the room, I go back downstairs looking for Tyler. When I don't see him in the clubroom I get concerned, but one of the prospects points me in the direction of the garage. I choke back a laugh when I find him. Another prospect is working on a bike, and the lad's kneeling on the ground beside him with a selection of tools. As I watch, he expertly hands his companion a spanner. It's the wrong one. The prospect is patient and explains what he needs. Tyler sorts through and comes up with the correct implement.

"Everything alright here?"

The prospect glances up, a smile on his face. "Yeah, got a new trainee as you can see."

As Tyler turns his face up to me, I can see he's got oil smudges all over it. His hands are filthy too, but there's a fucking big grin on his face. Wondering how the hell I'll get him cleaned up, I park that problem for later. He seems more than happy helping out.

"He okay with ya here?"

"Yeah, man. I don't mind watchin' him awhile for ya."

Giving a thumps up to show my thanks, I head back inside, relieved Tyler's fine and occupied for now, as I could do with a beer and a moment to myself. I'm wound up, hating Thompson for what he's done. Unable to understand how a man can be so cruel, and longing to have the man under my hands, planning on how much I can make him hurt.

A man comes alongside me. "Hey, you tappin' that black bitch?"

I grit my teeth. "No, Poke, I'm not."

"Don't blame ya. You forget to wrap it up you'll have a half-breed on yer hands." As he laughs at what he thinks is a joke my face tightens with rage.

Oh fuck. He didn't go there, did he?

Before I can get out a response an angry voice snarls out, "And what's fuckin' wrong with that?" Mouse was standing close enough to have overheard. His hands are fisting at his sides, his nostrils flaring.

Poke takes one look at him and holds both palms toward him. "Didn't mean no offence, Brother." He looks around quickly, as though seeking an escape route, then settles rather lamely for, "Well, I'll leave you to it. Things to do, ya know?" Then he walks off sharply with Mouse still glaring at his retreating back.

I take a swig of my beer. "Stupid fucker, that one."

"Yeah." Mouse sounds like he's still fuming, but as Poke disappears, starts to relax, and instead focuses on me. "Is he on the right track, Dart?"

"What?"

Mouse signals to the prospect, and once he's made his request known and has a drink in his hands, leans his back against the bar, resting his elbows on the wood. "Alex. What's holding you back? Is it the colour of her skin?"

I'm amazed he could ask that. The answer's simple. "Ain't gonna go there because she works for us."

"Not anymore," Mouse replies, almost under his breath, but I hear him loud and clear.

I told her she still had a job, but the more I think on it, I realise she was right, no one would want to watch a scarred dancer. However much I'd prefer to be able to think otherwise, there's no way she could strip for us. I'm gutted on her behalf, and enraged about Thompson all over again.

As Mouse stands quiet beside me, probably considering his own problems, I think about what he just said. Yeah, I fancy her, so what's holding me back? Is it that her heritage is different to mine? Am I so brainwashed to think white only goes with white? I've never considered myself racist, but perhaps somewhere deep down inside I am?

Nah, that's not it, I don't give a damn about the colour of her skin, barely register it anymore. She's Alex, that she's black just makes her uniquely her. The problem is, she'd want more than I could offer. A future and security for her and her son. Not just a romp where we both got our rocks off and then move on.

She's a special woman, I knew that from the moment I met her, her personality drawing me in. She's got backbone, an inner strength shown by the way she cares for her son. I reckon she'd be loyal to a fault for anyone she loved.

But she's not for me. I don't go for her sort. I like my women tall and slender, long legs that can wrap around me as I pound into them. Blond hair's always been my preference, long and smooth that I can wrap around my hands.

As I try to summon up an image of the type that does attract me, memories crash into my head of the first time I'd seen Alex dancing in the club—her suppleness and erotic moves, and immediately my cock starts to throb. Now *he* doesn't seem to mind she's short, plump, and soft with a great ass and tits…

She needs a man who's in it for the long haul, and don't come close to that. If I started anything I'd only be leading her on. Sure, I wouldn't turn down the chance to fuck her, just to see what it's like, but that's out of the question. Because she's an employee.

Not now she's not.

"You like her," Mouse observes.

"Of course I like her. She's a lovely person, good natured."

"And with a fuckin' good body. The money coming into the club can testify to that."

Not any longer. I frown. "Dollar's not gonna be pleased."

"Fuck Dollar," Mouse growls. "You didn't come across two states just to look after our investment."

Even I can't adequately explain why my first impulse was to jump on my bike to take on her ex on her behalf. I just thought it was unfair on her, that's all. *But would I have done that for any other bitch?*

"Why don't you just admit it and go for it, Brother? I seen the way you look at her."

Narrowing my eyes, I stare at him. "And what fuckin' way would that be?"

Mouse smirks and points towards Slick, who's currently deep in discussion with Poke, and by the tension in my brother's body, he's not enjoying the conversation at all. Wondering what they could be talking about almost makes me miss the implication of Mouse's next words. "Like the way Slick looks at Ella. Or Wraith looks at Sophie. Or hell, the way Drum is with Sam."

No I don't. There's no similarity at all. "I'm not fuckin' her, Mouse. Told ya that already."

He rolls his eyes. "You don't have to fuck her to have feelin's for her. Back in church, when I say I was going to play boyfriend with her, you clenched your fists."

Did I? I hadn't been aware of it. "Maybe I was just stretchin' my hands."

Again, his eyes rise to the ceiling then back down. "Just fuckin' listen to yerself. Yer makin' every fuckin' excuse you can to deny what's plain as the fuckin' nose on yer face. The real reason why you won't go there? You're scared you get one taste of that pussy and you won't want any other. And yer frightened of makin' that commitment."

Commitment and me don't go together. Yeah, I'd fuck her. But she'd be nothin' more than any of the rest. Once I've gone there I'll have had enough. And probably shattered the friendship between us. "I don't go back for seconds, Brother."

He smirks. "I'd put good money on it you would this time."

He's wrong. Completely wrong. But fuck it, my head's screwed up in knots. I eye Eva coming into the room, scantily clothed and swaying seductively, obviously advertising she's available for a quick fuck. *There you go fella, what about that instead?* Shit, now I'm having a conversation with my cock! But he twitches, which I interpret as he's telling me it's a fuckin' good idea, a way to get rid of my tension and those strange, inappropriate thoughts about the woman lying injured upstairs. And that's what I want to hear, not the rubbish my brother's been spouting.

I nudge Mouse and point towards the sweet butt. He gives me a strange look and a quick disappointed shake of his head. But I'm already moving, throwing a quick, "Keep ya eye on Tyler for me, will ya?" over my shoulder. I hear him huff as I move off.

"Hey, Eva. Up for some fun?"

Her instant smile and nod gives me the answer I want. She takes hold of my hand and leads me out of the room. I try to focus on the sway of her ass, but can't help but mentally compare it to another, the one I can't seem to get out of my mind. She pauses at a doorway and pushes open the door. I follow her inside.

"I've been looking forward to this, Dart." As she licks her lips she leaves me in no doubt what she's talking about.

I simply jerk my chin. I'm not being modest, no woman I've had has ever left with complaints. Reaching out, I cover her tits with my hands, already having seen she's braless beneath her tight top. Under my touch her nipples peak, pushing at the thin material. My cock seems to have lost interest. Maybe I need to see flesh.

"Take this off," I instruct her, using the commanding tone women seem to like.

Hurriedly she complies, tearing it off over her head. Yeah, her breasts are pretty enough, tanned and tipped with rosy red nipples. Lowering my mouth and putting a hand around her back, I pull her too me and close my lips around one of the hard peaks. She gasps loudly, an exaggerated and practiced sound. I give a little nip of my teeth, and she pushes against me. My cock twitches.

After treating the other nipple the same way, I take a step back and wave my hand. "Naked, now."

With a gleam in her eyes, she undoes the buttons on her shorts, hooks her thumbs into the waistband, and slowly pushes them over her hips. As she kicks them off, freeing her feet, she's wearing nothing but high-heeled shoes. No superfluous clothing here.

I've got a naked and very attractive woman standing in front of me. As I examine her, she flicks just the kind of long blonde hair I like over her shoulders. She puts a hand on her hip and a finger to her mouth, and sucks it inside. Having lubricated it, she trails it down her stomach, and circles her clit. Another twitch, and my cock's almost at half-mast.

What the fuck is wrong with me?

Grinning, I try to get my head—and dick—into the game. Placing my hand against her chest, I push her back towards the bed. When her knees hit the edge, I curl my arm around her back and gently ease her down. Expertly she spreads her legs, allowing me the see her glistening arousal. Her perfume is heady. I've got a willing woman ready and waiting for me. Instinct takes over. Pushing aside any other thought in my head, my cock pushes up against my jeans, now fully erect. *At last.*

Before he can have second thoughts, I straddle her body, pulling her up on the bed. I start working her with my fingers as my mouth finds her breasts, nipping and soothing with my tongue. I know my way around a woman's body, and soon have her writhing, alternately flicking, circling, and pressing on her clit with my thumb while my fingers work from inside her channel. With my free hand I take hold of her hair, pulling her head back on the bed.

"You gonna come?"

"Yes."

And then her body's tensing, her mouth opens as she cries out. I keep up the pressure until she's back down to earth again.

Standing, I take off my tee and open my jeans. Her eyes widen as they fall on my cock. Her tongue rims her mouth suggestively as I take out and slide on a condom.

"On your knees."

As she turns over she wiggles her ass in the air. With my hands on her butt cheeks I thrust forwards and then I'm inside her pussy. I start slowly, knowing women enjoy a gradual build.

She's encouraging me on. "Oh, yes, Dart. That's it. Fuck yes. That feels soooo good."

I fasten my pace.

"Oh baby, that's fucking good. Yeah, Dart. Oh Dart."

I start hammering.

"Dart! *Dart. Oh fucking yes, Dart!*"

I've got a reputation for giving a girl a good time. The sweet butts back home make a beeline for me, and hangarounds always try to come back for more. I've got stamina too, and that's fucking useful for once. She's come twice now, and I can't even feel that telltale tingling in my balls.

Pulling out I turn her onto her back, noticing her eyes are glazed over. I pull up her legs, thank fuck she's supple and I can push them back over her shoulders. I push in my dick, getting deeper this way.

My hips piston as I plunge in and withdraw, over and over again. I tune out her voice and close my eyes...

Suddenly I see a dark vision in my head, a girl with assets she knows how to use as she shimmies around the pole in the club. And there it is, at fucking last, my balls draw up and I'm emptying myself with little more than a feeling of relief that I've come at last.

Releasing her legs and putting my hand to the condom, I pull out. Removing the latex, I tie it off, and, standing up, put it in the pocket of my jeans. Yeah, I'm not looking for a paternity suit.

She's turned on her side to watch me dress. "Dart, babe. That was amazing." Sitting up, she reaches out her hand and touches my abs. "Expected it to be good, babe. But you blew me away."

Now what man doesn't feel proud getting praise like that. I wink at her. "Glad to be of service, darlin'."

"You know," she continues, still stroking my chest, "I didn't think I'd get the chance to take you for a test run."

"Really?" Zipped up, I'm pulling on my tee now.

"Yeah, thought you were with that black bitch you brought back with you."

Swiping her arm away I lean down, twist my hand in her hair to the point of pain and snarl, "You show some fuckin' respect. She's got a fuckin' name and you use it, you got me?"

Disgusted with her, and for some inexplicable reason with myself, I loosen my grip and leave the room, slamming the door behind me.

CHAPTER 17
Alex

For the past two days, I've done little but sleep, my rest aided by the drugs Doc insists on me taking to control the pain. Tyler's been coming to see me, but seems to be having a great time with his new friend, Lloyd—a prospect, Dart has explained—who has been keeping him occupied in the shop. My son's calling himself a mechanic now, which made me smile when I first heard it. As long as he's happy I don't mind what he's up to, even if he constantly seems to have a spot of grease somewhere on his face or hands.

Today I'm going to try to shower and dress, and maybe get out of this room for a while. Doc's arranged for Eva, the club girl who's also a nurse, to come help me get up.

I take another pain killer—a lower strength one now—to prepare for what I know will be an ordeal. Half of it's in my head, knowing I have to be mindful of my stitches and not over-doing things and making them to tear. I've not long to wait before Eva walks in.

"Hi, Alex. How are you feeling?" She's been in before, changing my dressing, but I've not really been up for having a talk.

"I'm feeling more with it today." I take a moment to study her, noticing how pretty and slim she is.

"That's because Doc's stopped your morphine. He's given me instructions. First, we need to get that catheter out." She's business-like as she's goes about her work, but sucks in a breath when she sees the evidence of what was done to my nether regions.

"Is it awful?"

A quick look at my face, then she replies, "Girl, it's not so bad, it's just the thought of it makes me cringe. And I'm a nurse."

"You're a woman."

She looks at me and grins. "Yes. That's what it is. But don't worry, like any other stitches that have been removed the holes will disappear in time, and no one will ever know what's been done." *I will. I'll never the able to forget.*

She disposes of the gloves she was wearing and moves something under the bed. "I'll be back to deal with everything later, but for now let's get you showered. You'll feel better after that."

I wince as I take the weight on my hands and gingerly pull myself into a sitting position.

Eva's watching me carefully. "That's right. Just take it slow. If you feel the stitches pulling, take a moment and relax. Now, can you swing your feet over the bed?"

I do, and touch the ground for the first time in days. I give her a little triumphant smile, and she nods back.

"How do you feel?"

"A bit dizzy."

"We'll give it a moment." She turns and opens a bag. "Got some things here for you to wear. You'll be uncomfortable wearing a bra for a while, so I got you a loose top. And I thought a skirt would be best, under the circumstances." She nods at my groin so I get the point. "Right, ready to try standing?"

"Thanks for getting the clothes, Eva." I express my gratitude as her arm goes around me. I put my weight on my feet and cautiously draw myself up. She helps me get my balance, and then slowly assists me into the adjacent bathroom. After a couple of steps I stagger, but she holds me up. "I'm sorry, Eva."

"Hey, no problem. You're such a tiny thing, you're no trouble." As she stands a head taller than me, I suppose I'm not.

At some point I've been dressed in a loose-fitting nightgown. Knowing she's seen everything there is to see, I don't feel any embarrassment as she helps me strip off. She starts the shower, and then helps me in. "Do you need help?"

I find I can't reach my hair as raising my hands pulls too hard at my stitches. Without blinking an eye, she takes off her clothes and gets in behind me. She shampoos and washes my tight curly locks, and then gets out and hands me a sponge. After she wraps a towel around me, she dries herself off, and I can't help noticing her fantastic figure. She's completely in proportion where I'm not.

Finished, feeling better now I'm fresh and clean, I allow her to finish dapping at the bits of me I can't reach, and then let her fashion a towel into a turban around my head. After she's carefully inspected the stitches on my chest, she puts a fresh dressing on.

"You know," she starts conversationally, helping me get a loose top over my head. "Before I saw you I thought you were Dart's old lady. He was so worried about finding you, and then distraught about the state you were in when you came back. And he stayed by your side until you regained consciousness. He cares a lot about you, doesn't he?"

I get a glowing feeling inside knowing how much Dart had been worried about me. But feel I have to deny any relationship between us. "I'm just his employee, but I think we've become friends."

"Yes. It seems you have. And you've got a wonderful little boy in Tyler. He's settled right in in the club."

"He's a good kid," I tell her proudly.

She sits me down and picks up a comb and starts teasing the knots out of my hair. "Now that I've seen you better, I can see how wrong I was about your relationship with Dart," she starts, conversationally, "and of course, he told me himself." She laughs. "You're really not his type, are you babe?"

Oh? Now how do I take that? "You don't think so?" I throw out the off-hand comment, hoping it sounds casual. *He's been speaking to her about me?*

She laughs. "No, I've got to know Dart very well, if you know what I mean." She winks at me again. "And I think I know what he prefers. Mmm mmm. That man in the sack. He certainly knows how to use his God-given assets."

I fight hard to keep all emotion off my face. Oh, I know it was stupid of me to dream, to imagine a mutual attraction that simply wasn't there. She's right, she's much more his type, tall, slim, pretty, and white. But I thought there was a spark between us, something that might only having needed a small push to flame. But while I've been lying injured he's clearly been fucking Eva. I feel like I've been punched in the gut, as though he's betrayed me. *But he owes nothing to me.*

I'd misread so much into the times he's been sat with me. And that over the past two days it seems every time I've woken up it's to find him holding my hand. I'd been so wrong and stupid to read any more into it than concern for me. As a friend.

I've gone quiet. My sense of pride tells me I've got to start talking before she suspects something. And then she'd probably have to disappear rather than burst out laughing to my face at the fat girl's audacity to think such a handsome biker would have the slightest bit of interest in her. "How long until I can get out of here, would you think?" I ask, my one thought to get as far away as possible from the man who, for some reason, I feel has been disloyal to me. One side of my brain says I've no right to expect anything from him, while the other remembers the heated promise in his eyes. *I've been so ridiculous.*

"As long as there's no sign of infection, and you feel strong enough, another couple of days should do it, if you take care." Eva seems completely oblivious to the fact she's just dashed my hopes.

The day I can leave can't come soon enough. She finishes my hair, and I just want her out of my sight. While she's done nothing wrong, I'm starting to hate her. *She's had my man.* But he was never mine. Tears prick in my eyes and I try to hold them back.

"Shall I help you downstairs?"

I put my hand to my head, feigning weakness. "The shower's taken it out of me, Eva. I think I'll just stay here and rest for a while. I'll try and make it down later on."

It's an easy excuse for her to accept. "I'll leave you to it then."

As she opens the door I remember to thank her politely, while vowing I'll work on doing everything for myself from now on, knowing I won't be able to get that image of her and Dart together out of my head.

Don't cry. Don't cry. Don't fucking cry. I bite my knuckles in my effort to hide back the tears.

I'm still fighting against breaking down when the door bursts open, and in runs my son. He skids to a halt in front of me, and a delighted smile splits his face.

"Mom, you're dressed! Are you coming downstairs now?"

Dart has entered more slowly behind him. He gives me a nod of approval. I turn my head away, but his attention's on Tyler. "Hey, little man. Be careful of your mom. She's still sore."

Ignoring Dart, I reach out my arms and pull Tyler into my chest, wincing as I hold him too tight, but ignoring the pain as I need the comfort. For a moment we just hug, something I've not been able to do for days. Then, when my wounds starting throbbing, I put him at arm's length and look at him carefully.

"You been feeling okay, Tyler?" He's got a good colour, his eyes are bright and shining. And I even think he's put on a bit of weight.

He brushes off my concern. "I'm doing good, Mom."

"And how's Momma today?" Dart steps up, his arm reaching out to tip my chin up towards him.

I rear my head back, then gasp as the sharp movement pulls at the stitches. Dart's eyes narrow, and he switches his attention to my son.

"Tyler, why don't you go and see if Lloyd needs help? Ask Slick or Mouse to take you out to the shop. I'll stay and see if I can't persuade your mom to come down and you can show her what you've been doing."

"You gonna come see, Mom?" Tyler's almost dancing on the spot.

I don't want him to go, don't want to be alone with Dart. Not when these tears are still threatening. "Why don't you visit with me a bit longer?" I'm being selfish, I know.

"He can come back later. Ty, I'd like to talk to your mom for a while. Lloyd was asking where you were."

And that's all it takes for Tyler to desert me.

Dart closes the door behind him. He leans back against it for a moment with his arms folded across his chest and stares at me. Then he comes over and hunkers down. He reaches out for my hands, I pull them away. Crease lines appear on his brow.

"You hurtin', doll? Need me to call Doc back?"

Yes, I'm hurting. But there's nothing that anyone in the medical profession could fix. "I'm okay, really, Dart. Just need some time to get my breath back after having a shower."

He nods. "You look better in some clothes and not lying on that bed."

I look down at my lap, just wanting him gone. While repeating the mantra in my head, *He hasn't been disloyal, he hasn't deceived me. He owed me no fidelity at all*, yet all I can think of is that unspoken promise I thought I could see in his eyes. That spark that was there until he'd found me, marked and cut up.

He places his hand under my chin, a forceful touch which I'm unable to evade. "Talk to me, Alex."

My eyes meet his, and as they do a tear escapes. While not letting me loose, his free hand wipes it away. His head tilts to one side. "What's wrong, doll?"

I can't begin to explain. He'd only laugh. The overweight girl who impudently thought she was enough to attract a handsome biker. I shake my head, making him drop his hand, and then look away. I feel my eyes watering, and there's nothing I can do to stop it.

He puts his hands lightly on my forearms and tries to pull me to him, but my body is stiff. "What's happened?" Now he's starting to sound annoyed.

"Nothing. I'm just tired."

But his lips press together as though he's not accepting my denial. He continues to stare at me while he wipes his hand over his face.

"Did Eva say something?" he asks, tersely.

And he's right on target the first freaking time. I suppose I should be glad he didn't run all the club girls' names past me first. But then, of course, Eva's the only one I know, and she's just been in here. It didn't take him long to put two and two together. While I try to stay impassive, the tensing of my body gives me away.

"Fuck it!" He stands and starts to pace across the room, then swings around and comes back, looming over me. "What did she say, Alex? Tell me what she fucking said."

All at once my spirit returns. "Only that you fucked her," I spit out. "Now if you want *conversation* I suggest you go find her."

"Fuck!" he exclaims. In an automatic action, he pulls the tie out of his hair and shrugs it down, lovely dark locks that flood over his shoulders, then almost as quickly scoops it up again, twisting it back into a bun. It's the first time I'd seen it loose, and my traitorous fingers itch to run through it.

"Fuck," he says again, this time more quietly. He looks at me quickly, and then away. Neither of us seem to have any more words. I've no business hurting, but he's too much of a gentleman to tell me that.

After what seems like eternity when neither of us speak, he puts his hand on the door handle. He turns just before he opens it to tell me, "It was a mistake, Alex."

And that confusing statemen is his parting shot.

I bow my head and know I'm going to give into my tears. But even as the first sob passes my lips, the door bursts open again. Dart comes back in, his face set. He stands in front of me, forcing me to look up at him. "It was a mistake. I knew it and regretted it. Even while I was fucking her."

But every word coming out of his mouth hits me like a bullet. *He regretted it? While he was with her?*

"It doesn't mean anything to me, Dart. I don't mean anything to you. You owe me nothing. Least of all an apology."

He pulls back his shoulders. "What if I told you I wanted you to mean something to me?"

"I'd say you've got a strange fucking way of showing it." I swear sparks flash from my eyes.

"I cocked up, alright? Fuck. You...This..." He waves his hand down to where my chest is bandaged under my clothes. "It was a way of relieving my tension."

Unable to prevent myself, I snap. "Other men would use their hand."

He looks at me incredulously and then barks a laugh. "Yeah, I suppose I could have done that. Look, Alex, I like sex. I'm used to getting it a lot. And that's what club girls are there for. Don't matter what club they're at, their Satan's Devils property, women for us to use…"

"You're a manwhore," I interrupt.

He shrugs, but doesn't deny it. And then says the words which come much too late. "I like you, Alex. I've been tryin' to deny it to myself. No girl I've seen lately can come close to measurin' up. And you're right, I could have used my hand. And I have done. But it's you that I find myself imaginin' when I do. And even with Eva, I couldn't fuckin' come until I closed my eyes and pictured you instead.

"Look, I reckon you're feelin' much the same way. Eva runnin' her mouth wouldn't have bothered you so much if you didn't. When you're healed up, what say you we give it a try? You and me, together."

I wince each time he says her name. All I can see in my mind's eye is the perfect blond and Dart together. Unsteadily I rise to my feet. His hands hover to help me, but I stand straight without needing his help. In fact, he takes a step back when he gets a look at the fury in my eyes. "It's too late, Dart. I am attracted to you. Or to put it more accurately, I was. But I'm a mother with a child. If I'm going to go with a man, it's someone who can at least give it a damn good try to make something of a relationship. I've already been tied to someone who thought I came second best. And I wouldn't want to compete with your whores."

"I'm nothin' like Thompson."

"Aren't you? How long until you get bored? Or would I be like Eva, something to cross off your list? Been there? Done that?" I take a step toward him, my finger jabbing at his ribs. "And what about my scars? Admit it. They're a turn off. You'll soon be back to preferring white, unmarked flesh."He moves back to get away from my prods. I advance and continuing stabbing at him. "Or would it just be the once so you can say you've fucked a black girl? Had you some dark meat for a change?"

"It's not like that!" he thunders. "And whether or not you've got scars doesn't matter!"

"What's it like then? You swearing undying love for me?"

That pulls him up. He stares, and something in his eyes fade. He closes them briefly. When he opens them, he says in a much calmer voice, "It would be all or nothin' with you, wouldn't it? You'd want to be my ol' lady, and I'm not ready for that."

And sadly, I don't think he ever will be. I'd read him correctly. He was interested in me, but not enough so he'd wait. No, while I'd been lying injured and hurting, he was in another woman's arms.

Someone else might forgive him and give him a second chance. But I won't.

This time, when he leaves, he doesn't come back.

CHAPTER 18

Dart

When I see Eva sitting with the rest of the girls, she preens and gives me a flirtatious wink. She's pretty enough, but now that I'm really looking at her and not being guided by my cock I see she's got nothing on the woman I've just left. She doesn't make my pulse speed up, or cause my blood to heat. She was a chance to scratch my itch, and available hole to shoot my load into. And it's cost me so fucking much.

I couldn't offer Alex a promise of anything permanent. But I'd be prepared to offer her more than I've ever offered any other woman in my life, and the thought of her riding bitch on my bike strangely holds attraction. I suspect Mouse is right, one time with her and fidelity, at least in the short term, wouldn't be a problem.

But from that one stupid action which I immediately regretted, I've put myself into the position where I'm unlikely ever to know what it's like to have behind me on my bike, or having her beneath me as I sink into her soft tempting depths. And once wouldn't have satisfied me, and that's possibly the first time I've ever thought that way. She's not a practiced whore, I'd place a bet Thompson was the only other fucker to have her. There's probably so much I can teach her, show her, and now I've lost my chance.

I can see why she's reluctant to forgive me, I can't see a way to exonerate myself. She'd put up with enough from her husband in the past, and strong woman that she is, she's learned her lesson, and isn't prepared to listen to excuses from another man.

Fuck it. I could have been a different man for her. While I don't have it in me to make a long-term commitment, I knew when I'd left Eva's room that until I had a chance to get Alex out of my system, however long that might take, no other woman would satisfy me.

I feel like someone being offered their first fix of cocaine, knowing it would be addicting, hesitating before trying it, but knowing I'll be unable to resist. And now, due to my own stupidity, my chance of trying the drug of my choice has been taken away. I left it too long to reach out and grab it.

I'm standing in the middle of the clubroom, staring into space. I hadn't noticed anyone approaching me until I feel a touch on my arm.

"Dart, I've got a couple of hours before I leave for work."

I wrench my arm out of her touch. "Been there. Done that, Eva. I don't go back."

Her eyes become slits. "But I thought…"

Yeah, just another club girl wanting to snag herself an old man. "You thought wrong. And don't go opening your mouth to Alex again."

I'm so angry, I'm shaking. But the blame isn't on her. It's on me.

Eva looks crushed. "You said she wasn't your woman."

She isn't. And now it seems likely she never will be. Leaving the club whore standing alone, I make my way to the bar.

Mouse comes over, takes one look at the expression on my face, then shakes his head. "You fucked up, Brother."

And I can't fucking deny that I did. Badly. And I've no idea how to mend it. I flick my eyes toward him. "Eva's got a big mouth."

Mouse rolls his head around, then puts his hand on my shoulder. He looks as if he's going to say something along the lines of he could have warned me I was making a mistake, but changes his mind at my glare. "Fuckin' sorry, man. Still think you should have gone for it."

Past tense. Seems he thinks my chances are shot too.

He calls to the prospect to get me a much needed drink.

I'm only halfway through my beer, which seems tasteless, when Snake comes out of whatever cave he hides in. He doesn't waste time getting to the point. "Got a call from Tinder, who's up by the cabin. Thompson's turned up with another cop. They went inside. An hour later another carload of cops turned up."

"Forensics," Mouse suggests.

"I would think so."

"I'd have given anythin' to see Thompson's face." Mouse laughs. "Alex missin' and a clean-up done."

A half-smile forms on my lips. "He must have been fuckin' beside himself. But he'll probably make sure they check for prints to find out who helped her escape."

"Let them. Is Alex fit enough to come with me today?"

I hadn't asked her, though that was the main reason that I went up to her room just now. But other things took precedence. Remembering how unsteady she appeared on her feet, I doubt very much that she is. "Best give it another day or so, Brother."

Mouse nods. "Well, it will give them a chance to pick up my prints from the cabin. Can't fuckin' wait to see their faces when they see us turn up."

"It all hangs on Alex being able to play her part. If she's not lookin' well, they'll sniff somethin's wrong." Snake nods at Mouse. "Another twenty-four hours will have her lookin' and feelin' stronger."

"Why can't she just tell them it was her ex?"

I roll my eyes as Poke joins us. He's working at his teeth with a wooden stick. "Because cops stick together. They'll be inclined to believe whatever Thompson tells them. They'll take his word over his wife's."

"But his fingerprints will also be all over the cabin…"

"Because he fuckin' went there at some point with his wife. He'll make some story up."

Poke's not going to give up. "Then we take him. If he disappears…"

Snake whacks him over the head. "And who do you think they'll come lookin' for first? We want to clear Mouse's name, not give them more incentive to dig." The prez looks at me and shakes his head as though he's apologising for his sergeant-at-arms. As Poke walks away, he confirms it by saying, "I'm convinced his momma dropped him on his head when he was a baby."

I wouldn't be at all surprised.

"Got company!" Lost calls out from over by a window. "Tucson boys wanna make themselves lost."

Snake moves fast, directing us to a room, and then to a closet where a panic room's hidden behind. If you didn't know it was there, you'd never see it. "We tried to soundproof it but ain't no guarantee. Try to keep quiet in there."

Don't think any of us are going to say a word. Probably try to stop breathing if we could. Snake leaves us to deal with the police and the inevitable raid. But before long the door opens again, and Alex is carried inside.

"Sorry, darlin', was quicker to carry ya," Grumbler explains as he puts her on her feet, Tyler runs in after them, then the door's shut again.

Fuck. It had slipped my mind she couldn't be found either, not in the state she's in today. And now we're all imprisoned together, nobody able to make a sound. To say the silence is awkward is a gross understatement.

Tyler crosses over to me. I take his hand and lean down, speaking softly. "You've got to be real quiet, buddy."

"Are there bad men out there?"

It's probably the easiest way to explain to him. "Yeah, the bad men who hurt your mom."

With a grown-up look, much too old for his age, he looks at his mom and then back to me. "My dad."

Alex's eyes open wide, and I give a violent shake of my head. No, I hadn't told him who'd hurt her. The kid had worked it out for himself. It gets me in the guts that a boy should know something like that about the man who sired him. Tyler drops his hand and goes to sit on the floor beside Alex.

There's not much room, and Slick moves so I can go to Alex's side. Ignoring his unspoken offer, I ease myself back into the corner instead, keeping what distance I can between us. Mouse narrows his eyes and shakes his head, then he takes charge, crossing to her and whispering into her ear. He then lends her a hand to help her sit down and get herself as comfortable as she can on the floor. He sits down on the opposite side to Tyler, his arm around her shoulder. I watch as she whispers a question into his ear, which he answers with a sharp nod, and I wish it was me she's turning too. But I've blown it.

She won't even look at me. Won't catch my eye. It physically hurts to see the way she's holding herself, trying to be so brave for son. And it cuts me to the quick when Mouse stretches out his legs, letting her half lie down to take the pressure off her injured chest. *It should be me.*

Slick's glaring at me, Mouse throws me dirty looks. But as we're trying to keep quiet, I've no chance to explain, or to plead my case with Alex. Though even if I could, I wouldn't know what to say. I can't deny I fucked another woman, and in the world Alex comes from, if I really wanted her, I'd have waited.

But that's not my world. Man's got urges, man gets them taken care off. And sometimes your hand just won't do. I'd made no commitment to Alex. So why the fuck am I wishing I'd kept my fuckin' dick dry? Maybe it's better not to draw her into this life. She'd never accept or understand it. Best she's never going to be riding bitch up behind me. Fuck, I'll never feel her at my back.

Damn it! I turn around and rest my forehead against the wall.

It seems like forever to me until the door opens again.

But Slick arches his eyebrow. "That was quick."

The man who'd given us our freedom puts his finger to his lips. "Snake wants you out of here. Cops are out in the main room questionin' the brothers. We're goin' out the back." I notice the name on his cut is Gator.

There's another man standing behind him with such a leer on his face, there's something about him to which I take an immediate dislike.

"Why aren't we safe in here?" Something tells me this is wrong. I don't trust these men at all. I make a gesture to Mouse and Slick to stay where they are.

"Come on. You're wastin' time."

"Get Snake, I want to hear it from him."

Now the second man steps in. Quick as a flash, he's got Tyler up and is holding him with a knife to his throat. "Take out your weapons and drop them," he rasps. "And don't think of shoutin' for help. You'll have a dead kid on yer hands in you do more than fuckin' blink."

Damn it, this is one time I didn't want to be right, but I don't see disobeying as any alternative. One look at Alex's face, her mouth open in horror, her eyes flicking wildly between us, and I don't hesitate. Carefully I slide my gun out of my cut and put it on the floor. Slick and Mouse do the same.

"Now your knives."

Mouse opens his cut to show he doesn't carry one. Slick and I take ours out, and the small pile of weapons grows on the floor.

"Turn around. Hands behind your back. I don't care for kids, especially a nigger brat, so if you don't want his head and body separated, then you do as I say."

His racist term hits me in the gut. He's signed his death warrant for calling Tyler that. But for the moment we've got no choice other than to follow the instructions, that knife at the boy's throat too much of a threat.

Next thing I know my hands are being tied behind me tightly with rope. I try to tense my muscles to allow for some slack, but Gator knows what he's doing with knots. When he's finished I can't get them free.

"Now come with me. And remember, Fang's got the kid."

I exchange glances with Slick. With Tyler's life at risk, there's not much we can do. Alex awkwardly gets to her feet, her body hunched over in pain. As soon as she's standing, Gator ties her hands too. Raised voices can be heard from the clubroom, help so near, and yet so far. Gator is wearing a Satan's Devils San Diego cut, but Fang's cut is bare, just jagged stitching where patches were stripped off. Looks like we're in the hands of an out bad member, a man with nothing else to lose.

Unwilling to risk even the slightest injury to Tyler, I and my brothers follow Gator out back where a blacked-out truck is waiting. As Gator opens the back he instructs that we move inside. Slick gets in first, followed by Mouse. Somehow, and with a lot of pain, Alex manages to heave herself up and roll in. While Gator and Fang watch her struggles with grins playing at their mouths, I take my chance and throw my body back, twisting so my head knocks into Fang's arm holding the knife. I feel it slice along my jaw line, but ignoring the injury, shout, "Run, Tyler. Run!"

The boy's fast to react, turning and disappearing back into the clubhouse.

For my reward, I get a fist to my already bleeding face, so hard it makes me see stars. Both men pick me up and throw me into the truck. The doors are slammed shut, Gator jumps in the driver's seat, Fang next to him. The engine is gunned, and we're off, crashing through the partially open gate, surprising the cop left waiting outside.

After a couple of minutes Gator asks, "Have we got a tail?"

Fang's studying the side mirror. "Nah. Most were inside. Fuckers can't get themselves organised."

At the moment I wish the police had got themselves together in time. But at least Snake will know we've been taken.

"Thank you," Alex mouths. I'd got her son safely away. Fuck me, hurt and injured, kidnapped and stolen, *yet again*, and this woman's so strong her only thought is for the boy. And all my concern is for her.

What the fuck have we got mixed up in now?

"The kid will have raised the alarm," Fang sounds angry. "I shoulda' killed him but he was too fuckin' quick."

"Fuckin' brat's too young to have picked up much. What can he say?"

"He might have our names…"

"Snake won't give a damn. We're followin' his orders after all. Probably gut the kid himself."

"The police are still there…"

"We know Thompson wants the brat. And the bitch dead. Kid will probably go runnin' straight into dear papa's hands. Now keep your eye on them in the back."

As Fang turns around and levels his weapon at us, he gives an evil grin towards Alex, and as his mouth opens I can see how he got his name. One of his top canines is missing, the other seems overly long. My fists itch to knock it out, and the smile off his face.

Alex is trembling, her head starts dropping. Awkwardly I move myself and try and put my body between her and the hard floor of the truck. She's doing that quiet as fuck sobbing thing again, and knowing her, it's the thought of Tyler in her ex's hands rather than the death sentence that's been announced on herself, that's causing her terror.

"It will be alright, doll," I whisper into her ear. "It will all turn out right."

She shakes her head sadly. She's come through so much, it will be breaking her all over again losing her son now.

Slick and Mouse aren't making a move. With our hands literally tied, and the unwavering gun pointed at us, there's nothing we can do now except try and communicate by almost imperceptible gestures. By their narrowed eyes, I realise they'd picked up on the comment about Snake just like I had. I take the time to run over conversations I've had with the man in my head. There was nothing to suggest that he hadn't been playing it straight with us. Perhaps he's a good actor? But why? That's what I can't understand. I try to pick at the threads.

Did Snake rat us out to the police? That doesn't seem likely if he's in league with Gator and Fang. *Why kidnap us at all?*

No fucking answers come to me. Snake's a Satan's Devils president. For the life of me, I can't see what he's got to gain. But next time I see him he better have some fucking answers. Glancing at Slick, and then at Mouse, it's clear we're all thinking along the same lines. And none of them are good.

Then I spare a thought for Tyler. I can see nothing else but him running back into the club to raise the alarm, only to be faced with a possible rebel president who doesn't give a damn about the kid, or, and I can't make up my mind which is worse, his father who's already tortured and tried to kill his mother. I told Alex it will be alright. Right now, I have no fucking idea how.

The truck's turned off the main highway and is going up some side roads, and shortly after, starts bumping down a neglected track. It comes to a halt at an abandoned warehouse. Fang wastes no time getting out, and he's joined by Gator as he opens the doors.

"Out."

The one word command backed up by the threat of the gun has us moving. Slick nudges me from behind, and I know what he's thinking. But so do the men who've taken us, stepping back smartly out of our reach and, bound as we are, we don't have a chance to go on the attack.

"Inside."

With guns at our back we approach the warehouse. Alex stumbles from weakness, and gets a fist to her side to encourage her to get to her feet and start moving again. No hand offered to help her up, no chance for me to try to knock Gator or Fang off their feet. I growl at the additional injury she's received.

We enter into a large room with machinery obviously unused for years. But the area itself has been used before, and quite probably recently. There's the metallic odour of blood in the air, and red stains at our feet. I half close my eyes. This room is much like our storage room back in Tucson, and pretty soon I'll most likely be on the wrong end of the type of treatment we dish out there. But we're not allowed to linger, and are pushed on through, into a room with no windows and only one door, it's bare with no furniture.

Having pushed us in, Gator and Fang make as if to leave. Before they can close the door, I take the initiative, turning to face our captors head on. "Who are you? And what do you want from us?"

"All in good fuckin' time," Gator replies, and then slams the door shut.

CHAPTER 19
Alex

My wounds are hurting, and now, in addition, my side is throbbing from the punch I received. But my overriding pain is the worry I have for my son. So choked up, it's hard for me to speak. *Did he run to this man, Snake? And would he really hurt him? We've got to get out of here. I've got to get back to my son.* Looking around the room we've been imprisoned in, there's not much to see. I heard the door being locked, and there's no window and no other way out. My only relief on a personal level is that I've not been separated from the men, that's some comfort at least. I'm not stupid, I saw the looks on the faces of the one's who've taken us, and heard the insults—they've no respect for the colour of my skin. Shuddering, I'm left in no doubt of the ways they want to make me suffer. *Are they in league with Ron? Is he coming for me again?*

I bite my lip to force back useless tears. I escaped my husband once, I doubt he'd give me another chance.

When the door shuts, leaving us alone, I try to see if there's any way I can loosen the bindings around my wrists. But they've been tied tightly, and already I can feel the strands cutting into my skin. Remembering the lewd looks they'd given me, I ignore the pain and keep trying.

"Here, Slick." Dart's voice interrupts me. "Let's get these fuckin' ropes off."

As if they've done it before, Slick and Dart both slide to the floor and sit back to back. Slick starts fumbling with binds around Dart's hands, quietly swearing as he does do.

Mouse watches them for a moment, then comes across to me, examining my face carefully. "You doin' okay?"

"I'm fine," I tell him, frantic with concern about my son. I'm ignoring the pain which is being made worse from having my hands fastened behind me, pulling at the wounds on my chest. "I just need to get back to Tyler. Mouse, I'm so worried about him."

"Know you are, babe. But look at the odds, there's two of them, three of us. We'll get out of here, sweetheart, and get back to your boy." Slick confidently throws over his shoulder while working the knots behind his back.

Dart's looking at me strangely. I turn away. He might be able to offer me sympathy, but I was so stupid to ever think he might want to give me anymore. I'm so embarrassed to think he'd ever have gone for a girl like me. And one lumbered with a child. A child who's in danger if he trusts the wrong man.

"Alex…" Dart speaks sharply while Slick continues working at trying to unknot the rope tying his hands together. Hampered of course, as his own are tied too.

I swing back around. "Nothing's changed, Dart," I hiss. "I need to get back to Tyler. If Ron's got him…" My eyes fill with tears as I replay what the men said. "Snake wouldn't really hurt him, would he?"

His own eyes fill with anguish, he can't reassure me at all.

Slick gets Dart's attention, talking to him as he works the ropes. "What ya think we're dealin' with here?"

Tilting his head to one side, Dart replies, "You notice anythin' about Gator?"

Slick shrugs. "Thought he looked familiar, but hell, I've probably just seen him around the club."

Leaving me, Mouse joins in. "What you gettin' at, Dart? Slick, I don't think I've seen him in the clubhouse before today."

Dart lowers his face and briefly closes his eyes as he works it through. "He hasn't been at church and we've had enough meetin's. Could have been on a run or somethin' and only just got back. He's not out bad, as he's still got his patch. Now, I might be goin' a stretch with this, but Gator's got the same eyes as someone we all knew. Same mouth an' all. Ouch, Slick. You ever cut your fuckin' fingernails?"

Slick shakes his head, ignoring Dart's complaint, and gets back on topic. "Not sure where you're goin' with this, Brother."

"Six months ago?"

Mouse freezes. He too looks like he's thinking. Then he whistles through his teeth. "Buster. He's fuckin' Buster's brother."

Slick starts, frowns, and after a pause, seems to agree. "Certainly a familial resemblance. You really think he is, Dart?"

"Brother or cousin. There's a likeness there. And if I'm right, he'll have no love for the Tucson chapter."

"And Fang? Who the fuck is he then? Another cousin?"

"Nah, no similarities there. But who else would want to take us out?"

Now Slick pulls his shoulders back, and a scowl appears on his face. "Man with no patches? Don't belong to no club?"

"He's either out bad…" Dart starts to add his thoughts.

"Or he's a fuckin' Rock Demon," Slick finishes for him. "It couldn't be, could it?"

"It's a possibility. And if it is, he's likely the one you've come here to kill. They were fishin' to get him into the club. Maybe they drew him in for their own reasons rather than ours and have been keepin' him under the radar."

Fuck. Kill? I knew they were rough, but to admit to murder? But when Slick continues, I realise he has reason.

"Yeah, I want him dead. Promised Ella the fucker who raped her would be taken out."

In a couple of seconds he's gone from murderer to avenger, and I risk a quick look at Dart, wishing he felt the depth of emotion for me as Slick does for Ella. Someone who'd be by my side and kill my bastard of an ex for me. Then the thought of Tyler slams into me, again. From the way the men had spoken, we can no longer trust anyone in the club. And I last saw Tyler running to them for help. Oh my God, these men are murderers and rapists, they could... A wail comes out of my mouth, as I can't even complete the thought in my head. These men talk about killing as if it means nothing. *My lovely boy.* I sink to my knees, my legs unable to support me anymore.

"Alex," Dart attracts my attention again, telling me emphatically, "Alex, if you're worried about Tyler, I'm sure he'll be fine. If Gator was right, Thompson will be there. He might not be the best father for your son, but he won't let any harm come to him, not with the other cops around. We've got time. Once we're out of here we'll get Tyler back. Don't cry, darlin'. Stay strong. Don't give up hope."

Half of the things Dart is saying to me go straight over my head. But he carries on talking, reassuring me that I will see my child again. I know he's right, I mustn't give up. But it's so darn hard. My heart's still beating as normal. Surely, if anything had happened to Tyler I'd know in here? I carried him in my womb for nine months, he's part of me. If he was no longer breathing, I'd feel it.

I swallow back a sob. "How are we going to get out of here, Dart?" That's the first step to get Tyler back. I start twisting my hands all over again, uncaring of the pain as I try to loosen the rope.

Ignoring my question, Dart glances at the two men on the floor. "How you doin', Slick?"

"Almost there."

"Yes!" Dart hisses, and his hands appear in front of him. Without pausing he swings around and starts untying Slick, a much easier affair as he's not working blind. Once Slick's free they make short work of freeing both Mouse and myself. We all take a moment to flex our muscles.

Dart's eyes narrow when he sees my wrists. "Shit, Alex, you shouldn't have struggled so much." rubbing my blood-slickened wrists to help me get the circulation back.

"Why d'ya think they left us?" Mouse is walking around the room, presumably seeing if there's anything he can use as a weapon. Slick's examining the door. "Why not start in on us right away? What the fuck is goin' on?"

Dart, his hand resting on my shoulder, replies, "I think they're waitin' for someone. How long's it been now, Mouse?"

Mouse looks at the watch he can now see. "An hour or so. You could be right there, Dart. But fuckin' who?"

"Buster got any more brothers?"

Mouse smooths his hands over his long dark hair. "Fuck if I can remember. I did the background check as I always do when someone joins the club, but I was lookin' at him, not his fuckin' family tree."

"Who's Buster?" I ask.

The men look at each other, and when Slick raises his chin towards Dart, it's him who informs me, "Buster patched over from San Diego. Tried to rape Wraith's woman."

I gasp. "Is he in prison?"

"He's dead."

"You killed him." I breathe, my hand going to my mouth.

"Now don't look like that, doll." Dart sounds annoyed. "Man showed no remorse, thought he had a God-given right to take what wasn't fuckin' his to take. We weren't gonna risk a court settin' him free."

They've admitted they've killed a man, and Slick's vowed he's going to take the life of another. I should be afraid of these men. Instead of a snap reaction, I take a moment to think. I don't condone violence, on the other hand, the thought of a rapist walking the streets is equally abhorrent. But if they're right, Buster's brother certainly doesn't agree. And it seems it's down to them murdering Buster is the reason I'm being held here today, with my son God knows where and in danger. It's them they want, not me. I'm just collateral damage. Not that that's going to help me. There was lust in our captors' eyes, and it certainly wasn't directed at my companions.

Slick's playing with the lock on the door, but without tools, doesn't seem to be having any success.

Mouse walks over to him, holding his palms face up. "Nothing we can use. I was looking for some overlooked tool or something, but the room's been swept clean."

"Right. We need to be prepared then." Dart eyes Slick up. He's easily the biggest man here. "You stay by the door, let us know if you hear anyone approach."

After throwing Dart a nod, Slick opens and closes his hands as if getting ready. "If it's three against two, I like those odds."

"But if it's more? And don't forget they're armed and we're not."

Dart scowls at Mouse. "We got them beat, Brother. Tucson chapter will top San Diego anytime. They think we're tied up. Just got to move fast while we've got the element of surprise and make sure we've got the upper hand." He stares first at Mouse, then at Slick. "We got this, brothers. We got this."

As two chins dip back at him, I just wish I had his confidence. And how long will we have to wait? How long until the men come back?

My injuries are throbbing, it's long past time I should have had more painkillers. I suspect the rough treatment, the way they'd pulled on the wounds when they tied my arms behind my back, may have torn them open again as I feel the pull on the bandages where fresh blood has dried. I start to get angry. *If only I'd never got that job in the strip club, I wouldn't have met these men and I wouldn't be here.* And then the alternative thought, *Ron would have found me anyway, and I'd have been left to die with no one coming to save me.* Then my eyes go to Dart, and another pain rips through me, this time like a knife through my heart. *I wish I'd never met him at all.*

One man stays by the door, the others hunker down as though conserving their energy. Another hour passes, and then one more. I'm shifting uncomfortably, my bladder full to bursting, but still no one comes.

"How long's it been now, Mouse?"

Again he consults his watch. "Three and a half…"

"Someone's comin'," Slick interrupts, then places his ear to the door, putting his finger to his mouth. In the silence it's easy to pick out footsteps approaching, and soon we hear voices too.

"Can't wait to get hold of that black bitch. D'ya see the ass on her? Just right for fuckin'. My big old cock gonna damn tear her in two." My eyes widen in horror as Dart glances at me and gives a shake of his head, his face set to reassure me that's never going to happen. But if they can't take the men out of action, they've just announced my fate.

"First I want to deal with the Tucson boys. Find out what they can tell us." Slick, Dart, and Mouse exchange looks, obviously recognising the newcomer's voice. Dart pushes me over against the wall so I'm out of the way.

There's the sound of a key turning in the lock. Slick's standing one side of the door. Mouse the other. As soon as a snicking sound shows the lock's been turned, Mouse yanks on the handle pulling it open. They hadn't spoken to arrange such a choreographed move, and I look on in amazement as Slick grabs the arm of the first man, taking advantage of his momentary shock to take the gun out of his hand, turning it on the other men entering as Mouse deals with the second in a similar way, then the butt of the pistol comes down on Fang's head and he collapses to the ground. Slick whips his weapon around the head of Gator, and he joins his prone partner.

There's one man left standing. I don't recognise him.

"Snake." Dart breathes.

And that's when I know who the stranger is. He's the president of the San Diego chapter. The men are pointing guns at each other. It's a stand-off.

"I'll kill you where you stand, I ain't got no time for traitors." Slick's coldly spoken words send a shiver down my spine.

"I was coming to rescue you." Snake sneers down at the men on the ground. "Got a sniff of what was goin' down, got myself invited along."

I don't know about the others, but I don't believe him for a moment. Then Slick does something strange, and starts to lower his gun. "Thought you were with them for a second." *What? Can't you see...* My eyes flick from one to the other, trying to warn Slick not to trust him.

"Nah, man. You know me better than that." Snake begins to relax. He takes a step to the side, his gun now pointing to the floor. "Let's get you out of here." He indicates with his hand that we should go past him.

Slick takes a step forward then, like lightening, his arm comes down, and Snake's weapon scoots across the floor. Dart picks it up and points it at Snake's head. He throws an instruction over his shoulder. "Mouse. Tie Fang and Gator up and make damn fuckin' sure they ain't gonna get free."

Another sharp nod, then Mouse is tying the unconscious men's hands behind their backs, and then for good measure, he ties them together back to back, wrapping and knotting the rope so it's impossible for them to escape. I breathe a sigh of relief.

"You're makin' a mistake, Brother. I came here to cut you loose."

Dart's gun is now jammed against Snake's skull. "Reckon I don't believe ya, *Brother*. You seemed overly friendly with these two. Now you better start talkin'. What you doin' with a Rock Demon in yer house?"

"You caught on fast. Didn't think you knew him." Snake sounds impressed. "You wanted to take him out, Slick. Well, now's yer chance. I've given him to you on a fuckin' plate."

I don't give a damn about Demons. I want to know what's happened to my son. I walk towards Snake, but Mouse moves quickly and holds me back. I make do with screaming from the middle of the room. "What have you done with Tyler? Where's my son?"

Snake looks confused for a second. "Done nothin' with the boy. Thought he was here with you."

What? Where on earth can he be?

"He ran back into the clubhouse," Dart says, his eyes narrowed as if he doesn't credit him with telling the truth. And neither do I.

Snake raises his shoulders. "Don't know nothin' 'bout that. Haven't seen the kid."

"I need to go back to the clubhouse, Dart. Now." I don't know whether it's a good thing or bad that Snake's denying seeing him.

Dart brushes hair out of his face. "Sure you do, doll. But we need to get intel first. We'll go find Tyler just as soon as we can, but with Snake behind this, we need to know what we're walkin' into. Okay?" He gets up close to the San Diego prez and snarls into his face. "Need to know whether the whole fuckin' club's turned bad or just these fuckers here."

No, it's not okay. But there's no point walking into a trap. Even I can understand that. I just can't bear to think my son is right in the middle of it.

At that moment, Fang starts to groan, his arm twitches, and then pulls at the bindings when he realises he's been secured. He isn't going anywhere. I watched Mouse, and the knots he tied were tighter and more complicated than the ones they had used.

Slick walks forwards and kicks him in the stomach. "Start fuckin' talkin', Demon."

Fang's eyes widen, and he looks at Snake.

"Don't look at him. He's busted as well." Slick hunkers down in front of him and draws a knife out of the captive man's belt, testing the edge against his thumb. "You were with the Rock Demons' Phoenix chapter, yes?"

Looking as cocky as a man tied to an unconscious person can, Fang lifts his chin and turns his head away. Slick moves so quickly I barely see the knife flash before the blade's been stabbed into Fang's leg. Blood immediately starts to well up. Fang tries to get away, but he's hampered by the dead weight.

"Need to get a tourniquet on that, *Brother*. Oh, fuck, you can't, can you?" Slick doesn't look at all concerned. Fang watches the blood soaking through the denim of his jeans and pooling beneath his leg.

"I'm gonna bleed out, man." His face has already gone white.

"Better start talkin' then. You tell us the truth and you may have a chance."

Fang looks at Slick, and sees no sympathy there. He swallows and then glances back at his leg and grimaces, then finally admits, "Yeah, I was at the Phoenix chapter."

Slick growls and lunges forwards, and now the blade's pressed against Fang's cheek. "You there at the Friday night party? Couple of weeks before the clubhouse exploded?"

Trying to move his head back out of Slick's reach, Fang looks surprised. "Probably was. Always go to parties."

"There was a woman there. She was new. You had her pullin' a train."

"Yeah, probably. Fuck, it's what we always did with the new bitches. You know what it's like."

I'm not sure what he's talking about, but his disrespect for women is clear. Something I hadn't seen in the Satan's Devils club. I can see veins popping on Slick's head, and his bald head looks slick with sweat. His hands are bunched, his muscles taut, and I read he's just as disgusted as me. Then in a measured voice he asks, "You take yer turn?"

"Yeah, probably man. We all would have."

Slick leaps to his feet, his face red, his breathing rasping through flared nostrils. "Untie him!" he shouts. "I wanna fuck him with his own fuckin' knife."

Dart pulls Snake into the room so he can keep his weapon on him while talking to Slick. "Ain't got time for this. Just finish him, Slick. Or leave him to bleed out."

Obviously undecided, Slick wipes his hands over his head. "I want him to suffer, Brother. Like Ella did."

My hand goes to my mouth. *Ella. He's talking about his wife, Ella.* Fang said they'd all take their turn. If I've understood it right, all the Demons had raped her, not just this one man like I had assumed. That would have been bad enough. Oh, my God. Poor Ella. No wonder Slick's so incensed.

Mouse takes Slick's place in front of Fang. He grabs his hair and twists up his face. "Give me a name, man, and I'll get Slick to finish you quick. The name of the other Demon who escaped."

"Scratch," Fang gasps out.

"Not his fuckin' road name. His real name, you asshole."

Fang shakes his head and looks like he's going to deny he knows it, but Mouse tugs back on his hair and his fist smashes into his face. Blood now streaming from his nose, Fang starts to sob. "Clint something. Martin I think. Something like that. Please, I've told you what I know. Please. Don't let him..." his eyes go wildly to Dart as though sussing he's in charge. "Please don't let him hurt me."

Mouse stands up. "He's all yours, Brother."

Slick eyes up the Demon. "You raped my wife. You think I'm gonna have mercy on ya?"

"I didn't know! No one knew who she was! She was just another bitch..."

Dart puts in mildly, "Should a' not treated any bitch that way. Finish him, Slick."

The knife Slick's holding flashes again, and is buried right up to the hilt just below his groin before Slick pulls it away. He must have hit an artery from the amount of blood spurting out. Fang lets out a piercing scream, then starts wailing and tries to fold over, but his movement's restricted by the man at his back.

Mouse comes to me, puts his hand around my head and presses my face into his chest. "Not something you should have seen, sweetheart. But I assure you, he deserved everything he got."

The dead man who just doesn't know it yet continues to cry, but his cries are getting weaker.

"Slick. Watch him, will ya?" I hear footsteps and then, "And you. You're awake. You can stop pretending now." I hear something I interpret as Dart's boot hitting the man behind Fang. "Yer what, Buster's brother?"

"Yeah. That's who I am. And you lot killed him." Gator spits on the ground.

I turn my head in time to see Dart sink down on his heels, staring intently into his San Diego brother's face. "He was a rapist. He deserved to be put down." Then he pauses to wipe the second globule of spit from his face.

"You bunch of motherfuckers! He did nothin' wrong!"

"Nothin' fuckin' wrong? He had his hands on our VP's woman." Dart stands up. His hair's come loose from his bun, and automatically he takes out the band and ties it back up. "Tell you what, Gator. We might let you live if you give us some info."

Snake growls and Dart rounds on him. "One fuckin' word and you go the same way as Fang." Slick puts the bloody knife to the San Diego prez's neck, then turns back to Gator. "You want to save yourself a world of hurt? Start fuckin' talkin'."

Gator looks wary. "What do you want to know?"

Dart indicates the blood pooling on the floor. "You were working with Fang. Obviously neither of you had little love for the Tucson chapter. You've started a war by takin' us. That Snake's here suggests the rot runs deep. What was it? Club decision?"

As Gator shrugs, Dart kicks him again. I hear the cracking of bones and reckon he's broken at least one rib. That gets him talking. "Nah, we didn't take a vote. Just Snake and a few of the trusted brothers."

"Suggest you give us the names, Brother."

Snake makes another noise. Slick's arm tightens around his neck. Gator's eyes look around shiftily. "I'll give you a couple of names just to show I'm willin', but I've nothin' to bargain with if I tell you them all."

Dart shrugs nonchalantly. "Ain't no way you're getting' out of this, Brother. You can go fast or slow. Slick here, he's got a likin' for cuttin' off dicks." Slick barks a startled laugh, Dart winks at him, then continues, "You want I should let him castrate you?

Want to get an up-close look at your dick before you go? Perhaps I'll shove it down your throat. Hey, deep throatin' yerself. Could be a new kink."

Throughout Dart's verbal deliberations, Gater's going paler and paler. I'm feeling ill myself.

His Adam's apple works in his throat, and then he screams out, "Poke and Shark, DJ, Crow..." He pauses as if counting them off in his mind. As Dart lifts his leg again he spits out, "Rattler, Tinder, and Bastard. That's all!"

"That's fuckin' all?" Dart swings towards Snake. "Your fuckin' sergeant-at-arms was on board with this?"

"It's near on half the fuckin' club, man."

"Yeah, Mouse. I got that." Dart thinks for a moment. "And how was it gonna go down?"

Gator shakes his head. "I'm just a foot soldier, Brother. I don't know the deets. Only know we were gonna take our chance and take the three of yous out. Then pick the club off one by one as they came lookin' for ya."

CHAPTER 20

Dart

So that was their fucking plan. Yeah, we go missing, and what would Drum have done? Snake would have had him all worried and concerned, and the Tucson prez would have rounded up the troops and sent brothers to help the San D crew search. Then when they disappeared, Drummer would have sent more. Fuck, the club would have been decimated without a clue who their real enemy was. He'd have probably sent Wraith and Peg first, who'd have walked straight into a trap.

"Finish him, Mouse." He's got no more to tell me, and I'm sick of looking at his face. As the gun shot sounds behind me, I focus my attention on Snake, knowing he's living up to his name, a snake in the fucking grass. "Why?" I ask, as I approach him. "For the love of fuckin' God, why?"

Snake shrugs, but keeps his mouth shut.

"Gotta warn, Drum, Brother."

Yeah, we sure have. "Bring him." I turn toward Alex, worried sick she's had to be here and watch this shit going down. "You okay, doll?"

Her arms are wrapped over her chest, and she looks drained. I need to get her somewhere safe, and fuckin' fast. And find out what the hell's happened to her son. As Slick leads Snake out through the warehouse, I go to help Alex, but she shrugs off my hand. Mouse nods at me, then sweeps her up into his strong arms. He must have noticed, like I had, she's dead on her feet and clearly hurting. As well as in shock, a woman like her isn't used to violence and blood.

Emerging into the brilliant sunlight, I see the truck we were brought in, and Snake's bike. Crossing over to it I open his panniers. Hell yeah. I find some zip ties. They'll do. Slick realises my intention and pulls Snake's arms together. While I'm making sure they're tight, I thank fuck Fang and Gator had been such amateurs as to use rope on us. These ties are nigh on impossible to get out of.

Putting my hand into his cut, I pull out a phone then push Snake into the back of the truck. Without being told, Slick sits in the front passenger seat, his body turned toward the back, and the gun still trained on Snake as a threat to make him behave.

"You want to drive and have me bring Alex on the bike?" Mouse asks.

The only one riding up front with Alex behind is going to be me. I shake my head, then wave the phone. "Can't put this off. I'm gonna ring Drum."

As Mouse nods in understanding, I place the call.

"Dart. We got a problem."

"What the fuck, Prez? How...?"

"Jesus Christ! Shit. Really?"

"What's your ETA?"

"One thing you need to know, Prez. Snake..."

"What the fuck you mean you know already?"

"Christ!"

"Mouse, com'ere. You can work this shit. Can you give Prez the co-ordinates of where we are?" As I pass over the phone, Mouse takes charge and is soon handing it back. "Texted him the info."

"What's happenin', Dart?"

I'm still shaking my head in disbelief. Keeping a careful eye on the unwilling passenger in the back, Slick slides out of the truck. I walk towards him, and Mouse follows. "Alex, come 'ere, doll. You'll want to hear this."

"Tyler?" There's a look half of hope, half of despair in her eyes.

"Prez is on his way here. As well as a fuck load of brothers."

Slick looks suspicious. "Snake give him a call?"

"Nope. Not Snake."

Mouse and Slick exchange mystified looks, so I put them out of their misery. I put my arm around Alex and hug her to me, this time not allowing her to pull away. "Tyler. Fuckin' Tyler. Kid somehow sussed there was somethin' wrong. Hid himself and somehow got hold of a phone. Called his aunt, who somehow got him through to Drummer. They've been rollin' for the past few hours. They should be here soon."

"Tyler's okay?"

Now comes the hard part. "He was okay when Drummer spoke to him. Drum told him to stay hidden. He's a smart kid, Alex. I'm sure he'll be fine."

"I want to go to him."

"Just hang on for a bit until the others get here. Prez will have some kind of a plan."

With her arms supporting her sore chest, she pulls away from me and stomps around to the driver's side of the truck.

"Hey!" Mouse has got to her before I can, gently turning her away before she can get inside. "Hang on a minute, babe. Prez will be here shortly, and we'll go get your boy back."

The tears rolling down her face feel like a punch in the gut. I take a few steps that close the distance between us. As I lift my hand to her face, she pulls away. Grasping hold of her chin, I pull her back around, forcing her to look at me. "Listen to me. Alex, I can't tell you how fuckin' impressed I am with your boy. Somehow, fuck knows how, but he got a message to the prez, who's on his way here right this very moment. You heard what

Gator said—as well as Snake—there's at least seven other brothers involved in whatever the fuck this is. Mutiny, takeover. Fuck, I don't even know what to call it. We storm into the club and might get taken out before we can even reach him. Just give us a minute to regroup, yeah? Hear what Drum has to say. He's the prez of the mother chapter for a reason, and you can bet your fuckin' life he's spent every one of those four hundred miles he's been ridin' thinkin' on how to play this."

"I'm scared." Her voice sounds small, lost. The phone call had given her some hope, my delay seeming to take it away again.

I can do nothing but pull her into my chest gently, so as to not cause her pain, and smooth my hands up and down her back. "I promise you, Alex, gettin' Tyler back safe is the top fuckin' priority."

The roar of pipes coming up the road echoes like thunder around the deserted buildings. Fuck me, Drum must have been pushing it, he's made the six-hour drive in just under five. I feel a wave of relief that no one's looking to me any longer, more than happy to take my place back the middle of the pack, glad to be shrugging off the officer role. I'm still holding Alex as they drive up, only letting her go when Drum kicks down his stand.

I walk over to him slowly as he dismounts and puts his shades in his cut. "Brother." At his greeting I smartly step forwards, grasping his hand and pulling him close, exchanging mutual slaps on the back. I doubt I've ever been so pleased to see my prez before. As I move away, Slick takes my place, and then Mouse, as I move down the line, greeting my brothers who've come to our aid.

Blade's taking out his smokes and, without being asked, offers the pack to Slick and myself. Fuck me, that's welcome. I'd lost mine somewhere along the line. I take a long drag, feeling the nicotine going to my head after all the hours of abstinence. Then I turn and see Alex gesticulating at Drum.

He's got his arm around her shoulders, but his eyes are on the man in the truck, and such a cold look comes over him it even makes me shiver.

"Prospect?" Road steps up. "Keep an eye on him, will ya?"

"Sure thing, Prez."

"Rest of you buggers, let's get into the shade. Been a hot, dusty trip." One by one we follow him into the warehouse.

"Gator's dead," I start to explain. "Fang probably is too by now." I lick my dry lips. "Gator gave us the names. Seven of the bastards are in it with Snake."

"Who?"

I tell Prez.

Wraith snarls as Peg spits on the ground. "Fuckin 'disloyal assholes."

Blade stubs out his light on the sole of his boot and throws the dead end away. "How we going to play this, Prez?"

Drum looks at Alex. "Your lad's done good. Hid himself away under yer bed. Got hold of a phone and called his aunt, who called the strip club, who called me. I got back to him and he told me what he knew." He points to me. "When yers were taken, he ran back inside. His first thought to get to the brothers to get help. But he heard his dad's voice, so made himself small. He heard what was said. Snake was tellin' Thompson that you," he breaks off and turns to the woman at his side, "Alex, were as good as dead. That's when he decided to hide. And fuck me, he thought of comin' to the club for help." Again he pauses, gives a short laugh and shakes his head. "Six fuckin' years old and he makes the right call. Gave us a head start even though you've sorted yerselves out."

"And given us the element of surprise." Peg's nodding. "Even if they thought we could have been warned, far as they know we're hours out yet."

Prez is looking directly at me, then looks at Slick and Mouse. "Yer all okay? Not hurt at all?"

"Not even a scratch," I confirm, then ruefully rub at the drying blood on my chin. Well, only a small one.

He dips his chin, then looks back up. "Hate to tell ya, but as you know the club better than us, and the brothers who," he breaks off, looking as pained as I've even seen him, "well, I hope to God there's still some who'll be trustworthy and stand by the club. Yers know them best so you've got a better chance of goin' in and gettin' the kid out."

Like Drummer, I hope there's still some loyalty in the club. I make a suggestion. "Lost doesn't seem like he's part of this. What if we can get him to come out? Meet him somewhere, let him know what's gone down."

"You sure he's clean, Dart?"

I shrug. "Can't be certain, but Gator didn't name him. Can't believe they've all gone bad, Prez. But can't say for a fact Gator wasn't holdin' back."

"Won't know much more until we get Snake to spill, but that could take hours." As I see Alex flinch by Drummer's side, he continues, "If your gut feel is that Lost is good, we'll go with that and get him to meet up." He toys with his beard for a moment. "Keep us being here to the three of you for now. Don't want to alert him we're in town until we know he's okay."

He's right. But he'll be putting Slick and Mouse at risk too. "I'll go in alone." I decide fast.

"Not lettin' ya do that." Slick's first to protest.

Mouse adds his agreement. "We've got yer back, Dart."

"I'll go too. I can help find Tyler…"

"Yer stayin' right here." When Prez fixes his steely gaze upon her, Alex is smart enough to shut her mouth. "Yer hurt, darlin'. Dart knows the boy, and Tyler trusts him. If you go you'll only be holdin' them up."

Visibly reluctant, she bows to the truth. "Dart, please, bring my boy back to me."

I make a promise I hope I can keep. "I will, doll. I will."

"Right. Give Lost a call. Arrange to meet up. Then you three get goin' while I have a chat with Snake here. Alex, I'll get Road to keep you company, you don't need to be here for this."

The shudder she gives shows she knows exactly how the chat's going to go down, and that she's seen far too much of how we do business already today. Seeing she's going to be looked after, I wander off to find some quiet, and place my call to the VP of the Satan's Devils San Diego chapter, then move back.

"Slick, Mouse. Ready to roll?" At their twin nods, I turn to Drum. "We'll have to take the truck."

"Yeah, just let us take the trash out of it first." Peg and Blade step up without being asked.

Once our unwelcome passenger has been removed, I get into the driver's seat, my brothers take their places, and then we're off. It doesn't take long before we're heading into a parking lot about ten minutes away from the club. Lost's sitting on his bike, pulling at his beard. He gets off and comes over as soon as he sees who it is getting out of the truck.

Slick slides the gun he'd taken off Fang out of his cut, and holds it down by his side. Lost's eyes open wide when he notices. Mouse also has a Glock in his hand.

Lost doesn't go for a weapon, a smart move on his part. He approaches with his hands held open. "What's all this Dart? Don't know of any problem between us. And where the fuck have you been? Come to get you out of the safe room and you'd all disappeared."

I give it to him straight. "Snake's defected. Along with Poke, Gator, Shark, DJ, Crow, Rattler, Tinder, and Bastard. Turned on the club, man. You any part of that?"

The expression on his face would be difficult to fake. "What the fuck?"

"Truth, Brother." Slick backs me up. "Gator and Fang kidnapped us, Alex, and Tyler. We managed to get free. Snake turned up, they were obviously actin' under his instructions. Gator dropped the names, with a little persuasion."

"Fuckin' Fang? He that Demon you've been chasin' down?"

"He was." Slick gives an evil grin.

"What the fuck's Snake doin' dealin' with the likes of him?"

"Long story, Brother. One we don't know all the ins and outs of yet. But we'll be questionin' your prez. We got a problem we need some help with." I continue to tell him Tyler's escaped and is hiding somewhere in the clubhouse, and that we need to find him and get him back to his mom.

Lost strokes his long beard again. "Can't believe what you're sayin'." He's still stuck on Snake. Then his expression changes from disbelief to anger. "If what you're tellin' me is true, I've been played like a fuckin' fool. The sergeant-at-arms and the prez? Fuck! Motherfuckers!" For a moment he seems to find the truck fascinating, but then turns back. "Ain't got no problem with the mother chapter myself. I've got your backs, brothers." He pauses to think. "Crow, Rattler, and Bastard aren't in the club. Poke's hangin' about, and I think I saw Shark and DJ too. But Grumbler and Smoker are there as well. I'll give them a call and see if I can't get Shark and DJ out on a job. You need a bit of space to search for the boy."

If Grumbler is straight, he'd be a good man to have on our side.

"Even if there's still question marks over the others, I'd stake my life on Grumbler and Smoker being loyal." After he's answered the question I didn't ask aloud, he breaks off and clears his throat, and I wonder whether he's thinking that just a few minutes earlier he'd have trusted his other brothers too. At last he begins to speak again. "What your drivin' is a club truck, won't be no surprise to anyone it turnin' up. Park around the back and we'll go in the same way as it seems you were taken out. I'll go in and distract any of the other fuckers we've got doubts about if Grumbler doesn't manage to get them all out." He pauses and wipes at his eyes.

I step forward, half to thank him, half to warn him. "Ain't no doubt in my mind, Lost."

"Shit." He looks at me sadly, correctly reading I've every belief in what I'd been told. He then takes out his phone and places a call, not giving details, just asks Grumbler to arrange for Shark and DJ to investigate another reported sighting of Fang up in Escondido. Even though they'll be laughing their heads off, thinking they know exactly where to find the rogue demon, it will get them out of the club. Then that will just leave Poke we'll need to avoid.

That settled, Lost passes out his smokes to give some time for them to get gone.

At last we're able to go get Alex's boy.

Last time I was in the San Diego clubhouse I thought I was surrounded by likeminded brothers who all bought into the same cause as me. This time I feel enveloped in betrayal, a feeling I never expected in any Satan's Devils club. Feeling sick to my stomach as I walk in through the doors, I nod at Lost as he goes to run interference and leaves us to our search.

"Drum said he was hidin' under Alex's bed in the room she was stayin' in. Let's get there first."

We make our way up the stairs, weapons drawn, not knowing what we'll be walking into. I'm hoping I don't have a need to fire on any man that, up to now, I've happily called a brother.

There's no one around as we reach Alex's room. Hardly daring to breath, I fold to my knees, then lie on my side to look under the bed. There's no one there. *Fuck! Have they found him? Where could he be?* For a second I envisage returning to Alex without her son in tow, and then realise there's no way I can return without him.

As I jump to my feet, shaking my head, my expression showing how gutted I am, an unwelcome voice intrudes.

"Dart! You're back. Come with me."

Narrowing my eyes at Eva, I give a short laugh and shake my head. "Not hangin' with you darlin'. Been there, done that. Caused enough fuckin' aggro."

She looks taken aback. "No, no. I'm not suggesting we fuck." She pauses to toss her hair back over her shoulder. "You weren't that special, Dart." She looks at Slick and Mouse, and then lowers her voice and adds conspiratorially, "It's the kid. He's in my room."

What? Stepping forward I put my hands on her shoulders, my fingers biting into her skin. "What you talkin' about? Why's he with you?"

"I'm not stupid, Dart. Alex and Tyler went downstairs and didn't come back. Found Tyler under her bed. He was shaking and crying, obviously scared. He thought Snake was coming for him. If that was true, this room would be the first place he'd have looked. Not so much mine. So I took him to be safe. Gave him my phone to use when he asked. "She studies our faces for a moment. "I don't like Snake. And lately he's been acting real strange." And with that she shows she's more perceptive than some of the brothers here.

If it wouldn't cause yet more problems with Alex, I'd kiss her. Instead, I resort to thanking her profusely. Just as I'm turning my thoughts to how to sneak Tyler out of the clubhouse, she puts her hand on my arm.

"Alex needs to know. He had an episode, probably brought on by being so scared. I got him through it okay, but I don't know if she's keeping track of them."

I wipe my hand over my eyes. Poor kid. And thank fuck it was Eva who found him. Being a nurse, she'd have known what to do. "I'll tell Alex. And, Eva..."

"It's alright, Dart. I'm just glad I was there and able to help."

Footsteps sound on the landing outside. Mouse glances quickly around the door and gives the all clear just as Lost appears. "Found the kid?" When I nod he continues, "Poke's with a club girl. Knowin' him, he'll take his time. Grumbler got rid of the other two. I'll keep an eye out if you want to sneak the kid out the back."

"I'll get him." Eva's not asking questions. That, and the fact she looked out for him makes her go up in my estimation.

Lost is looking tired, and older than I've seen him. "You'll keep me informed, Dart?"

"Prez will want to speak to ya." I don't need to clarify it will be our prez not his. He's unlikely to ever see Snake again. "Lost. Club will need its VP when this all gets out."

"That's what I'm afraid of," he mumbles.

"Keep our route free, then you and Grumbler better come with us. Drummer's on his way." I don't explain he's ready and waiting.

Lost nods at me sadly.

"Dart!" Tyler runs in and hugs my legs. Without thinking I swing him up into my arms, knowing I'm almost as pleased as Alex is going to be to find him safe and unharmed. The brave kid clings to me as we start to make our way out. We meet Grumbler guarding the foot of the stairs. He gives me a sharp look as I pass, doubts that anything could be amiss in his club written in his eyes, but also a promise of retribution for those he finds that have done wrong.

The return journey to the warehouse is uneventful, and I stand to the side watching as Alex has a tearful reunion with her son.

As she gazes adoringly at Tyler, refusing to let him go, I wish she'd have even one tenth of that emotion in her eyes when she looks at me.

CHAPTER 21

Alex

I've already seen how they question men who've gone against them, so when Road leads me away, I'm more than happy I won't have to watch what they do to Snake. I'm still stunned that he's turned against his own club, but what do I know about the dynamics of an MC? Perhaps it's not so unusual for them.

"Here, darlin'. Take a load off and sit before you fall down. You've been through a lot today."

Yeah, a lot over the past few days. Kidnapped twice in a week must be a record for anyone. I've been hurt and left for dead, threatened with rape, and lost my son for a second time. It all catches up with me, and before I know it I'm bent double as I sob. Each indrawn breath pulling at my newly healing scars. A strong arm comes around me and gently draws me into a leather clad chest.

"I got ya, darlin'. Just let it all out. Dart will find yer boy for ya." He pauses and rubs his hand up and down my back. "Soon this will be over, you'll come home to Tucson, and be back at the Satan's Topless Angels before you know it."

Wiping my tears away with the back of my hand, I turn to him incredulously and scoff. "Well that's not going to happen."

"Why not? The customers are missing you."

It's then I realise that as he's just a prospect he probably doesn't know. It almost hurts as much to explain as it did when I received the wounds, but it's not something I can hide. "Ron, my ex, well, he cut me up, Road. There's no way anyone will ever want to see my body again. He's scarred me for life."

Road looks shocked. He lets me go and paces away. By the rigid set of his shoulders, it looks like he's trying to get himself under control. I don't bother watching him, I've already accepted I've got no job and no way of earning money to put aside for Tyler's treatment. And if I'm no longer an employee, will the club still want to offer me help? I'm nothing to them now, just a damaged woman. And I've lost any connection to Dart.

Lost in my thoughts, I don't realise Road's come back until he clears his throat. When I look up it's to see this huge man standing in front of me, studying me closely. Then he sinks to his heels. "You've got blood on yer top."

Glancing down I see that he's right. "I think my stitches have pulled open."

"Can I see?"

As I nod, he carefully lifts up my tee. Looking down I see blood seeping through the dressings.

"Don't want to touch this, but fuck that must hurt. We'll get someone to look at this as soon as we can. Hold on a minute." He goes to his bike and gets something out of one of his saddle bags. When he comes back he's holding out a bottle of water and a couple of tablets. "Here. They're Tramadol." As I raise my eyes he says, "I've got them from when I last came off my bike."

I've taken them before, the first time Ron had hurt me, so thanking him I swallow them down with the water, hoping they'll soon take effect. Simply to pass the time I ask, "Last time? Do you make a habit of falling off?"

He grins. "I race trial bikes. Comes with the territory to take a few spills."

There's a short period of silence, then I can't help myself asking, "How long do you think before Dart is back?"

"It's hard to say. He's meeting with Lost, the VP first. Depends on how that goes."

I presume he means if he's turned traitor too. And if he is, how will Dart know? What if he makes the wrong call? Now I'm worrying about him as well as my son. Road can't give me the answers I want. Slowly the Tramadol starts to take effect. Tired with the stress of the last few hours combined with the pain having drained my strength from me, despite my worry, I close my eyes and doze off, only to be woken by the sound of bikes and the truck entering the parking lot. Woken with a start, I pull myself straight and gaze across, hardly daring to breathe.

The doors open, and oh my God! There's Tyler! Dart's spotted where I am, and has pointed me out. Tyler comes running over and throws himself into my arms. I don't want to let him go, but as I hold him so tightly I can't smother my gasp of pain. Dart's there and pulling him off gently.

"Careful, young man. Yer momma's still hurt, remember?"

This time he's more careful. Tears are once again running down my face, but this time they're happy ones, not sad.

Dart looks at Road. "Drummer inside?"

"Yeah. I'll stay with Alex and the boy if you're going to join them."

"Thanks, Brother." Dart runs his hand over my hair, gives my shoulder a squeeze, then disappears with Slick and Mouse, and two other men who've turned up on bikes.

I've got my son in my arms and that's all I need. Tyler's updating me on what he'd done, and I'm so proud of my boy and how he summoned help. I get a blast of envy when he tells me it was Eva who looked after him and lent him the phone, but if I ever see her again, know I'll have to bury my jealousy and thank her. Tyler's exhausted, and after talking himself out, drifts off in my arms in the warmth of the sun. I'm content to just sit here and hold him.

Sometime later men wander out of the warehouse. They're not particularly quiet, so I can hear every word that they say.

"We'll take him back to Tucson. Deal with him there. Want the presidents from our other chapters in on this to see what happens when one of our own fuckin' turns on us."

"Still can't believe this shit."

"Should have expected somethin' when he dumped that cocky fucker Buster on us. Reckon he was placed as a spy."

"What about Marvel? I like the man, but…"

"Yeah, Wraith. Hate to say it, but we need to be suspicious about any fucker who comes from this chapter."

A man coughs.

"Yeah, Lost, Grumbler. I reckon you're straight. Not that I have much trust in the fucker, but Snake confirmed you weren't a part of what was goin' on."

"Here's Snake's phone."

"Thanks, Dart. Right. I'll send them all a text, get them here. We deal with them once and for all, then get Snake—fuckin' lived up to his name, hasn't he?—back home. We'll take Poke along too. He being another officer, he deserves more than a bullet to the head."

"What about her?"

My ears prick up even more as I assume they're talking about me. I am the only female here after all.

"I'll come and talk to her."

As footsteps approach, I turn my face and try to pretend I hadn't been listening at all.

"Alex." Drummer raises his chin in greeting. I nod back. He lifts his leg and plants it on a crate and then leans forwards with his hands clasped over his knee. "Fuck, Alex, I'm so sorry you got dragged into our business. Specially after what happened to you."

There's no point in me ranting and raving about what can't be undone. At least I'm alive and haven't been raped, and Tyler's unharmed. I sigh, unable to bear any animosity. If it wasn't for them, I wouldn't be breathing. "It's all good, Drummer. Scary while it was goin' on. But it's behind me now. And I owe you a debt. It was your club who rescued me from the cabin."

His eyes seem to narrow as I remind him. He glances down to my bloodstained t-shirt. "How you feelin', darlin'?"

"A bit sore. Better after the painkillers Road gave me."

"I'm going to be sendin' you and Tyler back to Tucson. You'll be stayin' on the compound for a while, where you'll be safe."

Now it's my turn to frown as I brush back the hair on my son's now wide-awake face. "Tyler's got school. And after the past few days, getting back to normality would do him good."

But Drummer shakes his head. "Too easy for Thompson to try to take you again. Both you and he need to stay somewhere secure. Can you tell the school he's unwell or somethin'?"

"You really think Ron will try again?"

"Thompson was with the cops in the club. He's lookin' for the boy." Drum rolls back his head and then fixes his stare on me again. "Apparently Fang fucked up by takin' the boy. He should have left him locked up in the panic room for Snake to find and hand him over to his dad." His eyes grow cold. "We'll be sortin' yer problems out on a permanent basis. But you need to give us a while to get somethin' arranged."

I don't want to know what they're intending to do, but expect the worst. I can't bring myself to care. Ron left me for dead, I've no difficulty with anything they plan. And if it's only for a short time, Tyler can stay off school. It's the thought of Ron getting his hands on him which fills me with dread. "Okay, we'll stay on the compound."

"Good." I watch as he smooths his hand over his beard. "Before you go, there's a favour we want to ask of you."

I cock my head to one side in question, unsure of what I can do for them.

"Mouse's fingerprints were found at your old house. There's an APB out for him in connection with your disappearance."

Oh no. They'd been trying to find me, and Mouse has got into trouble because of it. I can't allow that. I'm sore, hurting, and really have had more than one woman should have to take. But I pull my shoulders back straight, they returned my son to me, unharmed. If there's anything to help, I must do it. "Drum, what can I do?"

He nods in approval at my quick offer to help. "You and Mouse go to a police station. The story will be you and he met in Tucson and got together. You came back to get some of your clothes."

My face falls. "The place was smashed up. All my clothes cut to pieces. That story won't fly."

He's quiet for a moment, thinking. "Just tell the truth. The house was like that when you arrived. As it had been vandalised, you moved on. You decided to stay a couple of days in the city to show your new boyfriend the sights. Mouse is makin' sure you, he, and the boy have been booked in to the Holiday Inn for a few nights. He's workin' on that now."

How can he do that? Leaving it aside, I wonder aloud, "Should I suggest Ron trashed the house?"

"I wouldn't go there unless you are pressed. Thompson's a cop, his colleagues will have his back. Don't make accusations with nothin' to back it up. You're just reportin' in to let them know you've not been kidnapped or harmed by Mouse. Put him in the clear. We've enough to watch out for over our shoulders, don't want that on us too."

I look down at my bloody t-shirt, and Drum follows the path of my eyes. "Road?" As the prospect jumps to attention, he continues, "Go buy a new top for Alex, will you?"

Open mouthed, I watch the prospect run over to his bike. He hasn't even asked my size.

"What about Tyler?"

"Take him with you. Hey, kid. You think you can pretend Mouse is yer Mom's boyfriend?"

Tyler looks at him, then at me. At my nod of encouragement, he grins. "Sure can, sir."

"Good lad," Drum praises, and Tyler gives him a chin lift. Then the prez looks at me again, his steely eyes softening. "We're sortin' out your attire, but what about your pain? You mustn't give away yer hurtin'. Think you can hide it?"

"If I have another of Road's Tramadol I'll be able to." I'll have to. These men stopped at nothing to find me and rescue me. If it wasn't for them I wouldn't be here today.

"The records show you've been listed as missin'. Strangely, Tyler has not—I'm presuming Thompson altered any record made of your sister's report. Snake was gonna give him to Thompson. When Snake assumed Fang and Gator had taken him, he told Thompson he'd be getting' him soon."

I shiver. Going back to Tucson under the protection of the Satan's Devils does seem the safest option. Being a cop, Ron's got too much power.

It doesn't seem long before Road's back. He's bought me a couple of plain tees in two different sizes. The first one's a bit small and shows the outline of my bandages, but the other is fine, and I grin as he smiles shyly and hands me something else. I nod my permission for him to give it to Tyler.

Drum's been speaking to Mouse, who comes over with some keys in his hand. "Ready to go clear my name?" Without waiting for me to reply, he holds out his hand. Once I've been helped gently onto my feet he leads me slowly over to the truck. He programs in an address, then turns to speak to Tyler, but laughs when he sees what's in his hands.

"Where the f… hell did he get that?"

Grinning to show my appreciation that he stopped himself from swearing, I give him the answer. "Road." I carefully twist to see the toy motorbike being lovingly examined in Tyler's hands. He's got a rapt expression on his face. I don't know much about bikes, but even I can see it's a Harley.

Mouse shakes his head, laughs again, and then we're off.

"I'm sorry," I tell him as we're driving down the street. "I didn't mean for any of you to get in trouble over me."

"Ain't yer fault. And no matter. Hopefully it will be simple to get this cleared up." He looks behind him as he speaks, flicks the indicator, and switches lanes. It doesn't take long before we arrive at a station house I've not been to before, and I breathe a sigh of relief. I'd been worried we'd go to the one Ron's based out of. Mouse finds a space and parks.

Noticing my look of concern, he gives my hand a reassuring squeeze. "Shouldn't take long, darlin'. Just a quick in and out."

As we enter the building, I'm unable to shake the feeling I'm putting my head into the lion's den. But I've promised I'll do this. He keeps hold of my hand as we walk inside, with Tyler alongside still holding his new toy. As we approach the front desk, Mouse pulls me closer and plants a kiss on the top of my head.

"What can I do for you?" the desk sergeant says in a bored voice.

"My name's Tse Williamson," Mouse begins. "Heard you're lookin' for me."

The policeman consults his computer, and his boredom rapidly seeps away. "Mr Williamson, please come with me."

Mouse makes no move to follow him. "I'd like to know what all this is about. My girlfriend, her son, and I have been spendin' a few days in San Diego. I have no idea why you want to speak to me."

"If you'll come this way, a detective will be with you shortly. And you ma'am, you can wait here."

I don't want to be separated. As I'm opening my mouth to speak, Mouse gets in first.

"Unless you're arrestin' me, we stay together," he states.

The cop looks confused. "And you are?" he asks me directly, and closely examines Tyler.

"Alexandra Thompson." I reply, as steadily as I can.

He consults his computer again, and his eyes open wide. "But you're missing!"

Mouse looks down at me and smiles. "Don't think you are, are you babe?"

Getting up from his desk, calling one of his colleagues to make sure we don't leave, the cop disappears. Quickly he returns, followed by a detective.

"Mr Williamson and Mrs Thompson, would you come this way please? We've a couple of questions to ask you."

"Is this going to take much time? We've got things planned."

The detective seems flummoxed. "No, er. It depends. Please, follow me."

We do as he asks and are shown into a plain interview room with seats on either side of the desk. Having seated ourselves, Mouse squeezes my hand again, and it's only then I notice his look of concern and his brief glance down to the wounds on my chest. I press my fingers to his to show that for now I'm doing okay, the Tramodol's doing its job. Tyler's over in the corner, tracing the chrome on his bike. Then he gives me a cheeky look and runs across to Mouse.

"Mouse, look at this." Mouse puts his arm around him and makes appreciative sounds as Tyler shows him the detail on the toy bike. I'm full of pride for my son.

The man with us coughs to get our attention. "I'm Detective Parker," he says, introducing himself.

As Mouse pats Tyler's arm and tells him to go play, I ask, remembering to use his proper name. "Why do you want to speak to Tse?"

"Well, Mrs Thompson, you've been listed as a missing person, and we've been following up leads. Mr Williamson's fingerprints were found at your residence, and at a cabin that belongs to your parents."

"Well, that's no surprise," I state, as if the answer is obvious.

The detective leans back in his chair. "Would you like to tell me what your relationship is?"

"Not that it's any of your business," Mouse speaks for me, "but Mrs Thompson, Alex, is my girlfriend. We got together in Tucson, where Alex moved to after she parted ways with her husband."

"And you're in San Diego, why?"

At Mouse's nod, I pick up the agreed story. "I wanted to collect some more clothes from my house. But when we got there, it had been vandalised. My parents had said I could use the cabin anytime, so we decided to go there for a couple of days."

"You know how it is," Mouse breaks in, raising my hand to his lips and kissing it. "New lovers and that. We wanted some time to ourselves, and for me to get to know her son. Then Alex wanted to show me her home town, so we came back to town and have been stayin' at the Holiday Inn for the past few days."

"Room number?"

Mouse gives it while I wonder what magic he's done.

Having written everything down, Parker leans forward. "Mrs Thompson. Your husband has listed you as a missing person."

I try my best to look surprised. "I don't know why he would have done that. We've been separated for months."

"Hmm. We're trying to contact your husband. I know he'll want to see for himself that you're okay."

Mouse sits forward, but I push him back. "Detective. I have absolutely no wish to speak to my *ex*-husband. Anything he wants to say to me can go through our lawyers. Now that you've met Mr Williamson and understand our relationship, and that which I no longer have with Ron Thompson, I presume we can leave?" Mentally I'm crossing my fingers. There's no way I want to be confronted by my ex.

"Can I offer you a coffee?"

And keep us waiting until Ron turns up?

"No." Mouse takes over. "Unless you've somethin' you want to charge me with, I presume we're free to leave."

"Going back to the Holiday Inn?"

Mouse shakes his head. "No, we're heading back to Tucson later today."

He doesn't like that. "And your address there?"

I give Celine's address. Ron already knows that.

Mouse nods at Parker. "Now, if you've got nothin' else, come on darlin', you wanted to show me Coronado before we get going."

I force myself to put an eager smile on my face. "I did, didn't I? Detective, Tse is never going to believe how close the planes fly to the buildings, and Tyler always loves watching them land. It's a great view from there, isn't it?"

Mouse stands up and offers me his hand. I lean on it a little too hard to help me to my feet, but all the time I keep smiling. The detective's frowning, he doesn't want us to leave. But his hands are tied. There's no reason to stop us.

"One last thing, Detective. You'll get that APB cancelled? We've explained my fingerprints, and you can see Alex is fine, and so's her son. Wouldn't want to be stopped and have the end of our vacation spoiled."

"Er, yes. Of course."

Mouse leads me out of the room, looking around to check Tyler's following, then out of the station house and helps us into the truck. I don't think either of us breathe easily until we're on the move again.

And then we look at each other and burst out laughing. I don't know about Mouse, but I'm envisioning Ron's confusion. After having left me for dead, I've just spoken to one of his colleagues alive and appearing completely unharmed. My wounds might still be hurting, the panic and fear not forgotten, but the thought of the look on Ron's face? That has me smiling.

CHAPTER 22

Dart

I'm driving an SUV Lost managed to find for me, Mouse is in the passenger seat, and Alex and Tyler are in the back. Glancing in the rearview mirror, it kills me to see pain etched on her face. I've already given Doc our ETA and asked him to be ready at the club to change her dressings and check none of the stitches have been pulled out. She's had a terrible few days, being put through emotional and physical hell. Currently she's twitching in a fitful sleep, but Tyler's happily amusing himself, playing on a tablet which Mouse had stopped off to buy for him, his new motorbike close at hand by his side. I only hope my brother's view of what's a suitable game for a six-year-old is the same as Alex's. He's enjoying it though, and it's keeping him quiet. Kid deserves a little spoiling after what he's been through.

Drum sent Mouse and I back with Alex, and Slick's staying on to help sort out the rogue chapter. I'd offered to stay and help, but he thought Alex would feel easier if I was with her back home. I'm yet to be convinced on whether he's made the right call, unsure that there'll ever be a way back from my stupid mistake. Staying behind dealing with traitors would probably be easier than making things right between us. Why is it you only realise you want something so badly when the chance has been taken away?

Even while I'm wondering there's any chance I can rescue my relationship with Alex, particularly now Thompson's giving her even less reason to trust a man, I can't help but think about what's going on at the warehouse we just left, suspecting there's going to be one hell of a showdown. Both loyal and disloyal San Diego club members will be shortly be receiving a text summons, supposedly from Snake, to gather them all together. Drum's not relying on Gator's info about just who was involved in the coup and who's not. His plan is to confront them all and watch who takes which side.

We might still have doubts about who, but we'd got to the bottom of why when we started questioning Snake. While Satan's Devils still run a few guns, nowadays we get most money coming in legit. What we don't deal in is drugs. Seen too many clubs go sideways when their members start sampling the product. Snake thought it was a sign of the mother chapter's weakness to insist on staying out of that trade. When he'd realised his game was up, he tried to tempt us with talk of the money he thought he'd be bringing in.

Out of the corner of my eye I see Mouse glancing over his shoulder. When he sees Alex is sleeping and Tyler otherwise engaged, he starts to speak. "I'll feel easier once we've crossed the border into Arizona. I've a twitchin' feelin' between my shoulder blades that Thompson's gonna be comin' after us."

"Yeah, the sooner she and the boy are on the compound, the happier I'll fuckin' be." Automatically I check in the rear mirror that there isn't a cop car approaching with lights flashing. Then, bringing my eyes back front, I concentrate on the road for a moment, overtake a slow-moving truck, and then continue. "Spoke to Drum about takin' Thompson out. However much I want to tear him to pieces with my bare hands, Prez is concerned about blowback on the club." I hate it, but Drummer's right. "Can't just disappear the motherfucker, Mouse, not with you on the cop's radar already."

"I overheard. Looks like he'll be havin' a nasty accident soon."

"Wish I could make him suffer for what he did." I bang my fist on the steering wheel. "Fucker mutilated her, scarred her. A clean death's too easy after what he made Alex go through."

"Dead's dead, Brother. Dead's dead."

"Yeah, I suppose." I don't like it, but can see Drummer's point. The sooner that motherfucker stops breathing air, the better I'll like it. "Fuck knows how we'll do it. I'd have left it to the San Diego boys if we knew who we could fuckin' trust."

"You thinkin' of goin' back down there yourself, Dart?"

"Don't know what the fuck is gonna happen, Brother. Just know all this shit goin' on doesn't rest easy with me. Snake! Who'd have fuckin' thought it?"

Mouse sighs and tries to stretch out his long legs. "Think he thought the mother chapter was weak, as we've called on his help a few times."

"Only because we were up against somethin' bigger than us. Fuck, man, Tucson weak? Not with Drum at the helm. Never in a million fuckin' years." And fuck anyone who thinks it.

We drive on another couple of miles, and then Mouse voices his thoughts again. "You reckon Lost will take the prez's patch?"

"Who else is there? Unless Drum's thinking of winding up the whole fuckin' chapter. It's so rotten, that could be in the cards."

"Didn't like leavin' our bikes there."

I grimace. "With you there, Brother. Drum's promised to get a prospect to drive them back." Again I signal and move out when it's clear.

The checkpoint comes up, and we go through without hassle. Once we're through, Mouse and I bump fists. I swear the Arizonian air smells different. I can physically breathe easier, and when I catch my first glimpse of a saguaro, I feel like I'm home.

It's full darkness by the time we arrive at the club. Jekyll's on the gate and slides it open. As most of our members are in Cali right now, the clubhouse seems quiet. Alex has slept most of the way, and Tyler had abandoned his game at some point and also nodded off. Now I wake them up.

Alex blinks her bleary eyes and looks around.

"Come, Slick's given me the key to his suite—he and Ella have rented a place in town while they look for somewhere to buy, and rarely use it now." I grin for a moment. Slick wanted to put some distance between Jayden and Paladin, but there's no need for Alex to know that. "The suite next to his is empty—it used to be Wraith's but he's living with Sophie. We'll get you settled in Wraith's and I'll stay in Slick's so I can be close by." Unless I get pulled back to San D of course. As she looks at me in confusion, I realise she's only been to the clubhouse before and hasn't seen any of our accommodations except a brief view from the outside, so it must sound like I'm talking gibberish. It's easier to just show her. "This way," I encourage. Tyler's awake, but only just. It feels natural to sweep him up into my arms. "Come on, little man. Let's get you to bed."

Alex follows me up the compound, her eyes open wide as she realises this is nothing like where she'd been staying at in California. No, nothing can match the standard of our housing. Blocs sitting side by side, two suites in each. We're the envy of a lot of biker clubs having this old vacation resort as our home. There are crash, or fuck rooms in the main clubhouse, but each Tucson brother has a suite of his own, most with amazing views of the desert basin and up over to the Tucson mountains opposite.

We come to the bloc containing Slick and Wraith's now redundant suites. The key to Wraith's is in the door. Turning it, I let her inside, then take it out of the lock and hand it to her. She takes it absentmindedly without looking, far too interested in examining the large space, noting the bed, closet, desk, and comfortable chairs, and then spies the adjacent bathroom. Her eyes widen when she sees the balcony and the view.

She touches my arm. "This is more than I expected, Dart."

I nod towards the bed. "The old ladies have made sure you've got clean linen. Tomorrow I'll get a prospect to go to your sister's house and pick up some clothes for you and Tyler."

"Can I give him a list? Tyler will need some of his toys."

"Looks like he'll be taking a truck." I grin, and then my smile fades. The way she's holding herself looks like she's in pain. "I'll go chase up Doc. He's probably here by now."

"Thank you. And I'll get him into bed."

The 'him' she's speaking about has his legs around my waist and his head on my shoulder. He's already falling back to sleep. She pulls back the covers and slips Tyler inside, then I leave her as she starts to get him undressed.

As I thought, Doc's already here. He's not a fully qualified doctor like Snake had on call, but his Army medic experience and my warning of what to expect means he's come prepared with a bag of medical supplies. After I take him up to Wraith's suite, I suggest he examines her in Slick's. I don't want Tyler waking and seeing what that bastard of a father of his had done to his mom. Then I leave them alone and go to my own room, collecting some of my clothes and essentials for the next day. By the time I return, Doc's got Alex's dressings changed.

"How's she lookin'?" I ask.

"Stitches were pulled, but didn't need to be redone. Healin' looks like it's goin' well otherwise. I've left some antibiotics just to be sure." Doc's eyes meet mine. He looks furious, but minds his tongue in front of Alex. He packs up his bag and walks to the door, inclining his head to show he wants me to accompany him. At the doorway he says softly, "Tell me the fucker's dead."

"Not yet. But he soon will be."

My answer seems to satisfy him. With a lift of his chin he walks off down the track.

Alex looks done in, despite her long sleep on the journey. She's sitting on the bed that tonight will be mine and popping a pill that Doc must have left. Damn it. She looks so right, right there. All I want to do is to hold her tonight, keep her close, know that she's safe. How stupid I was to keep finding reasons why I should keep my distance. And how beyond crazy I was to go with Eva to try to prove the non-sensical point that I didn't want her. That didn't work, and I lost the woman I do want in the process.

As I stare at her, I run my hands through my hair, pulling it loose from my bun, not missing the way her eyes sharpen with interest. *Have I still got a chance?* Fuck it, if I have, I'm not going to pass up on it.

Seeing my eyes fixed upon hers, she turns away a little awkwardly, and starts to get up.

"No, don't go. Stay for a moment." I've startled her. As she doesn't seem to know what to say, I give her more. "Alex, look, I fucked things up, okay?"

I go to her and sit close, taking one of her hands. "Shush, look, please. Let me talk? This last day we've both been through hell, a hundred times worse for you after your bastard ex did to you, I know, but today, the thought of Fang or Gator touchin' you made me realise I don't want any fucker like that to get their hands on you. Hell, that's wrong. I don't even want any of my brothers near ya, and that's been the truth since the first day you danced at the club. It's just not somethin' I've ever felt before, and doll, I swear I don't know what to do with these feelin's." I glance up, checking she's listening. She is. Intently. "I'd be wrong right here and now to promise you a forever, it's too soon, for both of us I would think. But I do think there's somethin' between us, and I want a chance to explore where it might go." I try to lay it all out on the line, hardly daring to hope my heartfelt words might have any success.

She's quiet for a moment, then wrenches her hand out of my grasp. "It's too little too late, Dart. If you'd asked me before, there's nothing I would have wanted more than to start dating you. I'm attracted to you, but I need a man I can trust." She breaks off and waves her hand in the rough direction of the club house. "There are club girls here too, aren't there? And you've probably fucked them all."

I can't deny that I have. My silence gives her the answer.

"Look, Dart, I'm all worn out. I don't want to talk anymore tonight."

I admit she looks tired, and mentally exhausted. Now I might be a bastard, but after cocking everything up, maybe my best chance is to strike while her barriers are down and she's got no fight left in her. "Doll, I won't fuck any whores while we're together. And that's not what I want to do with you."

I've caught her attention. Her forehead creases and worry lines appear as she asks, "What do you mean, you don't want to fuck me? Huh, I suppose it's because Ron fucked me up."

I rear back. "It's nothin' to do with your scars. And that's not what I meant, doll." I run my hands through my hair as I dig for the right words, then lean forwards and clasp my hands between my knees. "I've kissed you, darlin'. Never do that with whores. In fact, I can't remember the last time I actually kissed a girl. Probably not since I joined the club. Easy pussy is just that, babe. Easy. There to get some relief."

"Eva seemed satisfied."

I should have expected I've not heard the last of that. I give a half smile. "Hope she was, darlin'. I'm not a bastard that just takes." Undoing my hands, I risk touching her face, and fuck me if she doesn't lean into my hand. Ignoring that she's probably too tired to hold her own head up, at this point I'll take whatever she'll let me have. "This isn't what I do with the whores, darlin'. I don't hang around talkin' like this. Before I just want to get in there. Once I'm done, I'm finished and out. I've never held a woman and discussed feelin's and the like."

She turns and looks into my eyes. "Is that what we're doing here?" She pauses and bites her lip, then continues in a tentative voice as though she's almost afraid to ask. "What are these feelings, Dart?"

"Fuck me, doll. I can't explain them. But I tell ya, I'm feelin' things I've never felt before." I shake my head as I think how to describe it. "I don't give a damn who's in Eva's bed now or who was in there before." Now my smile becomes complete. "I'd know I'd want to kill any other man who was in yours."

Now I raise my other hand so I'm cupping her face between both palms. "I don't kiss bitches—women—doll. You must be a witch, babe. Every time I've had your lips you entrance me. You scare me so much, I vowed to keep away."

"We've only kissed twice."

"Somthin' we can rectify straight away, doll."

And fuck me, she nods. Encouraging her face up, I lean down. Her lips are as soft as I remember, and immediately I'm lost. When she opens her mouth and grants me entrance, my tongue sweeps inside, and that taste goes straight to my groin. I force myself to think of her injuries, and before I act on my desire to take this further, pull away, then lean my forehead against hers.

She's quiet, and once again those teeth are worrying at her lip. After a few seconds she says, "Dart. You've caught me with my defences down. I must be out of my mind." She's going to give me a chance. I feel like jumping out and shouting, but force myself to stay in place and listen to what else she has to say. "How do we do this? What do you want from me, Dart? I want to understand what you're asking. I can't...not yet."

And I wouldn't push her until she's healed. "Babe, the last few days have been hell for me as well as you. When you disappeared I was frantic. When I found you injured so badly I didn't know how to cope. And today, fuck, I wasn't scared for myself, but for you and Tyler. I want, no *need* you close. Just give me this, doll. Stay with me tonight. I know yer hurtin', so I'm not proposing anything other than keeping each other company." If I can get her to sleep in my bed it will at least give us a good place to start.

"Tyler."

Oh yeah, I knew she was going to come up with that. "He's asleep, darlin'. And we'll keep the door open and hear him if he stirs. You sleep beside him and he might roll on you and hurt ya."

"What's stopping you from rolling on me?"

I smirk. "I can keep my hands to myself as long as you can."

She forms a fist and punches my arm, but her lips have curved up. It looks like she's decided to stay.

Not wanting to give her time to rethink it, I move to the practicalities. "Come on, let's get you settled." I rummage in the pile of clothes I brought up with me from my room. "Wear one of my shirts." And my cock twitches at the thought of her wearing something of mine.

She hesitates, and then gives in, but the truth is she's so worn out she's too tired to protest, but right now I'll be a bastard and take anything I can. She gets up, takes the shirt, and goes into the bathroom. As she walks, hunched over like an old woman, I bite back a curse, and promise that now she's under my protection on my home ground, no one's ever getting near enough to harm her again. While she's gone I strip down to boxers and pull back the sheet. I'm just about to slide inside when there's a knock at the door. I open it to find Allie standing there.

"Hey, Dart. You're a hard man to find. Heard you were back but you weren't in your suite. Had to get Mouse to tell me where you were."

"Allie…"

Her hand comes out and touches my bare chest and her fingers do a dance against my skin. "Thought you and me could get together, hmm? I've been dreaming about sucking your cock. Mmm mmm. Doubt those Cali whores could satisfy you the way I can, let me in and I'll show you just how."

My cock isn't up for any such action, not from her or any of the sweet butts. The woman I want is currently getting dressed in my shirt in the next room. Fuck it! When the thought of Alex so close by and naked lodges in my head, my cock starts to stir.

Pointedly Allie looks down at my tenting boxers, and then up at my face. She smirks. "Feelin' it, aren't ya? You want me to get Paige and Diva along too? Or Pussy, and Jill? See who's available?"

The thought of the three overused whores going down on me helps me get my unruly cock under control. Before I met Alex, I'd have happily done one, two, or three of them, singly or all together at once, but now the thought turns me right off. As her hand on my chest starts to move lower, I grab it and stop her wandering fingers before they reach their target.

"No, Allie. Not tonight. Not ever." Shit, I'm burning my boats here, hearing words coming out of my mouth I never dreamt I'd be saying.

Her eyes flit to mine, and her mouth purses. "You aren't steppin' into the old lady trap, are ya? Not you as well. You're not the type, Dart."

I'm not. But if I was, a woman as brave as Alex is exactly what I'd be looking for. Someone so strong and so selfless. Unfortunately I'm still holding Allie's hand to prevent it exploring, when her eyes widen as she sees something behind me.

Oh fuck. I drop her hand fast. "Get out of here, Allie. And tell the other girls I don't want or need anything from them."

"You're with…*that?*" Allie's look of contempt is more than I can take. "Club wouldn't allow it, Dart. She's black, and she works for us."

And then suddenly there's a comforting hand on my back. "I don't work for the club anymore," Alex starts, but gives no explanation. "But yeah, he's mine. So back off." Then almost without a break she adds in a sultry voice, "You coming to bed now, Dart?"

I want to laugh. Want to fist pump the air. Apart from the whores who might fight about who gets my cock, no woman's ever been possessive about me before. Her declaration of ownership shows we're in a fucking good place to begin to explore this strange attraction between us.

Allie knows when to give up. With a huff, she makes an about turn and leaves. I swing around, my arms rising to take my woman in my arms…

"Don't get any ideas, Dart. I could have gone to my room and let you get on with it, but I didn't want to hear screams of ecstasy from in here all night."

Now my hands do land on her biceps as I can't help but chuckle. "Screams of ecstasy, eh? At least you know what to expect, sweetheart."

That wasn't what she meant at all, and her eyes narrow to let me know it. Doesn't stop me none though. "When your healed, I'll be happy to give you a demonstration."

She blushes, and then frowns. "Dart, I'm tired. I can't do this tonight. I've got no fight left in me."

"Don't want to fight you, Doll." Letting go of her arms, I wipe my hands down my face. "I know I've got a long way to go to get you to trust me again. All you've got to decide is if you want to start on that journey. I didn't ask Allie to come to me, and I sent her away. I'll *always* send her and any club whore away."

She's quiet, thoughtful. And then her tired shoulders slump. "I'm just staying in the same bed, Dart."

"I know."

Letting go of her arms, I put my hand to her back and give her a little push toward the bed, noticing, with a smile, that my shirt comes down to her knees. Touching her through the material I can feel her breathing has quickened, showing she's not immune to me at all, and the thought of me showing her just how loud I could make her scream makes my cock rock hard, despite knowing that her injuries make it impossible for now.

She pauses before getting onto the bed, but doesn't turn to look at me. "Did you mean it, Dart? You won't go with the whores?"

"Next and only woman I'm fuckin' is gonna be you, sweetheart."

I hold my breath, but she doesn't say no.

CHAPTER 23
Alex

Fang's leading me out of the room. Dart's hands are untied, but he's doing nothing to help me, just standing, watching. Looking over my shoulder, frantically trying to beg for help but unable to get words to come out of my mouth, I see Gator walking around, shaking their hands, thanking them for bringing me along.

In a room with black walls, Fang drags me over to a cold metal table and starts stripping off my clothes. I'm struggling, trying to escape, but when Gator comes in to help I haven't got a chance. They're too strong and soon have me naked and are pushing me back onto the unyielding surface. Fang's hands go to his fly and he starts to draw down the zip.

"Fuck, her pussy's stitched up. Give me your knife, Fang, and I'll cut them out." What? Who stitched me back up?

"You'll cut her with that."

"Gonna bloody her up anyway. A bit more won't matter."

I feel the cold metal of the knife and start screaming.

"Alex. Alex. Wake up. You're having a nightmare. Keep still, darlin', you'll pull your stitches."

Slowly I realise I'm lying in a soft bed not on a cold table, and it's not Fang or Gator's voices I'm hearing. It couldn't be, the two of them are dead, I saw that with my own eyes.

"Alex, doll. Oh, Alex. Don't cry."

I hadn't realised tears are escaping. Forcing open my wet eyes, I see a bedside light has been turned on, and Dart's looking down at me, his brow creased and his lips pursed. Reaching out my hand I touch his cheek, as much to anchor me to the present than anything else.

"Oh, sweetheart. Come 'ere. Let me hold ya." He moves so slowly, as if he doesn't want to frighten me, and gently wraps his arms around me, careful of the wounds on my chest. He pulls me to him and spoons around me.

My heart's still racing from the terror of my dream, my skin covered in goosebumps from the cool air blowing from the air conditioning unit. His warmth surrounds me, and as he softly strokes his hand up and down my arm, I start to relax. Until I feel a hardness against me. I try to move away, but he holds me back.

"Can't help it, darlin'. Just ignore it. Having a beautiful woman in my arms will do that."

"Having any woman would probably work," I snap.

I feel his mouth nuzzling the hair on the top of my head. "Not any woman, darlin'. Since I first saw ya dance I only get hard when I'm around you, or thinkin' of you. And that's the truth of it. Believe it or not, that's down to you. It's you that I want. Don't know how you done it, babe, think you must have put some kinda spell on me." He chuckles softly, and I feel the sound vibrating over my scalp. My resultant shiver is not from the cold.

But how could he want me? He might have before I was badly scarred. How can he now that Ron's left his mark on me? I hate that man who may well have taken my future away. Biting my lip, I try to stop more tears falling.

Dart must realise he's lost me, as his arms tighten. "Whatcha thinking that's got you so worried?"

"My scars. You couldn't…"

MANDA MELLETT

"Fuck, woman. I can deal, give me some fuckin' credit. You're still the same woman you were before." He lowers his voice and it becomes a gravelly growl. "You've still got the same tits and ass." As though making the point, one of his hands fondles my backside. "Mmm. I love this, ya know?" I should tell him to stop, but it feels so nice. Such a loving touch that I've never felt before.

We lie in silence for a minute, and then Dart speaks again. "What do you feel about tattoos?"

What? The sudden change of subject floors me. "What do you mean? You can get another one if you like. I like them." I've already seen his colourful chest and the big Satan's Devils tattoo on his back. More wouldn't bother me.

"Not me, doll. Though I'm pleased you approve. But for you." He pushes me over onto my back, and his hands move until they cover my breasts. I should stop him, but I don't. Slowly his fingers circle the tee shirt material covering my mounds. "Daisy chains or something. They'd look great." And hide the cigarette burns, I finish in my head. Couldn't be more pain than the way I got my scars in the first place.

"And here." His hand hovers over my chest. "You can think of a design to go here. A good tattoo artist will work around the scarring and make it disappear."

"The scars will still be there. And you'll feel them." Any man would, I hastily correct myself. And be able to trace the ugly word Ron had carved into me.

"Won't bother me none. Alex, you're not your scars, you're more than what that bastard did to you. You survived. Fuck, you were so strong to leave the first time. If you hadn't, you'd have already been dead. Feel my dick, darlin', he's hard for you as you are. Once you're healed you can take up dancing again. But only for me. Don't want any other fucker looking at ya."

"No, I'd frighten the customers away."

"I very much doubt that. Did I tell ya you've still got a fant-astic ass, babe?" Again he moves to cup that part of my anatomy, and I'm ashamed to admit I push my globes back into his hands. He explores and squeezes, then his fingers wander. I tense, but can't bring myself to push him away.

"Are you still sore, babe? Down here, where the bastard stitched you up?"

"Only a little." I shudder as I remember the indignity Ron had put me through. It's the thought of it that's worse and makes me cringe.

"Why don't I see if I can make you forget about that?" The fingers of one of his hands creeps down lower across my stomach.

As I realise his intention, I try to pull away. "No. You can't. I don't want anyone touching me there."

I feel him tensing, but when he speaks know he's not angry with me. "Don't let that fuckin' bastard win, doll. Don't give him the power. He's screwed with your head. You tell me no, you're doing exactly what he wants. Let me take the memory of what he did to you away." His fingers reach their goal, and just one touch ignites something inside of me.

I should be moving, evading his hand. Telling him to stop. He's right. If I'm squeamish and don't move on from what Ron did, I'll be giving in to him. And what Dart's doing feels so good I force myself to be still, neither pulling away nor speaking as he gently strokes between my lower lips. My mind might be objecting, but my body responds automatically.

"You're wet for me babe. Hmm, I like that." As his finger lightly probes, I can't suppress a moan, and I press against him. He raises his hand and brings it up, and I hear a sucking noise. "Doll, you taste so fuckin' good. Always wondered what you taste like. It's perfect. It's you."

His hand moves back down, and now he's making lazy circles around my clit. I suck in air and try to move my hips around. *I shouldn't be letting him do this, but it's so good I don't want him to stop.*

"Relax, just let me do all the work."

It's hard to relax as my muscles start tensing. A finger probes again, and then another. "You're tight, doll. You're going to strangle my cock when I get in there."

He's keeping up a gentle rhythm, enough pressure that my desire keeps building and building.

"That's right, babe. That's it. You're nearly fuckin' there, aren't you?"

I'm hoping he doesn't want an answer, as right now I can't speak. I hold breath in my lungs, my whole body going taut as he lightly pinches my clit. His expertise is unquestionable, and I try to blank out all thoughts of how he got to know a woman's body so well. *Just take advantage.*

And then I can't hold it in any longer, I'm rising and rising until I go over the top, gasping air down into my lungs.

"Dart!"

"Mmm. So good, doll. So good seeing you let go. Next time I'll be inside you, alright? And next time I'll make you really scream."

It gets better? I've nothing to compare it to. Ron never touched me like that. Dart's right, Ron was a bastard. His abuse started long before he raised his fist. What he did to me was horrific, but the man beside me is chasing the memories away. I *can* move past this. With Dart's help.

He's made me feel so good, he'll expect me to reciprocate now. I try to turn to face him, but his arms tighten, and he places a soft kiss to the back of my neck. "Go to sleep, now, doll. Just go to sleep."

Surprised, but also relieved he wants nothing from me right now, my body and mind fatigued from the long day, the stress, and what Dart's given me to process. Already limp in his comforting hold, I close my eyes.

Next time I open them, it's morning. Dart's hair's hanging long and wet, clearly having come from the shower. I feel my cheeks burn as the events of last night come back to me, and it's only after I've relived what happened in my head I'm ashamed to say I remember my son.

"Tyler?"

"He's down at the clubhouse with Sam and Amy. I let you sleep in, babe, as you had a disturbed night."

Again my cheeks flush as I remember just how he'd disturbed me. His lips curl up in a grin as though he's remembering it too. He comes over and perches carefully on the bed. "You sore this morning?" As he sits I can see the bulge straining at his jeans.

Here it comes. Now he'll expect me to do something for him. *Am I ready?* To delay the inevitable, I just answer his question, and honestly. "Not too bad." I flex my shoulders and pull them back, testing my scars. "In fact, it feels easier today."

"Good." Leaning down, he places a chaste kiss on my forehead. "If you want to get up and showered, I can bring you some breakfast."

He's waiting on me now? And isn't asking for anything? Perversely it makes me want to offer. "No, it's alright, Dart. I'll get ready and come down with you." I glance shyly at his groin. "Unless you want me to take care of that?"

"Don't tempt me, babe. But I don't want to hurt you." He gives a cheeky smirk. "And I followed your advice and took care of it myself in the shower."

As I watch, the denim covering his crotch seems to strain even more. "Doesn't look like it."

Ruefully he glances down at himself. "That's your fault."

My eyes open wide. "I've done nothing."

He taps his finger on my forehead. "You don't need to do anythin'. That right there, that pout. I get hard just imaginin' my cock in your mouth. Mmm mmm. The thought of my hard cock disappearin' into those luscious lips." Suddenly he stands and adjusts himself. "Your sex on fuckin' legs, babe."

Now what woman wouldn't preen knowing how much she affected a man, and especially one such as Dart. And despite my scars. I might still need to be convinced Dart's the right man for me, but every word out of his mouth makes me feel stronger.

"Do you need help in the shower?"

I shake my head, thinking where that might lead would be more than I could cope with. Doc had told me what to do, and he left new dressings with me.

"I'll go check on Tyler, give you time to get ready. Then I'll come bring some food back or take you to the club to get something. You must be hungry by now."

The thought of food makes my stomach rumble, which makes him laugh. When he leaves I make quick work of getting washed and dressed, and am ready and waiting by the time he comes back. His hair's been dried by the sun, and I watch as he ties it back into a bun. Every movement this man makes is sexy.

"Tyler's fine, he's got everyone fussin' over him." I appreciate his first thought is to reassure me. He nods when he sees my smile. "Oh, and I've spoken to your sister, told her you and Tyler are safe, but haven't told her where you are. That way she can't say if anyone asks her." If Ron asks her, he means. I shiver as he eludes to my ex. "I haven't told her anything about what happened to you. It's up to you how much you want to say."

The fact that he'd contacted her and put her mind at ease shows me what a special man he is. And for the moment at least, he appears to be mine. I still have some doubts on the wisdom of starting this journey with him, not having a clue where we'll end up.

"Dart." He turns to me and raises his eyebrow. "All I'm asking is that your honest with me. Don't keep secrets, like Ron. If we're going to give whatever this is between us a try, I want to know I'll be able to trust you." I pause and gather my thoughts. "You do something to hurt me or my son, we'll be finished."

He gathers me to him, his chin resting on the top of my head. "Babe, I'll be tryin' here. Never had somethin' like this before. Can't promise I won't do anythin' wrong, but I'll never intentionally hurt ya. Or step out on ya. If I don't feel it's gonna work, we'll talk about it, okay? And if you've got a problem with somethin' I do or don't do, don't keep it to yourself, babe. We'll thrash it out."

That's seems fair, and all I can ask.

I tilt my head up. "You think we've got a chance, Dart? A biker who doesn't do relationships, and a scarred woman who's come from an abusive marriage?"

Looking down at me, he smiles. "We write our own rules, babe. Make it up as we go along."

And that, I suppose, is as much as any couple can do. Couple. I like the sound of that. Having never had a proper relationship with Ron, I'm exploring new ground too.

When we enter the clubhouse, it looks quite empty until I remember most of the men must still be in San Diego. I follow Dart through to the kitchen, but don't really need him to lead the way, as the smell of bacon would have guided me there all by itself. Tyler's sitting at a table, an older woman beside him, and he's got paper and pens and appears to be drawing a bike. There's five women in all, and I think for once the women outnumber the men. Although I'd met them at the cookout. Sam, who I know is with Drum, and Ella, who's with Slick. My eyes flick toward her as I wonder how she recovered from her own ordeal. She's showing no signs of it now. There's Carmen, the hairdresser, and Sophie, who I think I'm remembering correctly, is with their VP.

As I'm nodding towards her, Dart gives a chuckle. "You'll have to forgive Sophie if she starts speaking garbage. She's from England and doesn't know how to talk proper English."

The woman in question flicks a dish cloth towards him, and he steps out of reach with a laugh. The last woman, Sandy, is sitting at the table with Tyler. She looks up and gives a little wave. As Dart pulls out a chair for me, I sit beside her and take a moment to praise my son for the drawing he's done. I also thank Sandy for looking after him.

"Ain't no problem," she tells me with a smile, "always loved kids. Can't wait for my own grandkiddy to be born." She grins toward Sam, who rubs her small belly. She then leans down to check on Amy, who's playing under the table.

Dart makes me a plate and soon I have more eggs, bacon, and waffles in front of me than I've seen in my life. Then he pushes a fruit bowl toward me. "I can't eat all this!" I say with a laugh.

"Expect you want this." And Sam sets a very welcome cup of coffee within reach. Dart starts in on his own breakfast, and I decide where to start tackling mine. Conversation flows easily.

When there's a lull I ask a question which has been eating at me. "The strange names, where do they come from? Do the men choose them?"

"Ah, right. I'm well chuffed you asked that. Allow me." Sophie pulls out the seat on the other side of me from Dart and sits down. "Now, Dart, you know why he got his name?"

I shake my head. Up to now I hadn't thought to ask.

"Well, he doesn't throw darts at a dartboard."

"I've been known to," Dart interrupts.

Sophie flicks her hand at him in dismissal. "Dart, do your thing."

Wondering what's going on, I watch as Dart stands. He undoes his hair and his long dark wavy locks flow down around his face. He then bows with an exaggerated flourish and a twirl of his hand, then says, "D'Artagnan at your service, ma'am." He looks up and winks. "And before you ask, I'm very good with my sword."

My hand covers my mouth as I laugh, and then I'm grateful for my dark skin hiding my flush as I remember how it felt against me last night. Although I've yet to experience it, I've no doubts he knows how to use what he's got. The other's might not have noticed my lapse, but Dart has. He gives me a wink.

Sam sighs. "My man's called Drummer because he *used* to bang everything in sight."

"Doesn't need to now, hun." Sandy gives what I've gathered to be her daughter-in-law a fond look.

The prez's old lady shrugs. "He knows I'd cut off his dick if he even looked at another woman." As the other old ladies echo Sam's solution, I give a pointed glance toward Dart and notice his hands go protectively to his groin.

Another man wanders in, stretches his arms up over his head and yawns, and then goes to grab himself a plate. While he's putting a mound of bacon on it, Sophie calls over. "Why you called Rock, Rock? Alex wants to know."

"What?" He must have had a good night, as his eyes are rimmed red. He grins, puts down his breakfast, approaches me and lifts up his shirt. "Hit me."

What? Dart winks to encourage me. I ball my fist and hit him in the stomach. Then shake my hand out afterwards. Yup, he's abs are as hard as rock.

Another man comes in and sits next to Dart and nudges him. "Shall I tell her how I got my name?" A stud flashes in his mouth as he talks.

"I think she can guess, Tongue."

Ewh!

CHAPTER 24
Dart

Leaving Alex chatting away with the old ladies and watching her son, who I last saw proudly showing Amy his new motorbike toy, I enter the clubroom, still hearing bursts of laughter coming from behind me. I suspect Sophie's still in her element explaining the names of my brothers. I just hope the old ladies keep to the PG version in front of Tyler.

It's good to hear them having a good time. That one of their number is no longer with us is still a raw wound, but at least they're starting to move past it, proving Crystal's no longer hovering around like a spectre. Heart's wife had such a huge personality it's still often a shock not to find her dressed in her colourful clothes cooking up something tasty on the stove, seeming able to relentlessly multi-task as she looked after us, her daughter, and her old man without breaking a sweat, and always with a smile on her face.

I still miss her like fuck, and thinking on it, can better understand why my brother's staying away—if it's painful for me, it must be ten, no, one hundred times worse for him. Even though the hospital visits were painful, I miss seeing him and talking with him. Heart having decided to recuperate with an old buddy leaves me wanting to offer support without knowing how. With that sombre thought in mind, I join Mouse at the bar.

Nodding at Hyde to give me a beer, I raise the bottle in salute. "It's good to be home, Brother."

"That it is." He glances around the room. "At least I can trust everyone here to have my back. We're both quiet for a moment, each reliving the horror of the previous day. Betrayal in any form is never good, but betrayal by a brother? It's going take some time to get past that.

Because he's been on my mind, I ask Mouse the question, "Talking of home, when d'ya reckon Heart will come back?"

Mouse thinks as he takes a swallow of his own drink. "I think the more pertinent question might be, if he ever does."

"You think he's abandoning his patch?" If I sound shocked, it's because I am. Very few people leave this life, voluntarily that is. And most, like old Digger, hang onto it as long as they possibly can. "What about Amy? Surely at some point he needs to start thinkin' 'bout her." I'm stating the obvious and not looking for an answer. Amy's a cute kid and we all tolerate her fondly. Perhaps other MCs wouldn't like a little'un running around getting under their feet, but she's got most of the men here wrapped around her little finger. And soon we'll have more babies around when Sam and Sophie pop theirs out. And then a picture comes into my head of a cute coffee-coloured kid...

My phone starts vibrating before Mouse can respond to my question. Taking it out I see it's the prez.

"Whatsup?"

"Yeah? Ok. See you then."

Mouse has an eyebrow raised, so I satisfy his curiosity. "Prez is on his way back. Wants to have church when he gets here. They're just starting off, should be here by early evening."

"Our bikes?" He frowns. Like me he'll be feeling adrift without his sled.

But I can put his mind at rest there, too. "Lost is coming with. He's driving the truck with our bikes and his. Prospect can take it back."

"Or they forfeit it. That lot of fuckers should lose everything they've got. Includin' their fuckin' bikes."

I wait for Mouse to finish his rant, which I have absolutely no problem with, and then continue, "Drum's put a call out to the other presidents. Red's comin' in from Vegas, Hellfire from Colorado, and Snatcher from Utah. They're bringin' Snake and Poke up."

"That's gonna be one fuck of an easy vote." Yeah. It definitely is. Can't see anyone objecting to a final solution. Satan's going to be having new recruits very soon.

"I'll get the girls to sort out the house at the top of the compound." We've got a place we keep for visiting officers from other clubs. It's conveniently situated next to where the sweet butts live. Yeah, us Tucson boys don't mind sharing. Then I feel my face tightening. There's one woman I'm definitely not going to be passing around.

Mouse and I play a few games of pool before he disappears back into his cave when Alex emerges from the kitchen.

"I think Sandy's adopted Tyler," she says with a smile. "He's quite happy playing with Amy. She's going to take them both to the pool." She sits herself down on one of the new couches we had to get after the police raid when they destroyed everything they possibly could. As she looks around the clubroom, nodding her approval at the walls freshly painted and the matching tables and chairs as well as the handy sofas, I hide a grin. Place even looks upmarket now. Fuck knows how long it will last though.

"You can trust her to keep an eye on them. Viper and Sandy couldn't have kids, you know? It was one fuck of a surprise when Sam turned up fully grown saying Viper was her father. Now that Sandy's going get a grandkid she's over the moon. Happier than I've ever seen her."

"That's sad." Alex's smile disappears. "Sandy's a natural."

"That she is." Sam's appeared and must have overheard what I said. "Hey, you need us to do anything, Dart? Drum's just called me and said he's on his way back."

I keep forgetting with the others away I'm the only acting officer here. "Yeah, Sam. We got three presidents coming in tonight, probably accompanied a man or two. Can you make up the rooms up in the guest house? Get the sweet butts on it."

She laughs. "I'd rather do it myself. Their lazy asses wouldn't get anything done, and they'll need to rest up today if they're going to be busy tonight."

That they will. The visiting officers will need some release after their long rides, and our boys will be all too ready to fuck too, after dealing with all the San Diego shit.

"Can I help?"

Sam puts her hand on Alex's shoulder. "No, you just take it easy. We've got this."

She doesn't need much persuasion. While I can see she wishes she was stronger, her body still healing is taking it out of her. She lost a lot of blood after all. But it's not long before she gets restless, so I take her outside to the pool and seat her in a lounger where she can watch the kids having fun under the careful eye of Sandy. The two women seem to be getting along well. Although we're light on men at the moment, and she's not getting the full Satan's Devils' experience, I'm thrilled at how easily she's fitting into the club. At least her ordeal with Fang and Gator doesn't seem to have put her off bikers.

After making sure she has a lazy afternoon, I keep a careful eye on her as she helps the old ladies cook dinner, which we then eat, saving a huge pot for the brothers who will be getting here any time now. And then it's just a waiting game until they arrive. It's impossible to miss the roaring as they all draw up, making the clubhouse windows rattle and shake, and then they're all backing into their parking spots.

Asking Sam to make sure Alex and Tyler get back to their suite later, knowing I'll be tied up the rest of the night, I wander outside.

"Dart! Can you make yourself useful and help Peg and Blade get our visitors up to the storage room?"

"Sure thing, Prez." Exchanging slaps on the back with my brothers as I pass, I go to the truck where Peg's just getting Snake out. I'm surprised that he's still able to stand on both legs, but notice a fair bit of damage has already been done. One eye's swollen shut, and his nose is crooked and bleeding. There's more blood on his clothes, suggesting Blade's been working with his knife. Oh, yeah, and last time I saw him he had two ears.

Behind him there's Poke, brought along as he's the other officer involved. I spare him a look of disgust before I help our sergeant-at-arms and enforcer drag them both up to the last room they'll ever see, the soundproofed and isolated location we call our storage room kept for precisely times such as these. After tying their hands to chains hanging from the overhead beams, we leave them alone with their thoughts. They know what's got to happen and it won't do them any harm to think on it for a bit.

By the time we get back down to the clubhouse our numbers have increased. The other presidents have arrived, and as I thought, each is accompanied by a man or two. Then it's a waiting game while men take plates and help themselves to some food, visit the heads, or grab drinks from a flustered Jekyll who's trying to man the bar and keep everyone satisfied, receiving no thanks and just being shouted at to hurry up. Yeah, we've all done our time as a prospect. He knows only too well, remaining stoic and taking all the flack thrown at him without complaint is the only way he'll ever get a patch.

At last Drum shouts for us all to go into church. Jekyll's now given instructions to find extra chairs.

As I go to take my customary seat, Drummer waves me to Heart's. When I raise my eyebrows, he shrugs. "Too many of us to have empty seats." We'd always left his space vacant as a mark of respect when we hadn't known whether he'd ever come out of his coma. Now, I suppose, it's a different scenario. Heart's not here by choice, not because he's unconscious in a hospital bed.

It seems all the visiting presidents have brought their VPs, which isn't really surprising. This must be one of the most serious matters the club has ever had to deal with. Crash takes a place next to Red, Hellfire's brought Demon, and Thor sits down alongside his prez, Snatcher. Drum bangs the gavel and we're ready to start.

"You know why we're here. Motherfuckers from San Diego wanted to take over the Tucson chapter and make a bid to have the mother title. And change the direction of the whole club."

A chorus of outrage greets his summation.

"First off, lets clear the air. Any other chapter have a problem with Tucson?" Drummer's steely eyes look around the table, ready to meet any challenge.

There's a shaking of heads and a few "fuck noes." Everyone sounds genuine to me.

Drum bows his head and takes a deep breath. When he looks up, a few lines have gone from his forehead. "Some time ago we all met and decided that we were gonna get out, and stay out, of the drug trade." He nods at Wraith, who lost a sister to crack. "If any of yers have changed your mind on that front, let's get it out in the open now."

Red waves his hand. "Far as Vegas goes, we agree with that decision one hundred percent. There's enough temptation on the streets without stockin' it inhouse. Seen too many brothers get tempted and dip into deliveries. I say we're out and stay out."

There's a rap on the table, then Hellfire speaks. "Agree with Red. Pussy and beer keep my crew happy. Don't have no desire to feed no other appetites. And I got kids, Brother. Don't want them brought up in a house where everyone's wipin' their noses and snortin'."

Snatcher's nodding. "Same goes for me. Without the kids that is, Hell." He lifts his chin to the Colorado prez while chuckles go around the table. "I'm too old to get into that lark. Drugs or kids," he emphasises, just in case anyone misunderstood.

"Motion carried. Satan's Devils stay clean on that front. Dart?" I hear my name, then remember I'm supposed to be recording things like this in the book. Hastily I pick up my pen and do so, ignoring Mouse's smirk.

"Movin' on, now we've got to discuss the situation in San Diego."

"We gonna vote on Snake and this fucker, Poke?"

"Yeah, Hellfire. That's what we're here for." Drum pinches the bridge of his nose, and after a second he looks up, his eyes full of emotion. "Never thought I'd see the day when we were voting on whether to send a Satan's Devils' president to meet Satan." He shakes his head sadly as Red, Hellfire, and Snatcher all echo his sentiment.

"Ain't got no option," Red says. "Can't leave them alive. Out in bad standin' is far too good after what they done."

"Getting the club deep in drugs would be enough by itself," Snatcher starts. "Tryin' to take out the mother chapter is something else."

"I agree," Hellfire says seriously. "Don't like it, Drum, but we've got to get rid of the rot."

Drummer drums his fingers on the table and takes a moment before he lets out a deep breath. "Let's vote on it then. Snake and Poke to meet Satan." His gaze turns stern. "This is a grave step we're takin' here, and know I don't do it lightly. Two members, two *officers* of one of our clubs. Take a moment, brothers. I need everyone in. One no and we discuss other routes."

Silence descends, broken moments later by Wraith, who says aye. Blade follows quickly. One by one my brothers pronounce the death sentence. The three visiting presidents are all in accord. When the vote gets to Drummer, he agrees with the rest.

I pick up my pen and record the grimmest decision ever taken by the club.

As the seriousness of the situation is sinking in, the quiet is broken by one word. "Prez?"

"Yeah, Lost. Spit it out."

Lost looks down at his hands, which are twisting together, and then slowly lifts his head as if it's become heavier overnight. One by one his gaze falls on every man at the table. Only when he's completed the circuit and met all of our eyes, he begins. "Fuckin' bad business. I want to assure you I had no idea we were runnin' a dirty club. Don't know how we got there, getting on for half the members involved, led by our prez and sergeant-at-arms. Fuck, I just don't know what to say, brothers. I must have been fuckin' blind not to see what was goin' down."

"You had no inklin' at all?" It's Red who's asked.

"None, Brother. Sure, noticed a couple had a habit of keepin' to themselves, Poke and Snake were gettin' close, but didn't think nothin' of it. You know how it goes? With the numbers we have we're not in each other's pockets all the fuckin' time." He gets a few nods at that. "Thing is, Prez, I think you should take my patch. I'm the VP, and I should have seen it happenin'."

As people start to protest, Drum bangs the gavel. His voice is cold, unemotional. "Lost is right. After Snake, San Diego is the VP's responsibility. If we find he's at fault, then he's out, and out in bad standin'." My eyes widen. Fuck, I didn't expect that. That sentence would mean he won't be welcome in any club. I glance at the man in question, only to see acceptance of his fate already written on his face. He seems to have shrunk and looks a shadow of his former self. To be kicked out of the brotherhood would be a damning result.

Drum continues. "I've questioned Snake…"

"Left anythin' for us, Drum?"

"Yeah, Hellfire." Drummer's resolute eyes glare at the interruption. "You'll get your chance." There's cracking of knuckles and men rolling their shoulders. Yup, we all want a turn at the man who betrayed his own club.

"Now focus. Snake was tryin' to turn his members. He was recruitin' carefully and under the radar. The plan was to use easy earnin's as an inducement, so he approached the men who could use a new source of income first. Poke is a gambler, heavily in debt. In fact, that was where it started. The sergeant-at-arms got involved by gettin' himself a loan from the cartel, and they suggested usin' the club as both mules and dealers to pay it all off. Snake himself was just greedy when Poke ran him through the numbers. Same with the other brothers they got on their side."

He pauses and sips the beer he'd brought in with him. He's drinking it slowly, as though wanting to keep a clear head. "Snake knew Lost's as straight as they come, which is why he was kept well out of it."

"What was the plan?" Hellfire again interjects. "What were they goin' to do with anyone they couldn't get onside?"

Drum's answer comes quickly. "Kill them, or turn them out bad."

Growls go around.

"As far as I'm concerned, Lost is in the clear. Can't know anythin' if it's deliberately kept hidden."

Lost goes to refute Thor's support, but Drum forestays him. "That's my impression as well. Lost isn't a drunk, he's not lazy.

He doesn't go around with his head stuck up his ass." He breaks off and looks around at everyone much the same way that Lost had done. "My gut feel is we need someone honest who we can trust at the helm. Lost keeps his patch."

Our approval is shown by stamping of feet and the banging of hands down on the table. I get out my smokes and pass them around, believing the tension has eased now that decision's made.

"I disagree."

I pause with my lighter halfway to my cigarette at the unthinkable objection from Snatcher. All eyes go to where he's sitting at the end of the table, others, like me, frozen in pose.

"I propose that we make him president of the San Diego chapter. As you said, Drum, brothers there will need a firm hand to guide them, and I've heard nothin' but good things about Lost."

"Not our decision to make, Brother. You know the rules, chapter votes their own president in." Drum closes his eyes briefly, then opens them again. "But we can make a resolution to let it be known he has our support. *All* our support." His eyes query Red and Hellfire, who send him back chin jerks.

Lost's sitting there as if he's, well, lost. There are tears in his eyes that not only has he got an unexpected reprieve and remains a member of the club, he's being put forward for top spot. His mouth works as if he's lost for words. Then at last he manages just to get out a stammered "Thank you, brothers." There's a wealth of emotion in those three words.

Drummer now turns his gaze on me. "I want you to go back down to San D, Dart. Lost is gonna need someone to have his six while he gets his house sorted. Long as the president's vote goes the way I expect it, as long as Lost's in agreement, I'm proposin' you for the VP spot until things settle down. Lost, got any objections?"

Lost turns to me and grins. "Fuckin' none at all, Prez. Dart's a good man to have at my back."

My mouth's opening and shutting like a fucking fish. On one hand, I'm thrilled Prez thinks so highly of me. On the other, and on a more personal front, I want to stay here and explore where I'm going with Alex. And there's no fucking way she can go back to Cali while that bastard ex of hers is still breathing air. Finally I manage to stammer out some words. "Fuckin' overwhelmed, Prez. Don't know I'm the best person." Fuck, I never considered myself officer material. I know I've been standing in for Heart, but there's a shitload of difference between secretary and VP.

"From what Slick's told me, you did everythin' right. You've been takin' charge and makin' good decisions. That's all we can ask of a second. Any of you fuckers disagree with me? Let's vote it. Mother chapter proposes temporary VP for San Diego is Dart."

There's a unanimous round of ayes, which take me by surprise. Then I hone in on one word he's said. "How temporary, Prez?"

Drum shrugs. "As long as it takes. Need you and Lost to decide what to do with Snake and Poke's supporters. We left them on ice at the warehouse. Then you'll need to kick the others into shape, sift through to find any more that don't smell good, and go on a recruitin' drive, get some prospects in or transfers from other chapters. Get SoCal back up to strength again."

That sounds like it's going to take months, if not years. I frown.

Prez is examining me carefully. "You don't want to leave your woman."

As I open my mouth to refute I've got any claim on her publicly, which would imply a permanency to our relationship, suddenly thoughts flash through my head. Not least the curves of her body, the way she felt in my arms last night, the strength she's shown with all the shit she's been through, and the guilt I'd felt after I fucked Eva. And then there's Tyler. Yeah, I've come to really care for that kid. I'd told her I couldn't make a commitment, but perhaps I was wrong.

Knowing I'm going to take shit for this, I let a smile come to my face. "No, Drum. I don't."

I've got the reputation as a manwhore, and rightly deserve it. With the good looks I was born with, I'm a target for the hangarounds when they come to the club. I only have to crook my little finger to get any woman I want. The incredulous looks of my brothers, with the exception of Slick and Mouse, who'd probably seen what was in the cards, almost make me laugh. Almost. I'd gone against club rules and touched an employee.

My thoughts come out of my mouth. "She can't dance anymore. She no longer works for us, Prez."

"That point's debatable, Brother. But I vote we let it pass. From what I've seen, you ain't going anywhere where you're not wanted. Anyone want to disagree?"

Luckily they don't. Wraith even goes so far as to say, "Alex is a good fit with the club. So you're officially clamin' her, Brother?"

Am I really doing this? Christ. I think I am. The corners of my mouth turn up as in front of the brothers from my club, and from other chapters, "Yes. I am. If she agrees, I'm gonna make her my old lady."

Drummer laughs as Red shakes his head. "And another one bites the dust. Is there somethin' in the water in Tucson?" I flip my middle finger toward the Vegas prez.

"Anyone against?"

"Don't know the bitch, so surely that's up to Dart." Hellfire lifts his chin at me. "Yer makin' the brother a VP, trust he knows what's best for the club."

Lost looks at me. "I want to get back to San D tomorrow. Don't want to leave things up in the air."

And as quickly as that I've claimed my old lady, and I'll just as fast have to leave her. But that's what I signed up for, to do whatever is necessary for the club. "I'll be with you, Brother." Even if I don't want to go.

"Dart's takin' an ol' lady brings us on to one more thing." Drummer says.

CHAPTER 25
Dart

The prez has got our attention. I wasn't aware we had much more to discuss. "Alex, Dart's ol' lady, is black," he begins.

Where's he going with this? What the fuck does her skin colour have to do with anything?

Before I can say anything, Snatcher leans back in his chair and says it for me. "Bylaws don't include bitches. If Dart wants to dip his wick in a black hole, that's up to him."

Demon nods at his prez, then looks at me. "You gonna have kids? They'd be…"

"Don't fuckin' go there." Mouse is out of his seat and has the Colorado VP out of his chair and up against the wall, his hand circling his neck. Demon flutters his hands in surrender.

"Didn't mean anythin' by it. Just pointin' out…"

"Sit down and shut the fuck up! Both of yers," Drum thunders. I swear his voice is so loud the room vibrates. Once they take their seats, and the prez has silenced them with a glare, he continues, "Talking of kids, Alex has already got one. A boy, six years old." He gives everyone *that* stare, as I sit wondering why the fuck he's bringing this up at the table. Suddenly his fist hits down on the table. "Tell you this, brothers. If it hadn't been for that kid's quick thinkin', *I* might not be sittin' here today, and we could have lost other good members of this club." Now he's caught their interest. No one speaks, and all eyes are upon him. Drummer's tense stance relaxes and he sits back. "Lad was upset, but knew somethin' was off. Managed to get a warnin' to me, so we got rollin' in time, and gave us the head's up we were steppin' into an ambush."

"Six fuckin' years old?" Thor's shaking his head.

I nod. "Yeah, the boy's been through some shit in his life. He's got an old head on his young shoulders."

"Boy did a solid for the club. If it wasn't for him we might not be having this meetin' today."

Slick throws me a chin jerk. "Good fuckin' kid there, Brother. He know that?"

"We should all thank him." Peg looks around. He knows if he hadn't have been warned, and Slick, Mouse, and I hadn't escaped by ourselves, he'd have been one of the first to put his head in a trap.

"I want to do more than thank *him*." Drum's emphasis is confusing, and again we give him our eyes. "Kid's got me thinkin'. He loves bikes, and thanks to Dart here, will grow up around bikers. Quite likely when the time comes he might want to prospect for us. Far as I'm concerned, I'd be proud to have him in the club."

Hellfire brings his hand down onto the table. "We're a white fuckin' club." He gives a side glance to Mouse, who's bunching his hands. "You look white, Brother. Hard to tell…"

I take a sharp breath, knowing how proud Mouse is of his heritage. I don't have to wait long. "This is an American club, and last time I fuckin' looked into it, my people were here long before yours."

Red starts getting to his feet as though to intervene, but sits down again when he sees it's not necessary as Drum takes control.

"Shut! Up!" Drum roars. "We're not fuckin' white supremacists, and as far as I'm concerned, our bylaws are years out of date. For myself, I don't give a fuck whether members are white, black, brown, fuckin' yellow, or purple. What's more important is I know they've got my back. How many of you were in the services?"

A number of hands go up, including Hellfire's. Drum's eyes narrow as he challenges him. "And how many times did a black have your six?"

Hellfire looks taken aback. "More than once," he admits.

"Covered you as good as a white?"

Hellfire can't argue. "Sure did," he replies honestly.

"What's the difference to having blacks in the club or in the service then? You sayin' they can't be trusted, can't fight by your side?"

Now Hellfire shrugs, and slowly a grin comes to his face. "Ain't sayin' that at all. Just that we've always been white."

"And we can't change that?" Drum strokes his hand over his beard. "We've got a black woman and kid at the Tucson Chapter. Don't want them to feel they are any less than any of the other ol' ladies and kids we have here."

"Don't bother me none. Long as they're a good fit in other ways." Red seems to have no problem with us opening the club up.

Listening to the debate, I'm overwhelmed that Drum's going out on a limb, and it's for my benefit. I hadn't thought what would happen if Tyler started saying he wanted to prospect for the club. Could even be in just a year or so knowing that kid. I didn't fancy being the one to say he couldn't just because of the colour of his skin.

"So," Drum begins, looking around the table, "I'm proposin' we remove the bylaw that restricts membership by colour. And I'm puttin' it to the vote. Anyone putting up objections better be ready to explain themselves."

I get a few sideways glances coming my way and know what they're thinking and can't deny it. By claiming Alex I'm forcing this vote. I pull the decision book towards me, expecting to be disappointed. But one by one the votes go around the table, and while some brothers think on it more than the rest, eventually it's a complete round of ayes.

"So recorded." Drum bangs the gavel on the table. "Welcome to the twenty-first century, brothers." He's rewarded by a laugh.

Red's nodding and beaming. "Fuckin' good move, Brother." He gives a chin lift to Drum.

Thor puts up his hand. "When I served my sergeant was a woman…"

Now there's shouts of derision and exclamations of disbelief.

Beef is the first to put it into words. "Ain't having any fuckin' bitches as members." And his comment is echoed by everyone, albeit in slightly different ways.

"We'll leave that to the twenty-second," Drum says drily. And we laugh once again.

"Had me a bit nervous for a while there, Drum." It's Snatcher who starts us all off again.

It's a release of tension, but Drum hasn't finished the meeting. He points towards Mouse. "Brother, you had something you wanted to say?"

"Yeah." He lifts his chin toward me. "Alex, and her ex. We know Thompson took out a life insurance policy, but not just on her, on himself too, to allay any suspicion. He dies, as they're not divorced, she benefits and gets a clear half a million."

"He's dead anyway." The sooner that man stops breathing, the sooner I'll have my old lady by my side. "Much as I'd like to tear him apart with my bare hands, we need to be clever about it." I nod toward Drum, and then at Mouse. It kills me I can't get up close and personal, but his death has got to be arranged so nothing comes back on the club.

"Another good reason for you going to San D," Drum states. "And once he stops taking in air, that money is sure gonna come in useful."

Mouse continues, "Probably not enough, so we'll have to help raise the rest."

Hellfire doesn't know any of this and looks mystified. "What the fuck you talkin' about?"

Now Drum takes over. "That kid, Tyler? We can thank him for what he did, but there's somethin' he needs more than words. He's got a fuckin' death sentence hangin' over his head. Fuckin' sickle cell disease. He needs expensive treatment, which could be a cure and save his life." He pauses for a moment to let that sink in. "Tucson club is gonna be doin' a poker run to raise money."

Now I know Snatcher's got no kids of his own, or none he's owned up to that is, but he looks thoughtful as he brushes his hand over his face. "Sickle cell? That's the thing black people get?"

"And Asians and Hispanics. But in the US, you're right. It's mainly blacks. And they're born with it." Alex had educated me on the subject. I give him more info. "Fuckin' bastard of her ex played the odds. Didn't tell her he was a carrier. If she'd known, she'd never have taken the risk." I don't go into the rest of the details. I've given him enough.

Others go to speak, the Colorado prez holds up his hand. "Christ. Your woman and kid have been through some shit. And a poker run to help? We'll be up for takin' part. There's some hobby clubs our way who'd be all over that too. Make a big splash, get people to make donations. Yeah, my club will be there."

Demon jerks his chin towards his prez. "Haven't done somethin' like that for a while."

"Well it gives us somethin' fuckin' positive to focus on for once, rather than watchin' our Tucson brothers' backs." This is from Snatcher.

Ignoring the snide remark, Drum nods his head. "Thank you, brothers. And time's of the essence. These things usually take ages to plan and we've got to work fast."

There's a few offers of help for that too.

Prez gives one of his rare smiles, and I know what he's thinking. This is the real Satan's Devils right here. One for all and all for one, just like the musketeers I was named for. It helps remove some of the bad taste left by Snake and his crew.

"All agreed then? We raise funds for Tyler's treatment and get his life insurance for Dart's ol' lady."

I grin. We're voting on Thompson's death. It's another round of ayes, and I record it. Fuck, this book's getting near filled up today.

Raising my hand, I draw attention to myself. "Just one thing, I don't want Alex to know about the insurance money. Want her to have a genuine reaction to anything that happens."

Nods around the table, they all know what I'm getting at.

Drummer looks pleased, and so he should be. He's prez of the mother chapter for a reason, and everything's gone his way today. He picks up the gavel. "Now, if there's nothing else?" When we all shake our heads, he brings it down. "Meeting fuckin' over. Now, Hellfire, Snatcher, Lost, and you, Dart, we've got business up in the storage shed. Blade, Peg, you come with too. And anyone else who wants in on this."

There's no doubt in any of our minds that Snake's remaining hours are numbered. But Drum's doin' this right. Until we take his patch, Snake remains the president of one of our chapters, and all chapters present need to take joint responsibility for his demise. We don't want the mother club getting a reputation for taking another prez and officer out on a whim. But the way

Drum's handled it, Hellfire, Snatcher, and Red are already convinced, the way they voted confirmed it. Now they just want to see the guilty men with their own eyes.

There's not one of the Tucson Chapter who's not come along. It ends up a bit of a squash as we take our places in the shed, watching the two men who, by their expressions, show they know they've got no hope at all.

But it doesn't stop Snake from trying. "Look, runnin' drugs will bring good money into the club. I've got connections with the cartel. I can get good shit."

As Hellfire raises his chin toward him, Drummer nods back and lets him have his say. "I don't want that shit in my club."

Red spits on the ground. "Seen what drugs can do. Don't want me a part of any of that."

Snatcher agrees. "That shit's for assholes. Not for this club. Bring the law down on us fast. Don't know what you were thinkin', *Brother*." He snarls out the last word as though it's left a bad taste in his mouth.

"But the money..."

Drum looks incensed. "Run yer fuckin' club properly and you can bring in good money legit. You just have to fuckin' work at it."

Peg steps up to Poke, his counterpart in the SoCal club. "Always shied away from honest work, didn't you, Poke?"

"Honest fuckin' work? We're a one-percenter club." Snake can't understand the other prezs' views.

Drum's face twists. "Yeah, we're a one percenter club. So you know what's comin', don't yer?"

"Are you puttin' us out bad?" Snake sounds hopeful.

"Gone too far for that. You had your eyes on the mother chapter. If things had gone down differently, you'd have started takin' us out. How ya expect this to end, Snake?" Without giving him a chance to tell us the answer, which must be written on all our faces, Drum turns around. "Peg, Blade. Get him down."

As our sergeant-at-arms and the enforcer do what he says, the rest of us form a circle. Yeah, he'd aimed to take down the Tucson club, so this is personal, and we all want a part of what's going on. Red, Hellfire, and Snatcher, along with their VPs, also find themselves some space.

Snake's a president, he knows what he's got coming, but he stands in the centre bravely with his shoulders pulled back.

"Strip him of his patch, Peg. We'll burn the cuts later."

The first real emotion I've seen from Snake is sadness as his worn leather cut is taken off his back. To make a point, Blade takes out his knife and one by one strips all the patches off, the one saying his name, the one denoting him as president, and the San Diego chapter patch on the back. Finally, he removes the centre patch bearing the Satan's Devils' logo.

As his colours are destroyed, the defeated man visibly slumps, he no longer looks like a man in charge.

Peg gets the full-strength brandy we keep on hand here, and Blade gets the blow torch to light. I turn away, swallowing to keep the bile down as the smell of flesh burning thickens the air. I have to give it to Snake, he makes no sound as his large Satan's Devils tattoo is burned off his back, taking with it some of his long hair. The pain must be unbearable, but he's got more to come.

When Blade steps away, Drum makes the first punch, straight to his face, Snake reels back and spits teeth onto the ground. Deferring to the presidents, Red's next, and a blow to his chest is accompanied by a cracking sound. By the time the higher--ranking officers have taken their shots, Snake's no longer standing. When I get my kick in, I don't know or much care whether he's still breathing or not

When everyone's taken their turn, Drum gets out his gun and finishes him off with a possibly unnecessary shot to the head.

Poke's been watching. His eyes rolling wildly in his head. When Peg and Blade step up to take him down, he shouts out, "Just shoot me, please. For God's sake. Shoot me!" The last words are a scream as he's pushed into the middle of the circle.

How this man ever made sergeant-at-arms, I'll never know. Instead of accepting his punishment stoically, he's crying like a bitch, begging for mercy as his colours are shredded. He screams as the blow torch is lit. But no one feels any mercy as the reek of burning skin once again fills the air. Like his now dead prez, this was the man who would have condoned Alex's rape by Fang and Gator, and if their plan had worked, Slick, Mouse, and I wouldn't be breathing, and other members of the club sent to find us dispatched to their maker as well.

Prez takes the first punch, and one by one my brothers step up. When it's Slick's turn he steps back, and aims a kick right into his balls. I suppress a smile when Slick winks at me. It takes time as we all lay into the traitor, and when it comes around to me, Poke is no longer able even to twitch.

When we're done, Drum raises his gun one final time. The bullet fires and it's done.

As we start to disperse, leaving the clean-up and burial to the prospects under the watchful eye of Peg, the events and outcomes of the meeting hit me with the force of one of the blows the two dead men had received. I've claimed Alex as my old lady, now I've got to convince her I've done the right thing. And in addition, that we'll have to delay starting our relationship, as I'll be leaving Tucson tomorrow.

As my brothers saunter away from the club, going off to drink, fuck, or both—individual coping mechanisms of their choice for what we've just witnessed, the brutality which brings primitive urges to the fore—I don't follow them. I'm feeling it just like they are, but it's not alcohol or a whore that's on my mind. I peel off, and rather than going down to the clubhouse, go to spend the limited time that I have left with my old lady.

We've spent most of the day in church and dealing with the aftermath. Evening's falling as I enter the bloc and see Alex getting Tyler ready for bed. I stand in the doorway, leaning against the frame for a moment, seeing with fresh eyes what I've just claimed as my new family. I'm going to be proud as fuck to be a dad to that special kid. Whatever his colour, I'm going to step up and be a better father than that bastard Thompson ever was, and do what I can to ensure he gets the treatment he needs to live a normal life.

Neither of them notice me as Alex tucks him in, then takes out a book and starts to read. I'm staying quiet, just listening to her sexy voice and enjoying the sight before me. But I give myself away by chuckling as she starts to mimic the animals in the book she's reading from. Giving me a quick grin, she shoos me away with a wave of her hand and nods at her son. Tyler's noticed me too, and now appears wide awake.

"Sorry," I mouth, and then go back into my room. The quicker she gets him to sleep, the sooner we can talk.

I'm sitting on my bed with my legs comfortably splayed, my chin resting on my hands when she eventually comes in. I've spent the time thinking through the implications of having an old lady, knowing I'll have to organise getting her a patch. It makes me rock hard to think of fucking her wearing just my cut saying 'Property of Dart' on the back. I never expected to see those words, but now that I've committed in front of my brothers there's no turning back.

Holding out my hand, I invite her to come across to me. "How are you feeling?"

"A little bit sore, but I'm healing at last."

Thank fuck for that. I thought we'd have more time, but tonight's got to be a goodbye.

Twisting my body, I take her face in my hands, look into her beautiful eyes, then lower my head. As my mouth touches hers she opens for me, and I sweep my tongue inside. I take control, kissing her harder than I had the night before. It's almost like she doesn't know what to do. Placing my hand on the back of her head, I hold her to me and take time getting to know her taste. When at last I release her, her lips are swollen.

Leaving my hand where it is, I wrap my fingers into her hair. "Alex," I start, not knowing quite how to proceed.

"Dart," she replies, a little smile on her face as she mocks me.

"Vixen." I grin, and then grow serious. "I'm done fuckin' whores. Won't be goin' there again. Ever."

"Don't make promises you can't keep... When we're finished."

"I'm keepin' this one and we ain't never gonna be finished. Don't want no other woman but you, Alex."

She's shaking her head. "You can't say that. You don't know... We haven't..."

"Don't matter. And I've had a taste. You've already spoiled me for anyone else." As she widens her eyes, I tell her the rest: "I've claimed you. Told my brothers I want you as my ol' lady."

She rears back in surprise. "*What?* Dart, you said you couldn't make a commitment."

"Been doing some thinkin'. Decided I'm not runnin' from this. Want us to be real, doll. Want my patch on your back, and you in my life."

She obviously doesn't know what to say. "Tyler..."

"Tyler will be my son, babe. Our boy. And I promise I'll be the best dad he'll ever know. Hey, I might make mistakes, but I'll never hurt him, or you. This sickle cell thing? I'll be right there beside you, fightin' for his life."

"Dart!" Her hand covers her mouth as she hears the totally unexpected words. "It's too fast, too much. Too soon. You said …"

"I know what I said, and I was an idiot. Not gonna chance losin' the best thing that's ever happened to me. Hey, we've been friends for a while, haven't we? Can't think of a better fuckin' basis to take this to the next level." Lifting her hand, I place it to my denim covered but clearly rock-hard dick. "You do this to me. No one else since I met you."

She frowns again. "Eva."

I close my eyes briefly. "That was the biggest fuckin' mistake I ever made. Told you already, doll, the only way I could do her was imaginin' it was you instead."

"I still don't understand how you could do that."

I roll my head on my shoulders. "Truth, doll? Didn't like that you'd taken residence in my head. Thought I could shake these feelin's I have for ya. Didn't fuckin' work, babe. You caught me well and good."

Raising my hand to her face, I stroke her cheek gently, pleased when she leans into my touch. Although I've released her, she hasn't moved her hand from where I left it on my cock. Her fingers start exploring, testing my length. I grit my teeth.

"Gonna come babe if you keep that up."

Her mouth twists cheekily, and fuck me if she doesn't sink to her knees, her hands going to the button of my jeans. As I look on in amazement, she glances up as though looking for permission. "Feel free, doll. Do what you want."

Biting her lip, she undoes the button and then takes down the zip. Lifting my hips, I allow her to move my jeans down. Needing no further incentive, my cock bobs out. I hear air whistling in through her teeth, then, fuck me. She's wrapping those gorgeous kiss-swollen lips around the head.

Gently I place my hand on her hair as she starts sucking and licking, knowing she's got to be tasting the pre-cum that's leaking out. She tries to take me down further, gags, and pulls her head up.

"You don't have blow me."

"I'm no good at it." When I turn her face up toward me, her eyes are watering. "I've only done it once before, and I know I'm not like other girls."

Unintentionally my fingers tighten in her hair. "The fuck you mean?"

"I wanted to please you. Like you did for me last night. But I can't do it."

"You don't have to, doll. Not everyone likes givin' head."

"Ron told me I, well, suck at it."

That makes me see red. "Ron's not here, babe. It's just you and me. And we do what we want. For the record, what you just did felt fuckin' fantastic." That's it. However Thompson meets his demise, I'm going to make sure it hurts.

She glances up quickly, her eyes wide in disbelief. "You liked it?"

"Yeah." *And that's a fucking understatement.* And the thought of her lips around me has me leaking again.

Encouraged, she lowers her head and takes me in once more. And fuck, seeing her dark hair bobbing over my dick has me almost ready to blow. "Steady babe, that feels too good, sweetheart." Realising she needs to know how she's making me feel, I keep talking. "Yeah, right there. That's it, that's the sensitive spot. Oh hell, sweetheart, you keep doing that…" She's nowhere near deep throating me, but her hands come up and circle the length she can't take in.

"Doll," my voice is unrecognisable. "Doll, pull away now unless…"

Fuck, it's too late. I've no control over myself with those lips wrapped around my cock and I lose it completely cum shooting into her mouth. She swallows and licks, taking everything I offer. I've just been given the best blow job of my life, and by my old lady.

CHAPTER 26

Alex

I'd spent all day thinking about Dart, and what he'd done for and to me in the middle of the night. How he made sure I was satisfied while taking nothing for himself, being so gentle and so caring. What had it meant?

And after dinner, when he'd left me, I wondered why he'd been gone so long and doubts started to creep in. Had he taken Allie up on her offer of last evening, or spent the evening fucking one of the other whores here? Taking from them what I'm not able to give, or not until I heal. While he told me he wouldn't be going with them again, left to my own devices, all my insecurities came flooding back, unable to understand why he'd want a scarred woman when he's got all the flawless women he wants at his beck and call.

But he'd come back. Oh, out of the corner of my eye I'd seen him watching Tyler, a sneaky sideways glance while he'd been transfixed by my son. His face had been as relaxed and happy as I'd ever seen it, as if seeing me and Tyler had given him a sense of being home. At the time I thought it fanciful thinking, but then I'd come into his room, and he told me he wanted me. Exclusively and permanently. While I still have lingering doubts that he can be faithful, I can see he's sincere in that he means to try.

He wants me to be his old lady? The way he said it, that's some kind of commitment in his world. *My world,* if I agree. To think that a handsome man like Dart wants me is utterly crazy. But last night he'd told me, proved to me, my scars don't matter.

When he'd placed my hand on his dick, I'd never felt anything like it before. White folks tend to believe the myth that black men have bigger cocks. If there's any truth in that, Ron must have been an exception. His dick was definitely on the small size, or possibly proportional, as he wasn't a big man. Dart, on the other hand, is tall, and his endowment matches his size. I'm ashamed to say as soon as I touched it I wanted to see it, to taste it. A reaction I've never had before.

When I did, I fast realised I didn't have a clue what to do. An inadequate performance once before in my life was no basis to practice on this man who's probably had dozens, if not hundreds of experienced blow jobs in his life. Quickly becoming embarrassed, I wasn't sure whether to continue, but then he reassured me, and he'd come so fast I knew I must have done something right.

My head is resting on his leg, and I turn my face to look at him. His cheeks are flushed, and there's a lazy grin on his face.

"Doll, you can do that anytime you fuckin' want."

When I'd tried with Ron I'd hated it. The taste of his dick was abhorrent in my view. Dart though, the scent of his pheromones, the salty taste of his cum, the power I felt when I realised I was giving him pleasure. I'll have no issue doing that again.

"Now, fair's fair, doll. You've tasted me, now it's my turn." He pulls me to my feet, then stands himself. His hands go to my tee and starts to pull it over my head. I hold onto the material. He's seen me naked before, but I prefer him to remember how I was when I danced in the club, before I was scarred. Now he'll be revealing the healing burns on my breasts and the bandages still covering my chest. He's claimed me as his woman, and I wish I could be whole and unmarked. My nerves that he'll realise he's made a mistake make me shiver.

Sensing my unease, he lowers his head and kisses me once again. He's so tall I have to crane my neck. But without words, his actions help me ease the grip on my shirt. Unable to wear a bra as it's so painful, soon I'm totally naked above my waist. Gently his hands trace my breasts, carefully avoiding the burns. He makes like he doesn't even see them as he breathes out. "You're fucking beautiful." He circles my nipples. "Just love the colour these are. Such a sexy dark brown, almost black. Sorry, doll, but I've just got to taste."

He doesn't appear repentant as he bends his knees and sucks one of my nipples into his mouth, sending a tingling sensation down my spine. When he does the same to the other, I let out a moan.

As if it's a signal, his hands wrap around me, picking me up and lying me flat on the bed. He pulls off the yoga pants I've been wearing, wasting no time taking my panties along with them.

And then he's kneeling on the bed, pulling my thighs apart. I do nothing to stop him, the wicked grin that he gives eliminates any awkwardness, and he shoots out his legs so they hang over the end of the bed, putting him just in the right position to put his mouth where I need it. His tongue slides from my ass to my clit, a lazy slow journey that has me clenching my thighs. He delves inside my depths, and I almost jump at the sensation. *Nobody's ever done this before.* I've read about it, dreamed of it, but never experienced it. Sex with Ron, on those few occasions we had it, was a perfunctory affair simply to get him off.

Dart's taking his time, my hands twisting into the sheet as he finds my clit and sucks it into his mouth. *I've never realised how it would feel.* I assumed it would have no more sensation than masturbation, but somehow the slight roughness and warmth of his tongue is quickly ramping up my desire.

"Dart, oh Dart!" I murmur, giving him verbal encouragement while both straining to reach my peak and not wanting it to end.

He puts a finger inside me, lifting his mouth to tell me. "Fuck, you're so tight." I refrain from admitting it's been over six years since I last had sex. "You're dripping for me. You want this, don't you, doll?" His eyes meet mine, and he corrects himself. "You need this." Redoubling his efforts, he adds another finger, then starts a motion which has me catching my breath. Then he touches something, somewhere inside me, and as his fingers curl round, he ramps up the attack on my clit.

And now I'm moaning, my body going tight. The feeling, oh the feeling, the strength so out of my experience. I think I'm going to die as he takes me up and over the top. I come hard with a loud cry around my hand that I've quickly stuffed into my mouth.

Now he moves up the bed, careful to keep his weight off my chest, and kisses me deeply, allowing me to taste myself on him. It's a strange, but not unpleasant sensation. When he pulls away he looks satisfied with himself.

I have to tell him. "No one's ever done that before."

His head resting on the other pillow, he turns and stares at me. "Never? No one's gone down on you?"

"There was only Ron, and he didn't want to."

"Fuck, woman, I'd eat you out for breakfast, lunch, and dinner if I could. I'll warn ya now, won't be able to get enough of your taste, doll."

Twisting my head to one side, I ask a question. "Do I taste different?"

He looks confused, then says, "To a white woman?"

I shrug. I suppose that's what I meant. And then I wish I hadn't asked as he replies, "Every woman tastes different, babe," and reminds me of just how he would know. But his hand comes out and smooths down my face. "Would it help if I told you I've never tasted better before?"

I don't think I believe him. But I can go with the lie. I smile.

"Doll, I wanna fuck ya. But I don't want to hurt ya." He frowns, then asks, "If you're feeling up for it, you gonna ride me?"

I shake my head. He stills my action with his hand. "Sorry, babe. I forgot how much pain you must be in. Are you alright?"

I put him right. "It's not that I'm hurting or don't want to. It's that, I, well, I haven't done that before either."

He sits up and brushes his hand over his hair. "What did that fucker do? A quick on and off in fuckin' missionary position?"

He's hit the nail on the head. Embarrassed, I nod and turn my head to the side.

"He's a crazy asshole." Reaching out he moves my head back so I'm forced to look at him. "Knew I was a lucky motherfucker gettin' you into my bed. But now I know there's so much I can show you. We've got so fuckin' much to explore with each other. And a whole fuckin' lifetime to do it."

There's that promise again. I still can't quite believe it. But Dart's a man of action, and his talking is done. He lies down on the bed beside me and pats his thighs. "Come sit on me. In this position, you control how much you take, and how you ride me. That way, hopefully, we don't pull your stitches out." As I'm trying to follow his directions, he keeps speaking. "If I fucked ya any other way I wouldn't be able to hold myself back."

I straddle him, and lift myself up. Taking his cock in my hand I'm not certain how I'm going to be able to accommodate it. He must see the worry in my eyes.

"Take it slow, babe."

"You're so much bigger…"

"Don't mention his name. Not now." Now he barks a laugh. "But babe, you sayin' I'm bigger than a black man?"

I grin. "You certainly are." At his wide grin, I continue, "And it's been a long time."

"Thought so, doll. You felt so tight. How long?"

Biting my lip, I tell him the truth. "More than six years."

"Before Tyler was born?" He looks incredulous.

"Uh huh." Wanting this conversation to be over, I place him at my entrance, and start lowering myself down. I take in the tip, and already feel the stretch. But he turned me on so much I'm well lubricated. I push down a bit, and then rise up. My teeth worry my lip as I concentrate on what I'm doing.

"That's it, doll. Fuck, that feels good."

I'm rising and lowering myself, gaining inch by inch. He holds my hips and starts to help me. I don't know what it's doing to him, but it's making me feel fantastic. Then his fingers move to my clit, and the further stimulation encourages me. But I still can't seat myself fully on his dick, and feel my eyes watering.

"Take what you can, babe. We'll get there in time. Don't worry." He reaches up to brush away a tear that's escaped.

After pausing for a moment, scared I'm going to be a disappointment, I start to move once again, realising he's got one thing right. In this position, if I ease myself forward it doesn't pull on my wounds. I only hope I've got enough of him inside that it's good for him too, as it's beyond amazing for me. I think even if I pulled out the stitches I wouldn't even know it, the feeling of him inside me, the sensations of him stimulating my clit, and seeing his face clenching as he moves closer to his peak.

"Fuck, doll. That feels too good. Tell me you're close and you're coming." He works his fingers harder, and I'm getting so near.

"Need you to come all over my dick, babe. Want to feel your juices fuckin' drenchin' me. That's it, babe. Fuck, you're so tight, your muscles are grippin' me so fuckin' hard."

His dirty words make me move faster. I throw back my head as I begin to feel like an overwound clock. My body is shaking, and as I come so hard, his hands both go to my hips and hold me up, taking over control and pulling me down hard on him. I feel him jerking as his cum shoots up inside me.

He sits up, wrapping his arms carefully around me. I can feel his softening cock still gripped by my inner walls. Resting my head on his shoulder, I try to recover my breath, knowing tears are falling down my cheeks.

I feel like a virgin who's been ravished by her first man. Nothing Ron had ever done with me had made me feel anything like this.

When our lungs stop heaving, he murmurs into my ear, "You on birth control, doll?"

It's a bit late for him to ask that. We'd both got carried away. But at least I can put his mind at rest. "Yes, I got the implant replaced a couple of years ago. I started using it after Tyler was born. I couldn't risk another accident with Ron." I know I don't have to explain why.

"How long is it good for?"

"Three years."

He grins, and surprises me. "Sounds like a plan. A year to get settled, then I'm gonna get you pregnant, babe. Reckon Tyler would like a brother or sister, don't you?"

He wants children? "Dart, isn't it too early to talk about that?"

"Early? Fuck no. I've got ya now, doll. I ain't lettin' ya go. And if you think that's early, you should know Drum got Sam pregnant a week after he met her." His grin widens. "Going bare with you was as hot as fuck. That was a first for me, babe. So you don't need to worry on that score. In the past I've always gloved up."

It should have occurred to me, but it didn't. Instead I'm thinking what a child of ours would look like. Mmm. Coffee-coloured skin, probably dark hair, which I hope they'd inherit from their dad, as mine's too afro and curly. And what colour eyes would our baby have? Still resting my head on his shoulder, I realise I'm quite taken by the idea.

"You need me to check on Tyler?"

"No, he's okay. I'll hear if he stirs."

Dart looks towards the open door to his suite, and the open one to the room where Tyler's asleep. He chuckles. "Lucky he's a deep sleeper. You got a bit loud there, doll."

Suddenly I feel insecure. "Dart, was it... I couldn't..."

"Babe," he admonishes, "it was fuckin' fantastic, okay? Just the feeling on being skin on skin got me hard as fuckin' steel. You just got to get used to me, right? It's been so fuckin' long for ya."

"Is this a case where practice makes perfect?" I grin at him.

"Definitely, doll. Definitely."

"Hmm." I snuggle into his side. "Better keep my strength up for tomorrow.

He sits up, his legs drawn up, his hands around his knees. "About that," he begins. "I'm really sorry, babe, but I'm going away for a while."

Even though tightening my stomach muscles pulls on my stitches, I force myself up so I'm sitting beside him. "What, Dart? What was all this then?" I wave my hand between us. Were all those words simply to get me into bed? My uncertainties return in a flash.

"That was me claimin' my ol' lady. And before you get any ideas, I don't want to leave you. Fuck, if I had the choice I'd be stayin' right here and startin' a new life with you and the boy."

"So why, Dart? And where are you goin'?"

"San Diego," he throws out. Looking me straight in the face. It's the one place I know I can't go. I can't take the risk, not while Ron's there. "Drum's asked me to go with Lost as their temporary VP. You know what went on, babe. Half their men betrayed the club and he wants me to help Lost sort out what to do."

"VP? That's vice president." I almost squeal. I might not know much about club life, but I know that role's important.

"Yeah, don't know why the fuck Drum thought I was officer material, but there ya go." Dart looks so proud of himself.

I do. He's proved himself to me, and I'm thrilled on his behalf that his president's seen his potential too. But selfishly, while I know I should support him, I don't want him to go. "How long for, Dart?"

"A few weeks, maybe a couple of months. I don't know for sure. But I'll be comin' back every chance that I get. I won't leave you for that long, you can be certain of that. Drummer will make sure you're safe here."

I've no worries on that score. From what I've seen, I like all the men and the old ladies here in the Tucson club. Perhaps not so much the whores, but I can live with that as long as they stay away from my man. I lie back down again, my action causing him to do likewise. Turning into him, I rest my head on his shoulder. "I wish Tyler and I could come with you. The doctors here in Tucson try to help as best they can, but they don't see much sickle cell disease. Our old doctor in San Diego was great. It was his area of expertise."

His arms tighten around me, and he doesn't speak. I don't need him to tell me it's impossible.

"I don't want to leave ya. Understand that, doll." He tries to reassure me again.

I'm worried, but try to suppress it. If he was stayin' with me, maybe we'd have a chance. But he's going to be four hundred miles away, and while I want to trust him, in my mind's eye, all I can see is the temptation of a beautiful woman called Eva.

CHAPTER 27
Dart

L ost calls church as soon as we arrive in San Diego, and manages to get all the boys around the table in not much more than an hour. Being stunned and confused with the events of the past couple of days, everyone was hanging close by to find out what the fuck is going on.

The first matter of business is dealt with fast. There are unanimous ayes when we take the vote that makes Lost prez of the chapter, and that no one queries his suitability to sit in the chair seems to take him by surprise. I hide my smile. It's not unusual for a good man not to recognise his own worth.

When the congratulations die down, it's only minutes later when he introduces me as his temporary VP, and that goes down better than I'd thought as well. To be honest, my new band of brothers seem to be in such shock they're just happy someone's stepping up and taking charge. As I cast my glance around the table, I see various expressions of disbelief and disenchantment. This chapter's lost so many men, it's vital the numbers don't get further depleted. I make a mental note that keeping those that remain from giving up and walking away will be my number one job. These men have lost those they'd called brothers and friends. They'll all be feeling betrayed. As my shoulders pull back I sit up straighter, getting ready to carry the load.

When I was here a few days ago, some of those now around the table had been out on a run, so they're still strangers to me.

When one starts to speak, I ask him to introduce himself. When he does so, as Pennywise, I can't keep the smile from my face. That's a fuck of a handle if ever I heard one. I raise my eyebrows, and Lost explains.

"Our old prez, Bird, went through a spell when he had a likin' for Stephen King novels. Pennywise was unlucky enough to be patched in durin' that clown phase." I vaguely remember the old prez who had died, Snake only held the top spot for a couple of years.

"I got my name from him too." Salem, the enforcer, puts up his hand. I hadn't made the connection before.

The conversation gets half smiles, which quickly fade. Not surprising, as Pennywise takes the floor and starts on the topic foremost on all of our minds. "What are we going to do about the…" he breaks off as though he can't bring himself to say the word brothers, but hasn't an alternative at hand.

"The traitors?" Lost supplies, then looks around the half-empty table. "That's what we are here to discuss and will need to take a club vote on." He runs his hands over his shortly shorn head. "Goes without sayin' Snake and Poke were the ringleaders, and they got what they deserved. Stripped of their patches and dispatched to meet Satan. That was the decision of the mother chapter. Now we get to decide what to do with the rest." He looks stern as he regards his brothers. "One thing's for certain, Poke's no longer around, so we need a new sergeant-at-arms. I'm proposing Grumbler."

The man in question nods towards Lost, and doesn't look surprised. I reckon he's already had a quiet word with him before coming into the meeting. No one objects, so he seems to be the obvious choice. Token, who appears to be their secretary, as well as their computer go-to expert, notes it on his tablet.

Lost looks tired, and I don't think it's all down to two days of hard riding. "Gator's already swelling Satan's ranks, now we've got to deal with Shark, DJ, Crow, Rattler, Tinder, and Bastard. I know what I want to do, but I'd welcome your thoughts."

"Out in bad standing," Salem suggests. "The only other officer was DJ, and he was only the treasurer because he could add up." He points to a man aptly named Bones. I've noticed before he eats like a horse but never puts on any weight. He's more like a skeleton covered with skin. "Bones here would probably do a good job in his place."

"I'll take your suggestion on board, and we'll vote on it later. For now, we've still got a man in that post until we make a decision."

"Not happy letting any of them come back," Blaze, who I know is their road captain, puts in. "Not sure as I'd ever trust any of them again."

I'm on his side. That's the way I'm leaning as well.

"Anyone want to speak up on their behalf?"

The silence that follows Lost's question is deafening. The prez raises his chin toward me, and I nod back. It's the moment of truth. "We've got two options. One we make them disappear for good, and the second, as Salem suggested, they're out bad. Let's take the first option first."

He pauses and looks around, his expression showing the severity of the decisions we're going to make. For some of us death is preferable to losing our patch, the loss of the brotherhood being more than we could reasonably take. It's not easy to become a member of a club, the year or so prospecting while shits thrown at you from all directions means many don't make the grade. You earn your place to ride with your brethren. To lose that place is losing more than a way of life. I've known men who have committed suicide, as they can't take living outside of the club.

"First vote. Should any, or all of the traitors, meet Satan. If there are any ayes, we'll come back to discussing individuals."

"No."

"No."

The man named Kink seems to think seriously for a moment before shaking his head and saying clearly, "No."

It continues around the table. I give my negative answer, and then Lost adds his. "Record that will ya, Token?" Lost seems to relax a little. "Second vote. That all, or some, are out bad. Again, we'll come back and discuss individual members if there's a need."

There's no need. Everyone agrees, all the traitors are out in bad standing. It really doesn't surprise me. Trust is hard earned, and once lost, nigh on impossible to recover. Nevertheless, it's a hard day for this club.

"Snake's mother? She going to stay in the club?"

"She's got a house in the city." Lost seems to be thinking aloud. "Let's leave it to her. She's done nothin' wrong, but she's lost her son. I doubt she'll want to come back."

And there's another moment of sadness for the woman who'd apparently mothered the whole club, albeit without a smile on her face.

Leaving the compound unmanned isn't something we like to do, but Eva's around, so we give her strict instructions about not unlocking the gate. Out of all of the club whores, she's got the best head on her shoulders. The others are lazy, and rely totally on the club. Unlike in Tucson, no one's yet taken an old lady. The old prez's wife had moved away after he'd died.

The three prospects have been watching over the group of men kept in the warehouse since Drummer went back to Tucson, and it's Lost's decision, to which I give my full support, that all of the remaining San Diego brothers should be part of what needs to be done. That way, no one can raise any objections after the event. In the end, he doesn't even have to give the instruction, no one wants to be left out. As we ride to the warehouse the mood's much the same as for a funeral. No one wants to go, but nobody wants to stay behind, all feeling they owe it to the club to take their individual responsibility for what is about to happen.

The men who've been held prisoner haven't given the prospects any trouble. They've been kept locked up, but fed and watered, and awaiting their fate, probably hoping Snake would turn things about. When the doors are pulled open and we bring them out into the sun, they're all blinking their eyes as they haven't seen proper daylight for thirty-six hours. After giving them a moment to acclimatise, Lost steps up.

Twelve eager eyes look at him. A few more hopeful than others, a couple already resigned.

"Snake's gone."

They've been brothers long enough to read between the lines. After a moment, while that sinks in, their new prez adds, "And Poke's gone the same way."

"What the fuck, man? Shark steps up, and quickly moves back into line when he's faced with Salem's gun. "That's fucked up, man. They had good plans for the club."

"Plans we have no wish in followin'. It's in our bylaws that Satan's Devils don't deal in drugs."

"Yeah, but it makes good business sense." DJ, their previous treasurer argues the point. "Just look at the kind of money we'd bring in."

"And look what interest the cops would have taken in us. You'd have dragged the club down into the mud."

They're casting wary glances at each other, as the point sinks in none of us are going to listen.

"You gonna kill us?" Bastard sneers. "Take us out like the prez?"

Lost is keeping his calm. "I'm the prez," he updates them. "And no, we're not." He nods toward Grumbler, who's the new sergeant-at-arms, and at Salem, who retains his position as enforcer. "Start strippin' their cuts."

Twelve eyes open wide. Six men start protesting. But Salem and Grumbler just go down the line, taking off their leathers, some more forcibly than others, some more easily as the traitors give up. Soon there's six leather vests on the ground.

Lost nods at a prospect who rolls over a metal barrel. Salem picks up the cuts and puts them inside. Another prospect has a can and soaks the contents with gas. Lost himself steps forward and lights a match.

Each of us stand stoically, our nostrils flaring at the stringent burning smell in the air, but none of us making a move. We're probably all thinking what it would be like to see our own cut being burned. Two of the men who've lost their status and insignia are wiping tears from their faces.

In the midst of the flames shooting up from the barrel, Lost addresses the men. "It's the decision of the club that you're out in bad standin'. Ain't no way back from this, so don't even bother to try." He pauses, then repeats from the club rules he knows by heart. "You may not wear the club colors or participate in club activities. You undertake to get your ink blacked out as soon as fuckin' possible. You may not ride with the club. Since you went against the bylaws of the Satan's Devils charter, you may not affiliate with any other Satan's Devil's chapter.

"If any of you are seen by members of this chapter or another, you will be beaten and run off." This means they will need to leave their home city if they want to stay unharmed or even alive. "If you're seen wearing our ink you'll have it burned off. You may try to join another club, but if they find you have left in bad standin', and they leave you alive and let you in as a member, that club will become our enemy." Which means it will be very difficult for them to find another biker home. And difficult to hide what's happened with a blackened tattoo on their back. Realistically, this is the end to them being a member of any biker club.

Crow drops to his knees with his head in his hands, sobs quietly.

"Is there any comin' back from this, Lost? Will you let us back in after, say, six months?"

Lost rounds on the man who's spoken. "Tinder, you fucked up. You threw in with someone who you knew was breakin' club rules. You know Satan's Devils don't deal in drugs. You went against the regulations and had made plans to take our Tucson brothers out."

"Didn't know about that." But the way Tinder's eyes flick away from mine makes it pretty clear that he did.

Rattler calls out, "Don't do this, Brother. Please. Snake misled us."

Lost is impassive. "It's done." And he turns to walk away.

Shark is obviously out of his head. He runs to Lost and grabs him by the shoulder, swinging him around and drawing back his arm. Before his punch can reach its target, he's pulled back and several remaining members of the chapter give him a severe beat down. The other five men look nervously at his unconscious body on the ground. From their expressions, it's sufficient warning and they're not going to copy his actions.

"Get them out of here," Lost directs Salem, then when he glances at me I see the pain in his eyes. In forty-eight hours, he's seen his prez and sergeant-at-arms killed, I dispatched Gator, and now, Shark, DJ, Crow, Rattler, Tinder, and Bastard are out in bad standing. His club's been decimated. My job is to help build it back up. And that starts with supporting the prez.

I slip a friendly arm around his shoulder as we walk back to our rides. "We go forward, not back. No point regrettin' what can't be changed."

"Easier said than done, Brother." Lost steps astride his bike and waits while the other men come up to their sleds. As they're sorting themselves out, he continues, "These men, I trust them all with my life. But two days ago I'd have said the same for any of the other nine, too. Difficult to see how we can come back from this."

"You try. Of course, there's always the option to disband the chapter. But," I indicate the men getting ready behind us, "do you really want to kick them out of the home of their hearts as well as their bodies? No, I didn't think you did. We build on the trust that's there already. Maybe we'll all have to work at it a bit harder, but we *will* come back." As I talk it hits me how long that might take, and how much of my life I'll end up giving to this chapter.

"I'm biased, Dart. Fuck knows why Drum made me the prez. I'd have *died* for any of those men, and now I have to accept, as I'd never have agreed with the direction Snake wanted to take the club, let alone with startin' a war with the mother chapter, they wouldn't have turned a hair when they killed me. My judgement is fucked up." I go to speak, but he lifts his hand. "Need your help, VP. You don't know the men in the same way I do. Speak to them, see what you think. Were any others involved? If we've got any more bad apples, I want them out of the fuckin' barrel."

Suppressing the surprise I still feel at hearing the VP title from his lips, and the warm glow of pride it gives me inside, I nod my head. It makes sense that I can be more impartial with men Lost has been riding with for years and who he trusted to have his back. "Lost, we got this, man."

He reaches out his hand and I clasp it in mine. "Yeah, we got this, VP. We got no fuckin' choice."

CHAPTER 28
Alex

Dart left early this morning, trying not to disturb me as he dressed. Unsuccessful, seeing I was awake, he took my lips in a blistering kiss as though he wanted to brand himself on me to ensure I wouldn't forget him. He'd taken one last look at me, lust flaring in his eyes before ruefully adjusting himself in his jeans.

"This isn't the end, Alex. This is the beginnin'." And with that he turned, the set of his shoulders making it clear he was reluctant to leave. I didn't call him back, didn't stop him, giving my man the space to do what he needs to do.

He's only been gone a couple of hours and already I miss him like hell and wish we'd had more time to explore this new step in our strange new relationship. He claimed me. Then left me alone.

Tyler's up and dressed, and as hungry and impatient for breakfast as any young boy of his age. Ruffling his hair, grateful I've got him for company, I follow him down to the clubhouse. A few nods and looks are thrown at me by the men who returned yesterday. Knowing they've all sworn to protect me gives me a warm feeling inside. Though I might miss living with my sister and her husband, I know it's far safer to be here, secure in the knowledge that even if Ron found me, there's no way he'd be able to get past these bikers.

In the kitchen I find some of the women. Sophie, her pregnancy clearly showing, is standing by the stove, and the welcome smell of bacon once again wafts through the air. Ella's setting out plates, and Carmen is bending down, searching for something in the fridge.

"Ty!" An excited shrill pitched voice calls out.

Letting go of my hand, Tyler crawls under the table where Amy is playing. The teenage girl walks in, followed by the young-looking biker who never seems far away from her. Jayden glances around, then gets on her knees. "What are you two doing under there?"

"Jayden, can you get them up to the table, please? Palladin, you can sit opposite. Breakfast is about done. And Alex, how you feeling today? Want to sit with them and I'll fix you a plate?"

"Thanks, Ella. I'm getting better every day." My scars make me feel ill every time I see them when I change my dressings after a shower, but all that matters is that Dart is able to ignore them. Taking my seat, I ponder his suggestion of getting tattoos, and I wonder if it's possible to make something beautiful out of what at the moment looks so gross. But I've got time to think. I might not know much about marking my skin, but even I know the scars will take a long time to heal before I need to make any decision.

"What's got you so deep in thought?"

Sophie's question brings me back to the present, and I answer her honestly. "Dart suggested getting tattoos to cover my scars."

Placing a piled plate in front of me, she stands back with her hands on her hips. "Might be a good idea, hun. Replace the memories that bugger left you with, with something you actually want to look at."

Sam comes in, followed closely by Drummer. His normally steely eyes seem to twinkle as they fall on me. "So, how's our newest ol' lady doin'?"

"Old lady?" Sophie squeals. "Alex? You and Dart?"

"I didn't see that coming," Carmen mumbles, and my gaze immediately shoots to her. Why not? Am I so far from being old lady material that the thought of me and Dart together is a joke. She must notice my expression, as she comes to sit beside me. "Hey, nothing on you, babe. I didn't expect to see Dart tamed and on a leash. You must be one special lady."

And she's voiced my fear. Despite Dart's promises in the dead of the night, once he's surrounded by club girls again, can he really be faithful to a short girl with a fat ass?

There's easy conversation around the table. Making sure Tyler eats and doesn't get distracted takes my mind off worrying about what Dart's up to. Men wander in, taking seats, or when all those are taken, disappearing into the club room with over-filled plates. It's an easy atmosphere, and everyone tries to include me and make me feel at home. It's at the end of our meal when Drummer turns to me.

"Got a moment, Alex? There's something I'd like to discuss with you."

Drummer might have been friendly enough, but he's the prez of the club, and up until recently was my employer. Though nothing's been said officially, any idiot can see I won't be wanted at the club as a dancer any more. But hearing I've been sacked will just make it final, but I can't imagine there's anything else he'll want to speak to me about. After checking Sam's going to keep an eye on my son, I follow him into his office.

"Take a seat." He points to one of the chairs in front of the desk as he walks around it to take his own. He stares at me as if he can see right down into my soul, and I fidget uncomfortably. Just when I've almost given up on him speaking, he starts. "Couple of things, Alex. Firstly, you and Tyler. You settlin' in okay and got everything you need?"

"Tyler needs his medication in case he has an episode. I've got the prescription at my sister's house."

"Hmm. Getting that filled in Tucson would alert your ex to where you are. You got enough to last you a few days?"

"There's a bottle at Celine's…"

"I'll get a prospect to pick it up. Anythin' else ya need while we're at it?"

I look down at myself and my borrowed clothes. "Dart said a prospect would be able to pick up our clothes, and Tyler's toys."

"Fuck yeah, little tyke needs to be kept amused. But I don't like the idea of doin' much more than a quick in and out at your sister's in case Thompson's got it surveyed. I'll speak to the girls and get them to go shoppin' for you. Don't want to raise suspicion if someone's watchin' your sister's house."

"You really think Ron would do that?" I bite my lip.

He rolls back his head, circling it around his shoulders as if to remove some stiffness there. "Thing is, Alex, we're dealin' with a cop. They've got networks all over. I'd rather not give any sign you've come back to Tucson." His sharp eyes find mine, and realises I need reassurance. "Don't worry, they'll not be settin' foot on the compound. As far as they know you're in the wind with Mouse."

Now he sits forward and places his hands on the desk. "What I really wanted to talk to you about is where you go from here."

"I won't be working at the club." I say it for him.

"Not as you were before," he says enigmatically. And then appears to change the subject. "Dart told me you wanted to be a lawyer. Did your first year of the course?"

"That was a long time ago, and another life."

"But if you had the chance, would you still want to do it?"

Of course I would, I love Tyler to bits, but it's been suffocating just being a wife and mother. My mental capacity of necessity just shut down while I was with Ron. All I've been doing is vegetating the last few years. But I don't tell him all that, I simply shrug. "I'm not going to get hung up on impossible dreams."

"What if it wasn't impossible? Look, I'm not gonna beat around the bush here, but our club lawyer's gettin' close to retirement. It won't be too long before we look for someone else. And we pay him an arm and a leg." He rubs the short beard on his chin. "Makes it look like we're a bunch of criminals havin' a lawyer on retainer, but we're not as bad as all that. But the law's got a downer on us, and we need legal advice far too often, even when we ain't done nothin' wrong."

I keep quiet, not at all sure where this is going.

"What if the club offered to put you through school, and you come and work for us after? You could take on your own clients as long as you gave priority to us."

My eyes widen as a bubble of excitement churns inside me. "I always wanted to help people who found it difficult to get representation, or who couldn't afford someone to be on their side."

"Sums us up nicely, doesn't it? So what d'ya think?"

I bite my lip. "School starts in August. That's ten months off. Drummer, I won't lie. What you're offering sounds attractive, but what if I'm not still with Dart? I won't be anything to the club. And I don't know why you're offering to help me. I've done nothing but bring trouble."

His hands hit the desk. "Have you any idea what it means for a brother to claim an ol' lady?"

Again, I have no answer but a shrug.

"It's not somethin' done lightly just on a whim. It's a lifetime commitment. Dart's made the decision he wants you in his life, and that's as good, if not better, that any civilian marriage in our eyes."

A lifetime commitment? The words make me angry. I had no choice when my parents forced me into Ron's hands. And now Dart's claimed me, and again without giving me a say. When I agreed to be his old lady, I didn't realise how significant it was. He'd told me. Not asked.

"What's got you all riled up?"

"I thought it was like it meant we were going steady or something. I didn't realise it was permanent. I've had enough of having decisions being taken out of my hands."

That gaze has now turned steely. "You like Dart?"

More than that. "Yes."

"Then I don't see what the problem is."

I'm not sure why I'm suddenly feeling annoyed. I'd like nothing more than to think Dart and I have a future. But there's still this niggling doubt that he won't be faithful, and after those years I wasted with Ron, I never want to feel second best again.

Drummer's watching me closely, as if he can read my thoughts. "Dart's a good man, Alex. One of my best. I've known him for six years and never seen him treat a woman bad, and he's always been fair with the men. That's why I chose him to go to San Diego. He's not going to turn on you like Thompson. And seems to me, you chose him yourself. Poor man didn't have a chance once you'd shaken your ass at him."

I still have difficulty believing I attracted Dart in the first place, and it's even harder to think I could keep him. "Look at me, Drum. I'm not the type of woman that a man like Dart goes for."

"Think it's too late to say that." He raps his fingers on the desk. "But for the record, I agree. You're not the type of woman he'd go with just for a fuck. You," now he points at me, "are the type that a man like Dart makes an ol' lady."

I stare at him, still unconvinced.

He sighs. "You know how I got my name, Alex? I'm not ashamed to admit I'd take easy pussy wherever I could find it. But once I met my ol' lady, it was easy to put that behind me. She's the only woman I'll ever want. With club whore's there's something missin', one is as good as another. There's no emotion involved. What you've got with Dart is very different. Oh, he fought it, that's plain to see. But from the moment he met ya he wanted to give both you and your boy a better life. You've got to stop comparin' yourself to any of the club girls, and realise what Dart's offerin' you."

I look down at my fingers twisting in my lap. Am I always going to let the insults Ron repeated until I believed them rule my life? Am I always going to think I'm not good enough for the man that I want. Or can I stand straight, and take what I'm being offered. Isn't it about time I started thinking more of myself and giving Dart credit for doing what he's said? Drummer gives me a few moments to process, and I use the time wisely.

Coming to a decision, I raise my head. "Alright, Drummer. Working on the assumption Dart and I will work out, I'd love to take you up on your offer." Then I start thinking about transferring my credits and the practical side, and that flicker of anticipation starts burning again.

"In the meantime," Drummer waits until I return my attention to him, "I take it you've a good head on your shoulders. With Dart gone, we need someone to manage the club. Road will take over some of it, but how about you help us out and work alongside him? Schedulin' the girls, dealin' with when they want the night off. Fuck, when the babysitter lets them down or some other crap. You won't make the same in tips, but we'd pay you a decent wage."

I could do that. Eagerly I nod. "That sounds great, Drum. But isn't it dangerous for me to go off the compound?"

"You need time to heal up, darlin'. Don't expect you to make an immediate start. But there's ways around it until your problem's sorted. You can go in the back way and keep to the office when there's customers in."

They keep alluding to a future time when I'll no longer have Ron coming after me. As Drum says, I'm not stupid. But I feel no remorse hoping their suggesting a permanent solution to my problems. He tried to kill me after all. But I don't dare come right out and ask him.

"In the meantime, there's something else to keep you occupied. We're arrangin' a poker run as you know, and that's somethin' you can help with. Couple of the brothers have been involved in that before, and Sam's goin' to throw her hand in. You up to gettin' in on that?"

As it's for Tyler's benefit, I don't see how I can refuse even if I wanted to. And it will give me something to do rather than just hanging around waiting for Dart to get back. I answer quickly, "Sure, Drummer. I don't know what the hell I'll be doing, but I'm in."

"Check with Sam, she'll let ya know how far she's got."

I leave Drummer's office feeling more light-hearted than I have for a while. He seems pretty certain Dart was serious in the commitment he seemed to be making last night. How on earth did I get so lucky as to land myself such a man? And now I've got a purpose in life and can look forward to having a career that I've always wanted. In the meantime, he's given me a job. And while I heal, something to do. If it wasn't for the fact I haven't physically got my man at my side, I'd be walking on air.

After checking on Tyler and discovering Jayden's got both him and Amy happily doing some colouring, I go into the clubroom and see Sam sitting at a table drinking some coffee. Grabbing a cup for myself, I go and join her.

She looks up at me with a grin. "Drum's told you I volunteered you, I take it?"

Smiling, I sit down. "Seeing as it's for Tyler, I'm happy to help. Just don't have a clue what needs doing."

"You and me both. Wraith's joining us in a few. Rock and Lady are coming along too. They've all been on charity runs before, so can give us some ideas."

"When we planning this for?"

She laughs. "I've got no clue. Soon as possible, as you need the money, but it will take time to organise, I already know that. Hey, here come the boys now. We can start getting some answers." She pulls an iPad towards her and winks when she sees me eyeing it. "Mouse said it's was best to keep notes on here. That way we can print them out for everyone to see."

"Want me to be note taker?"

"Oh, if you would. I'm better at tuning an engine than tapping on a keyboard." She sighs gratefully as she passes the tablet over.

"So, ladies," Wraith grabs a chair and turns it around and straddles it, "we're talking poker run, right?"

Sam nods. "First we just need to throw around some thoughts about what we need to do."

Rock and Lady settle themselves down. Rock waves towards Hyde and gestures for him to bring beers. I decline, having only just had breakfast. Surely it's too early for alcohol? But the boys clearly don't care, taking the bottles Hyde puts down in front of them.

"When you thinking of?"

"Soon as possible, Wraith."

The VP thinks for a moment. "Best ones take six months or more to plan, but I reckon we can do it in three if we push hard. Time's of the essence, isn't it, Alex?"

"It is," I agree. "But can I ask, exactly what is a poker run?" I've always thought you don't get far if you try to hide your ignorance. Best be up front about what you don't know.

Rock, for some reason, takes a gun out of his cut and places it on the table in front of him. He proceeds to spin it with his hands. Then nodding at Wraith and Lady, says, "I'll take this, shall I?" At their nods, he continues, "It's a run where the winner is the person who ends up with the best poker hand. The run should be long enough to be interesting, but not so far as to put people off. We should aim for about seventy-five miles to a hundred.

"We sell tickets. Each entrant gets given his first playin' card at the beginnin' of the run, then there's usually five checkpoints, and at each of those participants will draw another card and have it marked off on a score sheet. At the end of the day, the person with the best hand takes home the prize." He pauses to take a swig of his beer. "Now the bit you're interested in, Alex, is how it makes money. Obviously, first off is the entry fee, but set that too high and people won't enter. The idea is to get them to empty their wallets during the day."

Lady takes over. "Auctions are good. If we get people to donate prizes. And competitions."

Wraith butts in. "We need to decide somewhere where people can assemble, somewhere like a restaurant is a good starting point. And at the end, something to make people stay and part with more money. A band and a beer tent, or somewhere that provides food and drink."

I swallow, only now realising how complicated this is. I've been trying to take notes but they're all in a muddle. "Hold on a minute. There's a heck of a lot of organising to do. Can we go slower so I can start making a list? Then it sounds like we need to assign people to do various tasks."

Wraith nods. "Makes sense. Right, where to start?"

"Date and route," Rock suggests. I wish he'd stop spinning that gun, it's making me feel nervous.

"Will the end of January give us enough time?"

"Yeah, I'll check what else is going on at that time. Don't want to clash with a run from another club."

"I'll talk to Joker about plannin' a route, as he's Road Captain, that's his job. We'll sort out the start and end points, and talk to the police."

I'm busy scribbling it all down. *End of January. Road Captain plans route.*

"We need someone to approach sponsors. The Harley shop in Tucson might be on board. We'll need to check insurance at the properties at the start and end, and at the waypoints. And permits if we need them."

"I can do that." After years of disuse, I'm looking forward to getting my brain working again. And while it seems a mammoth task, I'm starting to enjoy myself.

CHAPTER 29
Dart

I've been in San Diego a week now. Everyday I've spoken to Alex, who's been roped into organising the poker run. She seems to have taken to it like a duck to water, and at least I don't have to worry about her brooding. It's never easy to maintain a long-distance relationship, and one so embryonic is even harder. I'm trying to find some space to make that promised visit home, but it's difficult as my VP duties seem to be taking all my time.

There are now only thirteen patched members at the club, fifteen counting myself and Lost, and I know a couple have been thinking about leaving. I've spent more than one evening expounding the virtues of the Satan's Devils Motorcycle Club, even though after all that's happened it's hard to sound convincing. Having a president, an officer, and several members go their own way is a dark cloud hanging heavy over everyone here.

And then there's the workload. Like the Tucson club, San D runs an auto-shop, a strip club, and several small businesses, including one that particularly interests me for future reference, a tattoo shop. Being nine men down, work's piling up, and grumbles increasing at the end of each day. Lost and I have moved men around, but we are loathe to close down any of the businesses. I floated the idea of employing civilians until we can get our membership back up, and so some of my time has been spent interviewing candidates.

To date I've taken on two new mechanics, we'll just have to see how they shape up.

It's taken longer than I hoped, but today I hope to find some space to work on my own pet project. Taking out Thompson and setting Alex free for once and for all. Salem and Pennywise—shit, I can't get over those handles—are joining me for a beer and to try to pull together a plan of action. I'm pleased to find as I walk down from my room, they're not only ready and waiting for me, but have also got beers lined up.

Salem waits for me to sit down, then gets straight down to business. "Right. You want this cop taken out. How we going to play this? What ya thinkin'?"

I push back a strand of hair that's escaped from my bun, tucking it behind my ear. "The cops know his wife's shacked up with a man from the club." They do, they just don't have the right man. "We don't want any suspicion to fall on the Satan's Devils."

"Okay, so how do we stop the po-po from finding out?" Pennywise doesn't seem overly concerned that we're planning a murder.

I've been giving a lot of thought to that, and while I long to take out the fucker in the most painful way possible, putting my personal feelings aside and thinking of the club, there's only one answer. "It's got to look like an accident."

"Any ideas?" Salem asks.

"Some, yeah. Pennywise, you're a sniper I hear."

"Sure am. Got the unit's record at 1500 yards." I know there's been longer shots, but at only just under a mile, that's an impressive achievement.

I let them in on my initial thoughts. "We track his regular routes. Find a spot. Basic idea is to shoot out his tires. Need to try and sort it so he somersaults over the guard rail."

"I'd like to make some adjustments to that, VP. Take too long trailing him, and he might get wise to a tail. How's about we get him on a route we've planned and set up for instead?"

Salem looks thoughtful. "He's still got a hard on for yer bitch, VP. If he's after her, and he's plannin' to take her out, he won't tell anyone where he's goin'. We could use the lure of her as bait."

I nod at them both. "As long as we don't put her in danger. She's stayin' in Tucson, ya hear? You're the expert, Pennywise. And both of you know the terrain around here better than I do."

Stroking his chin with one hand, Salem cocks his head on one side. "What about the Lake Wohlford road from Escondido to Valley Center? We can take him out where there's a drop off on left before the paintball grounds."

Pennywise is nodding. "That would do. But it means we'd have to get him on the way back down."

Salem hasn't finished. "How's about we let him know she's been spotted up somewhere up near Valley Center? We'll drop you off, Pennywise, get you in position early. Then we'll stake out where we want him to go, get exact details of what he's drivin'. When he's finished his wild goose chase, you can get him on his way back down to Escondido."

"Can you do it with one shot?" I ask, creasing my brow. I don't doubt that he'll hit it, but banking on a blowout which will take him over the guardrail could be down to luck."

Pennywise grins, an evil looking leer. "I'll use a dumdum bullet. One that expands on impact. Got a fella who makes my ammunition for me. That fucker will explode and he won't have a chance."

"Any chance of them findin' evidence of the bullet?"

A shrug. "Can assure you there won't be much left of the tyre other than shredded rubber. The bullet will have disintegrated, but of course there's always a slight risk. There's a chance, of course that they might find a fragment, but even if they do, it won't point to us. My guy's too clever to leave his signature. And a cop as rotten as Thompson must have a fuckload of enemies."

Salem nods. "Even if they were suspicious, the Satan's Devil they know of is in Tucson with your old lady. Thompson was the only one who knew she had anythin' to do with this club, and he'll be long gone before they start investigatin'."

We seem to be covering all the bases. Of course, there's a fuck of a lot of things that could go wrong, but it's the only clean way I can think of to take Thompson out. It still leaves a sour taste in my mouth like I can't make him suffer like he did my woman, but dead's dead in the end, as Mouse had told me.

Pennywise wants some time to scout an exact location to set up, Salem volunteers to look for somewhere we can lure Thompson to. While I'm anxious to get this matter over and done with, I agree that we need to take time to scope it all out. But I itch with impatience. At the forefront of my mind, after all, is the thought that once we've accomplished this, there's nothing to stop Alex coming back to San Diego as a grieving widow. And my old lady. And with enough money so she can start on the road to get treatment arranged for Tyler. The benefits weigh up well against the downside that Thompson's heading for too easy a death.

As I've at last got some free time, I decide that next weekend I'll be making a visit back home. I've rarely gone so long without sex before, and while I'm steering clear of the club whores— particularly Eva—my hand's getting a twice daily workout in the shower, fuelled by thoughts of exactly what I'm going to do to Alex next time I see her. There's an upside to this forced time apart, as it means she should be healed up by the time I return, and I can start giving her some real biker loving. Just the thought of her luscious lips around my cock, or the idea of me working my way into her so tight cunt never fails to have the predictable reaction.

I'm just adjusting myself in my jeans having spent the last few moments thinking about my woman when Lost meets me at the bar. Opening my mouth to tell him of my decision to go home, he forestays my words with a sentence of his own. And just like that, my plans to get fucked anytime soon turn to dust.

"Dusty and Scribe are looking to leave us."

"Fuck." I've not had much to do with that pair. They've been keeping themselves quiet and out of the way. "Think they were mixed up in Snake's shit?"

Lost shakes his head. "I really don't think so. They're just twitchy, wonderin' what's going to happen to the club. Someone's put out a rumour that Drummer wants to close us down. We're losin' money, Brother, as some of the businesses are runnin' on a skeleton crew, and they're also afraid their pay packet's gonna get lighter."

"But we haven't got as many mouths to feed. Their take home shouldn't drop much."

"Just as long as the rot doesn't extend any further. Lose more men, a business may have to fold."

I think for a few seconds. "They tight with anyone else, other than themselves?"

"Scribe used to hang out with Rattler."

So he'll be missing his brother. "Want me to have a word?"

"Yeah, VP. That would be useful. Need you around to keep an eye on them. We don't want them influencin' anyone else."

Weekdays most of us work, weekends is the time they're more likely to get into corners and plot. Reluctantly I realise I'll have to put Alex off for another week if I'm going to take my role seriously here. As Lost continues to sit beside me, each of us lost in our own thoughts, I try to turn my mind away from the disappointment that I'll have to wait longer to see my old lady, and instead consider the problem at hand. As I drink my beer, I start to think on the reasons why we all joined the Satan's Devils in the first place, and why we endured the long twelve months or more of the prospecting stage to get to be a fully-fledged member. The love of riding bikes, the brotherhood. And not forgetting pussy and alcohol on tap.

Lost is staring morosely into his bottle. As the solution comes to me I pat him on the shoulder. "Arrange a run. Saturday. Somewhere we can have a barbeque, on the beach, perhaps? Get the girls there, perhaps gather up some of the hangers on? A good ride on their sleds, food, beer, girls, and companionship might remind Scribe and Dusty what they're thinking of givin' up."

Lost takes a moment to respond. When he finally turns there's a sparkle in his eyes which wasn't there before. "Fuckin' good idea, VP." Then without wasting a moment he cups hands around his mouth and hollers, "Run, Saturday. Leavin' sharp at noon. Everyone's comin'. Mandatory attendance."

There's a moment of silence, then somebody cheers and someone else says, "About fuckin' time."

The prez gives me a wink before crossing to his office and picking up the reins of business again. Guess that's my job as VP, keeping everyone's morale up.

"I suppose that was you?" Salem comes up and slaps my back. "Lost's been, well, lost since he took top spot."

"Cut him some slack, Brother. He's got a lot on his plate."

"Not criticising him, but with you watchin' his back we've got quite a team here." I nod absentmindedly. Sure, I miss my brothers back in Tucson, but this group is turning out to be a good fucking bunch. Any I hadn't taken to at first were among the lot that are now out bad. "So where we goin'?"

Realising Salem's still talking, I bring my attention back. "No idea, man. Don't know this area too well as yet."

Salem turns around. "Blaze. Com'ere man." Blaze is the road captain. "VP's organisin' a run and beach barbeque with fuck all idea where to go. Help him out, will ya?"

With a nod at me and a gesture towards Al, one of the prospects, minding the bar, he takes his bottle of beer. "How far away d'ya want?"

"Far enough to get our engines warm, not so far that we spend all day on the bikes."

Blaze taps his beer bottle against his mouth. "Sixty-miles or so do ya? I'm thinkin' Doheny State Beach. It's got picnic areas and grills for barbequin'. Been there a few times before and always had a good time."

"Sounds good, man!" I slap his back. "Sounds fuckin' good."

Once we've got an outline of arrangements, I'm just about to push away from the bar when this time it's Pennywise who comes over, pulls me to one side, and speaks in a low voice. "Reckon we could combine the two? You, me, and Salem go sort Thompson out, then go join them at the beach. Got a whole load of brothers who'll swear we were with them the whole time."

I like the idea. I like it very much. "Any idea on location?"

"Yeah, I'm thinking of heading out tomorrow and having a look around, find the right spot." He pauses to grin. "If my boss gives me time off work, that is."

I'm his boss, so I give a broad grin back. "I'm sure he can arrange somethin'."

"Can I make a suggestion, VP?" At my nod he continues, "We're best off not ridin' our bikes when we do the deed. So get the prospects to ride them. Anyone counts up the bikes, we'll all be accounted for. On the way back they can drive the crash truck."

"And who drives it there?"

He nods his head to where the sweet butts are coming in. "Ask Eva. She'll do it as long as she hasn't got a shift at the hospital."

The one person I don't want to speak to. It's not that I don't trust myself, I just like to keep a distance and not encourage her to be friendly. When Alex can come to this chapter, I don't want any rumours around that I've been getting close. Funny enough, I feel worse about what isn't even a betrayal to Alex than I do about an unknown prospect riding my bike.

As the woman in question catches me looking at her, I realise putting it off isn't going to make it better. Instead of ignoring her as I normally do, I approach. "Eva." I raise my chin in greeting.

"Dart." Her face splits into a welcoming smile. "We haven't spoken since you got back." She points at my VP flash in my cut. "Congrats on that. Does that mean you're stayin' here a while?"

"I'll stay as long as necessary."

"And while you're here, how about you and I get together?" Moving closer, she manages to brush up against me. Immediately I take a step back and decide it's time to put her completely straight.

"I'm with Alex. She's my ol' lady."

She makes a fuss of looking around her, and then puts her hand on my arm. "She's not here, is she? Where is she? Back in Tucson? And you, poor baby, must be in need of some company by now. I know you haven't been with the other girls, so you must have blue balls."

Not having old ladies at the San Diego chapter, the club girls haven't seen how faithful a biker can be once he's found the right woman. After her indiscreet disclosure to Alex last time, and all the damage that caused, in the extremely unlikely event that I had a fancy to go with a whore it certainly wouldn't be her. I remove her hand from my arm, not feeling the slightest stirring in my cock.

"I told you, I've got an old lady. She gets my dick, nobody else."

Eva pouts, obviously unhappy.

Not understanding what attracted me to her in the first place, hell, then I wasn't concerned with her looks or her character, just wanting to get my rocks off, I decide to end this confrontation and fast. "Need you to do somethin' for us, Eva. You gonna be free Saturday afternoon?" When she nods and tilts her head to one side I tell her what we need.

"A barbeque on the beach sounds fun. We haven't done anything like that for a while. Sure, I'll drive the truck and follow you guys. You want I should bring the other club girls as well, rather than leaving them to make their own way there?"

Might as well. The prospects can return in the truck Pennywise, Salem, and I will be using. "Yeah, bring them with you if they want."

"And perhaps you and I can have some fun?"

She doesn't give up. I shut that down fast. "No chance of that. I'm not cheatin' on Alex, not today, not Saturday, not ever."

I don't know if it's promotion to VP status or simply finding the right girl to take as my old lady, but suddenly, as I speak to Eva, I realise I've grown up. I'm no longer the man who doesn't want to be tied down. I'm the man who wants to make Alex my wife, do everything properly, adopt Tyler, and eventually add a couple more kids into the mix. And that's the thought that gets me hard, not the idea of variety and a different girl in my bed every night.

Leaving her standing and disappointed, I turn away and a smile comes to my face. I never understood how the likes of Drum, Wraith, and Slick could tie themselves to one woman before. And Heart's devastation at losing his soulmate, well I'll give him a pass on that. If anything should happen to Alex... Just the thought turns my stomach sour.

CHAPTER 30
Alex

Dart had to go to San Diego for reasons that weren't his own, and while I'm proud on his behalf that Drummer proposed him for VP, I hate this distance apart. I could spend all my time tense, worrying he's being unfaithful. Or I could remember, that time when he went with Eva, he'd made no promises to me. Now that he has, unless I trust him, I'll just get myself tied up in knots. I resolve to give him the benefit of the doubt.

And that's not as hard as it seems. While I'd hoped he'd have returned for a visit by now to explore our fledging relationship, he never fails to call every night and gives me the gist of what's going on down in San Diego. Although he doesn't tell me anything that comes under the category of club business, I hear enough to know he's run off his feet.

He asks a lot about Tyler and, unfortunately, I've had to admit he's had another couple of episodes. They seem to be happening more frequently now, the stress of seeing his father again seems to have triggered them off. Dart sounds more worried than me. I learned long ago I just need to make it as easy on my son as I can, and not to waste time agonising over what I can't prevent.

I do what I can. Once Tyler had an episode in the clubroom, witnessed by Dart's brothers. The men have been great, the temperature in the clubhouse has been turned up a few degrees so Tyler doesn't have such a shock walking in from the outside.

When I've apologised for causing them discomfort, they shrug it off, saying I, and by extension, Tyler, belong to the Satan's Devils now, and their protection extends to looking after his health. When they'd seen Tyler collapse in pain, Paladin, the youngest of them all, carried him up to my suite, and the burly Beef followed, his jaw clenched with concern.

No, worrying about it won't make a difference. What will is getting Tyler back to San Diego to talk with the specialist he was seeing before we had to leave. The frequency of his episodes is increasing to the point that some action needs to be taken. If I agree to a blood transfusion to help in the short term, I say goodbye to the chance of success for a permanent cure.

I've lived with the worry about Tyler for six years, and have learned constantly dwelling on his health isn't good for either of us. It's best to remain positive for him, and keep my worry and fear for the future hidden. I help him through his episodes and then move on. And I've got so much to do here, it's not too hard to try to put his disease to the back of my mind, concentrating on the positive things I can do instead, such as trying to raise money.

In the past few weeks the arrangements for the poker run have started to take shape. We've sorted the route and have applied for the necessary permits from the counties the run will be going through, and from the police. We've got a number of sponsors who've agreed to donate prizes, and a local and popular tribute band have agreed to take part.

We're starting at a restaurant and ending up in a park where we've got permission to set up a marquee. The Wheel Inn will be doing some of the catering, but with the numbers expected they're having to bring in outside help. We've enlisted an army of catering vans, selling anything from hot dogs and pizzas to candy floss and ice cream.

Sam and Wraith have even done an interview with a local radio station, who have gotten interested in the cause and that it was to help a young boy. We got a firm who print t-shirts involved, who're going to produce versions celebrating the event and sell them at the park. Other vendors are stepping up too, all interested in taking part.

People are already registering, and the ten-dollar entrance fees we decided to charge have started to trickle into the bank account Dollar has set up. We'll be running a raffle and giving prizes for all manner of things. And we've contacted the area's car and motorcycle clubs who are going to come and set up a show.

With Tyler's health deteriorating, I've tried to keep him quiet, and have had him helping me designing flyers and the like. He's taken quite an interest, especially when Wraith suggested he judges some of the competitions, like those for the longest beard and longest ponytail.

"Wow! I'm exhausted." Sam comes and flops down into the chair beside me. After heaving a sigh, she sits up straight. "Right, I've been to the printers and got a whole batch of tickets and flyers, and dropped them off at the Harley store. Also a couple of other biker shops in Tucson."

"Rock's going to take some up to the Harley store in Phoenix as well. I rang them today and they're happy to assist. Oh, and I've got the prospects delivering them to the other chapters."

"It's going good, girl." Though tired, Sam manages a smile. I don't think any of us knew what we would be taking on when we agreed to manage this. The club has already had to find room to store the donated prizes.

"Glad to find you here." Dollar, the treasurer comes over. "Had an idea. Young Tyler's story is one that would touch a few hearts. Reckon we should set up one of those Just Giving or Go-fund-me accounts. Want me to look into it?"

I bite my lip. A poker run is one thing, but asking strangers to donate? And so far, we've kept the details of who it's for and why out of it, just in case it gets back to Ron. "It's a good idea, Dollar, but that makes it public. Surely we'd have to put details of Tyler's sickness and identity up?"

He looks at me sharply, opens his mouth, then snaps it shut fast. He looks around the room, then turns back and pats my hand. "An idea we'll revisit shortly." And with that enigmatic statement, he gets up and leaves.

Sam raises her eyebrow and watches him go. "He knows something we don't."

"He does that," I reply, thoughtfully.

Drummer appears from the direction of his office. "Alex? Got a moment?"

"I'll watch Tyler," Sam offers. "I was just going to get Amy from Jayden and give her some lunch."

Thanking her, I go to see what Drummer wants. As I enter his office, he directs me to sit down.

"Sam tells me that the arrangements for the poker run are goin' well." After making his statement he examines me. "And you, Alex. You healed up now?"

The stitches have been removed, and now it's just a waiting game for the last remaining soreness to go. "Mostly, yes, Drum."

"We discussed before you doin' some of the management activities at Satan's Topless Angels. Are you ready for that?" His fingers toy with his beard. "Road's gettin' into a bit of a muddle. He's okay with the money side, but the girls are runnin' rings around him, all wantin' the best slots or take the same time off, and he's unable to say no."

I suppress my smile. I might not have been there long, but I had got to know the girls a little. And I knew exactly what he was talking about. Later in the evening when drink has loosened their wallets, the tips can be bigger. No one wants to go on in the earlier slots if they can help it.

I really don't mind helping them out. As long as I keep my clothes on, that is. There's only one concern. "What about Tyler?" Before, when I was working, I had no concerns leaving him with his aunt.

"I've spoken to Sam. She's happy to watch over Tyler while you're at the club. Schedulin' can be done before the club opens, and you don't need to stay there late, just long enough to sort out the girls. And, Alex, I'm hopin' this won't be for long. You've heard about Heart?"

Of course I have. The girls all miss Crystal and have told me about her, and of her husband who's yet to come to terms with her loss. He's Amy's father, but sadly he's had nothing to do with her since the accident. So I just nod.

"Well, I've just had a conversation with him. Heart's comin' back, and I want him to replace Dart at the club, and the work ain't physical so it won't be too taxin'. It will do him good to have some focus again. He'll be back next week, so this will only be temporary. If you can work this week, and then until Heart knows enough to take over."

Actually, I'm relieved this won't be a permanent position. "That suits me fine, Drum. As the date for the run comes closer it's going to get really hectic."

"Of course it is. And I don't want Sam overdoin' it. Fuck me, she'll be more than six months pregnant by the end of January."

"I've noticed her looking tired, Drummer. I'll watch her more carefully and make sure she's not doing too much."

"Appreciate that, Alex. Fuckin' appreciate that."

There's no point in delaying, so I decide to start my new job that afternoon.

Aware eyes might be on the club looking for me, I drive down with Road in a discreet SUV and park around the back. That first step into Satan's Topless Angels is harder than I expected, and the prospect puts a comforting hand on my shoulder as I stop dead, my eyes going to the poles on the stage. While I hadn't enjoyed taking my clothes off in public, I had loved the freedom that twirling around the pole gave me, and have to admit, had been inspired by the adulation I'd received. It was the one thing I could do, and now that had been taken from me.

As I stand, unable to move, realising I'll never again be entertaining people and showing off my pole dancing skills, Road squeezes his fingers.

"Tomorrow we'll come earlier," he says. "Bring a leotard or something you can dance in and take some time on the pole. Keep your hand in, at least." Today I'm dressed in a skirt and blouse, wanting to give off a managerial vibe as if I know what I'm doing, whereas in truth I'm banking on my brain to get to grips with work that I've no experience with.

I gaze up at him in amazement, surprised he'd so quickly sussed how I was feeling and the reason for it. "I'm not sure I can do that yet." My hand gently rubs at the still healing scars on my chest.

He turns me to face him. "Whenever you're ready. Hell, anytime you want I'll open up for you and you can dance to your heart's content."

His caring offer puts a smile back on my face. "Hey, I think we've got work to do. Want to show me what I'm supposed to be doing?"

His mouth turns up at the corners, and he does a mock bow to show me the way. "After you, boss."

While we're not open it's safe for me to go anywhere I want in the club. When the customers come in, I'll make myself scarce and stay in the office. Acquainting myself, I quickly find the scheduling is indeed in a mess, and quickly have a plan for the next few days. Then, when the girls come in, I present it to them, to a chorus of protests and excuses.

"Hey, I can't do the first spot tomorrow. I've got to go to the parents' evening at the school."

"And I need to leave early tonight. My kid's got tonsillitis."

Now that one I can slap down. "Bambi, your son had his tonsils out last year." I clearly remember her telling us in great detail. She's more likely got a hot date tonight. "And Karma, if you needed time off you should have told us in advance." No wonder Road had such difficulty with the girls.

But I'm firm with them. I leave them sulking, but sense I've gained their respect as soon as they saw I wasn't going to back down. They definitely need someone who'll keep them in line, and I hope Heart's up to the job when he takes over. Having heard the girls talk about him, he's got a reputation for being a big softy. *If he is, they'll run him ragged.* Knowing Heart was so named for his big heart, I do have to wonder how he'll get on deflecting the excuses the girls fling at him. I look forward to meeting the man and finding out.

Dart laughs when I tell him next time he calls, and seems pleased I didn't take their nonsense. He's also over the moon when I tell him Heart's coming back, but like me, he has some concerns about how he'll adjust to being back in the place he last lived with his wife.

CHAPTER 31
Dart

I don't get much sleep Friday night. In my head, I've been going over and over our plans, trying to think of everything that could go wrong, and if it does, what we can do to manage it. I'd been worrying most about getting Thompson to the destination we'd planned, but Lost was the one who'd come through on sorting that out.

Unlike the Tucson chapter, where we avoid having anything to do with the cops and have none on our payroll, Snake had decided to pull a couple into the San Diego fold. For now they're still getting a retainer, remaining ignorant for now that the new president is considering cutting them loose. He's managed for one to arrange to report a sighting of Alex directly to Thompson. He's sure to believe another cop, so we've little doubt he'll be hot off the mark to follow that lead up. Thompson should be given the info just after eleven. We're leaving at ten to be at the Valley Center location well ahead of him.

As I enter the clubroom brothers are already milling around, and there's an air of excitement about the run later today.

I reel as Lost slaps my back. "Look at this, VP. Brothers are already awake and getting' their shit organised. You made a good call. Needed somethin' like this to make us feel like a family again."

Yeah, from the general atmosphere, it's all looking good. Even Scribe's grinning as he talks to Brakes, and Dusty is laughing at something Token has said. Seeing Salem walking in through the door, I check my phone. Time's getting on, it's almost ten o'clock now. When Pennywise enters, pushing the three prospects in front of him, I go to join them.

I feel like I'm stripping naked as I slide off my cut and hand it to Al. Salem gives his to Lloyd, and Pennywise's goes to Dave. If anyone checks any CCTV later, they'll see the right number of bikers, and if they look closely enough, all the patched members' cuts.

"One scratch on my bike and you'll never patch in," I warn Al with a growl.

With equally serious faces, Salem and Pennywise issue similarly dire threats of their own. Then we all pass our bike keys over. If everything works, my reward will be a world without Thompson in it, and Alex a free woman later today.

"Good luck." Lost comes over, and that's all he says. No one but him knows the detail of what we're doing today.

And then that's it. With no fanfare, we quietly leave.

We're silent in the truck. Having gone over the plan so many times before, there's no need for further discussion. We drop Pennywise off and then continue up to the empty cabin Salem had found, hiding the truck in a hidden-away parking spot he suggested. Using a handy tool, I disengage the lock and go inside the cabin. Putting on latex gloves, I then proceed to make it look like somebody's been staying here. Once I'm happy, I carefully place a pamphlet from the hospital Tyler used to go to, and an appointment card for this afternoon in a not too obvious place. It's the bait to get Thompson chasing back to the city.

Then I go outside, and prepare to wait with Salem.

We were right. The tip-offs got Thompson responding fast, obviously not wanting to lose Alex again. He arrives minutes before we expected him to. We grin at each other and place bets on how long it will take. Salem wins, Thompson was faster than I thought, running out of the cabin and back to his car, which tears out of the driveway, spinning gravel and dust. Once he's away, I run back inside to check, before making my way back to our truck.

Thompson's found the lure I'd left and plainly swallowed it up.

With no need to follow him, I wait until he's out of sight before pulling the SUV out of its spot.

Salem's grinning like a loon as he picks up his phone. "Phase one completed, Brother. And he's comin' your way fast. Best get yourself in place. He's speedin'.'" He then tells him the colour and make of the vehicle he's driving.

As he ends his call, I frown. "That shot's not gonna be easy."

"Pennywise is fuckin' good at this. He'll make it okay. Spot he's chosen is only five hundred yards away. Piece of cake, VP."

I wish I had his confidence. After everything, if Pennywise misses, all our planning was for nothing.

"And anyway," the enforcer continues, "the speed we saw him go out of here will increase the chances that tire blowin' out has the results we're looking for. That's a dangerous road to take fast, Brother."

I need to know for certain and see with my own eyes. I increase the speed, but keep to the limit, not wanting to draw any attention today. Ten minutes later and Salem's phone rings. "I'll tell him."

Unable to discern anything from the tone of his voice, I slap my hand on the steering wheel and demand impatiently, "Just tell me already."

"Worked like a charm."

And fuck me, we're coming up on the evidence now. The guardrail's bent where the car must have clipped it when it went over. It's a long fucking drop. There are no other cars around, so I allow myself to slow.

Salem's craning his head out of the passenger window. "Can't see the car, but there's black smoke billowin' up. Car's burnin' up, Brother. Couldn't have asked for a fuckin' better result."

Burn well enough there won't be anything left to investigate. Best fucking outcome I could have asked for. I'd like to have made sure, but the likelihood of Thompson surviving the crash was extremely small. And we can't stop or hang about.

We go on to the pick-up point and pull over. Pennywise is nowhere to be seen.

"What the fuck?"

Salem's phone rings again. "Okay, we'll stay put." He turns to me. "Got your wish, Brother. Pennywise decided to jog down aways to check it out. Thompson was thrown clear, and from the way he's landed he obviously broke his neck. No fucker can survive with their head facing backwards."

I'm still letting out a deep sigh of relief as the back door opens and Pennywise gets in. He's panting from exertion having had to run a third of a mile and then back.

As soon as he catches his breath he tells us, "It's burning up fast. Best get out of here in case someone comes to investigate. Oh, and, thought you'd want this, Dart. It was in his pocket."

As a piece of card flutters onto my lap I see it's the appointment card I'd left as bait. The fake evidence that could have exposed it wasn't an accident. I don't have the words to thank him. He shrugs it off and tells me to get moving.

He doesn't need to tell me twice. As I shift into drive and put my foot down, I almost can't believe it. Thompson is dead. And Alex can come out of hiding.

"Fuck, that was fun, VP. He must have been doing a hundred or more. Didn't have a fuckin' chance when that tire blew up." Now breathing easier, Pennywise seems hyped up.

Salem and I exchange grins.

When we draw up at the beach we find the prospect, Lloyd, who's been left on duty watching the bikes. As we draw to a stop he runs to the truck and approaches us carrying our cuts reverently in his hands. While we slide them on, he also hands over our keys.

Salem goes across and inspects his bike. "What the FUCK!"

Lloyd goes pale.

Stomping back over, the enforcer's face is thunderous. Then he smirks. "Just fuckin' with ya, Prospect."

I double over, chuckling at the look on Lloyd's face. I think he was close to shitting himself. When my mirth fades and I straighten, I see a man checking out the bikes parked up. There's a Harley that's not one of ours a little further along the beach, an older model Sportster. The man's wearing jeans and motorcycle boots, but no cut.

Lloyd notices what I'm looking at and steps forward with a scowl.

"I got this," I tell him. As Salem and Pennywise head on down to the beach I walk to join the newcomer. He's a tall man, probably my height, and has muscular arms which are covered in tattoos. As I get closer he notices me approaching and raises his hands as if to show he's no threat.

I lift my chin and flick my wrist, signalling that he needn't be concerned. He waits for me to get close enough to speak, and now in range I can read some of the writing on one of his arms, *Live to Ride,* and above that, the words, *Semper Fi.*

I nod towards his bike. "Early '90s?" I admire it. It's in factory state, hasn't been altered or customised at all. Hard to find a blank canvas like that.

"Yeah, I've just got it. Fucker who owned it kept it in fairly good shape. No gimmicks at all, just how I like it. 883 bored out to 1200. Didn't take much more than a service to bring it up to scratch." He jerks his head towards our Harleys. "Nice selection here."

"You ride with a club?"

He grins and looks around him. Yeah, pretty foolish question as there's no one else there. "Only clubs that I know are into too much shit for me. Or are just full of weekend warriors."

Well, we were into shit, but we're now trying to stay clean. "We're having a cookout on the beach. Wanna come join us for a bit?"

He steps back and looks at me sharply, obviously thinking I'm setting him up to walk into a trap.

Ignoring his reaction, I continue. "Satan's Devils is all about the brotherhood. We eat live and sleep bikes." I've become pretty good at summing people up, and something tells me that might interest him.

"And what else are you into?" he asks, suspiciously.

"Earning an honest wage."

He looks incredulous.

"Some of my brothers work in the auto shop. We got a lot of custom work going on." I point to his arms. "Nice work, there. We've also got a tattoo shop, and a strip club."

His face relaxes into a quick grin at the last. Yeah, he's just a man as much as the rest of us.

"Hey, what say you come join us? Grab a bite to eat, talk bikes with the boys?"

I've almost got him, but then he steps back and makes a move to his bike. When he walks he favours his left leg. I want to keep him talking, so I wave my hand toward it. "Get that overseas?"

He sees where I'm looking and pulls up his pants, allowing me to see a prosthesis, similar to the one Peg wears. "Nah, stupid fuckin' woman knocked me off my bike when I was on leave. Compounded her error by runnin' over my leg. I was going to be a lifer, but they gave me a medical discharge."

"Noticed the tattoo. Marine?"

"Yeah." He looks into the distance, and regret passes over his face. It's easy to see he misses being part of a team.

"Look, I'll be straight with ya. It's up to you, but I reckon you're lookin' for a home. A brotherhood to belong to. If I'm wrong, I'll apologise to ya."

He shrugs, and there's that look of longing on his face again. "Can't say yer wrong."

"Then come join us, see if we've got somethin' you like. Won't lie to ya, we don't accept new members easy. See that guy there?" I indicate Lloyd. "He's happy to do that shit job of looking after the bikes. We may, or may not, let him down for some food. He's a prospect, and given all manner of shit jobs for a year or so, until we have sufficient confidence and trust to vote him in."

"You served?"

I nod.

"Then you'll know anyone who has can put up with a whole heap of the smelly stuff."

I've almost got him, now I just have to reel him in.

He's still wary. "Saw your boys ride in. You're a white club. And there ain't no getting away from the colour of my skin."

I shade my eyes as though giving him a look like I hadn't noticed he was black until he'd pointed it out. Then I grin. "Dart," I tell him, holding out my hand for him to shake. "I'm the VP, the vice president of this chapter. And I'm on the lookout for new members."

He looks a little more interested now I've explained my rank.

"Ain't gonna kid yer, I've just taken an ol' lady, and she's got the same colour as you. She's got a young son which forced a decision on the club. We changed our bylaws to accept all members, black, white, purple, or fucking blue. You come with me? You'll be our first black member. Not gonna lie and say there won't ever be any awkwardness or that it will always be easy, but there ain't nothin' stopping ya becoming a part of the club."

He straightens his back and flexes his impressive muscles. "I can handle my own." And he looks like he can.

I give him a few moments to process what I've told him. Then his mouth quirks, one side turning up followed by the other, and then a full smile appears on his face. As he holds out his hand I grasp it, and pulling him to me, slap him on the back.

"What's yer name?"

"Simpson. Niran Simpson."

"Well, Niran, sounds like we've got a party to go to." I turn and walk off. After just a second's hesitation, Niran steps alongside me.

CHAPTER 32
Alex

Ron's dead. I was wary at first when Celine contacted me saying his department was trying to get in touch. I wasn't sure why they wanted to talk with me, and I certainly had no desire to be tricked into talking to Ron. I checked with Drummer, who said it was okay to call them back. I made the call in Drummer's office, sitting across from him.

It hadn't taken me long to get through, and once I got through to the right person, his captain I think he said he was, well, he gave me the *sad* news. An automobile accident he said, assuring me Ron had been dead on impact and hadn't suffered.

It took a long time to sink in, I couldn't even tell Drummer for a second. When I looked at him, his features were set, and his eyebrow raised as if he had no idea of the news I'd just been given. But a feeling told me he already knew. And I was one hundred percent alright with that.

A big smile split my face as I told him, almost jumping up and down with excitement. Ron's gone. He's really gone. And will never hurt me or Tyler again.

And then I couldn't wait to tell Dart. Drummer left me alone for that call.

Dart's still unable to come home, but when I spoke to him he'd suggested there was no longer a reason preventing me going to San Diego, and that I should join him as soon as I could. And I'd have gone like a shot, except for one thing.

Drummer's pleased with the work I'm doing at the strip club, it's running more smoothly now I've knocked the girls into shape, and wants me to stay on until Heart can take over.

How could I say no after all he and the club have done for me? Giving me the job in the first place, and then saved me and subsequently offered me their protection, and now I suspect are responsible for ensuring my son and I are safe for good. I can't just walk out, it's not in me to be so selfish.

Dart wasn't happy, but, for the moment, both of us are stuck due to our obligations to the club.

Ron's dead. I shouldn't want to dance around cheering every time I think of it, but that man scarred me for life and had left me for dead. I won't even pretend to be sad.

Tuesday afternoon I leave for the club early, and as Road had suggested, I dress in yoga pants and a tee so I can get in some practice on the pole. I won't be able to do much, and if it hurts I'll stop. But just to do a couple of minutes will feel amazing.

Road's at the bar that he should be cleaning, but he stops for a moment, resting his elbows on the wood and his chin on his hands. "You want me to put some music on?"

"Not yet, Road. Just going to start with something simple."

"Okay."

I wait for a second, but he doesn't move. "Could do without an audience."

When I narrow my eyes, he chuckles. "Okay, darlin'. I can take a hint." He picks up his cloth and starts polishing again.

I wipe down the pole and put chalk on my hands, then look at it as if it's an obstacle as high as a mountain. Gingerly, I pull myself up and attempt some experimental moves. Yes, I can feel the scars pulling at my chest, but not much more than any exercise would do. Climbing the pole, I then let myself twirl around to the bottom, thinking I won't do too much today, as I don't want to push it.

I'd ignored the door to the club banging open, thinking it's just more staff coming in. But I can't ignore the loud, horrified shout.

"Who's that fucking fat assed bitch on the pole? You lettin' your girlfriends in for free, Road?"

I drop down, landing lightly on my feet. There's a biker wearing a Satan's Devils cut, but I don't recognise him. He's got long blond hair tied back in a bun, but one side of his head is mismatched and covered in much shorter hair. Realising immediately it's not deliberately styled that way, I gasp with surprise, this must be the reportedly mild-mannered Heart.

Road's standing with his mouth open, gaping like a fish, while Heart takes a step toward me. "Get off the fuckin' stage, bitch." Then over his shoulder he adds, "I can see why Prez wants me to take charge here. Place has gone to the dogs. Fuckin' black ones at that."

I walk down the steps and confront him. "I got this, Road," I start, while my eyes are fixed up at the biker's face. "You're Heart, I take it. Let me introduce myself. I'm Alex, and I'm Dart's old lady."

Instead of looking contrite, he looks even more annoyed. "Dart wouldn't take an ol' lady. Don't know what you're on about, bitch. And he certainly wouldn't take one of your fuckin' kind."

"I suggest you shut up until you know the facts of what you're disputing. Drummer asked me to manage the place until you arrived to take over."

He's not appeased. "Don't look like you're doin' much managin' to me. You're just fuckin' playin' around."

I don't even attempt to defend myself by saying I got here early, nor explain I don't have set hours I need to work, and only need to stay until what I've got to do gets done. I just put my hands on my hips and glare at the man.

Road's come out from the bar. The look on his face is both bemused and dismayed. No, this man, Heart, doesn't resemble the person who'd been described to me at all.

The prospect tries to help. "Heart, you need to speak to Drum. He'll tell you everythin' about Dart and Alex…"

"I certainly will. And I look forward to seein' Dart's face when he hears how you think he's claimed ya." He takes a menacing step toward me. I stand my ground. "Whatever you believe, you're fuckin' mistaken. Dart would never get caught in the ol' woman trap. He's got far too much sense for that. And yer not his type. Never would or fuckin' will be."

This man frightens me, which is strange. I've never felt nervous around any of the other club members. A cold shiver runs down my spine. If what I'd been told was true, his accident had obviously changed him. And it's only remembering that he's dealing with the loss of his wife that helps me keep my temper.

"Do you want to see the books now?" I offer.

It only brings a deeper scowl to his face. Turning away from me, he addresses Road. "I'm off to the club. Just stopped in on my way to remind myself of the dive Drum's asked me to mind. I'll be sure to tell him how your both slackin' off." Then he storms out the door, making as much noise on his way out as he did when he came in.

Road's staring after him. "Hey," I put my hand on the back of his cut. "Drum's not going to pay any attention to what he has to say."

"I'm giving no thought to that. I'm just worried about *him*. Fuck, Alex. That man's changed. Wouldn't have believed it if I hadn't see it for myself."

"Going to give Drummer the heads up?"

Slowly he nods. "I think I better."

The rest of the afternoon and evening passes without incident, and when I drive *myself*—I don't have to hide anymore—back to the clubhouse, I find I'm half curious to find out how Heart's been with everyone else, and the rest of me is worried about coming into contact with such an unpleasant man again.

After I park up behind the clubhouse, I make my way to Drummer and Sam's house at the top of the compound. She sees me coming and has the door open. Tyler's watching something on TV. I can see at once she's upset by the expression on her face, and that she's been crying, which is surprising. Sam's one of the strongest women I've ever met.

"What's up?" I ask, stepping inside and making sure Tyler's occupied.

She beckons me into their kitchen. "Heart's back."

"Yes, I know. He came to Angels on his way here."

"He doesn't want anything to do with Amy."

"What? He's her father."

She humphs. "You wouldn't think it. She saw him, ran up to him. He just pushed her away and carried on talking to Drum. Poor child doesn't understand it. She ran back to me in tears. I brought her and Tyler up here, and we've stayed here ever since."

It's then the door pushes open and Drummer steps in. He looks as tired and worn as I've ever seen him. He nods at me, then looks at Sam. "I've tried talkin' to Heart."

I take it that's my cue to leave, so start moving away.

"No, stay, Alex. I take it you've already met him." His mouth twists distastefully. "After my little chat with him, I can guess how that went."

"He wasn't particularly impressed."

Drummer looks at me carefully. "I understand he was probably rude. But don't take it personally. Don't think there's one person he hasn't upset. He's only been back a few hours."

"He's already upset Amy."

Drummer turns to his old lady and notices her reddened eyes. "And you, darlin'," he says softly. "I'd tell you he doesn't mean anythin' by it, but his head's all fucked up. I don't know who he is anymore."

"His head injury might have affected him."

Drummer nods, but in a way that suggests he's already thought of it. "Alex, we'll keep to the plan if that's alright with you. But I want another brother with you when you're workin' at the club and showin' Heart the ropes. From the words he was sayin', he'd obviously got some insults in. Dart wouldn't be happy if I didn't protect you from that."

"I don't care about me, I can handle it. But I don't want any nastiness around Tyler."

"I'll get everyone here to be on the watch out for Heart upsettin' the boy, but I know they don't really need tellin'. We all like Tyler, he's a great kid. And I'll watch out for you, Alex. Heart will go no further than words, but taunts can be hard to shake off. It's the least I can do for Dart while he's away."

"Dart's got enough on his plate, Drum. I won't tell him if you don't."

"Don't like keepin' anythin' from a brother. But if he'd heard what he said to you he'd be back here in a flash."

I take in a breath and let it out slowly. "Coming back here must be hard for Heart. Losing his wife, well that's a wound that will never completely heal. But returning to his home must be like pulling a scab off and starting it bleeding again. He might just need some time, Drum, to come to terms with what he's lost."

Drummer gives a wane smile. "Now I know what Dart sees in you." He gives a cheeky wink towards his old lady and adds, "Apart from the obvious that is."

"Drum!" Sam is forced to laugh, and it relieves the tension a bit.

"Mom! We going?"

Looking down, I ruffle the hair on Tyler's head. "Program finished?"

"Yeah."

I take hold of his hand. "We're off then. And we won't say anything more about it for now."

To my relief, Heart doesn't come to Angels for a couple of days, and it appears while he's in the club he stays up late drinking himself into a stupor, and then staggers out of his suite late, or out of one of the crash rooms if he doesn't even make it that far, so it's not too difficult to keep out of his way.

We've taken over Dart's room to do the planning for the poker run, and I suspect it's an excuse for people to keep out of Heart's way. He's certainly not making it easy on anyone here. No one can say the right thing, and he argues every point that is made. There's a downer over the whole club, the atmosphere completely changed.

While we plan, Tyler plays with Amy in our room. Occasionally she'll ask where her daddy is, but as she's got used to him being away, seems to have adapted to seeing him around and has learned quickly not to go to him. All the other brothers overcompensate, going out of their way to play with the little girl, and as for the women, well, we all spoil her rotten.

My luck runs out on Thursday. I'm at Angels, just firing up the computer to sort out some nights off that Vida and Karma have requested, when the door to the office opens and Heart walks in. True to his promise, Drum's obviously asked Dollar to come keep an eye on things, as he's not far behind.

"So, you gonna show me the shit you haven't fucked up?"

"Hey, man. Alex has worked her ass off to keep things runnin' smooth." Dollar glares at his brother, bristling on my behalf.

"And what the fuck are you doin' here?"

Dollar shrugs, winks at me behind Heart's back, before informing him, "Drum asked me to go through the accounts with ya."

Well, it sounds plausible enough to me, and obviously to Heart too. And at least the treasurer's presence seems to temper Heart's belligerence some. I show him everything, then checking the time, take him out to the dressing room where the girls are arriving. I introduce him. He gives them a onceover, sneers, and then takes himself out.

Vida shivers. "I don't take to him, Alex. You say he's taking over from you?"

I lean back against the door. "Yeah, that's what Drummer wants. And give him some slack. He's just lost his wife. Drummer wants him to keep busy and not have too much time on his hands."

"We all might end up with nothing to do if he treats the customers like that."

"He'll be fine," I reassure them whilst mentally crossing my fingers. "He just needs to find his place. Once he's involved with getting you lot organised, he won't have space to think."

They give a dutiful laugh, but I don't think I've got them convinced. I change the subject. "You okay with the schedule tonight? Tinker? You ready to go on first?"

"Yeah, fine," she grumbles. I like all the girls, but she's one of the best, and she'll have a couple of later spots too. She might not be a great dancer and not that good on the pole, but she's blessed with an incredible body and a cheeky face, and the customers love her.

"You staying around, Alex?"

At Karma's question, they all look at me hopefully. I don't know how they expect me to be a buffer between them and Heart, but I'm willing to try. It's his first night, and it might help if I'm here to ease the way. "As long as I can get someone to have Tyler, I'll be here, okay?"

I leave the dressing room with their thanks ringing in my ears. A quick phone call and Tyler's sorted. He'll be staying with Drum and Sam for the night. I end the call having heard the excited yells of Tyler happy to have a sleepover with Amy, and Drum's thanks as I explain why I'm staying.

"Thought you ran off before the club opened."

I swing around, already tensing as I recognise the voice speaking to my back. "Sometimes I stay to make sure everything's running smoothly." I don't, but I don't want to tell him the truth, that I'm here to check how he does.

"Well, get behind the bar and make yourself fuckin' useful then. And don't walk around on the floor. Don't want to chase the customers off."

Before Ron got his hands on me, the customers used to scream to watch me dance. Tears come to my eyes as I know all he's seeing is a short stockily built girl that nobody would want. As the insecurities which Dart had chased away come flooding back, I feel tears prick in my eyes. I turn away from him, and obediently go behind the bar.

"You shouldn't let him talk to you like that. I'll get Dollar—he's still out back."

"No, he's hurting, Road. Just lashing out."

Road's jaw is clenched. "He still shouldn't have said anythin'. I'll tell him..."

Yeah, a prospect reading a patched member the riot act. I can see how that will go down. "Road, no. I said no. Now leave it. Words can't hurt me."

He gives a quick shake of his head. "If Dart heard him..."

"Dart didn't. And doesn't need to know. Okay?"

Looking unconvinced, Road turns away and goes over to check on the bouncers.

Della, the bartender, is standing with her hands on her hips. For some reason, I feel embarrassed she heard all that. She nods her head in the direction that Heart disappeared. "I don't like him."

I just shake my head. If I admitted it, I don't either, but I'm trying to keep in mind that he's Dart's closest friend. But how long are we going to keep making excuses for his behaviour? Sure, he's hurting, but he can't keep lashing out.

Realising I'm not going to discuss him with her, Della shows me the ropes and I get a quick lesson in tending bar. It's busy, so in between watching the girls on the stage, I'm doing my best to keep up with the drink orders. The dancers come on quickly, one after the other. When one is finishing up, another is waiting in the wings. I know the schedule like the back of my hand, so when Tinker doesn't appear, know immediately it's her who's missing. She doesn't normally get muddled up.

"Della. Play Karma's music, Tink's missed her cue. I'm just going to see what's up." I look around for Heart to explain what I'm doing, but he's nowhere in sight.

Running to the dressing room I push the door open, throwing a quick instruction to Karma. "You're up, sweetie. Tink hasn't gone on stage."

"Why not?"

"That's what I'm gonna find out. Just get out there, will you?"

The others give each other worried glances. "I didn't see her leave. Her bag's still here."

"I'll go check out back, she might have gone for a smoke and lost track of time." I try to hide it, but I'm getting concerned myself.

Going to the back door of the club, I push down on the bar to open it up. Philby is standing outside. He's the bouncer who makes sure the girls can come out for a crafty cigarette or get to their cars unmolested. It's normally a boring job unless customers try to find their way around the back, and so he alternates with Fergus.

"Hi, Philby. I'm looking for Tinker. You seen her?"

"Seen no one. I've been here…" he breaks off and gives me a guilty look. "Tell you the truth, Alex, I just went inside to the head. I…"

"I said get off me! Get off." A scream comes, a shouted swear word in a male voice, and then nothing again.

Philby and I look at each other and run around the corner and come to a dead stop. Heart has Tinker pushed up against a wall, his hand over her mouth. She's struggling, her cover up that she uses over her costume is down by her ankles, as are her panties. Heart's other hand is up between her legs.

"Get him off her."

Heart might have been introduced to Philby as his new boss, but I'm his old one. He's got a soft heart for the strippers, and has no hesitation pulling Heart off Tinker and putting himself protectively between the two. I go straight to Tink, and pull the sobbing woman into my arms.

"What the fuck? She's a whore. A stripper. I was taking what she offered."

A small voice gasps. "I'm not a whore."

"I know you're not, sweetie." I glare at Heart. "Get out of here now."

"Bitch, you can't tell me what to do."

"If she can't, I can. Get your ass back to the fuckin' compound, Heart. I'm gonna have to take this to Drum." I've never been so pleased to see Dollar. I hadn't realised he'd stayed at the club. He's standing beside us, vibrating with fury.

"Look, all the girls go for patched members. You know that. She offered, I was just fuckin' pickin' up what she was puttin' down."

Tink gasps and shakes her head.

"Get back to the compound. *Now*."

For a moment Heart looks like he's going to continue to argue, but then throws both hands in the air before sauntering off. After a few seconds, we hear the roar of his bike.

"What happened, Tinker? Tell us exactly how this, whatever this was, went down."

Philby picks up her robe and passes it to her. Then picks up her panties, but doesn't know what to do with them, as they're clearly torn and useless. She wraps the robe around her, then snatches them from his hands, twisting them between her fingers.

"I came out for a quick smoke, I was due to go back on." She looks at me, her makeup smeared over her face, tears running from her eyes. "I'll take the next slot, Alex. I'll do my bit."

"You're going straight home." Bullet says gently. "But first, explain what Heart did."

"I didn't encourage him," she says quickly.

Bullet touches her arm. "We know that."

"I was lighting my cigarette, and he must have followed me out. Philby wasn't here, I didn't think nothing of it."

Philby looks down at his feet.

"Heart grabbed me, put his hand over my mouth, and pushed me up against the wall. He started tearing my robe off, and then my pants." She gulps. "He told me I was a whore, and that I should be grateful I'd got me a biker to fuck. I tried to kick him, to fight him off. I couldn't scream 'cause of his hand. So I bit him." Her eyes flick around wildly as she relives it. "When I screamed he tore off my panties... And then, thank God, you turned up."

Bullet hugs her to him, then his angry eyes turn to me. "Get her sorted. Alex, give her what time she needs to recover. Make up her lost tips from the till. I'm straight back to see Drummer. He'll probably want to talk to you too."

CHAPTER 33

Dart

San Diego has just about three times the population of Tucson. Whites only just outnumber Hispanics, and Blacks make up less than seven percent of the population. While not numerous, you're still more likely to come across people of Niran's heritage in this city than back at home.

Unaware of the dynamic when I introduced Niran to the Cali chapter that afternoon, I knew I was taking a risk leading him down to meet my brothers. Back in Tucson there had been little debate and general agreement on widening membership to the club. But here, when the topic had been introduced, I'd been unable to pick up the prevailing vibe. Hoping my brothers weren't going to let me down, preparing to speak with my fists if anyone started in with any racial slurs, it's true to say I was more than a little apprehensive as Niran walked by my side down to the beach.

White supremacists are known for regarding MCs as sharing their sympathies, but fuck me, I've got a black old lady, our bylaws have been changed, and I don't want to be associated with men who regard colour of skin as any type of privilege.

As it turned out, my worries were for nothing. I'd introduced Niran as an avid biker who'd served as a marine and who was looking for a new home. Within moments he was brought into the fold with barely the twitch of an eye. Breathing out a sigh of relief, I was pleased to see it was his qualities that mattered, not his heritage.

Surprisingly, he seemed to be adopted by Scribe and Dusty, and when later that afternoon the later approached me and said he'd be prepared to sponsor him as a prospect, I felt elated. It seemed to be too easy, but Niran had been given the chance to become the first black member of our club, getting off to a flying start as he'd been put forward to step on that first rung of the ladder. I promised we'd discuss it at the next church, as we would anyone wanting to join, but from the reactions I'd seen around me, I didn't think there'd be any objections.

This is the brotherhood I wanted to be a part of, and the lure I'd held out in front of our new hangaround.

"He's gonna fit in well." Lost salutes me with his beer bottle. "That the way you usually pick up new prospects, VP?"

Laughing I shake my head. "First time. It was somethin' about him, you know?"

"This run's been a fuckin' success, Brother. Made everyone remember what the club stands for." He points towards Scribe. "Now he had a quiet word with me. If Dusty hadn't stepped up, he wanted to speak up for the new guy. Seemed they've got mutual friends from when they served, and he'd heard of some of the things he'd fuckin' done. That man there saved lives, he's a fuckin' hero. Come back home, and given nothin' at all." He pauses for a moment. "Scribe told me he'd been thinkin' of throwin' in his patch, but today's shown him the club is movin' in a new direction. He'd have definitely left if Snake had brought drugs to the table, and told me none of the men we've got left would have supported that either. Seems a visible sign that we're movin' forwards, and not back, has had him rethinkin' his own position."

"You know," I tell him, "you've got good men in this club. We've just got to show them we've got their backs if we expect them to have ours."

"Truth, Brother. That right there's the fuckin' truth."

"Fifteen brothers, now potentially four prospects. Bit out of balance. Any of them ready for the patch?"

Lost thinks about it for a moment. "Reckon we could bring Al to the table, maybe Lloyd too. We'll discuss it when we discuss Niran."

A prospect to be patched in needs a unanimous vote to show everyone trusts them. Hopefully Al and Lloyd have proved they've got what it takes.

As night falls and bonfires die, we trudge back to our bikes. Glancing behind, I see Niran riding along with the prospects. The party's not over, just been moved to a different location, and he's been invited to get a better insight into the life that we lead. I'm just happy to see he seems to be fitting right in.

Over the next few days, my new project becomes a fixture at the club. Currently out of work, we give him a job in the auto shop where he proves how handy he is with a wrench. When I do my regular walk-through while checking up on all of our businesses, he looks up and I can see longing as his eyes fall on my cut. I can't make any promises I might not be able to keep, but personally I think he'll be a shoe-in when we're next around the table. And it's Friday, so that will happen tonight.

But as it turns out, that's a meeting I'm not destined to be part of.

Re-entering the clubhouse, I'm pleased to notice the atmosphere seems to have lightened since Saturday's run, Lost approaches and taps me on the shoulder.

"My office. Now."

If I wasn't VP, I'd be worried by the serious look on his face, but knowing I've done nothing wrong, my concern isn't personal, but what's heading for the club. "What's up, Prez?" I ask, even before my ass has hit the seat.

"Drum needs you back in Tucson. Emergency church. They need all members to take a vote."

"On?"

Lost shakes his head. "No fuckin' idea, VP. But it must be serious if he wants you back."

Wondering why Drummer hadn't contacted me himself, I offer, "I'll give him a call, see what's up and whether I can proxy my vote."

"Not this time, Brother. He wants you there in person. That's why he called me instead of you direct. It's not something he wants to discuss over the phone."

Shit. A serious vote needing all members present?

"He needs me today?"

"Soon as you can, Brother."

At least tonight I'll be holding Alex in my arms. My cock jumps in anticipation.

"I'll top off my bike and then leave. Oh, and I'll stay on for a day or so in Tucson, if that's okay with you, so you've got my proxy for gettin' Niran on board as a prospect. And patchin' in either of the other two or both. Far as I've seen, they'll make good brothers."

"So noted, VP. And you bringing that woman of yours back?"

Depending on what Drum needs me for, I can't promise I'll be returning to San Diego at all. But there's one simple answer that satisfies any alternative, "Ain't gonna be separated from her again."

"You've always got a place here, Dart. I'd be happy to make the VP spot permanent."

For a second I'm stunned, only able to stammer out my thanks, knowing he's given me something I'll be thinking on, and feeling fucking thrilled he thinks so much of me. When I get up he comes around the desk and pulls me to him. After we've exchanged hugs he looks me in the eye. "You've had my back, Brother. Gotta thank you for that."

I leave San Diego with some regrets. In Tucson, I'd just been rank and file, here I had to step up and play an officer role, and an important one at that. Can't say I've regretted it any at all, and realise I'd feel disappointment if that was taken away. Casting one last look at the city in my rearview mirror, given the chance, I know I'd like nothing better than to come back, and take that new step in my life as a full member of the San Diego chapter. And this time with Alex and Tyler at my side

Six hours later I'm pulling into the familiar compound that for once doesn't have quite the same feeling of coming home.

"Hey, Dart! Good to fuckin' see ya, Brother." Beef comes over and slaps me hard on the back.

"Well ain't you the fuckin' sight for sore eyes." Rock's not far away.

As we exchange greetings, I can tell something serious is going on. They might be pleased to see me return, but there's a shadow hanging over the club, an atmosphere you could almost cut.

"Alex? She about?" I'm not particularly hopeful. From what she's told me, early evening's she's usually working at the strip club.

But I'm to be pleasantly surprised. "Yeah, she's here. In the clubroom with Tyler."

Throwing a quick lift of my chin over my shoulder, I walk quickly through the clubhouse doors. And there she fucking is. Sitting at a table with Sam, Amy, and Tyler. And fuck me if it isn't the boy who notices me first.

"Dart!" He runs across and throws his arms around my legs, hugging me as though he doesn't want to let me go. Now that's a welcome, and one that puts a broad smile on my face.

"Dart? Dart!" And then my surprised woman is coming across. She tries to get as close to me as she can without squashing the boy. Pulling her to my side, I lower my head, turn her face up to mine, and give her a long, drawn-out kiss such that it draws a round of protests from the room.

"Get a room!"

As Alex pulls away, those tell-tale cheeks a darkened purple, she bangs her fist against my arm. "Why didn't you tell me you were coming?"

"Only knew a few hours ago myself. Thought it wasn't worth wasting time on a phone call when I could get here minutes earlier instead." Yes, when I realised I'd been given the chance to see Alex again, it pushed everything else out of my head. This is the reason I'm glad to be here. Wherever Alex is, that's my home.

And tonight? Well, as I try to adjust myself discreetly, my cock is already anticipating where he'll be.

"Now we're all fuckin' here. Church."

As Drum's voice thunders out, I give an apologetic smile and a kiss to my woman. And then tilt my head. There's tears in her eyes. "Hey I won't be long, doll. Then you and me got some catchin' up to do." I throw her a wink.

But as she turns her head side to side and puts her hand on my face, something tells me her watering eyes aren't because she's losing me again. *What does she know? And what the fucks going on?"*

"Dart!"

The bellow makes me realise I'm the only one who hasn't responded to Drum's call. With one last lingering look trying to interpret the expression on her face, I leave her for now and go into church.

The sombre atmosphere I'd picked up on outside is even more discernible here. Whatever I've been called back for is significant. And I'm apparently the last one to know.

Without delay Prez bangs the gavel. "Let's get this started." But after his pronouncement, he wipes his hands down over his face. If I didn't know better I'd say he'd aged in the time I'd been away.

"We all, except for Dart, know what we're fuckin' here for. Dollar, you were there and have debriefed me. The rest of you know just by rumour. This is a sad day for the club, and we're about to make a possibly far-reaching decision. For that reason, I'm gonna be callin' some witnesses into church."

Suddenly I realise someone's missing. I'd been told Heart was back, but his chair's been left empty. *Has it got something to do with him?*

"Paladin, can you show Philby in, please?"

As our newest member vacates his chair and goes to do what he's asked, I'm wondering why the hell they want to question the bouncer at the strip club, and feel an icy chill as I wonder how Alex is involved. That she is, I've suddenly no doubt. There was a reason for those tears in her eyes.

Philby comes in and stands at the end of the table, shifting from one leg to the other, while his eyes look anywhere but at the president.

"Tell us what happened last night." Prez looks tired and worn.

After coughing to clear his throat, Philby starts. "I'm sorry, I could have prevented it. It was all my fault." After pausing to let his admission sink in, he continues, "I'd left my post, gone for a, well I had to take an unscheduled bathroom break." His face tightens as he waits for the disapproval. But none comes. You can't really fault a man for having to deal with a personal emergency. "Anyway, when I came back out, Alex was looking for

Tinker. And we found her. Being molested by Heart. Some of the other girls had alerted Dollar that Tinker was missing. He came out as I was breaking it up."

Heart? Molesting an employee? That can't be right. My brother would never do such a thing. She must have led him on.

"Thank you, Philby. You can go. Ask Alex to come in next, please."

Now my woman's standing at the end of the table. She looks so small and lost that I want to go hug her. But then she draws her back straight and looks Drummer in the eye. "You want to know what I saw?" She draws in a breath. "I was looking for Tinker, who'd missed her spot. Unusual for her. Thought she might have forgotten the time, so when I couldn't find her inside I went out to see if she was having a smoke."

As Alex describes the screams for help and then how she'd found the stripper, I'm shaking my head. *It's not possible.* Heart's not capable of that.

When she finishes, her place is taken by Tinker. The stripper, one of our best, sobs as she relates the incident.

"I'm not a whore." She impresses on us. "I take my clothes off, but never even give lap dances. I know people consider strippers easy game, but I'm not like that. I only do it so I can put food on the table for my kids. If there was anything else I could do I'd do it.

"Heart said I asked for it. I didn't. He pulled me around the corner, and I thought he was gonna criticise my performance. He wasn't proving an easy boss. I prefer Alex...or Dart." Her eyes flick to me as if she wants to hear that I'll be getting my old job back. My heart breaks for her. She's been with us a year, and pulls in a good crowd. Now I'm wondering whether she'll be going back.

My eyes go to Drum. *We've let her down.* Though he can't know my thoughts, he nods back.

After she's gone, Dollar raises his hand. "I was there when Philby was tryin' to break it up. Heart showed no remorse. I sent him straight back to the compound. There's no doubt in my mind that what he's broken club rules. He put his hands on an employee. And more than that, looked like he was tryin' to rape an unwillin' woman. Certainly had his hand where no man's should go uninvited."

A collective gasp as it's put so strongly. We're not angels by any stretch of the imagination, but we've enough easy pussy that to think of taking something that's not offered freely is repugnant. As brothers start talking at once, Prez bangs the gavel.

"We've heard the eye-witness accounts. Now we've got to speak to the man himself. This has been hard hearin', brothers. Any of ya want to take a quick break, grab a beer, go do it. I'll get the prospects to bring him on down." As most of us get up to leave, taking the opportunity to relieve the tension for a moment, Drummer picks up his phone and sends a text.

CHAPTER 34

Dart

When we reconvene, Road escorts Heart into the room. I stare at the man who'd I'd last seen lying in his hospital bed. There's no sign of repentance as he loosens his shoulders like he's physically shaking off the touch of the man who'd brought him here. He doesn't attempt to take his seat, but stands at the end of the table, looking defiantly at Drummer.

"You've put hands on an employee." Drum states. Heart simply shrugs. "And were stopped from raping an unwillin' woman."

"I wasn't going to rape her. She's a whore. Just like the others who work at the club."

That makes me see red. If Alex hadn't been injured she'd still be there dancing. *Is that what he thinks my old lady is?*

"Dart." Drummer notices me tensing and stops me as he growls my name. Then his attention falls on the man standing at the end of the table again. "Even whores are entitled to say no."

Heart's changed. He says nothing to defend himself, just stands, back ramrod straight. He looks more hardened now, his features seem to be fixed in a scowl. He looks nothing at all like the man I'd prospected with. He's kept his hair long on the side that hasn't been shaved, the hair on the other side starting to grow back. It's adds to his demeanour of imbalance.

Drummer seems to have had enough. He's texting again, and now Hyde and Jekyll appear. "Take Heart outside and wait in the clubroom. Make sure he doesn't go anywhere. And," Drum's eyes flick to me, "keep him away from the women. Especially Alex."

"What don't I know, Prez." I say through gritted teeth as Heart is led away.

Drum strokes his beard before letting me in on some other facts. "Heart's been sayin' some hurtful shit to your woman. She said nothin', but Road told me what he heard."

"Her ethnicity?"

"Yeah, other personal comments too. And the fact you wouldn't be faithful."

Heart should have minded his own fuckin' business. "Thanks for the heads up."

Drum bangs the gavel. "I'd ask if you're all ready for this, but I know you won't be, 'cause I'm not. Can't put this off. We've got to discuss Heart's fate. What he's done can't go unpunished."

"He gonna lose his patch?" Fuck. I might be mad at him for insulting my old lady, but would I really want to see that happen? And where would we go from there? Out bad, like the men at San Diego, or worse, put down like rabid dog as we'd disposed of Snake and Poke? Christ, now I know why I was called back. I *need* to be part of this decision. I'm closer to Heart, or was, than any of my other brothers. Like Road, Jekyll, and Hyde, we'd prospected alongside each other. Doing the type of unsavoury stuff together which forms a strong bond.

The VP raises his hand. "Heart's been through some shit, and it's changed him. His brain injury might account for his behaviour. Whether it's temporary or permanent, there's no way of knowing. But that man who was just standin' there without any remorse? I barely recognise him." As he finishes, Wraith shakes his head.

"PTSD?" Marvel makes the suggestion.

"Or survivor's guilt. And now he's trying to get hurt. Or givin' us an excuse to finish what the accident didn't." Mouse looks concerned.

"So there's mitigatin' circumstances." Drum's listening to the comments.

"Or he could just be being an ass," Beef grumbles.

"And there's that." A few chuckles, but they're half-hearted. Drum waits for quiet again. "I'll remind you. We can take his patch, put him out in bad standin', or we send him to meet Satan. Ain't no other option I can think of."

"I know, *knew*, him best, Prez." When Drum lifts his chin, I continue, "The man that he was lived for two things, his family —his wife and child—and for the club. He's already lost one part of that. If we take the other away I don't think he'll survive."

"He wants nothin' to do with the kid. Poor child can't understand why her daddy's ignorin' her." Fuck, I didn't know that was still the way of it. My eyes go to Wraith's, and he nods as if to confirm his words are the truth of it.

Fuck, I need a cigarette. Getting out my pack, I pass it around, then flick my lighter and inhale deeply.

Prez gives those of us with a nicotine addiction time to fill our lungs. "I agree with Dart. Heart might not thank us now, but I don't think he wants to lose his patch. I've had several conversations with him before he came back. I wanted him here for Amy, and perhaps I pressed him too hard and he returned too soon. Should have left him where he was for a bit longer."

"This ain't on you, Prez." The VP's quick to admonish him. "This is all on him, and the choices he made."

"He knows the rules." Slick appears to be thinking aloud. "And he went against them. He wants to force our hand and get him out of the club."

"Or dead," Mouse emphasises again. "Crystal was more than his ol' lady, more than his wife. She was his soulmate. He probably can't see a way to move on."

"And buryin' her while he was unconscious couldn't have helped. He didn't have a chance to say a final goodbye."

"His head's all fucked up. Can't make final decisions on a man who's not in his right mind."

Drum puts his elbows on the table and lowers his head into his hands. Apart from a couple of softly murmured conversations, the rest of us are quiet, giving the prez a chance to think things through. I'm almost holding my breath as I wait for him to pronounce my brother's fate. If there's a chance that the real Heart will come back in time, I don't want to have to vote on a permanent solution. If Mouse is right, and he's trying to provoke us into killing him, well, I don't think I could give my assent to that. Christ, what a fuck-up to come home to. *Heart, how could you have been so stupid? You must have known the club couldn't accept your behaviour.*

Time ticks by. My leg's bouncing under the table, and my hands are clenching. Memories of Heart and I at everyone's beck and call flood through me. Heart was the one who boosted my spirits when I'd thought I'd had enough and couldn't take it anymore. Heart had been there for me through every one of those hard days prospecting, and every day since, until that fatal day he was deliberately knocked off his bike. His actions over the last few days can't wipe all of that out. I'm not going to vote on something that's final. I simply can't.

At last Drummer raises his head, and his steely grey eyes roam around the table. He looks tired, worn. My heart sinks, almost afraid to hear what he's going to say.

"I've got a proposal," he starts, and all faces turn to him, and all other conversations cease. "I can't have Heart at this club, that's for sure. And he doesn't want to be here, we've already discussed that." He pauses and takes a breath. Looking at my hands, I see they are trembling, anticipating the worst. "Man needs time to recover from a loss such as Heart's, and on top of that, fuck knows what effects his brain injury might be havin'. Yes, he went against our rules, and our moralities. Or that's how it appeared. You say he was stopped in time, Dollar, he didn't actually rape the woman. Was he bankin' on someone steppin' in? We can't know that answer. But I'm not proposin' we dispatch him to Satan on an intention we can't prove."

My sigh of relief is echoed around the table.

The prez hasn't finished. "If we send him out in bad standin', he's finished. He can never return to the club. Which brings me to Amy. I can't take away the chance that one day she'll have her father back."

Wraith taps his fingers against the table. "If he's out bad, he might take her with him."

"I don't know that he would, Wraith. And if he does, what kind of life could he make for a kid, with no home and no job?" Drummer shakes his head. "At the moment, Amy is better off with us. At least Sam and I can give her some kind of normality. But one day, I hope, Heart will wake up and remember what a great kid he has." Suddenly a look of determination appears on his face. "My suggestion is he becomes a Ronin. For six months. Then he returns and we re-evaluate at that time."

I sit up straight, and my eyes meet Slick's, who's raising his eyebrow. Ronins, so named after the Japanese Samurai warriors who no longer served a particular lord, travel alone. They have no affiliation with any club, but often carry a token which means they are given a level of respect by dominant clubs in the areas they travel through.

"He'd have to follow protocol, Prez. He can't expect respect in return if he doesn't abide by the universal rules that govern a biker's life. Could he do that? In the state he's in?"

"The old Heart would," I reply to Blade.

Drummer nods at me. "He's got a choice. Become a Ronin, or out bad."

"Why not just transfer him to another chapter?" Marvel asks, frowning. The idea of sending Heart out as a lone biker not settling well with him. "If he's havin' difficulty copin', don't like the idea of him being on his own."

Neither do I. But I don't see any other option. For now, at least, he's burned his boats here.

Drum is quiet for a second, giving the suggestion his careful consideration, and then responds. "Don't like the thought of transferrin'. Can be a problem." He looks pointedly at Wraith, who's nodding his head, and I reckon what happened with Buster is top on his mind. "I can't take responsibility for him, not how he is right now."

Our faces are all sombre, but we're all nodding.

"Okay. I don't see there's much more to discuss. Ready to vote? Heart is given the chance to become a Ronin?"

Sending my brother out on the road with no back-up or base, and no one to call on? Leaving him to the mercy of any wolves that might find him? That doesn't sit well with me, but neither do the alternatives. As I sit pondering, I realise the votes started. As each man says aye, I find I'm joining them. Beef, who appears to have taken over the secretary role in my absence, records it.

"Shall I get him back in?" Wraith asks.

"No. We can't overlook the important point. Whatever the outcome would have been if Heart hadn't been stopped last night, we've got a stripper who thought she was gonna be raped. If Tinker can't put this behind her, we'll have lost a fuckin' good employee and some of our income from what he's done. Club rules are there for a reason, and Heart knowingly broke them. I can't allow him to get away scot free."

My eyes narrow as I contemplate what he's thinking, but he doesn't keep us waiting long.

"Hate to say this, brothers, but the man we just seen deserves a beat down. I know how much the man we knew and loved meant to ya all, but that's not the man that was just standin' in front of us."

"He's only just recovered, Prez. Don't you think that's too harsh?"

I'm surprised when Drummer grins. "While I'm thinkin' another blow to the head might help put him right, we'll avoid hittin' him there, just in case."

"You're suggestin' we take it easy on him?" Blade, as enforcer, looks like he disagrees. I toss him a glare.

"Not that easy, but yeah, hold your punches some, and don't muddle his brain worse than it is." The prez grins wider. "Anyone here who's taken a beat down knows anticipation is half of the game. He probably won't even suss we're just givin' him bruises to remember us by."

Half an hour later we assemble in the gym at the back of the clubhouse, this isn't something old ladies should witness. Heart is brought in, Jekyll and Hyde each have hold of one of his arms, and Road's following behind.

As we circle around, Heart stands in the middle. Once again, he stands stoically, his shoulders drawn back, his feet apart and his hands held by his sides. He stares at the prez impassively, but I can see the glimmer of fear in his eyes.

He thinks this is the end, and he doesn't want to die. In that moment, I get my first inkling that he might eventually recover.

"Vote's taken," Drummer informs him without preamble. "Take off your cut."

A brief flash of regret, then he shrugs off his cut, letting it fall on the floor before kicking it towards his prez. Drum's eyes blaze at the disrespect, and he bends, picks it up, folds it, and passes it to Wraith, who puts it safely on a piece of equipment.

"Club voted. Want you away for six months."

Heart starts, as though that was the last thing he expected. But I can't tell from his expression whether he's happy or not. "Prez?"

Drummer continues, ignoring him. "You're to become a Ronin. If you agree, you leave here in the mornin'. No fanfare or fuckin' send off.

After a moment, Heart takes in a deep breath. When he lets it out, he asks, "Six months?"

"Far as I'm concerned, until your time's up you don't call the members of this chapter 'Brother'. You hear me? You're out on the road on your own. You fucked up good, Heart. And left us with a mess to clean up."

That gets to him. And to me. He's been my brother for six years. I swallow down my sadness and try to keep it from my face.

Taking a step toward him, Drummer continues, "You promise me now, that if you do this, you don't bring disrespect on this club, or any other. If I hear, and I will fuckin' hear, you've been causing problems elsewhere, then you won't even be out bad. You'll be dead."

After swallowing a couple of times, Heart nods. Then follows it up with words. "I hear ya, Prez."

"That's yer fuckin' choice, Heart. Out in bad standin', or Ronin."

He brings his hands up to his head and links his fingers behind his neck and stands with his head bowed. After a moment, he brings his arms back to his sides and pulls his shoulders up straight. "I'll become a Ronin." It's said with determination.

Prez nods. That's done. Decided. But for Heart, it doesn't end there. "Can't let you go without lettin' your brothers show how fuckin' disappointed they are in you, Heart. You fucked up. Can't let you walk away unmarked."

His body stiffens as it dawns on him what's about to happen.

"Now you going to take it like the Heart we used to know, or do I have to get the prospects to hold ya?"

That's an insult, and Heart knows it. He's never been a coward.

"Give me what you got, Prez."

"I ain't your prez. Not until six months have passed. And then we'll see where yer head's at then." As Drummer's speaking he steps up. I can tell he's not put his usual strength behind it, but it still causes Heart to involuntarily double up.

When he straightens, it's Wraith's turn, then Peg, then Blade. Dollar follows after. One by one the men step up, each eyeing him up carefully before placing the blows, and all of them avoiding his head and the left side of his body. Although they're pulling their punches, Heart's gasping for breath and on his knees by the time I take my turn.

As I step forward, his eyes meet mine, and for a second I'm unable to pull back my arm, certain I see the remorse in his eyes, and memory of our special relationship. Then the corners of his mouth turn up and he gives a twisted grin. "Heard you've got a taste for that black bitch's ass. By the time I'm back you'll have got tired of her and I'll have me a piece of that."

Even as my arm swings I know he's done it on purpose, riled me up so I'd play my part, but that doesn't stop my rage getting behind the blow. My fist connects with his chin knocking his head back.

"For fuck's sake!" Drummer roars.

Shit. I shouldn't have done that.

"Just finish it up." At least prez sounds more weary than angry now as he looks at the man I've laid out cold.

The rest of the brothers give a few half-hearted kicks, and then it's done, and Heart is still flat out on the ground.

"Jekyll, Hyde. Get him to one of the crash rooms. And get Doc here to give him a look-over. Road. Take all the patches off his cut. I think we've got a Ronin one around here somewhere."

He waits until the prospects all nod, then as Prez goes to leave the room he belts me around the head. Well, I deserved it. As I straighten again he shakes his head sadly. "He knew. I knew. You weren't gonna be able to bring yourself to touch him. He gave you a reason, Brother. There's enough of him left inside to give you that."

I stare at Heart, who's starting to come round with a groan. "Know that, Drum. Know that."

CHAPTER 35
Alex

When Dart walked in and kissed me, any doubts I had about our new relationship disappeared. I couldn't miss the bulge at his jeans that showed I can still make my man stand to attention. And on my part, at least, my heart leapt when I saw him, emotions I'd tried to even hide from myself came to the fore. Maybe it's that the shackles of having a husband are no longer weighing me down, but now I admit the depth of feelings for him, and can even put a label to the emotion I've only ever felt for Tyler before. *I love him.* And best of all, I'm a free woman and can do what I want.

And what I want to do now, is my man.

Damn, Road! He told me that he'd spilled the beans to Drummer about the insults he'd overheard Heart throw at me, and I'm certain Dart will have been updated by his prez. My joy at so unexpectedly seeing my man back was overshadowed by what his reaction will be. The last thing I want to do is to come between him and one of his brothers, and especially Heart, knowing their relationship had been so close.

Anyone with half a brain would have realised the reason Dart was summoned back was to discuss the events of yesterday evening. That I was called to give evidence only confirmed the fact. Their meeting could go on for hours, and I'm afraid of the outcome. While I don't much care what happens to the man who behaved so dreadfully yesterday, I worry about the effect it will have on Dart. To me it seems obvious just from how Heart had been described that the death of his wife has knocked him completely for a six. To my mind, he shouldn't be overly punished for something that's down to his injury and loss.

When I'd come out of the meeting having said my piece, there wasn't much else I could do. Anyway, it was time to put Tyler to bed, so I brought him up to the suite and settled him in. He was out like a light. He's been playing all day, and it's understandable that he's tired, but it's more than normal childhood fatigue.

A mother knows their child well, learns early on every nuance of their expression, every little changing pattern of behaviour. We watch them develop the ability to crawl, to walk, and to run. We watch them with the finely-honed eyesight of hawks, particularly if they are unwell. And Tyler's not been a healthy child the whole of his life.

Relaxed in sleep, his mouth slightly open as he gives out gentle snores, enabling me to see the inside of his lips is paler than normal, though touching my hand to his forehead there's no fever there. Suppressing my instinct to panic for something that might be nothing at all, but on the alert for the tiniest signs which might begin to add up and indicate that something is more wrong than usual, I pull up a chair by the side of his bed and just watch him sleep. It's hard to live with the knowledge I could lose him at any time, making every moment I have with him precious.

I'm sitting in the dark when the light between the two suites is switched on, and the silhouetted figure of Dart appears in the doorway.

"He okay?" he asks softly.

Getting to my feet, I nod. I'm not exactly answering the question, but I don't really know the right response myself. As I reach him he takes my hand and pulls me into his suite. "Sorry, doll, but I've got to get inside you now. Ain't nothing but my hand touched this cock the last few weeks, and I'm hard as steel just at the thought of sinking into your cunt."

It might not be the most romantic speech I've ever heard, but it's works to turn me on.

"Get naked, babe." As he speaks he strips off his cut and lays it reverently on the chair, then reaching behind his neck takes hold of his tee and pulls it over his head. Transfixed, I watch him divest himself of the rest of his clothes. Finally, he stands fully naked and sees me watching, His hand sliding along the length of his cock, turgid and ready.

"Your turn. And make it quick, babe. You see this? It's primed and about ready to go off. You take too long and I won't be able to wait."

Unconsciously licking my lips, just as eager as he is to feel him inside me again, I pull down my pants and underwear in one go. And then freeze as I remember. *My scars aren't covered by bandages any more.*

My eyes flick to his, and he sees the concern there. Closing the gap between us in one stride, he pulls at the hem of my shirt. Knowing he'll see sooner or later, I let him take it off. Then reaching his hands around my back, he takes off my bra.

Suddenly I'm in the air, lifted and dropped down on the bed, an 'oomph' coming out of my mouth.

"Told you I was in a hurry, doll."

Completely ignoring my scars, he clambers over me to take my lips in a scorching kiss. His tongue dives in deep, curling around mine, both of us duelling, refreshing our memory of each other's taste. As his hands clasp the side of my face, I raise both arms and put them around his neck, holding him to me. He fills all my senses—the smell of leather, of oil, and the soap he uses are intoxicating, his touch so gentle but dominating at the same time, his taste of beer and of cigarettes, and I feel his long hair brushing against my arms. Opening my eyes, I see him gazing at me with an expression that seems to suggest pure adoration.

My stomach muscles clench. This man wants me. And I'm his old lady. Which means he is mine.

Lifting his head slightly, a small smile plays on his lips. "Whatcha thinking?"

"That I won the freaking jackpot."

His forehead touches mine briefly, his hair now tickling my cheeks. "Not sure if you have, doll, but I certainly did."

"I love you, Dart."

Shooting up his hand he clasps me by the chin, and ensures I'm looking straight into his eyes, it's as if he's confirming the truth in my words. Then he's moving downwards, taking a moment to toy with my breasts, sucking and laving my dark nipples. I can't take my eyes off him, his gorgeous white skin so different than mine, and there's something decidedly sexy about the contrast. As his head moves lower, he gently kisses my scars, the gesture showing he's not pretending they're not there, but that he accepts them.

And suddenly the word that Ron so cruelly left behind goes to the back of my mind as Dart's fingers find their way in between my legs. He wipes at my slit then rests his chin on my stomach, checking I'm watching him as he greedily licks my moisture off his fingertips.

"Hmm. That fuckin' taste right there, doll. That's what I've been dreaming of. And I want a lot more. I'm takin' everythin' you've got to give."

And then he moves lower, his mouth settling so firmly around my clit that my head and shoulders come off the bed. "Dart!" I cry out, before stuffing a hand in my mouth when I remember Tyler's asleep in the next room.

He might have got blue balls waiting for me, but I've been suffering from the female equivalent. Just one time with Dart had got me impatient to be with him again, which must be the reason that almost immediately I start to tense up, my leg muscles locking, my stomach contracting, and when he curls his fingers inside me, I'm gone.

I'll leave teethmarks in my fist as I'm biting down so hard. Dart doesn't stop his ministrations, gently bringing me down and then taking me up and over again. This time I'm still quivering as he licks one more time and raises his head when I go to pull away.

"Gonna fuck ya now, Alex. And I ain't going to be gentle."

I'm ready for him. God, how I'm ready. He made it sound like a threat, but to me it's a promise. He's going to love me properly for the first time, no longer needing to hold back because of my injuries.

I watch as he rises to his knees and then pulls me down the bed with my hips angled up and toward him. He lines up his white cock and watches as it homes in on my dark depths. Then, with a strained look on his face, he thrusts in hard.

It's a new angle for me, and different sensations. I watch as he thrusts again and again until somehow he's stretched me and I've taken him all in. My head rolls back on my shoulders, I feel so full.

"Doll, I can't hold back. I've got to move…"

"Move!" I instruct him. And then I'm taken on the ride of my life.

As he starts hammering, pure sensation takes over.

"Fuck, doll. You're so fuckin' tight. Feels like my cock's in a fuckin' vice." He keeps pumping in, his face contorting with effort. "Doll, you're fuckin' perfect. I ain't gonna last long. Fuck, doll. Are ya close? Are ya comin'?"

For an answer, I clamp down with my muscles, he lets out a groan. Then, punctuating his thrusts with words, he stammers out, "Best. Fuckin'. Pussy. I've. Ever. Had."

The tell-tale rippling of all my nerve endings tightens my muscles all over again. "Dart!" I cry out around my hand. "Dart, please."

He puts his finger on my clit and starts rubbing furiously. I go to tell him it's too much when I realise it's not, it's just right. And then I'm flying, soaring, almost out of my mind, and hear his shout as though from a distance.

"Fuck, babe. Fuck!" he roars. His pumping slows but he's still moving, smaller thrusts now, but I swear I feel bursts of cum hitting my cervix and shooting up into my womb. For a second my floating mind wishes I didn't have an implant and we could celebrate our reunion by the conception of a child.

As our breathing starts returning to normal, he pulls out and disappears to the bathroom, returning with a cloth to clean me up. I'm so sated and drained I do nothing to help him. Then he comes back, lies down by my side, and turns me to him.

As his hand strokes gently up and down my arms, he murmurs into my ear, "We gotta talk, babe."

I tense. Yeah, there's things I need to tell him, but surely this can't be the brush off talk? Not after what we just did? *He didn't say he loves me back.*

He senses me freezing, and at last gives me the words. "Hey, I love ya doll, you must know that. You know what? Pussy offered itself to me on a plate in San D, and I wasn't interested one bit. You're it for me. Might have taken a while to see it, but you're my port in a storm. You're my home." As such beautiful words come from such a beautiful man, I'm rendered speechless as he continues, "I know Heart said some stuff to you, and it probably hurt. Don't need ya to tell me as I can guess. But if he said I wasn't in it for the long haul with ya, he was totally wrong. He's hurtin' so much, babe. That's not the brother I know and love that was speakin'."

"What's going to happen to him, Dart?"

"He's goin' to be a Ronin for six months."

I twist so I can look into his eyes. "What does that mean?"

Dart sighs and puts his arm over his head. "He'll be out on the road on his own. Prez has told him none of our chapters for more than a couple of days. It's a risk ridin 'solo, can't deny that. But it gives him space and time to come to terms with what's happened. We're hopin' it will clear his head."

"If he's having so much trouble dealing, surely he needs the support of his brothers." I purse my lips, not certain they've done the right thing.

"He doesn't want to be here, babe. He needs to detach himself from his memories. It's the best thing we could have done in the circumstances, and certainly not the worst. Drum could have taken his patch. At least he knows he's got a home here to come back to. Anyway, movin' on. How's Tyler?"

I bite my lip. "Not good, Dart. He keeps getting pains, and the episodes are taking their toll on him. I want to take him to his specialist in San Diego. The doctors here are okay, but they're not experts. Now that Ron's gone, it will be safe, won't it?"

I don't understand why his hand reaches around the back of my head and pulls me in for a kiss. Until he replies, "Not only safe, doll, but just what I wanted. I love my brothers here in Tucson, but at San Diego, I'm the VP, involved in everythin' that goes on at the club. Lost offered to make the position permanent, and I'd like to make that move. But I want you with me. Both you and the boy."

Wow. It's the answer to my prayers. I've liked living in Arizona and have made friends here, but Tyler needs medical supervision by someone who knows how to treat him.

"Not asking you to live at the club. We'll find a place off the compound soon as we can."

I glance at him, holding back the smile for the moment. "You, me, and Tyler?"

"Yeah, babe. Our little family." He moves his arm and places his hand on my stomach. "And when you're ready, we'll be addin' to it."

"I'd like that," I say shyly.

"Good. 'Cause on my part I can't think of anythin' I'd like better. Now I want to fuck. Babe, you don't know how much I've thought of holding onto your luscious ass when pounding into you." As he speaks he sits up and leans over me. His words make me giggle.

"You think that's funny?" He's grinning too. But when he moves his talented fingers to my pussy, my mirth comes to an abrupt halt.

"Dart!"

It doesn't take long as he circles my clit with those talented fingers while pinching my nipples, and soon I'm coming again. Immediately he picks me up and turns me over, positioning my ass in the air and my head to the bed.

"I've never…"

"Another first? Fuck, that man was an idiot." As he speaks he's kneading my ass with his hands. "This right here, doll, fuelled my fuckin' hand in the shower more times than you could believe. I've been dreaming of this."

As he speaks, his fingers move and circle my puckered hole, and he leans forward and says softly in my ear, "Not here, not now. But one day…" He gathers my moisture and pushes his lubricated finger in the entrance, leaving me no doubt what he means. "All your firsts are now mine," he says, and I know I'll let him do anything he wants to me.

"No more talking, babe. Time to fuck."

His hands take my hips and he pulls me back, pushing in with his cock in one practiced move. He seems to go deeper than ever, but my gasp of shock quickly turns into a moan of pleasure as he fills me up. It's such an intense feeling.

"Wish you could fuckin' see what I'm seeing, babe. My white cock going in and out of your cunt, sliding between your black cheeks. Fuckin' amazing. Best sight in the fuckin' world. Would die a happy man if this was the last thing I saw."

Then he shocks me by giving my butt cheek a slap, but the sharp sting seems to send a tingling to my clit. He spanks the other side, and I push back.

"You like that?"

Is it wrong to admit that I do?

He repeats his actions, and by God I'm close to coming already.

"Answer me babe." There's amusement in his voice.

I think my body's provided sufficient response, but I rasp out the word. "Yes."

He spanks me again, and then he increases his pace, hitting that spot inside me. As his thrusts deepen and intensify in their force, I'm totally lost.

"Come for me, doll."

He's in total control of my body as I push my face into the mattress to muffle my scream.

"Oh fuck, fuck. That's it. I'm coming babe. Oh fuck. FUCK!" After a few little pumps he stills. "Fuck, babe, that's feels so fucking good."

We stay locked together, until at last he pulls out. This time he lies spooning behind me. "Give me a second doll, I need to get my breath back, then we'll go take a shower and get cleaned up." My heart could do with a moment to slow, so I just nod.

"Doll, I never understood how men with ol' ladies could give up other pussy. But with you, I know. I won't need anyone else, as I've got the fuckin' best."

I turn my head and offer my mouth for a kiss, he doesn't disappoint. My lips are swollen by the time he pulls away. "Dart, what you do to me? I couldn't imagine anyone being better."

"Doll, you're not going to have a chance to find out. You're mine. I'll kill any fucker who dares to look at you."

"You put that dick anywhere it shouldn't go, I'll cut it right off. And I promise you, a bitch looks at you wrong? She's not going to live."

We stare at each other, then for some unknown reason, the intensity of our declarations has us both laughing.

CHAPTER 36
Dart

Until we know for certain that Thompson's life insurance is going to pay out, I hadn't wanted to raise Alex's hopes. But the large policy he'd taken out in order to benefit from his wife's death had backfired. Of course, the reason he'd taken out a policy with reciprocal benefits was to leave one less pointer toward him in the event of her death. But it now won't be him who reaps the rewards, and unless the insurance company finds some way to wriggle out of it, Alex is now five-hundred-thousand-dollars richer.

Having found Thompson's death was indeed declared a tragic accident, Mouse has started looking into sorting the paperwork out for her. And while he's at it, he'll be helping Alex sort out her enrollment in the law course in San Diego. As she's coming back to Cali, she'll be able to go back to her old school, with no need to bother about transferring her credits. I'm proud as fuck that hopefully she'll eventually be the Satan's Devils lawyer, working for whatever chapter needs her. Fucking good call on Drum's part if you ask me.

We stay on in Tucson for a few days while I square things with Drummer, but I don't want to delay too long before returning to Cali. Tyler's had two episodes quite close together, and the sooner we can get him expert help the better. Alex is worried she's leaving the poker run team in the lurch, but Sam assures her the bulk of the work has already been done. We'll be returning for that, and I expect I'll be bringing some of the San D brothers with me. They won't want to miss out on the fun.

The night before I leave for good, I sign the transfer papers with Drum with mixed emotions. I'm going to miss that fucker, and all the brothers in the club, however much they behave like assholes at times. But I'm reassured I'm doing the right thing the moment I walk out into the clubroom and see Alex, *my old lady*, now wearing the property cut I'd brought back with me, waiting alongside my brothers, and the old ladies, who are setting out food on the tables.

My face widens into a grin. They might have kept it quiet from me, but they're throwing a going away party for us.

Peg chooses the music, of course, and we're treated to a night of Bob Seger. Whenever anyone attempts to put something different on, Peg chases them off. Fuck, I don't care, and I'll miss the fucker and his strange eclectic taste of tunes.

I do the rounds, saying my goodbyes to Wraith, who takes a moment to enlighten me on the ups and downs of being VP, and then move to Dollar, who tells me he's always on the end of the phone to give help. Blade gifts me one of his knives, then stands waiting, expectedly, so I get my smokes out with a grin. I'm going to miss that tight-fisted asshole.

Ella kisses my cheek, while Slick scowls and grunts, Tongue flashes his stud as he wishes me luck. Viper and Bullet shake my hand then pull me in for a hug. Rock nods his farewell, and Beef clenches his jaw and says I'll be missed. Shooter and Paladin pause their game of pool to say they hope it all goes well. Lady and Joker tip their beers toward me, and Marvell spends a few minutes giving me the lowdown on his brothers who remain. As we speak, I watch and listen carefully, but there's nothing to suggest he was a supporter of Snake, and Drummer's already reassured me he'd come to that conclusion himself.

Being kidnapped together helps form a special bond. When I approach Mouse, we exchange chin lifts, then both move at once, hugs and back slaps exchanged. He promises to be at my beck and call for anything Token can't handle.

When I come to the prospects who have their work cut out keeping drinks flowing, I toss them a glare, then grin, and say I hope everything works out for them. After all the dedication he's shown to the club, I've got a sneaky feeling that Road might be patched in before his twelve months.

Then I come to Drum, who gives me a penetrating stare. "This is what you want, Dart? I know we've got the paperwork sorted, but that's all it is. Change your mind and I'll tear it up in a minute. Gonna miss you, Brother."

Out of the corner of my eye I spot Alex, laughing with the girls. She's holding the hand of the boy I'm going to adopt. "My ol' lady's my home, now, Prez. And it's best for Tyler to move where he can get specialist help. The brothers in San Diego are a good bunch, and Lost is doing well as the prez."

"Got your work cut out there, though."

I nod, knowing that only too well, and inadvertently straighten my shoulders as I reply, "Seems I like a challenge."

"Always knew you had it in you, VP." He surprises me by honouring me with my San D rank. "Only way an officer spot would open up here is if we lose a man, and I fuckin' hope that's not gonna happen, or is a long way off. But I want you to know, if it did, it would be your name I'd be puttin' forward."

I've always known Wraith, Peg, Blade, and Bullet had their roles for life. But I hadn't known my name was next in line. That Drummer's told me, chokes me up.

Blinking my eyes rapidly, I try my mouth. "What about the secretary?"

"Beef will carry on with it until Heart comes back. And then we'll see."

I'm glad Drum's not ousting Heart in his absence. That causes us to discuss my now Ronin brother for a second, and to wonder how he's getting along, and then the prez is grasping my hand, and with his other arm comes around me. "You take care, Brother. Any advice or help ya need, don't hesitate to call, okay? I'm relyin' on you and Lost to knock that chapter into shape. And if things don't work out, well, you've always got a chair around this table."

We hold each other for a few seconds, and I'm all but overwhelmed with emotion. This is the man who first gave me a home, who'd welcomed me to the brotherhood the day I got my prospect patch. When I pull away my eyes are wet, and his own look unnaturally bright.

Then one side of his mouth turns up. "Best go and enjoy your party."

I start to look for Alex, my intention to join her, but then I remember one last thing I want to say. "Prez. If you're ever on the lookout for a new prospect, that bouncer at Angels, Fergus, well he's a good man."

Drummer raises his chin. "Appreciate the, Dart. And I'll keep it in mind."

I pause for a moment, swallowing down the rush of emotion that this is the last time I'll be a brother in this chapter. Then I look to my future, standing with the other old ladies and a smile comes to my lips, and any regrets about transferring fade.

Leaving the Tucson compound the next morning again gives me a moment of regret. The San Diego clubhouse isn't situated in anything like such a nice spot as this one, and apart from the location, saying goodbye to the brothers who I spent the last six years with is difficult to do. But as I pull out of the gates following Alex's car, I realise that from now on, wherever she is, that's where I'm going to be. And when Tyler turns around and waves out of the back window, I raise my left hand and wave back. *My son.* There may be benefits for me in the transfer, but even more so for Tyler. There can be no doubt I'm doing the right thing.

We pass through the checkpoint and soon afterwards stop at a rest area to give Alex and the boy a chance to stretch their legs, then soon we're off on the final part of our journey. And fuck me, when we arrive it's to find they've cobbled together a banner saying in big letters, "Welcome Home VP." Fuck me, I've only been gone a few days, but of course now I'm here as a permanent fixture. I may have left one set of brothers behind, but I'm greeted here by another. And fuck it if knowing that VP handle is mine for keeps doesn't give me a warm glow inside.

The one upside to having lost a few members is that there's more room here now, and I'm astounded to find they've already prepared two adjacent rooms, one just for Tyler. And that's been decorated especially for him, the bed covering having a motorcycle pattern, and pictures of Harleys put up on the walls. Well, Drum had suggested he might want to become a prospect, and I reckon this lot here are already leading him in that direction.

Holding on to my old lady, I bend down and laugh into her hair. "Hope you don't mind our son growing up a biker, babe."

But she doesn't laugh, just clutches my hand, and as Tyler excitedly explores his room she says, "I just want him to have the chance to grow up."

Her statement sobers me, and I vow to do all I can to ensure we address his health problems. Together.

Then the next thing she says surprises me. "Who do you think did all this?" I've got a sneaking suspicion, but I'd rather not say. But then she goes on and answers her own question. "I reckon it was Eva, and if it was, I'm gonna thank her."

Now that had been bothering me, whether the women would get on or whether I'd need to step in and break up trouble, but after the last few nights in my bed, Alex seems to have grown in confidence and accepted she's got no competition. As VP that's going to make my life easier.

"You're a great ol' lady."

She turns in my arms and looks up. "I'll try, Dart. I'm new at this, remember."

She is, and she's the first old lady at this chapter, or at least in recent years. I'll give her all the support and guidance I can.

"Hey, VP. Party downstairs to celebrate you officially taking the second spot. The three of you coming down?"

Lost is standing at the end of the corridor, so I shout back, "Yeah, we'll be there in a few."

"Party? Again?"

"Seems that way, doll. You ready to meet all the crew?"

She laughs. "Don't think I've got a choice. Com' on Tyler, let's go meet new friends."

I swear if anyone else puts their hand to my back I'll have bruises, as I'm greeted the same way my Tucson brothers said their goodbyes. Pennywise is first, and when he leans in to give Alex a kiss, my growl makes him step back. He good naturedly laughs, and I introduce my woman to Salem and Bones. Then to Kink, Smoker, and Blaze. Grumbler puts a welcome drink in my hands, and Token asks about Mouse, seeming grateful he's got an offer of help if he needs it. Dusty and Scribe seem more settled now, and Brakes slaps me with oil-covered hands, then, noticing what he's done, apologises and walks off hopefully to clean up.

Niran's behind the bar, and he raises his hand, grinning when he sees Alex and Tyler. Then the newest patched member, Al, now having, for a reason that escapes me, picked up the handle Deuce, appears and gives me his hand, thanking me for giving my vote that meant he got patched in. Apparently they decided to wait a while on Lloyd, but his time will come.

And fuck me, that's the lot. Oh, except for the said Lloyd and Dave, who are hovering and anxiously seeing to everyone's needs.

Alex leans into my side. "Happy?" I ask.

"Happy," she confirms.

And she's happier still the next morning, when Celine rings her to say a letter has arrived for her. She tells her sister to open it, and nearly drops the phone when she finds she's going to get half a million dollars from Thompson's life insurance policy. She ends the call unable to talk any longer, completely lost for words, and then jumps up and puts her arms around my neck. As my hands go to support her ass, she wraps her legs around my waist, with the predictable result that I'm immediately hard.

"Dart, this means…"

"I don't know if it's enough, babe. But it's a good start. And the money the Tucson crowd will bring in from the poker run will boost it a bit more."

But will it be sufficient?

As well as settling into the new chapter, Alex gets on with sorting things out. We get an early appointment, and only have to wait a few days before we're spending most of a day at the hospital, with Tyler patiently going through all manner of tests that he must have had done before. Such a brave little boy, just turning his head when they stick yet another needle in his arm. After everything's done, it's the moment of reckoning, and while Tyler's sorted with his iPad and happily playing a game at the nurses' station, I stay with Alex as the consultant goes through our options.

Dr Crowther is African-American himself, and Alex has already told me he's dedicated himself to dealing with the sickle cell condition, as he'd lost a member of his family to it. His compassion and understanding are clear by the expression on his face as we take seats across the desk from him. He's got an open folder in front of him, and more notes on the screen to his side.

"It's been a while since I've seen Tyler."

Alex nods. "I had to go away."

"Yes, your physician in Tucson has been in contact with me." He takes off his glasses and takes out a polishing cloth. "I don't like the increase in Tyler's episodes," he says, almost conversationally as he cleans the lenses. When he replaces the glasses on the bridge of his nose, he directs his gaze to the woman at my side. "It's time to do something, Mrs Thompson. We can't put it off any longer. You know what might happen if those sickle cells cause a blockage in his heart. The other matter which I was going to discuss with you, are the results of the transcranial ultrasound we carried out. Unfortunately, it showed Tyler is at a higher risk of having a stroke."

Alex grasps my hand and squeezes it.

"If he was older we could start medication, but there are contra-indications if it's given to someone of his age. I suggest we look at blood transfusions."

"Dr Crowther." Alex's voice sounds hesitant, "We've saved my daughter's stem cells for this very reason, and you tested she was a match at the time. I want to look into doing a stem cell transplant."

He doesn't immediately answer, just consults his notes, and then shakes his head. "Unfortunately, that path should have been explored some time ago. Stem cells are only considered viable for five years, and it was over six years ago that we harvested them."

"From what I've read, Doctor, new research suggests they could be viable a lot longer, even up to fifteen years."

I expect him to refuse to even consider it, but he taps a pen against his teeth.

Alex continues, "It's not that long past five years."

He tilts back his head and is silent. Then he looks at her again. "I'll talk to the technicians. If they consider they've still viable, then, yes, we can consider that route. Mrs Thompson, if you've looked into it, you must know that there's a five to ten percent chance of Tyler not making it through the procedure. He's going to need intense chemotherapy, which will destroy his own bone marrow first."

I start. I didn't appreciate exactly how grim this was going to be. Turning to the woman at my side, I'm surprised she still looks set on this path. In fact, as her fingers slip away from mine, she leans forward and puts her clasped hands on the desk. "A stem cell transplant is the only cure for sickle cell disease. Medication and blood transfusions are only temporary help. He'll have to continue with those for the rest of his life. And the chances are, with the problems that are already showing, his life span won't be long."

"Yes, Tyler is symptomatic, which causes me concern. And which is why I'm even considering this path. When did his episodes start? Let me see." He looks through the notes again. "He was only a few months old."

"He could suffer organ failure at any time. That's what you told me when you first started seeing him. Something because of the haemoglobin levels in his blood."

The doctor nods. "It does concern me he was showing signs of being very anaemic today. I expect you've noticed him getting easily fatigued. As you know, some sickle cell sufferers don't show symptoms of their condition. But Tyler does, and he is getting worse. But now we come to the hard part. If we go ahead with the transplant, you know how serious it is. He'll have to come in before, and he'll be hospitalised for between one and two months afterwards. Possibly up to three if he has complications and it's expensive. Will your health insurance cover it?"

Alex shakes her head. "No, and I'm not even certain about what happens with the policy now, or whether I'm still insured. But they previously said they'd pay for treatment, but not the transplant." As she explains, her mouth twists. I'm incensed yet again that a man in a suit distanced from reality made that decision based on cost. "My husband has just died." She explains why the policy may have lapsed.

The doctor looks sympathetic, but I know the next words out of his mouth will have to do with the money. But Alex forestalls him. "The good news is, I've got half-a-million-dollars in life insurance to come, and," she glances at me and smiles, "a bit more on top of that."

She's referring to the poker run. But there's something else we need to look into. Why it hadn't occurred to me before I don't know, but suddenly I remember Thompson owned the house that his girlfriend is living in. That must belong to Alex now, as he died intestate.

"We'll find whatever's necessary," I inform him in my most confident voice.

He looks at me, as if to check my sincerity, and what he sees must satisfy him. He nods. "If that's the route you wish to explore, I believe you already understand, we can't perform a blood transfusion or do anything else to help him right now. I suggest you go away and think long and hard about the matter. You've a lovely boy, but he is at the risk of organ failure or stroke, and if we don't take this option, he will need regular blood transfusions and medication when he's older. All of which will mean constant medical monitoring and, I'm afraid, expense. I have gone through with you before all the other health issues he could be looking at in his future."

Alex nods, she must already know.

"While you're thinking I will do my own research on the likely viability of your daughter's cells, and we'll meet once again when I have determined the position." He stops and looks at me. "I'm glad you've got a friend to support you. In all the time you've been coming here, you came on your own."

I reach for her hand again. "Alex and Thompson were separated for a long time before his death. We will be getting married, and Tyler will be my son. I care for him too, and want to be fully involved."

Alex turns sharply; I give her an apologetic smile. Well, I suppose it was a bit audacious of me to assume anything, and I should have asked her before announcing it to her doctor like that. But she's agreed to be my old lady, and I take that even more seriously than a ring on her finger.

"Married? Hmm. And will you be considering more children?"

"Yes," Alex says firmly.

"No doubt you know, Mr...?"

"Lowe," I tell him. "Colin Lowe."

"Well, Mr Lowe. You'll need testing to see if you carry the sickle cell gene."

I'm surprised. "But I'm white, Caucasian."

"I might need to clean my glasses every so often, but I can see that quite clearly." The doctor chuckles at his own joke. "It's a fallacy only certain races have the trait. Blacks, Asians, and Hispanics are more likely to be affected, but I assure you, Whites can be carriers too. After all, thousands of years ago we probably all came from the same ancestors. And in the circumstances, I'm sure Mrs Thompson will want to take every precaution now that she knows what she's dealing with."

"I'll get tested today."

He smiles. "It will take a bit longer than that, but I'll make a note to get the appointment set up as soon as I can. I know how important this will be to you both. And my office will be in touch to set up an appropriate time when we can meet again. In the meantime, Mrs Thompson, any issues which worry you about Tyler, bring him straight in."

"What about his anaemia?"

"Just keep him quiet, feed a well-balanced diet. His type of anaemia often rights itself on its own."

I take Alex's hand as we leave the office. Once outside, she pulls on my fingers. "You want to marry me?"

I give her a sly glance. "Yeah. You gonna say yes?"

She considers it for a moment, but I reckon she's just kidding. "Only if you go down on one knee and give me a ring."

"Yeah?" Cheeky minx. "Any particular ring you prefer?"

"Nope."

Hmm. Seems like I need to find one myself.

"And your real name's Colin?" She grins.

"It might be, but you're not gonna call me that, babe. Col, if you must. But Colin, no way. Pussy name if you ask me."

"And I'd be Alex Lowe?" She pauses and says, "That's got quite a nice ring to it."

"Is that a yes?"

"Didn't hear you asking."

I laugh softly, already planning a surprise in my head.

But the moment of levity fades when Alex's eyes fall on her son waiting for us to collect him. It's the first time I've appreciated what an enormous and difficult decision she has to make.

At our next church, I'll be filling in my brothers. Alex will need all the support she can get.

CHAPTER 37

Alex

I leave the doctor's office as I normally do. Downhearted. Even the knowledge that Dart wants to marry me doesn't bolster me for long. I take a moment to wipe a traitorous tear from my eye, then put a smile on my face and go to collect my son from the nurses' station.

"Ice cream?" Tyler looks at me eagerly.

"Yeah." It's his standard treat after being so good for the staff.

Dart's deep in thought as he follows me out to the parking lot. Having successfully managed to put a smile on my own face, he needs to put one on his own. I refuse to let Tyler have an inkling of how worried we are, he's got enough to deal with as it is. I nudge him and point to Tyler, and then to my face.

He realises immediately. "Do I get an ice cream too?"

"Has he been good, Mom?"

I tilt my head as though I'm considering it, and then relent. "Yes, he's been good." My lips curve up in a grin. In fact, he's been excellent. Him being there means he knows it all, and I can use him to bounce ideas off as I prepare to make the most difficult decision of my life.

It's a fairly warm day, so we head down to La Jolla and walk along the boulevard to see the seals and sea lions on the beach. Tyler loves it here, and their behaviour always makes him laugh, even if it's just the way they wriggle themselves on their stomachs up the sand.

Dart seems almost as entranced as my son. "Hey, buddy. That one's waving at you."

When we've had enough seals for one day, Tyler switches his attention to watching the squirrels eating the shrubbery that lines the path.

Dart clearly notices how much he likes the wildlife. "Let's take him to the zoo one day. Has he been?"

"That's a great idea. I did take him when he was younger, but doubt he remembers much." I can't believe I have a man at my side who wants to do all the normal family things. It goes without saying Ron never did.

"Doll, I've been thinking. You know the house that you lived in was rented." Of course I do. Glancing at Dart, I don't know what he's getting at. "Well, the house he lived in with his girl-friend, he owned that. And that now must come to you."

My eyes open wide. *I own a house?*

"He ever mentioned anyone called Belle or Belinda to you? Winscott's the name."

"That her?"

"Uh uh."

"And she's living in the house?"

"Yup. According to her she's been there six years."

I look across to check on Tyler and call out, "Not too far. We're going to be heading back soon." Then switching my attention back to the topic at hand when I see I've been heeded, I sum up my thoughts. "I feel sorry for her, you know? If he was better to her than to me, she's lost her man and now could lose her house."

"*Will* lose her house." He corrects me. "You can't afford to be soft. Not with the boy to look after. I don't know Alex, whether the house was paid off, or whether he's got a mortgage outstanding, but any profit from it will go towards Tyler's treat-ment."

He's right. I wonder why Ron stayed with me all these years. Why keep up the pretence of our marriage when he had someone else on the side. A thought occurs to me, and I frown. "He must have paid for the house with the money my parents gave him." While I lived in a rented home. He'd told me it was all he could afford on what he was making.

"What you thinkin', doll?"

As Dart looks at me with concern, I bite my lip. "When he took me to the cabin he told me about the money he was getting. And said he'd made other arrangements now that it would stop with my death."

He nods. "You'd left him, babe. The money from your parents was gonna stop. He took out a hefty life insurance policy to compensate some for the loss."

Rolling my head around my shoulders, I try to take it all in. "I hate that it explains everything." My voice sounds heavy. "I was never anything more than a commodity to him. He never wanted me, not even from the start." My eyes flick toward Tyler. "That's why he got a girlfriend so early on, but kept up appearances so the money would keep coming in."

"Babe..."

"He didn't have to torture me, Dart. Didn't need to pretend. If he'd explained, we could have lived separate lives."

"Doll, he was trapped. Probably part of the bargain he made with your parents."

My head snaps back around to Dart, my eyes flaring. "Are you making excuses for him? Justifying how miserable he made me? He fucking hurt me, Dart, that night before I ran. And he threatened Tyler..."

"Doll, darlin', no." Dart looks out over the ocean, as though wondering how much he can say to me. "Thompson was a sadistic bastard, that's got nothin' to do with you. If he'd been a proper man there could have been a way to work things out. But believe me, babe, he was a man who liked causing sufferin', mental or physical. If anyone's to blame, it was on your parents for not checkin' him out." He pauses, clears his throat, and then continues, "Club's come up against him before. He was responsible for the needless death of one of the members. Can't tell you more, babe. Club business."

I shut my mouth. I was told Ron had, what was for me a happy accident, but I already thought Dart and his brothers were responsible in some way. Now that I've learned they had their own reasons for hating Ron too, I'm convinced of their involvement. It should bother me more, but it doesn't.

Dart's hand comes to rest under my chin and he turns me to face him. "He might not have got physical until the end, but I reckon you've had a hard time of it, ain't cha doll? I'm going to make up for every one of those six years. Both for you and for Tyler."

"He's gone, it's over. Done with. You don't owe me anything at all."

"Yes I do. I owe you the best life I can give ya." He stares down, then looks back up. "Ty. Come on, son. Time to get going."

Son. He called Tyler, son. My heart misses a beat. Ron's gone, but Dart's here. And he's proving to be everything I ever wanted.

On the way back to the car he asks, "Do you want to stop off at your house on the way home? Give a heads up to Belinda that she needs to get packing?"

I glance at Tyler, but if I'm just going to talk to her on the doorstep, he can wait in the car, the day's not too warm for him to do that. And Dart's right, I need all the money I can get if I'm going to pay for Tyler's treatment. While it goes against the grain to think of turning someone out of their home, for the sake of my son I can't afford to be generous and let her stay on. I straighten my back. I'd rather never meet the woman who'd been my competition, but with Dart at my side, I can do anything.

"Okay. No point putting it off."

Putting the car in drive, Dart turns out onto the road. He drives across town without consulting a map or programming the GPS, letting me know he's been here before. After a while we pull up at a neat one-story that looks like it might be a three-bedroom home. Much nicer than the one Ron had rented for me. And I deserve to have the proceeds from this house that he bought. After all, it was the bribery from my reasonably well-off parents that had paid for it.

"Wanna do this, then?" Dart's expressive eyes look concerned, both of us expecting a difficult conversation.

"Might as well. Tyler, you wait here, you hear?"

"Sure, Mom." I glance over my shoulder. At least his game is keeping him amused once again.

Dart and I get out, we've parked right outside the gate to the front yard so I can see the car from the front door. We approach and ring the bell.

It's opened by a white woman, which takes me by surprise. She's tall, willowy, and has beautiful blond hair and blue eyes. I can immediately see why Ron preferred her. I risk a peep at Dart, but he looks unaffected. She notices him though, and her mouth twists in disgust.

"You're one of those bikers. You kidnapped me."

What?

"It was an emergency. We needed to find Alex before Thompson killed her." Dart's completely unrepentant.

She looks down at me, my presence seems to relax her a little, though she isn't smiling as she takes not too wild a guess. "You're Alex?"

I really don't know how to play this, especially now I know she's met the bikers before. *Kidnapped?* I'd hoped to avoid getting confrontational. "I'm Alex," I confirm, while wishing Dart had told me exactly how they'd gone about trying to find me before we'd come here.

She stares at me for what seems like ages before her frown disappears, and she asks, "Do you want to come in? I think we need to talk."

Exchanging surprised looks, Dart answers for me. "Tyler's in the car."

She looks behind me as if to prove the truth of my words. "Bring him in with you. I can get him a juice or something if he'd like?"

It's certainly not the reaction I expected, especially now knowing she's no reason to want either me or a biker in the house. I look between the woman and Dart, but she looks resigned rather than upset.

"Look, there's things you need to know, Alex." She looks at me carefully. "I admit, I spent six years hating you, but now? I don't. Not any longer. Please come in, we can't talk on the door-step."

Dart shrugs, leaving the decision to me. When I nod, it's him who goes to get Tyler, then we all step inside.

"Go play with your game, Ty. Us adults need to talk."

Seeming unable to lift his eyes from the screen, Tyler plonks himself down in a chair. Belinda waves us over to some chairs around a table.

"Can I get you something to drink?"

"No, thank you."

Again, that intense stare at me, and then she looks toward the man at my side. "I was angry when you kidnapped me...er..."

"Dart."

"Dart. But things with Ron deteriorated from that point. Though I wasn't expecting him, Ron came home that day, changed his clothes and chucked the old ones in a bin bag. I thought it was odd. But I was still fuming about what you'd done to me. As far as I knew, you and your biker friends had questioned me for no reason."

"It wasn't for no reason. They saved my life."

Slowly she nods. "Okay, that might have been a stretch too far for me at the time. Now I believe he would have hurt you. But not then, no. I didn't accept it when Dart and the other bikers told me Ron had been violent toward you. The story he'd always given me was you refused to give him a divorce."

I'm confused, if so, her non-combative attitude is surprising.

She continues, "That day, I ignored his odd behaviour, too intent on telling him what my own experience had been and, of course, that you'd taken Tyler. I was unhurt, but I'd been taken, detained against my will. I'd been scared, and still was to some extent. I was looking for sympathy, and at first, I thought I'd get it. He changed immediately, his body tensing with fury, which I thought was on my behalf. I expected him to immediately call it in—he's a cop after all, and his son had been kidnapped by bikers. But he didn't." She pauses and swallows, and throws me a knowing look. "He lost his temper, grabbed me by the neck and threw me against a wall. Sometimes he'd be a little rough with me when he lost his temper, and God help me, I always found an excuse for him, but Alex, nothing like this," again she breaks off and looks straight into my face, "at that moment, I was terrified of him. He had this look in his eyes, a wild expression."

Now it's my turn to dip my head, knowing only too well exactly what she's describing.

"He didn't seem to give a damn about Tyler, but just wanted to know exactly what I'd told you. He kept on and on. Then something must have clicked that I hadn't been able to tell you anything of any real use. He kept on about a cabin, had I told them about it? Of course I said no. I never knew of a cabin. In the end, he seemed calmer. He let me go and told me to get dinner.

"I was too frightened to bring the subject up again. But I remember what you, Dart, had said. And for the first time I started to wonder whether there was anything in it. His complete lack of concern about where Tyler was floored me, though I didn't dare ask him why he wasn't more upset.

"When he went out the next day, I looked into the bag of clothes he told me he was going to discard. They were covered in blood. I remember staring at them for ages. I didn't know what to do. I was scared. I even thought about going to the police, but what could I say? I could show them the bruises on my throat, and the blood on the clothes, but I had no idea what that meant."

She looks over to Tyler, who's still engrossed in his game. "I decided to wait and confront him. I mean, he'd only hurt me badly the once, he wouldn't do it again, would he?" It's a rhetorical question, so neither Dart nor I answer. "He was missing for a couple of days. I thought perhaps he was trying to get Tyler back or something. But when he returned, I'd never seen him in such a mood. He kept mumbling that 'that fucking bitch got away'."

Again, she glances at my son. "I knew he was talking about you. And I was glad you escaped from whatever he'd done."

"He hurt you again." I'm already certain.

"Yes, he did. For the last time. I walked out. I only came home a few days ago when I got the call that he'd died."

"You want to see what he did to me?" I pull up my top and showed her the scars on my chest, but don't bother to show her the burns. Neither do I mention the cruellest thing that he'd done.

"Am I wrong to be glad he's dead?" Her hand goes to her mouth as though she's shocked the words had escaped from her own mouth, but adds with grit, "He couldn't have been allowed to look after that sweet boy."

Reaching out my hand, I cover hers. "If you're wrong, I am too. The world's a better place without him, and now I can concentrate on looking out for my son." I wait for a moment, then, "There's a reason I'm here today. Tyler's a very sick boy, he needs expensive treatment."

"That wasn't a lie?" she asks, tilting her head to one side. "You weren't making his illness up as a plea for attention?"

"No. This house, as it was Ron's and we didn't get a divorce, well, it belongs to me. And I need to sell it to raise the money. I'm sorry…"

She smiles. "I knew I wouldn't be able to stay here, and didn't want to. It doesn't hold good memories, not any more. I've already started packing boxes. If you can give me a week, I'll be gone."

Dart and I look at each other in disbelief. I don't know how much this house is worth, or how much is owed on it, but there must be something significant that will add to my funds.

"Thank you, Belinda."

"Belle, please."

"Belle. That's a weight off my mind." I break off and think. It might be strange, but there's something about her. "Here, take my number, and if you ever want to call." I don't know why I made the offer, and I doubt she ever will. I'd come here prepared to despise her, be jealous of her, but she seemed to have been caught in the same trap that I was, though for her it was of her own making. On my part, I didn't have much of a choice.

Dart stands. "Let Alex know when you've moved out your stuff." Then to me, "Come on, doll, let's go home."

I get Tyler, we say our goodbyes, and then go out to the truck. As I'm getting Tyler settled in his booster seat, I realise there's something I've got to do if I'm ever going to have peace in my life.

Dart's holding the passenger side door open for me, and I place my hand on his arm. "I want to go see my parents."

His eyebrows rise. "Really, doll?"

"I need answers, Dart. Everything that's happened to me comes back to them. I want to know the reason why."

"You sure you're up to it? You've had a fuck of a day so far."

He's right, I have. But perhaps that's what gives me the strength. I can't put this off for another day. "I'm sure, Dart. And, you'll be there to give me moral support."

He lifts his head and looks up as though the sky might provide inspiration, then when his eyes come down again, they crease at the corners. "Woman, fuck you constantly amaze me." His fingers rest under my chin. "Come on then, let's get this over and done with."

We're quiet on the short drive to my parents' home, I, for one, deep in thought. When I direct Dart up a driveway his eyes open wide. "Fuck, Alex, I didn't realise you came from money." He parks off to the side, next to two other cars, both a lot more expensive than mine.

Tyler for once looks up from his game. "We're gonna see Grandma and Grandpa?" He doesn't sound particularly happy about it.

"Just for a moment."

"Can I stay in the car?"

I would prefer he didn't hear what they have to say, so I quickly agree. "You going to be okay, sweetie?"

"I'm nearly at another level."

Sounds like he'll be fully occupied then. While wondering if I'm a bad mom to let him play so long on his game, and vowing to give him some one on one time later, I get out. Dart takes my hand as we walk up to the porch. When the door opens, it's my mother standing there.

She looks long and hard at Dart, and at our joined hands, then sneers. "Your husband's barely cold and you've taken up with that?"

"Can we come in, Mom? We're overdue for a long talk."

"I don't think we've anything to discuss." She brushes me off.

Surprising me, Dart reaches down and lifts my top, my scars on my chest coming into view. "I think you need to rethink that statement. See this? That's what the monster you forced Alex to marry did to her."

She stares for a moment, her eyes widening. "Alexandra?"

She's asking me if it's true. "Yes, Mom. And I think I deserve some answers. Including why Tyler and I were living in dump of a house while Ron bought a house and had his mistress living there. For the past six years." And then it hits me, how to get the answers I need. "If you don't want your friends to know how you basically sold me to an abusive man who tried to kill me for insurance money, I suggest you start talking."

I pause as her mouth opens and shuts, knowing after all these years, at last I've got the upper hand. "Actually, let me tell you. You paid him to marry me, and have been giving him money ever since."

She doesn't deny it, and her face tightens. "The money was for you and for our grandson."

"Tyler needs expensive treatment. But I didn't see a penny of the money you gave Ron."

"Why, Mrs Argent?" Dart's hand grips mine, a silent message that he's taken over for now. "What did Thompson have over you?"

"He had nothing. He was a respectable man. Not that you gave him any respect, Alexandra. You didn't even go to the funeral."

"I think you can see why. She was recovering from the injuries he inflicted. They've been separated for months, but Ron didn't tell you that, did he? Just kept taking whatever you were paying out."

She's flustered, her hands won't stay still, her fists are opening and shutting. "Alex, we did it for you. We didn't want you to go the way of your sister. We met Ron when we had that burglary, you remember? He was the policeman who came along. He seemed such a nice man with a respectable occupation." She puts one hand on the doorframe as if she needs help to keep upright. "We told him we'd support you both if you got married." She nods towards the truck where Tyler's looking out. "We offered to increase the payment if he gave us grandkids."

And that explains why Ron impregnated me and didn't give a damn about the consequences. It was always the money he was after, never me or my son.

"Mrs Argent, Tyler's a very sick little boy. Alex…"

"What are you to Alexandra?"

As always, my mother's not happy unless she's directing the conversation. Dart raises my hand to his lips and brushes his mouth over it. "We going to get married."

She tries to shut the door, but Dart's ready, and his strong arm pushes it back open. With a sneer she looks at me. "Then you're dead to me, Alexandra. If you go ahead and marry a white man…"

"You're going to disown me? Like you did Celine? Neither of us live up to your expectations?"

"You've got a son, Alexandra. You need to think about him."

"And Dart will be the father Ron never was." Frustrated, I brush my hands over my face. "You know what, Mother? Real people don't give a damn about skin colour. But you're a racist. Tyler's suffering because you never gave me a chance to make my own choices. Now I've made my own choice, and I'm proud to be with a white biker."

"If that's your decision, we have no more to say, Alexandra."

"Hold on a minute." Dart waves his hand at the house. "You've got money. Tyler needs an expensive operation, at the very least you should pay Alex what you were paying to Ron."

"Money. Might have figured that was what you were after." Dart's face goes dark, and I throw him a pleading look. Mom's oblivious and simply continues saying slyly, "You can come back to us, Alex. We'll find a suitable husband for you, and pay for whatever Tyler needs."

"Alex…"

"It's alright, Dart." After giving him a reassuring look, I turn back to my mother. "And give you another chance to ruin my life? I've got a new family now, Mother. True friends who are doing all they can to help me out. You don't want to give your grandson his only chance at a normal life because of the colour of the man I'm going to spend the rest of my life with, and how that will look in your circle of friends. Well, you know what? If they knew the truth about you…"

"Doll, that's enough. This bitch ain't worth giving the time of day. Come on." Dart gives me the full force of his warm eyes. "Let's go home."

But I've not finished. "I'm as dead to you, Mother, as I would have been had Ron succeeded. And you'll never see your grandson again. Oh, for good measure, seeing as colour matters to you so much, you might like to know that while I never saw a penny of that money you were paying out, Ron was using it buy a house for, and live there with his girlfriend." My hand goes to my mouth but I can't stop the giggle from escaping. "You've been supporting Ron and his *white* girlfriend for six years, Mom."

She gasps, obviously shocked, and looks around to check nobody is within hearing. "You say one word to anyone, Alexandra..."

I don't let her finish. I turn and walk away and go back to the people who don't give a damn about the colour of my skin, or that of the man who, although I haven't actually told him yet, I *am* going to marry.

CHAPTER 38
Dart

"Niran's fittin' in well, VP."

We've come to the table for another Friday church. It's been a month since I returned, and the chapter's settling down. I never thought I could replace my brothers in Tucson, but there's men here I've come to trust and like almost as much as those I left behind in Arizona.

"I'm pleased he's working out."

"Yeah, you were right. He was looking for something. Haven't found nothing he ain't willing to put his hand to." Grumbler's looking happy, and the rest of the men around the table are nodding. I'm pleased I was right that day on the beach. Briefly I think back on that meeting with that bitch of Alex's mom, and the difference between her and these men, and how easily they accepted him as though they didn't even notice his colour, just the man underneath. Alex's mom hadn't bothered to see me, just stopped at my skin. It had been a strange feeling, and one which helped me better understand my woman's challenges in life.

"So, VP. You wanted to bring something to the table?"

"An update is all." I lean forwards and rest my chin on my hands. "You know Tyler's condition." They've all been witnesses at one time or another to one of his episodes. "I want to thank you all for what you've done." Yeah, there's been some changes around here. No one smokes in the clubroom any more—it had only take Salem's brief conversation with Alex for him to use his enforcing role in that direction, and fuck it if these hardened men hadn't objected once they understood how it could trigger a serious reaction from the kid. Even Smoker didn't complain, though it does mean he spends most of his time outside.

Likewise, the air conditioning had been turned down with hardly a grumble. They're good men here in San Diego. After they've accepted my gratitude with nods or chin lifts, I give them the news. "Tyler's doctor has given the okay for the procedure to go ahead."

"That's fuckin' ace, isn't it?"

"Yeah, Prez. But it's gonna be hard. There's a small chance he might not survive the process, and if he does, we have to keep everything crossed that it's a success. He'll be in the hospital for a month or two after."

"But it's being done here, in San Diego?"

I slowly nod. "Alex has confidence in Dr Crowther and his team at the university hospital, and they're consulting with experts in the field in Boston."

"We got your back, Brother," Pennywise offers.

"Whatever time off ya need, VP, just let me know."

"Thanks, Prez."

That's all I can tell them. They don't need to know all the hours Alex and I have been thrashing out what's best for Tyler. It's a terrifying decision to make, the chance of a normal life on the one hand balanced against the possibility it might not be a success on the other, and the worst, that we might lose him. When Dr Crowther had confirmed the stem cells were viable, Alex didn't know whether that was good news or not. But she's again shown me her grit, trying to leave her emotions aside and to do what's best for her son.

"Okay. Let's move on. The road trip to Tucson."

"Fuck yeah. Can't fucking wait." Dusty's enthusiastic input is picked up by the rest.

Most of the chapter will be making the ride to Tucson next Friday night, staying over in the compound, and then taking part in the poker run the next day.

"Blaze, anything you want to say?"

The road captain nods at the prez. "Just ride safe, brothers. And Kink, try to stay shiny side up, will ya?" He adds the last drily.

That gets a laugh. Kink took a corner too fast week before last and parted company with his bike. Apart from a few scratches on his ride and a small patch of road rash, he'd escaped relatively unscathed, only to become the butt of many jokes.

We discuss some of the details, and then round the meeting up.

In the clubroom, Alex is talking with Niran, obviously having already put Tyler to bed. As my brothers file past her, they all say a word or give her a nod, and as usual I'm blown away at how easily she's fitting in here. She's the only old lady, which gives her top spot, and while I had doubts at first, she's managed to gain the respect of the sweet butts. And any fears I had there might be bad blood between her and Eva have disappeared, and they're often found together, discussing Tyler's condition, his forthcoming op, and the aftercare he'll need. I have to smile as I recall Bones telling me early on that he'd witnessed a blow-up between them, and overheard what Thompson had done to Alex would be nothing compared to what she would do to Eva if she caught her sniffing after me again. Yeah, that seemed to do the trick. Eva barely looks in my direction nowadays if she can help it.

For a few seconds, I simply stand and admire Alex. She's squeezed into leather pants, and oh fuck, that ass as she bends over. I notice Deuce, the newly made-up prospect, is eyeing her up, and slap that fucker around the back of the head. "That's my ol' lady you're ogling."

"Sorry, VP. But she's a stunner."

As I raise my fist he puts his hands up and backs off grinning. Yeah, she certainly is. And she's mine. All mine. And watching her ass give a little wiggle as she talks makes me want to get away and take her somewhere private. Approaching her, I curl my hand around her shoulder and pull her back into me. "Want ya, doll."

She turns and comes into my arms, attuned to me as I am to her. "What you got in mind, old man?"

"Showing you I'm not old for a start," I tell her, then lift her up, and as she wraps her legs around my waist and arms around my shoulders with a squeal, I carry her up and into our room.

"I was talking…"

"And now I want your attention. Get naked, doll, and on the bed. You can put that pretty ass in the air for me."

I've given her a lot of firsts, but there's one thing I haven't yet tried, and unless she has any objections, tonight's the night. And fuck me, she's winding me up. She's done what I asked, and while I'm standing her admiring the view, she's waggling that luscious ass at me. She has no fucking clue what she's asking for.

Stripping off my cut and tee, and then dispensing quickly with the rest of my clothes, I close the gap between us and bring my hand down on her butt.

"Ouch!"

"That's what you get for teasin' me."

As a response, she wriggles again. And gets another smack. She giggles.

"Think that's funny, do you? You've no fuckin' idea what yer gonna get for temptin' me, doll."

"You're keeping me waiting, Dart."

She's become so much more confident in the privacy of our bedroom. I lean over her, letting her feel the warmth of my chest on her back. "Whatcha want, doll?" I put my lips to that pulse on her neck, and her breathing starts to speed up. Reaching my hands around her, I palm her gorgeous breasts, and then can't resist pinching her nipples. She pushes herself into my hands.

"Dart…"

"That's my name. Whatcha want, hmm?"

"Lick my pussy."

I've no problem with that, but take a moment to enjoy the feel of her tits, but I don't need anything to encourage me, my cock is already primed and ready to go. But I'll take care of her first. I want her so turned on she won't care what I do.

Sliding down, I part her ass cheeks and stare at that puckered hole. It looks like it's waiting for me. My tongue comes out and circles around, and then I push in, just a little. Her musky perfume is all I breathe in, and fuck me if I don't get harder.

And then I lower my tongue, and she's already wet. I lap at the sweet salty moisture, the taste driving me crazy as I get into the routine that I've learned she likes, bringing my hands into play. I tease her clit, push my fingers inside her slit, and it's not long before her legs clench and her muscles begin to quiver.

"Dart! Please…"

I don't keep her waiting, just give her what she needs, and soon she's releasing over my hand. I continue to fondle her.

"Dart, no, stop."

I ease my touch a little, but don't give up, and quickly another orgasm makes her drop onto the bed. While she's panting and trying to recover her breath, I open the drawer of the bedside table and extract something I'd left there, leaving one item that will be too much for today.

Pulling her ass up, I again part her cheeks, and dribble some lube down her crack. She yelps at the coldness, and starts to tense as I rub it around the hole.

"Shush, babe. Let me play."

Gradually she begins to relax, then tenses again as I use more lube and push a finger through that tight ring.

"Relax, babe."

"How can I relax? You've got your hand in my ass!"

That makes me laugh. "Not my hand, doll. Just one finger for now."

I add a second, and this time she squeaks."

"Go with it, babe. Feel the sensations. Don't overthink it." As I speak I start scissoring my fingers inside.

"Dart! Dart, I…"

With my other hand, I reach around and finger her clit. She might be surprised at the unfamiliar feeling, but it's brought her close to another peak. It doesn't take long before she's coming again. I risk a third finger while she's distracted, and at the same time tear open the condom wrapper with my teeth and extracting the latex, one-handedly smooth it over my very hard cock, then smother it with lube.

Before she can come back to her senses, I start pushing inside. She tenses, I smack her lightly. "Relax, you can take me."

"Dart, you're too big."

"Bear down. Let me in." Another smack, with enough force that she likes. And fuck, she's trying for me, and in goes the head.

"Is that it?"

"Got a little way to go yet, doll." I chuckle. Actually it's quite a lot. "You feelin' okay?"

"It burns."

"Is it too much?" A pause and I push in a little more, and at the same time, finger her clit.

"Dart, I…"

I what? Hate it? Like it? Don't want to admit to enjoying me invading her forbidden place? Hoping it's the latter, I decide to push in more. "Tell me to stop if you have to." And fuck me if I'm not all the way in. "That's it, babe." I pause for a moment to let her get used to the alien sensation. "I'm gonna move now."

"Thank God for that!"

Shit! Even in the middle of initiating her into ass play she can make me laugh. But the smile on my face doesn't last long, as I slide out, then back in again slowly, the feel of her gripping me so tightly is making me count the cables on my bike in an effort to stop me blowing my load too soon. *Brake cable, throttle, battery lead to…*

"Oh, Dart. Oh, God, that feels so good."

I quicken my pace.

"Dart! I never. Dart!"

I play with her clit again, and when she tenses up, start moving faster, thrusting in and out. Fuck, I'm not going to last. She feels so fucking good.

"Dart!" she screams out, and I feel her shaking, and her orgasm ripples over my cock. I lose it. Hammering in, the tingling starts in my spine, cum churning up from my balls and shooting out into the condom. Fuck, that was probably one of the more intense and best orgasms of my life. Oh, I tried ass play before, but it's never been this good before. Everything's better with my ol' lady.

"You like that?"

She shudders, and I can't interpret the answer.

"Doll?"

She takes a deep breath. "I don't think I'm supposed to, but yes, I did."

"Hey, there's no right or wrong, you know that? What we want to do in private is up to us, okay? And," I lean over and wait until she turns her head, then press my lips to hers, "I've got another toy for another day. A vibrator to fill up your pussy while I'm taking yer ass."

Now I know that shiver's one of anticipation. Oh yeah, I'm gonna enjoy my old lady. Going back to a sweet butt? Hell, no. Never. No way. They just can't compete.

CHAPTER 39

Alex

"How many registrations is that?"

"Two-hundred-and-fifty-eight. Fifty-nine," a very pregnant Sophie corrects as she takes the money from a biker who's just appeared as I stare around, amazed to see such large numbers milling around, some on their own, but the majority mingling in groups with men wearing the same patches on their cuts. As well as Satan's Devils from all different chapters, there are a number of other clubs represented, and many unaffiliated bikers just along to enjoy the ride. It's an incredible turn out, and far more than I expected. Quickly I add up the ten-dollar entry fees in my head. That's over two-thousand dollars, and that's just the start. Even allowing for paying out for the prizes, that's still more than I'd hoped.

Blaze has left our group and is chatting to Joker and another man who Dart introduced me to as Shadow from Vegas. Along with some others, it looks like the road captains are getting together and finalising how they're going to cope with the numbers. There's a couple of police cruisers, but they're not worrying anybody. In fact, two of the cops are out of their cars and talking to Drummer, oh, and there's Lost with them. There's a happy atmosphere here today, everyone excited about the run.

"You changed your mind, doll?" Dart comes over, grabs the sides of my cut with the patch on the back saying 'Property of Dart'.

I shake my head. Seventy-five miles is a hell of a long way to go riding pillion. I've started riding up behind my old man, but only short distances so far. And after the new game he tried again last night, I was so full. And a bit sore today. "I'll go in the truck with Tyler."

"Okay. If you're sure." He gives me a cocky and knowing grin, and in return I mock punch his arm.

"I'll have Sam and Amy with me," I remind him. Sam's a bit disappointed, but at nearly seven months pregnant there's no way she can ride her beloved Vincent.

Sophie's checking the time on her phone. "Right, I've given the stragglers a few extra minutes, but I'm closing up now. Oh, hang on." She smiles up at another pair who've only just arrived, joking they're just in time, before handing out their two-part tickets and their first playing card. One part they give up as they're counted out, and it will go into the draw for a prize, and the other is their record sheet to record the hands they draw. They look at their cards, one isn't happy. Sophie cheerfully lets him redraw.

His face impassive, whether it's a better card or not, he's keeping to himself, and I grin, thinking I'm watching a poker-faced rider setting out on a poker run. Apt. Then Drum gets up on a hastily built stage and yells for quiet.

"Welcome!" he starts. "Thank you all for takin' part today. And I'd like to thank our hosts for lettin' us use their premises as a startin' point. If you've not sampled them yet, fuckin' good burgers for ya here." He waves at the burger joint, which as well as a parking area, has extra land, which is able to accommodate the bikes. "You've all been given a map and should know where you're going. There are five stops in all where you will draw your cards, and then get the last at the end. If anyone's got any questions, just find one of the Tucson chapter—you'll know them as their cuts have the word Tucson on the back." There's a laugh as he points out the obvious. "Now y'all wanna get goin', understand that. We go in tens, so as not to upset the cops too much. I know that means some of yer will have to wait, but as I said, fuckin' good burgers available here." Another laugh.

"This isn't a race, so keep to the limits. Ya don't get no prize for comin' in first. Right, all that's left for me to say is good luck to y'all. And may the best fuckin' hand win."

As men start going to their bikes, I kiss Dart goodbye, take Tyler's hand, and go to get in the truck where Sam's already waiting. We'll be getting to the other end before the bikers, as we won't be making any stops. Carmen and Sandy are already there with the rest of the Tucson chapter who aren't at the start, and they've all been overseeing arrangements to make sure it's been set up as planned. Ella and Sophie are riding up behind their men, a Tucson biker is going with each of the groups of riders to make sure they don't get lost.

I've felt guilty that I wasn't around to help in the later stages of planning, but I'm thrilled with what's been done. And seeing the numbers of people that have turned up, elated that the day's looking set to be a success.

Having passed the time making small talk, it doesn't seem long before we're pulling into the park and the first things I see are the marquee and the beer tent with tables inside and out, so hopefully can cope with anything the weather throws at us today. But the blue skies above us suggest it will be fine, and the temperature is just touching seventy, which will be great for the ride. The band's on the stage and already tuning up.

There must be fifty or so vendors setting out their wares, and numerous stands selling all manner of food and soft drinks.

I wave at Carmen and Sandy and then go over, seeing them setting out the items that have been donated for the auctions. They've divided them into two different competitions, hopefully so people will buy tickets for both. There's a well-stocked liquor basket as one major prize, with bottles of spirits for second and third place, and motorcycle paraphernalia as the other, including an expensive-looking helmet and a good leather jacket for the winner.

Then there's the booth and ring where various competitions will be judged.

"The vendors are giving a proportion of their proceeds," Sandy explains. "Tyler's story has touched everyone's heart. All of the entry prizes have been donated too."

Tyler's tugging my hand and pulling me over to a stand where commemorative t-shirts and baseball hats are being sold, each one carrying the words, 'Satan's Devils Poker Run'.

I widen my eyes and turn back to Carmen, who explains, "Sophie arranged that."

As Tyler pulls me again, I go across to the stand. Carmen's come along with me. As I go to take out my wallet, she puts out her hand to stop me. "Let me get this. I want to do my part."

"Carmen, you've already done more than enough."

But she won't be stopped, and soon Tyler's swapped his plain tee for a black one with the Satan's Devils logo, and she also gets the vendor to throw in a child-sized baseball hat. The beaming smile on his face seems to be all the thanks that she needs.

A roar in the distance alerts us, and the DJ starts up the music. The sound gets louder and louder, and then the first bikers are through the gates and parking up. They must all have had a good ride, as when they dismount their bikes their laughter mingles with the ticking of cooling engines and the scent of burning oil.

Participants wander over, passing through the checkpoint and drawing their last card. Having deposited their completed hands in a barrel, some go straight to the beer tent, others go to get food, and a couple start wandering around the stalls.

Bullet and Viper are with the first two groups, and go to stand with Carmen and Sandy, who will be selling tickets for the auctions. With hopefully a lot of money changing hands today, they want to make sure they're old ladies are protected.

For the next couple of hours, the groups continue to arrive, and there's good-hearted bantering going on everywhere. Then there's a long gap, and a last bike appears with a pop and a bang as it misfires and rattles its way into the park. The rider's greeted by cheers and slaps on his back.

"Jeez. We've got to give a prize for the oldest bike." Sam's come alongside me. "That's a thirty's Harley. Beautiful, isn't it?" Then she leaves me to go inspect the bike, and in no time at all is chatting to its owner. I smile as I see Drummer pushing through the throng and hurridly going over to join her.

All the Tucson chapter have been assigned roles, and there's nothing for me to do. Dart appears at my side, and we wander around the stalls. Tyler gets a burger and then a candy floss, and I have to refuse his plea for ice cream, fearing he's going to be sick. Next, we go to see the car and bike show, gleaming machines which their owners proudly display. I don't envy the person who'll be judging that, all of them look fantastic to me.

Drummer's back at the stage now, a mic in his hand. I watch him nod to someone, then a loud feedback whistle pierces the air. Well, it gets everyone's attention. The music turns off.

"Welcome again, all! I'm glad to report everyone's checked in safely. First prize to be announced is to Bob, who wins for the last man in and oldest bike."

A ripple of good-natured laughter accompanies the man as he is pushed towards the stage. Drummer leans down and hands him an envelope. "Think you might be able to put that to good use, Brother. Perhaps towards new pipes for ya bike?"

When the mirth dies down, Drummer continues. "We'll be checking the poker hands for the winner as soon as we can. I hope you'll stay around and enjoy the day, and part with your hard-earned cash at the auctions and stalls which have been set up. Won't kid ya, we want to take as much from ya as you can afford to support our good cause."

Dart's nudging me forward as Drummer's eagle-eyes land on me.

"I'd like you to give a welcome to young Tyler." Bewildered, not expecting to be called up, I walk up onto the stage, accompanied by my son.

"Sorry about this," Drummer speaks away from the mic. "Occurred to me seeing Tyler might make them freer with their cash. Then he turns back. "Tyler here is six years old and was born with sickle-cell disease. He looks fine today, but his health is failing. The only cure is an expensive procedure. And we all know about health insurance."

There's a roar from the audience. Yes, everyone knows what he means.

"His insurance would go for the option that may keep him alive, but wouldn't be a cure. Ya'll know how companies wriggle out of payin' what they should."

Now there's roars of agreement and protest. Reckon most of them understand that.

"I hope ya'll get a chance to meet young Tyler. He'll be judgin' some of the competitions today. And I think, if you do, you'll agree with me. He deserves to be given a chance of a good life."

Tyler's looking at me completely wide-eyed. "Yes," I tell him, "they're all here for you."

He beams. "To help me get better?" I've explained what he can expect, how he has to be brave and go into hospital. I can't hide anything from him, it wouldn't be right.

As we've been speaking there's been cheering from the crowd. Drummer takes Tyler's arm and leads him to the front. "I won't keep you away from the beer much longer, but first I'd like to introduce Lost, the President of the Satan's Devils San Diego chapter. He's got something to say."

Lost comes to the stage carrying something in his hands. It's a small child-sized leather cut. Drummer passes him the mic. Lost clears his throat, and then starts to speak. "Satan's Devils' chapters are full of good men. And sometimes we transfer between chapters. Drummer here is our national president as you all know, but I have been lucky enough to wrangle Tyler from him and get him to California. From what we've seen, we've got a good member in the making, and following the vote of the San Diego club, today he's becoming a junior prospect for us."

He holds the cut up, and those close enough can see those exact two words written on the back. Tyler stands completely bemused as Drummer and Lost both help him put his arms through the leather. I thought he'd been beaming before, there's now no words to describe the expression on his face. Especially as Drummer picks him up and puts him on his shoulders. Cheering and laughter bursts out, as well as a round of applause.

Totally engrossed in my son, I don't notice Dart has come onto the stage until Drummer lifts Tyler down, and picks up the microphone again. "Now I think you'll agree, every kid deserves a daddy. So I'm passing the mic to my brother, Dart, VP of the San Diego chapter, and let's see if we can't do that today."

What's he talking about?

Lost has moved behind me, and is pushing me to the front as Dart takes the mic from Drum.

My hand goes to my mouth. *He isn't, is he? Not here and now?*

"I'm not gonna take long," he pauses and grins, "I hope. But I just want to say Alex is my ol' lady, and I want to make her my wife. And ask Tyler if he'll allow me to be his daddy." He gets down on one knee and holds out his hand to me. I need a little prod from Lost to realise I should move across and take it.

"Alex, both you and Tyler mean the world to me. I want you in my life and on the back of my bike for the rest of my life. Will you marry me, doll?"

"Yes!" I scream out, having no need of amplification to get my point across as I throw myself into Dart's arms. To the sound of hollers, cheering, and shouts, Dart puts the most glorious, and big, diamond ring on my finger.

As Drummer disperses the crowd to their activities, Dart whispers in my ear, "That romantic enough for ya, doll?"

Well, he just proposed in front of a huge audience, almost all his brothers from all chapters are here. "What if I'd said no?"

"Then I'd have taken you home and spanked a yes out of ya."

I swallow. "Can we do that, anyway?"

Dart bursts out laughing and swings me around him. "Fuckin' perfect, doll. Abso-fuckin'-lutely perfect."

"Are you my daddy now?"

We both stop laughing and look down at Tyler. Dart reaches out his hand to him. "Yes, Junior Prospect. If that's what you want."

Then the three of us are hugging, not bothering that Drummer and Lost are looking on with smirks on their faces.

"Daddy," Tyler begins, and Dart's eyes flash with emotion, "I'm going to judge the competitions."

Not missing a beat, though he sounds choked up, he nods at Tyler. "No problem, son." Then he signals Drum.

"Entrants for the longest beard competition to the judging tent now."

CHAPTER 40

Alex

Dart and I sit with Tyler as long as we can. I hardly recognise my little boy any more, he looks so tired and wan. His hair has fallen out, and he is constantly sleepy. Yesterday saw the end of what they call the conditioning treatment, high doses of chemotherapy to destroy his existing bone marrow cells. The process has taken it out of him, and it's so hard for me to look at the tube that's inserted into a vein close to his heart.

Though Dart and I have been allowed to visit, we've gowned-up and masked to avoid passing on any infection. A process I'll need to get used to.

I defy any mother to not break her heart at the thought of any serious treatment being given to her child. This is not as simple or as necessary as having a burst appendix removed, this is an elective procedure that I could have decided against. But with Tyler's condition worsening, those damn wrong-shaped cells of his could stop his heart at any time, and that's the risk I'm not prepared to take.

Today he's having the actual transplant, and then it will be a waiting game. Tyler's going to be hooked up to a machine as the stem cells are passed through a tube into his body, hopefully working so he starts producing normal cells of his own. I'm allowed to stay, Dart has to leave.

Tyler's in a special germ-free room. He wanted to bring his cut with him but wasn't allowed. Nothing that might hold bacteria could be brought in. Dr Crowther's explained to me the things that might happen. If he experiences vomiting or doesn't want to eat, he may have to have a tube running from his nose to deliver nutrition directly to his stomach. Depending on his red blood cell count, he may need blood transfusions and/or regular transfusions to top up his platelets.

It's all such a lot for such a small boy. When the transplant is over, Tyler goes to sleep. The nurse tells me he'll probably be out for a while. I leave the sterile room and take off my protective clothing, feeling a hundred years old.

Dart lets me cry, understanding the angst that I feel. By allowing him to have this procedure, I might have just said goodbye to my son for the last time. There could be any number of complications that could take him away from me.

And his recovery will take a long time, at least one or possibly two months or more in the hospital, while he's kept free from infection and monitored carefully, hoping his sister's cells work to multiply and take over from his own. I spare a thought for my daughter who never drew breath, and hope somehow, some-where, she knows that while she had no chance of life, that she existed at all has provided this chance for her brother.

Dart doesn't give me platitudes, he can't tell me it will be alright. He's holding me close, his chest moves under mine, a tell-tale he's affected like me. Tyler's been calling him 'Dad' since the poker run, and the bond between them already closer than it had ever been with my ex.

"He'll be out for a few hours." Dart reminds me what I'd been told. "What do you want to do? Stay here?"

I know he'll let me do whatever I want. I'm not hungry, or thirsty, and I won't be able to concentrate if I try to read. What does a mother do?

"The primary procedures went well," he reminds me. "They'll let you spend as much time with him as you can, but you must look after yourself. "Shall we go into the waiting room? Or outside to get some air?"

I'm reluctant to leave, wanting to stay as close to my child as I can, while understanding it's foolish. He's in the best hands, there's nothing I can do.

A nurse comes along to go into the anteroom I just left, and gives me a sympathetic glance. "Go get a coffee, or better still, something to eat. You've got to keep your strength up to. If we need to contact you, you'll have your phone on you, won't you? We'll get in touch immediately if there's a reason."

Anything would cause my rebellious stomach to revolt. But I nod. I just don't know how to get through this torturous time.

"This is the turning point, doll. Up to now it's been the preparation, but after today Tyler can start moving forward. You've got to take some time to look after yourself. I, or one of my brothers will come and sit with Tyler any time you take a break."

He's right. I can't afford to get weak, or I'll come down with something that I could pass onto him. I force myself to follow Dart to the hospital cafeteria, and then to eat something that I don't really want. I've got to stay strong. For my son.

Over the next four weeks we can do nothing but wait and hope. Tyler has so many catheters all over him. They are either constantly taking blood or feeding him cocktails of drugs. The doctors give me encouraging words, but don't give me a definitive answer as to whether it worked. Today I've got a meeting with Dr Crowther to go over Tyler's progress to date.

Tyler's gone back to sleep, he's such a tired child, but he's getting stronger each day. I wipe my hand over his head and kiss his forehead. Then I go to see if Dart's arrived, as he wants to be with me when I hear what the doctor has to say. Reliable as always, he's already waiting for me, just outside the door.

He's got one hand pressed against the wall, he looks tired and drawn himself. "The house is all done now. Every surface has been cleaned and sterilised. The new furniture is in, and everything set up." Dart's been wonderful. He's bought a new home for us, and has set it up to be as clean as possible when Tyler's able to come home. We knew we couldn't take him back to the clubhouse, it would only take one person to get a cold and Tyler's health would be threatened, not the least to say it's hardly the cleanest place in the world.

This man of mine has done so much, it's hard to know how to thank him. "Dart, that sounds great. I can only hope for good news today."

"When we seein' the doctor?"

"In about half an hour."

"Do you want to go to the waitin' room, or to get a coffee or somethin'?" He places his hand under my chin and turns it up to face him. "I know he's not out of the woods yet, but while I'm no doctor, I'd say he's doing great. He likes that new game I bought him." I nod to agree, he certainly does, well anything concerning motorcycles is bound to be a hit. "Can't wait for him to come home and see his new room. Oh, and I can't wait to show you our bed, doll." He winks, and I place my hand on his chest. I've been missing my man too. I've slept beside Tyler for the last four weeks on a bed provided by the hospital, hardly ever leaving his side. Dart or one of his brothers takes over for short periods to give me a break, which means I've not seen much of my fiancé at all, and certainly not quality one on one time.

"Let's go to the waiting room." I come to a decision. And then my eyes fall on what Dart's carrying. Tyler's cut. The leather vest that he wore, only taking it off to sleep up—and then only reluctantly—until he was admitted to the hospital.

Dart sees what I'm looking at and pushes it into my hands. "Brought this in case he's allowed to come home. I want to be prepared."

Raising it to my face, I inhale deeply. Along with the leather, I detect the scent of my son. What I wouldn't give to see him wearing it again. Clasping it to me, I let Dart lead me into the waiting room which is crowded to the point of overflowing. Pennywise, Salem, and Grumbler have commandeered seats at the back, with Bones, Kink, and Blaze are along one side, Token, Dusty, and Scribe along the other, and Brakes and Deuce are sprawled on the floor.

Eva's sitting next to Salem and she gives me a little wave, and there's question in her eyes. I give her a small nod, then my eyes widen as I notice Candy, Tits, and Pearl, the other club girls standing just inside the door.

As a hand lands on my shoulder, I turn around to see Lost. "We wanted to be here to hear the news with you, Alex."

My jaw nearly drops onto the floor. I didn't expect anyone to be here, let alone *everyone*. Fresh tears come to my eyes at the unexpected support.

"He'll soon be back and wearing that cut," Lost continues, and nods at the leather in my hands.

"And getting under our feet." That's from Grumbler. But he smiles as he says it.

"And helping in the shop," Salem puts in.

"And making us smile." Eva laughs.

I've been around the club for a while now. I like all the men, and even got a grip on how to handle the club girls. But this is the first time it's really sunk in. It is one big family. They're not just here for Dart, they're here for me and my son too.

"Now who's going to shift their ass and give Alex a seat?"

Pennywise stands and waves me over. Dart gets there first, and I sit down on his lap, Tyler's cut in my arms, and Dart's hands on my hips.

"Everyone's here." I breathe.

"Niran's downstairs watching the bikes. He wanted to be close, doll."

"And Lloyd and Dave are back at the compound. They sent their best wishes for good news today."

I thank Lost, and again look around. Businesses are running without the Satan's Devils, or must be closed up. The thought's overwhelming. Everyone's here for Tyler? If the outcome could be influenced by the good vibes coming his way, he'll sail through this.

"Right, who wants coffee? Seein' as I lost my fuckin' seat," Pennywise pauses to look down and wink at me, "I might as well make myself useful."

"Could do with visitin' the head. I'll come with." Salem gets up, and Blaze and Kink stand too. Having taken the orders, including one from me, everyone being here is helping to settle my nerves, the men depart.

A cup of coffee later and the hour hand of the clock on the wall shows that it's time. Dart and I stand and go to keep our appointment. I pass Tyler's cut over to Lost for safekeeping.

When we come back I open the door to see that Grumbler has started a poker game with Brakes, Bones, and Kink. Somehow, they've managed to squeeze four chairs around a low magazine table and look very uncomfortable. Pennywise is looking through a bike magazine, and the others are chatting in low voices.

All their faces look up expectantly as we walk into the room and go quiet. I feel completely stunned, unable to get my head around the news I've just heard. What I most wanted to hear, but what I didn't dare expect.

"Well?" It's Grumbler who's the most impatient. "What did the doc say? How long until Tyler comes home?"

Lost waves him to be quiet. "Is he doing okay? Dart? Alex? What's the verdict?"

"His blood count is up," I start to say, flicking my eyes up to Dart. "He's got to have regular checks and follow-up appointments, but he's turned a corner and..."

"He's fuckin' comin' home today!" Dart can't keep quiet any longer. "My son's comin' home!"

I'm surprised no one from the hospital comes to investigate the noise in the room. They cheer, holler, slap each other's backs, hug me, Dart, and each other. The club girls are laughing, and Eva comes over and clutches me tightly.

"Anything I can do, Alex, you've just got to ask. I know you won't want to leave him yet and he's still got a long way to go, but when you're ready and you want a babysitter so you and Dart could get out, just call me, okay?"

"I will do, Eva. Thank you."

It's a few minutes before I can escape and go tell Tyler the good news.

The leaving procedure is lengthy, paperwork to be completed and signed, instructions given and prescriptions filled. When I go to the pharmacy, I notice through the open door that the waiting room is empty, but I'm not surprised. The men have given up more than enough time already today. No point everyone hanging around as we go through the formalities.

It seems like ages before Tyler gets dressed in street clothes and a wheelchair is brought in to take him out. For my part, I can't wait to escape. I don't think I'll ever get the smell of antiseptic out of my senses, but it's worth all we've been through just to see that big smile on Tyler's face.

The nurse wheels him down to the reception area and pushes him through the doors. As she comes to a complete stop, Dart takes over. I bump into the nurse's back and, looking around her, see what brought her to such a sudden halt.

There's a double line of Harleys all waiting, with the brothers sitting on them waiting for us, the club girls up behind some of them. There's clapping and cheering, and they start the engines up, twisting the throttles, increasing the sound of roaring around the hospital parking lot.

Dart goes to Lost and collects something which he holds behind his back. Then he marches back to Tyler. As he hands him the leather cut, my little boy, already smiling at the bikers lined up, slips his arms through the sleeves with the biggest grin I've ever seen. As Dart wheels him through the bikes lined up as a guard of honour over to the waiting car, Tyler waves at the men who throw chin lifts back, rev their engines again, and give him a thumbs up.

We get Tyler in the car, and while Dart disposes of the wheelchair I get in the passenger side. When Dart comes back he gets into the driver's seat, but turns to look over his shoulder before driving off.

"Ready to go home, Son?"

"You bet, Dad."

Dart grins at me and then waves his hand out of the window. Eight of the bikers come and position themselves in front, the rest, with Niran at the back, pull in behind. Lost, in pole position, signals above his head, and then we're all moving.

Tyler looks around, his eyes open in wonder as we're given a Satan's Devils escort to our new house.

"Dart?" I don't know what to say. I can't thank him or his brothers enough.

"You're mine, and so's Tyler. And that," he points forward and then back, "that is our family. Nobody wanted to miss out on this."

Yes. That's *family*.

There's still a long way to go until we can say Tyler's been cured, but with the goodwill surrounding us, I'm feeling more optimistic as I'm driven toward our new home and new life. And with this man by my side, I feel together we can conquer anything.

"Family," I repeat.

"Family." Dart nods.

I look at him, his long curly hair tamed into a bun, his eyes shining with hope, still wondering how it is I'm so lucky to have him fall for me. I didn't realise I'd been musing aloud until he barks a laugh.

"Doll, I tell ya. I might as well have had a target plastered to my back. The first time I saw ya up on that pole, it was like someone had shot an arrow straight through my fuckin' heart."

I glance over my shoulder at my son, who's entranced by the bikes in front of us and behind, seeming unable to stop looking forward and back to keep them in sight. A sob comes to my throat as it sinks in, perhaps for the first time, that he's now got a chance to live like any normal boy. Dart reaches out his hand, takes mine and squeezes it. When I look at him, he just nods, and I swear his eyes are glistening.

We continue to hold hands as we drive to our new house and our new life.

HEART
Broken
SATAN'S DEVILS #5

Heart

When you find your soul mate and make them your old lady, you don't expect they'll go before you. Losing Crystal destroyed me, and I wanted nothing better but to join her. I didn't have it in me to take my own life, but if I kept taking chances, I might get my heart's desire.

Banished from the club for my outrageous behaviour, I head off out on the road, a lone biker, one man against the world. And I wouldn't have survived were it not for one person who kept me sane. A voice on the end of the phone.

Marc

*I know only too well what it's like to lose everything you
hold dear. There one minute, gone the next. It was easy to
tell Heart was close to the edge that first time I spoke to him,
and I did what I could to help him back down.
Over the months we became friends.*

*When I knew he was missing, there was only one place to go
for help. The Satan's Devils MC. But cops and bikers don't
mix, so how could I even get them to listen to me?*

SATAN'S DEVILS #5: HEART Broken

OTHER WORKS BY MANDA MELLETT

Blood Brothers

A series about sexy dominant sheikhs and their bodyguards

- *Stolen Lives* (#1 – Nijad & Cara)

- *Close Protection* (#2 – Jon & Mia)

- *Second Chances* (#3 – Kadar & Zoe)

- *Identity Crisis* (#4 – Sean & Vanessa)

- *Dark Horses* (#5 – Jasim & Janna)

  There will be a new book in this series in 2018

SATAN'S DEVILS MC

- *Turning Wheels* (Blood Brothers #3.5, Satan's Devils #1 – Wraith & Sophie)

- *Drummer's Beat* (# 2 – Drummer & Sam)

- *Slick Running* (#3 – Slick & Ella)

- *Targeting Dart* (#4 – Dart & Alex)

Coming soon:
- *Heart Broken* (#5)

Sign up for my newsletter to hear about new releases in the Blood Brothers and Satan's Devils series:
http://eepurl.com/b1PXO5

ACKNOWLEDGEMENTS

One night, two friends of mine were sitting discussing my novels. As an outcome of their conversation, I received a message asking, why don't you write about women who aren't model thin and classically beautiful? It made me think, and the idea of the woman I wanted for Dart came into my head. To show my gratitude, I named my character after the person who gave me the idea. So, thank you Alex.

Targeting Dart was a challenge for me to write, touching on some sensitive subjects. It was important to me that I got the balance right, and in this case, relied heavily on the contribution of my fantastic team of beta readers. A massive thank you to Brandy, Danena, Zoe, Colleen and Alex. And, as always, a special thank you to my husband, Steve, for his help with motorcycling details, and his encouragement.

A special shout out must go to the amazing MariaLisa DeMora, who helped me with a few facts. Now if I've misinterpreted the information she gave me in any way, that's down to me and certainly not on her. MariaLisa's got a couple of amazing MC series that you might like to check out, Rebel Wayfarers and Neither This nor That. If you're looking for a good read, you won't be disappointed.

I love working with Brian Tedesco, my editor, it's always a pleasure and we seem to have a few laughs along the way. I'm so grateful that he can keep up with my tight schedule. His suggestions and input have certainly helped shape this book.

Lia Rees, what can I say? You're always there to format my books and the covers you produce are just great. Enjoy working with you.

A new person to thank is my PA Deb Carroll. Love your ideas, Deb and your encouragement, and our (for me) late night message exchanges. Looking forward to working with you in the future.

And last, but certainly not least, I'm so grateful to everyone who takes a chance on my books and reads them. Particularly to those who take the time to write reviews, or messages me to say how much they've enjoyed them. It's a nail-biting experience after you press that publish button wondering how your book's going to be received. You, dear reader, are what keeps me writing books.

STAY IN TOUCH

Email: manda@mandamellett.com
Website: www.mandamellett.com

Connect with me on Facebook:
https://www.facebook.com/mandamellett

Sign up for my newsletter to hear about new releases in the Blood Brothers and Satan's Devils series:

http://eepurl.com/b1PXO5

ABOUT THE AUTHOR

After commuting for too many years to London working in various senior management roles, Manda Mellett left the rat race and now fulfils her dream and writes full time. She draws on her background in psychology, the experience of working in different disciplines and personal life experiences in her books.

Manda lives in the beautiful countryside of North Essex with her husband and two slightly nutty Irish Setters. Walking her dogs gives her the thinking time to come up with plots for her novels, and she often dictates ideas onto her phone on the move, while looking over her shoulder hoping no one is around to listen to her. Manda's other main hobby is reading, and she devours as many books as she can.

Her biggest fan is her gay son (every mother should have one!). Her favourite pastime when he is home is the late night chatting sessions they enjoy, where no topic is taboo, and usually accompanied by a bottle of wine or two.

Photo by Carmel Jane Photography

Made in the USA
Columbia, SC
16 November 2017